a Jack the Ripper
Time-Travel Thriller

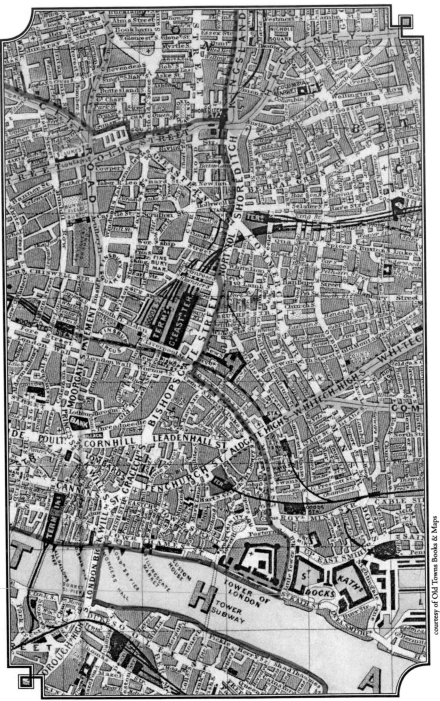

a Jack the Ripper Time-Travel Thriller

BY SHELLY DICKSON CARR

For information about permission to reproduce or transmit selections
from this book in any form or by any means, write to
NEW BOOK PARTNERS
48 Ware Road, Newton, Massachusetts 02466

Library of Congress Control Number: 2012949760
ISBN 9781939003003

Book & Cover Design: Jon Albertson | New Book Partners

Illustrations: Chris Gall

Would you like to meet the author? Bookstores, libraries, and other
organizations may contact the author at shelly@ripped-book.com for
readings and discussions.

Visit www.ripped-book.com to ask the author a question or say hello on
her Facebook page: Shelly Dickson Carr.

First Edition

To Steven Edward Karol
Now and For Always

CONTENTS

Cockney Slang

In Victorian London, Cockney rhyming slang was used as a secret "insider" language to confuse outsiders, especially peelers (the police) and toffs (the nobility or gentry). Cockney expressions have changed over time, but many remain exactly as they were in 1888, when Jack the Ripper terrorized London. The premise is this: A phrase that rhymes with the word a Cockney means is used to convey the word. The most famous example is "apples and pears," which means "stairs." Instead of saying, "I'm climbing the stairs," a Cockney would say, "I'm climbing the apples and pears." Often the rhyming word is dropped, so that "pears" (which rhymes with "stairs") is omitted, leaving only apples. "I'm climbing the apples."

Cockney Rhyming Slang:

Ankle and Foot	Soot
Apples and Pears	Stairs
April in Paris	Ass
Bacon and Eggs	Legs
Bag of Sand	Grand
Billy Goat	Coat
Boat Race	Face
Boiler House	Spouse
Bread & honey	Money
Bricks and Pates	United States
Brown Bread	Dead
Church Pews	Shoes
Fife and Drum	Bum
Flip Flap	Trap/Mouth
Frog and Toad	Road
Grady Moore	Door

19th Century expressions:

Blimey! .... Expression of surprise

Bobby .... Police officer

Born on Wrong Side of Blanket .... Born to parents who were not legally married

Chit .... Girl/Female

Copped It .... Croaked/Died

Cor Blimey! .... Similar to Blimey

Extra Ready .... Extra money

Little Kipper or Wee Nipper .... Child

Mate or Matey .... A friend

Old Boy .... As in: "I say, old boy!" Form of endearment

Old Sod .... A fool, an idiot

Peeler .... Police officer

Scotch Warming Pan .... Girlfriend

Toff .... High society

Take a Gander .... Look at something

Top-Drawer .... High quality

Cockney accents can still be heard in London as well as all across England. But in the 19th century, a true Cockney — with the right to use the secret rhyming slang — was someone born within earshot of the church bells of St. Mary le Bow, the area in London where Jack the Ripper stalked his victims.

Part I:

The
Chamber
of Horrors

Chapter One

Oranges and Lemons
say the Bells of St. Clements

FLICKERING AFTERNOON SHADOWS gathered around fifteen-year-old Katie Lennox as she strode barefoot across the shaggy white carpet of her London bedroom.

Stepping over mounds of crumpled T-shirts, wrinkled jeans, and school blazers strewn across the floor like a giant jigsaw puzzle, Katie picked up the pace and began to hop from one foot to the other over the piles of dirty clothes, careful not to topple them. *Step on a crack and you break your mother's back.*

Halfway across the room, she bent down and, balancing on one leg, scooped up a wicker laundry basket filled to the brim with vintage trolls — the soft, rubbery kind with round bellies, pinhole belly buttons, and heads sprouting tufts of rainbow-colored hair.

Clutching the prickly handles, Katie swung the basket past her bureau with its purple lava lamp and plunked herself down on one of the twin canopy beds. Her sister so rarely came home — if their

3

grandmother's house here in London could be called home—that Katie alternated between the beds, using first one, then the other, for homework and sleep, depending on her mood. The headboards were carved with the family crest of a unicorn flying over a large stone, with the Latin motto *Alta Alatis Patent*, "The sky is open to those who have wings."

Katie lifted a troll from the top of the pile and breathed in its worn eraser smell. *If I had wings, I'd fly far, far away.* Just then, the clock on the fireplace mantel chimed the half-hour. Twelve-thirty. Still plenty of time before her cousin Collin arrived. He was taking Katie to Madame Tussauds, the wax museum, to see the new multimedia extravaganza—*Jack the Ripper. See It If You Dare!*—about a serial killer who terrorized London in the nineteenth century.

Katie glanced from the clock on the mantel to the oil painting above it. Yesterday, her grandmother had taken the painting down from under the eaves in the attic and, after dusting it and polishing the frame, had hung it above the fireplace. The portrait, unsigned but dated 1888, showed a beautiful young woman smiling mischievously out from the canvas.

Katie's eyes wandered around the room, taking in the glass-fronted bookcase in the corner and her bureau with the purple lava lamp. On the window wall was a poster of the Metro Chicks. With blotchy red lipstick, fried white hair, greasy eye makeup, and a safety pin in her cheek, the lead singer, Courtney, was the antithesis of the girl in the painting. Courtney also happened to be Katie's twenty-three-year-old sister.

Feeling the all-too-familiar pang of sadness twist up in the pit of her stomach, Katie tugged her gaze away from the poster and stared out the window at the line of crooked chimneys skimming across the London rooftops like a row of blackened teeth. The chimneys, dark with age from centuries of soot, brought to mind the smoky black lipstick her sister wore at concerts.

I miss you, Courtney! I miss you so much.

If only Courtney would come home, Katie thought. But that wasn't about to happen any time soon, and not because Courtney was as famous as Lady Gaga now and constantly on tour, but because Courtney and Grandma Cleaves weren't speaking to each other. Their grandmother, though outwardly charming, with silky white hair framing a face unlined by wrinkles, was, on the inside, as prickly as the bejeweled scales painted on the dragon tails of Courtney's electric guitar.

Grandma Cleaves disapproved of Courtney's seemingly drug-induced lifestyle (which Katie felt sure was just media hype) and outlandish lyrics.

"Your sister's songs" — Grandma Cleaves's ice-blue eyes had flashed daggers at Katie only this morning — "are illiterate, ill informed, and historically inaccurate! Her latest travesty of an album, or CD, or whatever you young people call records these days, makes ridiculous reference to Napoleon's wife saying, 'Let them eat cake.'"

Katie, trying in a neutral tone to defend her sister, had answered that Courtney was merely poking fun at historical figures. "Everyone knows it was Marie Antoinette who said that. Courtney is just goofing on —"

"Goofing! Is *that* what you call it? Anyone would think your sister hadn't a brain in that miscreant skull of hers. I shelled out what amounts to a king's ransom for your sister to attend a proper girls' academy in Boston because your parents could ill afford it at the time. And this is how she uses her top-flight education? By joining a rock and roll band?"

"Technically it's not rock and roll —" Katie had tried to explain, but her grandmother cut her off.

"Why I even bothered financing her schooling at the Winsor School is beyond me, especially when I knew perfectly well that it was you, Katherine Lennox, who would be the academic one. A natural-born historian down to your teeth. Just like your poor, dear parents, *God rest their souls.* You have a gift, Katie. An innate appreciation for history and the way the past informs the present."

Katie didn't know if this was true, especially about the past and present, but she did love reading historical novels. And like her parents, she planned on majoring in history when she went to college. Her mom and dad had met at Oxford when her mother, an American, spent a year abroad. They'd fallen in love and moved to Boston, Massachusetts, where her mom taught history at Wellesley College and her dad wrote award-winning books on the American Civil War (though he was British). Katie and Courtney had been raised on Beacon Hill until a car accident killed their parents. Now, living with her grandmother, and a year ahead of herself at school, Katie was going to apply to Wellesley next year. If she got in, she'd search the campus for the beech tree where her parents had carved their initials.

Katie smiled at the thought of their initials carved deep in the bark of a tree. She wasn't sure where the tree was, except that it was near a lake.

Last year, Courtney had written a song as a sort of ode to their mom and dad, but with a name Katie hadn't really liked, "Dangerous Love." The lyrics were pretty creepy, especially since it was supposed to be a tribute, but at least Courtney had included Katie in the music video.

My one minute of fame, Katie chuckled to herself. DreamWorks had filmed the video in LA last summer. Slathered from head to foot in blue body paint, feathers dangling down over her face, Katie had sprouted out of Courtney's digitally enhanced backpack, only to fade into the background moments later with the rest of the blue-painted dancers.

Katie didn't crave the limelight the way her sister did. Courtney sought publicity as relentlessly as a hungry cat chases mice. Katie liked nothing better than to curl up with a good book. *What does that make me?* she wondered. *A total dork?*

The eraser smell of the troll wafted upward as Katie squeezed its pinhole belly button. "If only Courtney would come to London. Just to visit," Katie whispered into the troll's orange hair. *I wish we could be together again, like the old days when Mom and Dad were alive.*

Katie hadn't seen her sister since last summer. *I love you, Court. I miss you so much. I'm so lonely without you. Why don't you ever call me? Or Skype? Or text? I wish you were here!*

Katie clamped her eyes shut and rubbed the troll's round belly. "If wishes were unicorns, maidens would ride," she muttered under her breath. Then her eyes flew open. Why had she said that? It was an old nursery rhyme their father used to recite. She hadn't thought about it in years.

If wishes were unicorns
Maidens would ride
If you call forth dead ancestors
They shall abide
But long ago ghosts
From their graves shall collide
So if wishes be unicorns
Please do not ride.

Katie smiled, remembering her father's baritone voice as he recited that poem. Maybe Courtney could use those lyrics in one of her songs, with a more edgy intonation and a steampunk beat. Courtney had used children's rhymes in the past, changing the words slightly and using menacing double entendres. "Music by the Metro Chicks is sickly twisted," posted one blogger before the band became famous.

From the open window now came a burst of sunlight that streamed across Katie's lap and spilled over the side of the bed onto the white carpet, then splashed against the glass-fronted bookcase, illuminating shelf upon shelf of leather-bound books. As if through a magnifying glass, the light grew and blazed with such intensity, Katie could easily pick out three of the titles: *The Picture of Dorian Gray* by Oscar Wilde, *Dracula* by Bram Stoker, and *Strange Case of Dr Jekyll and Mr Hyde* by Robert Louis Stevenson.

The sunshine flared to an almost blinding glare, then rippled away as if tugged by unknown forces outside the window. The bright light, gone now, left a void against Katie's eyes, inexplicably painful. She dropped the troll and clamped her fingertips to the throbbing skin above her eyelids, still puffy from yesterday's crying jag.

Yesterday was the third anniversary of her parents' deaths. She'd waited all day for a phone call from Courtney. But it never came. "Stiff upper lip, Katie," Grandma Cleaves had chided. "All the crying in the world won't bring them back."

But it wasn't her parents Katie wished to bring back, it was her sister. *My parents are gone forever.* Katie plucked the troll from the folds in her bedspread and placed it on top of the jumbled pile in the wicker basket. After the accident, Katie was shuttled off to London to live with her grandmother. And it was here, in this bedroom (her father's when he was growing up), that Katie began immersing herself in old books, trying to lose herself in the past. She'd read so many Victorian novels that she was starting to feel she'd have been better off in that time period. It was safer and much more romantic.

What would it be like to live in the nineteenth century? Katie wondered, not for the first time, as she stared out the window at the long row of chimneys stretching across the city skyline. This townhouse had been in her grandmother's family for generations, and though smaller than the original Georgian mansion because it had been cut up into condos, it still had a turret room with a secret passageway and lots of old woodwork.

Her own fireplace was carved with garlands and roses and flanked by stone gargoyles — looking more like sad, skeletal trolls than jagged-tooth beasts meant to guard the hearth. When Katie's eyes flashed to the portrait above the mantel, she was struck once again by the contrast between the girl in this painting and her sister in the Metro Chicks poster. Total opposites. Or were they?

Katie jumped off the four-poster bed, strode to the fireplace, and read the brass inscription on the ornate frame. *Lady Beatrix, 1865–1888.*

Both Courtney and Lady Beatrix had beauty marks above their top lips, but their hairstyles and clothes were different. Courtney's bleached white hair spiked straight up from the top of her head, and she was dressed all in black leather studded with metal nails and chains. The girl above the mantel had golden curls cascading to her shoulders and full, satiny sleeves on her lace-trimmed gown. Coiled around her throat was a black velvet band pinned with an oval cameo.

Katie stared hard at the portrait. Though it was faded, with tiny cracks in the surface, the face appeared animated, with a haunting, disturbing sort of beauty, like Courtney's. And just like her sister's music star persona, Lady Beatrix had an arrogant air, chin raised defiantly at an angle that accentuated her beauty mark. And there was something about the eyes. Did a hint of accusation look out from those eyes, so dark a blue they were almost black? The same as Courtney's. "Blueberry eyes," her father had called them.

A shiver of apprehension tingled up Katie's spine. She took a step closer. The face in the painting was arresting, but it was the attitude and expression that drew you in. The golden hair, flowing in thick ringlets to the girl's shoulders, seemed almost too heavy for her slender, velvet-banded neck...similar to the spiked dog collar around Courtney's throat, too heavy for *her* slender neck.

Lady Beatrix, 1865–1888. She had died at twenty-three.

Was Lady Beatrix an ancestor? Katie wondered. Who was the artist? Why was it unsigned? When she'd asked Grandma Cleaves yesterday, her grandmother didn't seem to know, which was odd because Katie's grandmother knew the history of every painting, every antique vase, all the tapestries hanging in the entrance hall, the swords and old armor in the library, and even the tiniest of the porcelain figurines in the drawing room.

"*Katie!*" She heard Collin's voice in the distance. "Hurry up! We're meeting my friend Toby at the Chamber of Horrors at one o'clock sharp! I don't want you to make me late — *again*."

"Coming!" she shouted back, tugging off her flannel pajama bottoms and wriggling into a pair of rumpled jeans that she snatched off the floor. She jammed her feet into red high-top sneakers, scrunched her long, brown hair into a messy ponytail, and headed for the door.

A draft from the open window made her glance back. White eyelet curtains billowed above the window seat, then fell back, only to swell out again with the breeze. Katie wrapped her fingers around the crystal doorknob, turning it slowly.

A floorboard creaked beneath her sneakers as she trotted down the hall. Wood snapped again as she leaned over the carved oak banister. "Can we stop at Starbucks, Collie?" she hollered to her cousin who paced impatiently below. "I'd kill for a mocha Frappuccino," she shouted, enunciating her words in a playful, mock-British accent.

Though raised in Boston for the first twelve years of her life, Katie could easily affect an English accent, but she couldn't give up her American addiction. *I guess I wouldn't make it as a Victorian,* she chuckled, envisioning a plump Queen Victoria sucking down a Starbucks Frap.

"Don't call me *Collie.* I'm not a bloody pet dog." Her cousin scowled up at her, his thatch of red hair catching the light from the domed glass ceiling high above. Large brown freckles dusted his sun-burned face, as if someone had gone over his pink skin with a nutmeg grinder.

"Sure, *Collie.* Whatever," Katie whispered, biting back a smile. Her cousin, though two years older, was way too serious. And as fond as she was of Collin, she was fonder still of kidding around with him, hoping he'd lighten up. He never did.

Katie was halfway down the oak staircase when she remembered her grandmother's warning that it might rain. "Hold on a sec," she called out, and bounded back up the stairs. Grandma Cleaves was adamant about shutting windows and locking them if the forecast predicted storms.

After closing the diamond-paned window, which snapped shut like a small door, Katie glanced over her shoulder and watched a glob of purple plasma in the lava lamp heave and split in two.

Just like my life, she thought. Split apart from the people I love. And she hadn't even been back to Boston to visit her best friends. Not since the double funeral.

Katie turned to look at the portrait above the mantel. "I wish I lived in *your* century," she said to Lady Beatrix. "Life was so much easier back then."

The blue-black eyes in the painting seemed to shift and flicker. *A trick of the light?* Something soft as a kiss brushed against Katie's cheek. She jerked back. The muscles in her shoulders tensed. A strand of hair falling from her ponytail had skimmed her face. *That must be it,* Katie thought, and raced out of the room.

Chapter Two

Bull's-eyes and Targets
say the Bells of St. Margaret's

KATIE AND COLLIN stood in the gleaming glass lobby of Madame Tussauds, waiting in a long line to buy tickets for the Chamber of Horrors. This Jack the Ripper exhibition was the most popular attraction in London, with three-dimensional holograms; walls that closed in with spikes and knives; and real actors who "came alive" during the presentation, screeching and screaming.

"There he is. That's Toby," Collin said as a guy in a long, black trench coat strode through the revolving door. Collin raised two fingers to his wide mouth to let out a shrill whistle. "Toby! Over here!" He waved his friend over and introduced him to Katie.

"Hey," she said, nodding a greeting as she slurped up the last gurgle of her mocha Frappuccino. The tall, dark-haired boy looked to be sixteen or seventeen. He had a chiseled face with cliff-hanger cheekbones and penetrating eyes that gleamed like polished chestnuts.

Katie quickly averted her gaze and read the sign over the entrance door:

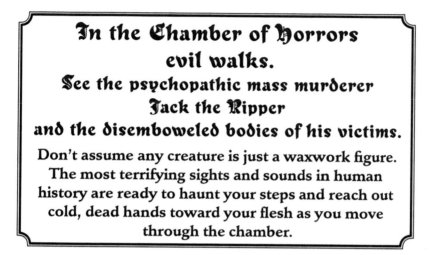

In the Chamber of Horrors evil walks.
See the psychopathic mass murderer Jack the Ripper and the disemboweled bodies of his victims.
Don't assume any creature is just a waxwork figure. The most terrifying sights and sounds in human history are ready to haunt your steps and reach out cold, dead hands toward your flesh as you move through the chamber.

The line, or queue, as the English said, inched forward. Katie found herself studying Toby, who was talking excitedly to Collin about some new, supersonic jet that ejected a microfiber parachute from its fuselage if it took an unexpected, terrorist-induced nosedive.

The two boys were total opposites, Katie thought, as the pair discussed the merits of titanium versus Teflon microfiber. Collin, with his red hair, sandy eyebrows, and beakish nose, was what their grandmother called "a level-headed" young man. His high forehead and narrow jaw showed intensity, but those solemn eyes reflected no humor, and his face was seldom animated *except*—Katie smiled to herself—when he was angry. Then he'd screw his face up, go bright pink all over, and rail at the top of his lungs like a malevolent gnome.

Toby, on the other hand, was tall and muscular. A mass of black curls framed his strong, dimpled chin and the crooked smile that played around his generous mouth. Unlike Collin's serious, coppery eyes, Toby's dark ones shone with a sort of secret amusement. He reminded Katie of one of those characters in the books she liked to read, carrying with him an energy that drew others into his sphere.

He was definitely hot, Katie had to admit, but maybe she thought so because she didn't meet many boys. She attended an all-girls school, which was okay, but sometimes she yearned to hang out with a guy, other than her cousin who was totally self-absorbed. Whenever she texted Collin, his messages (when he got around to texting her back) were short, dour, and to the point.

Poor Collin. It wasn't his fault he took himself so seriously. He couldn't help being the favorite, coddled son. Collin was the model of soft-spoken integrity and unerring exactitude, according to his mum, Aunt Pru, whose greatest delight in life was poring over picture albums of infant Collin.

Courtney liked to joke that if Collin wasn't careful, he'd grow up to be a "decayed little prig." Katie laughed at the thought.

Hearing her laugh, Toby looked at her, his face breaking into a wide grin. Katie bent her head and began to suck furiously on the tip of her empty straw.

"So you're American," Toby said. "Lucky you."

"Lucky because—"

"Hmmm. Let's see..." He stroked his chin. "You Yanks have J-Lo, Beyoncé, and the super hot Courtney of the Metro Chicks. Need I say more?"

Katie shot a furtive glance at Collin, who motioned back a barely perceptible no. Katie let out her breath. Collin hadn't told his friend he had a famous cousin. Two points for Collin. Or two points against. It was possible Collin was embarrassed by Courtney's music, especially the lyrics of her hit single "Dangerous Love."

Toby turned back to Collin and began to compare American and British actresses. By body type, not acting ability.

So much for Toby's eyes, Katie thought, feeling the unpleasant sensation of heat creeping up her face. *I pegged him all wrong!* He was obviously the type who knew everything about movie stars, rock stars, and super models and nothing about current events or world politics. She'd met plenty of boys like him in LA. Shallow and empty-headed.

"Smashing set of bacon and eggs on that one," Toby pronounced, nodding toward a girl in line who wore a polka-dot miniskirt, fishnet stockings, and high-heeled ankle boots.

"Bacon and eggs?" Katie realized too late she had spoken the question aloud.

"Smashing set of legs. Bacon and eggs. It's Cockney rhyming slang. You been here before?"

"To London?"

"No. Madame Tussauds."

Katie shook her head.

"Know how Madame Tussaud got started?" Toby pressed.

Katie shrugged and scanned the room, attempting to look bored. Across the lobby, tourists laden with cameras were asking the guard at the front door for directions.

"It began with the French Revolution," Toby said. "How many waxwork museums were around back then, do you think?"

"Let me see..." Katie rolled her eyes. "I can probably count them on one hand. Zero."

Toby laughed, a deep, rich but not unkind laugh. *For a boy who probably chugs beer, plays video poker, and reads nothing but comic books.*

"They *do* teach you about the French Revolution in the States, don't they? No?" He grinned in mock surprise. "They should, you know, because Thomas Jefferson was here in London at the time, secretly supporting the off-with-your-head revolution."

"No way."

"*Yes* way. Bet you a mocha Frappuccino," Toby said, reaching for her empty cup.

Katie thrust her hand forward to shake on it, but when he raised a fist to bump, she brushed her knuckles against his. "You're on," she countered. "And since you're going to owe me big time, how *did* Madame Tussauds get started? Don't tell me Thomas Jefferson was in on that, too?"

"If I tell you, you'll squirm and squeal like a bleedin' girl."

"As if," Katie said with a pitying expression. She glanced at the tourists by the exhibit entrance and with a start realized that the guard on duty wasn't real. He was a wax figure. *But he looked real.* She had walked past the guard when they arrived, and his skin and eyes *looked* real.

Collin roused himself and, turning to Katie, began in his slow, methodical way to lecture her. "During the French Revolution, Marie Tussaud was thrown into prison. She shared a cell with the future Empress of France, Josephine—"

"As in Josephine and Napoleon," Toby cut in, grinning at Katie and enunciating slowly as if to say *ever heard of them?*

"I know all about Josephine and Napoleon." *Duh.*

"Marie Tussaud was forced to make death masks to prove her loyalty to the cause," Collin continued, his face unsmiling, his voice grave. "She had to pick through piles of corpses, most of them friends of hers."

"Brown bread friends," Toby put in.

"Brown bread?"

"Dead. As in: Chop chop. Off with your head." Toby made a theatrical slashing gesture across his throat.

Collin nodded. "Madame Tussaud took the severed head right out of the guillotine box and made a mold, then plugged the victim's own hair into the wax skull, and painted and sculpted the face until it looked lifelike. Her most famous heads were of Marie Antoinette and—"

"Her idiot husband," Toby interrupted, his eyes bright with amusement. "After escaping across the channel, Madame Tussaud set up shop in London, charging people tuppence and a ha'penny to see her heads, and *voila!* she was off and running like a true American capitalist. Like Donald Trump. But when the pickings got slim and people grew tired of the French Revolution, she opened a special room with gruesome exhibits of famous criminals and weapons of torture, and called it the Chamber of Horrors. Charged extra bread and honey just to enter."

Katie raised an eyebrow. "Bread, meaning—"

"Money." Toby grinned, chucking her empty cup over the heads of people in line. Cup, straw, and melted ice sailed through the air toward the ticket counter, landing with a rattling thunk in a rubbish bin overflowing with chocolate wrappers and ticket stubs. "I'm Cockney. Can't you tell?"

"Is that where the word 'bread' for money comes from? Cockney slang?"

"She's bleedin' fast, this cousin of yours," Toby mocked, a gentle smile playing on his handsome face. *Too handsome,* Katie thought, as Collin nudged her forward in line.

"So," Toby continued. "Are you ready to see the Ripper victims? Up close and personal. In your face, as you Americans say."

Did Americans say that, or was Toby making fun of her again?

"Katie's not just here for the Ripper exhibit," Collin announced. "She also wants to see the London Stone."

Katie shot Collin an annoyed look. She'd confided in him earlier, thinking he'd keep it confidential. But it didn't matter. Collin knew that she wanted to rub the stone but not why. There was an ancient legend attached to the limestone rock, that if you rubbed it—

"The Stone of Brutus?" Toby asked. "You want to see the Druid altar?"

Katie shook her head. "It wasn't a Druid altar. It was part of a pre-Roman stone circle. Like Stonehenge."

"Bloody Druid altar," Toby repeated.

"And you know this because . . .?"

"I'm a history buff."

"And I thought you only cared about—"

"Movie stars?" Toby grinned, reading her thoughts. "History's my tripe and fashion. My passion. Course I'd trade it all in for Courtney and the Metro—"

"You like history?"

Toby nodded. "But my true passion is crime. Gut-wrenching, knuckle-biting crime. Think Scotland Yard. Think CID."

"Is that like *CSI?*" British cable TV showed reruns of *CSI Miami.*

"Sort of," Toby answered. "'CID' stands for the criminal investigation division of Scotland Yard. If I pass my A levels, I'll have a crack at it."

"And it won't be difficult," Collin sighed. "Toby has a full scholarship at Eton. Rocket-scientist brain."

Toby winked at Katie. "And you thought I liked nothing more than ogling the bacon and eggs of beautiful twist 'n' swirls. Well, I do like ogling —"

" — the legs of beautiful girls." Katie finished his sentence with a throaty grunt. *Hopeless. All boys are hopeless.*

"Cockneys always rhyme. If I say I like your mince pies, it means —" He stared pointedly into her eyes.

"Eyes," Katie said.

"Right." He pronounced it *roit.* "And if I say my strawberry tart belongs to you," he clamped his hand to his chest. "It means my heart belongs to you. If I say I like your harper and queens, I like your jeans. Rum and coke means joke. I'm having a good rum and coke with you right now. Tit for tat means hat. Got it?"

In spite of herself Katie smiled, then hastened to add, "It's not exactly rocket science. I'm a twist 'n' swirl —"

"Or a lamb to the slaughter."

"Lamb to the slaughter?"

"Daughter."

Katie shied back. She wasn't anyone's daughter. "How do you say...dead?" she asked quietly.

"Brown bread."

I'm no one's lamb to the slaughter, Katie thought, *because my parents are brown bread...*

Chapter Three

Brickbats and Tiles
say the Bells of St. Giles

COLLIN LEANED TOWARD TOBY and whispered something in his ear.

Toby looked startled, then fastened his eyes on Katie. His face was flushed and grim when he turned to her. "I'm a jabbering ass, Katie," he spoke softly, sounding sincere. "I talk a lot of rot, mostly. Can you forgive me?"

Katie stiffened. "Nothing to forgive." She shifted on her feet and wrenched her gaze away from Toby's intense dark eyes. Collin had obviously just told Toby about her parents' accident.

At the front of the line now, they handed their tickets to an usher and moved through a mechanical turnstile. With dozens of others, they climbed a set of stairs before entering the first gallery leading to the Jack the Ripper exhibit. Several life-size Victorians who had resided in London in the year 1888, during Jack the Ripper's murderous rampage, were on display in this antechamber.

Queen Victoria stood at the entranceway as if to be first to greet visitors, but for all her real hair and soft-looking skin, this version of the queen didn't look real, not like the guard at the front door. Instead, her face appeared textbook imperious, and slightly smug as she clutched the royal scepter in her bejeweled, sausage-plump fingers. Dressed in the actual ermine-trimmed gown Queen Victoria had worn at her Diamond Jubilee, a tiara anchored on her ash-grey head, the wax figure reminded Katie of a glum troll. Same worn-eraser skin, strawlike hair, and mothball smell.

Next to the queen was her son, the Prince of Wales, dressed in striped trousers and frock coat, a monocle squeezed into the doughy folds around his marble-blue eye. Arthur Conan Doyle stood beside the future king, looking wiry and vital in deerstalker cap and plaid cape that matched the clothing of his fictional character Sherlock Holmes.

Toby strode past Katie toward a tall, motionless figure with high cheekbones, a broad forehead, and crisp, curling dark hair. He was dressed in a velvet smoking jacket, scarlet knee breeches, and flowing opera cape. A spotlight ran up his face, emphasizing glassy-brown eyes that had an odd quality of watchfulness. Katie had the distinct impression they were staring at her.

She scooted closer to read the inscription: Oscar Wilde.

"Katie?" Collin said, circling the wax figure of the famous writer. "Remember last year when I was in Oscar Wilde's play *The Importance of Being Earnest?*"

"Uh-huh," Katie said, remembering how stiff and wooden Collin's performance had been.

"Wilde was a genius," Collin said reverently, still circling the black-caped statue.

"Too bad he was sent to prison for being straw and hay," Toby said, then to Katie, "Ever read Oscar Wilde?"

"A little," Katie answered, though she'd read everything he'd written. Her favorite novel was *The Picture of Dorian Gray*, about a man who makes a deal with the devil never to grow old.

The three teenagers moved past Lillie Langtry, who looked as if she'd just stepped out of a Pre-Raphaelite painting, her beautiful gown spilling to the ground. One gloved hand clutched a lace parasol, the other a bouquet of lilies. Katie thought that of all the wax figures Lillie Langtry looked the most lifelike, as if she would gladly step into the room and escort them to the next gallery. Her skin was silken and soft-looking, her lips curved upward in a playful smile, and she smelled strongly of rosewater.

They moved past Bram Stoker, whose vacant, sightless eyes in a mild-looking face gave no hint of the famous vampire character he had created. Except for a drooping left eyelid, he appeared to be the picture of happy optimism, his lips puckered as if about to whistle a tune, one hand positioned rakishly on a hip.

They proceeded under an archway painted with winged cherubs that were being strangled by two-headed serpents, down a winding corridor sectioned off by velvet ropes, and toward a room with flashing lights and a peal of screeching, howling noises.

"*Enter if you dare!*" blared a voice, followed by a high-pitched scream. Smoke billowed up through the floorboards. A bright light momentarily blinded Katie. She heard the sound of glass crunching and the shrill blast of an air-raid whistle. She reached out in the dark, disoriented. Toby took her hand.

You are about to enter a life-size model of a condemned cell from old Newgate Prison, made from the original bars and timbers of the actual cell that held prisoners on their last night on earth.

Be advised! A true history of blood and villainy surrounds many of the exhibits you are about to see.

Katie flicked Toby's hand away, but he stayed close as they moved through a cell like the one in which Jack the Ripper would have spent the last hours of his life had he been caught.

Inside the cell, Katie was startled by how real it felt. Duskily lighted, the small room was a grim hovel, with the original door from Newgate, heavy with rusty bolts. The walls had been reconstructed from the original stones, with a small, barred window showing a shadowy glimpse of the gallows in the distance. On the side wall was a display of actual manacles, leg-irons, and instruments of torture used on the condemned, with framed broadsheets of famous executions from the nineteenth century and grisly ink drawings of the criminals walking to the gallows, below the words "God Save the Queen."

A creak of the floorboards and a faint groan made Katie shiver. Toby took her hand again. Such a show of machismo would normally have irritated Katie, but at this moment, in this gloomy reconstructed cell, it felt reassuring. A real prison smell of dampness and decay seemed to cling to the dusty stone walls, as did a sense of the despair that must have infused it more than a century ago.

Moving quickly out of the Newgate Prison cell, Katie felt instant relief, as if she herself were escaping the gallows. They walked past shrunken-faced, wax effigies of prisoners in ragged clothes about to be executed, and farther on, those same figures lying in coffins. The bodies suddenly sat up in their caskets in a pathetic attempt to scare. Katie couldn't shake the feeling of gloom that had begun to engulf her.

A hologram of a woman's severed head turned slowly, suspended in a giant glass globe. This was a re-creation of the Demon Duchess of Devonshire, the famous Victorian ax-murderess. Strained faces appeared, then disappeared, sweeping past on a wave of grey mist. Some looked crazed, some drunk, others frightened.

A rise, stamp, and fall of organ music floated in the air.

When the next set of doors swung open, Katie, Collin, Toby, and a dozen others stepped into smoke-filled darkness. At the far end of the misty corridor they came upon a bank of elevators, where they squeezed into an already packed compartment. The uniformed operator pressed a button, and the doors rattled closed.

At first the elevator descended normally. Then it lurched and began to plummet in what felt like free fall. Katie's stomach dropped along with the elevator, followed by a rise of nausea.

The elevator shuddered to a halt. Somebody screamed. It went pitch black. A man behind Katie flipped open his cell phone and held it up for light. Several others followed.

The elevator operator turned slowly. "*Welcome,*" he grinned, his face transformed by a fright mask complete with blood-shot eyeballs, flubbery lips curled around massive buckteeth, and a lolling rubbery tongue. "The chamber is not for the squeamish," he chuckled. "Enter ye brave souls into the dark crypt of Madame Tussauds. Let the living nightmare begin . . ." He laughed, a silly cackling sound, more Disney World than horror chamber.

Katie turned to Collin and rolled her eyes. The cell phone man muttered under his breath, "Bloody stupid stunt. Scared the bejesus out of me — er, my wife here."

When the elevator doors rattled open, everyone pushed forward in a panic to get out. Katie was jostled from behind, then shoved forward. Toby took her elbow to steady her, but let go when she flicked her arm in annoyance.

After the crush of the packed elevator they stepped into more smoke-filled darkness and followed a greenish light that flickered over what looked like rough stone walls on either side of a dark passageway. Katie walked behind Collin, beside Toby, down a pebbled path that swam in greenish twilight from a source Katie couldn't see. Like a pea-soup fog, it distorted the stone walls on either side, where waxwork figures stood motionless behind iron bars, peering out. Some were cartoonish. Others were amazingly lifelike, with twisted facial features, despair etched forever on their wax faces. A London police officer, a bobby, stood stiffly to the side. Was he real? Katie wondered.

They continued along the corridor, the slow green tentacles of light picking out iridescent slime and moss on the rock formations. Grim pools of light punctuated the darkness ahead, illuminating a tall waxwork man in a red opera cape and glossy stovepipe hat. As the three teenagers approached, the man's robotic lips began to open and shut above a grey, rat-tail beard.

His voice, a kettledrum baritone, boomed forth like a circus ringmaster's. His wax fingers beckoned.

"Enter, ye who dare, into a bygone era where you will come face to face with the verisimilitude of evil. Each waxwork victim you are about to encounter is an exact replica of the actual young woman, painstakingly assembled by Madame Tussauds' team of forensic artists using death masks, old photographs, and cutting-edge digital technology."

The mechanical man gave a hinged bow and pointed the way into a dark passageway whose walls swelled in and out. Katie felt the pinch of claustrophobia. Just the effect the museum wanted, she reminded herself.

"Like being in a bleedin' Edgar Allan Poe story," Toby whispered, as they moved through a foggy sort of mist until they came to a giant hologram of a woman floating in a halo of silvery light. Her grey hair was tucked under a lace cap, her soft-looking skin wrinkled like an overripe apple's.

"Come. Follow me," came the hologram's disembodied voice, high and raspy like an old church organ.

Katie, Collin, and Toby followed as the holographic woman floated backward.

"Imagine if you will," quavered her shrill voice, "that you are entering the Victorian world of horse-drawn carriages, flickering gas-lights, cobblestone streets, and steam-engine locomotives."

A black-and-white projection of a fast-moving train tore toward them, making Katie and Collin duck as the three-dimensional optical illusion howled past, puffing great, billowing clouds of black smoke.

"The industrial age is reaching its zenith," the apple-skinned woman continued, her face floating overhead. "Queen Victoria has just celebrated her Golden Jubilee. Hot air balloons, bear baiting, and Punch and Judy shows are all the rage. Young men in shiny top hats saunter down the boulevards of Mayfair and the Strand, accompanied by fashionable young ladies wearing the latest Parisian bonnets and bustled skirts."

In the distance the train whistle shrilled, echoed, and died away. An odor of boiled potatoes wafted through the air.

The hologram woman continued. "Steam-powered technology has brought progress and prosperity to the middle class, making for an attitude of self-satisfaction and smug complacency. Londoners, from the most regal duke to the humblest chimney sweep, feel that, in the British Empire where the sun never sets, 'God is an Englishman.'

"But all this is about to change, isn't it, Doctor Llewellyn?" twinkled the hologram woman.

"Yes, Mrs. Llewellyn," boomed the rat-bearded man, popping out from a blanket of darkness to their left, his mechanical arms moving jerkily up and down. "Yes, indeed. On the last day of August, in the year 1888, under a bright, treacherous, full moon, Jack the Ripper began his one-man reign of terror, murdering and disemboweling girls in the Whitechapel district of London."

"Starting with poor, dear Mary Ann Nichols, whose body was discovered in the gutter of Buck's Row, isn't that right, Doctor Llewellyn?" asked Doctor Llewellyn's holographic counterpart.

"Indeed, Mrs. Llewellyn." Again, the hinged fingers unfurled to point the way.

The teenagers walked toward a glint of fake moonlight that spilled over the hunched shoulders of a large, hooded man who stood in the doorframe of what looked like a narrow little house. Dead vines clung to the brickwork around the door. A crooked window sagged overhead.

As they approached, the cloaked figure's snakish, beady eyes peered out at them through the slits of his black mask. His arms were wrapped around the wax figure of a girl in a low-cut velvet gown.

Wavering lamplight glinted across the rise and fall of the girl's pale breasts. The visitors inhaled a puff-cloud of cloying perfume.

In the brief flicker of hissing gaslight, Katie could just make out the silky gleam of the girl's black hair. Again, the man's bloodshot eyes fixed on her, glared, and turned away.

Collin was standing on one side of Katie, Toby on the other. Together they watched transfixed as the waxwork man dragged the head of the girl to his chest, and mechanically rumpled her hair. Swinging shadows threw brightness on the bulging outline of a knife handle sticking out of his waistcoat pocket. And as he swiveled and pivoted, the torn mouth of his mask showed a smiling ridge of discolored teeth.

A rattling creak came from the crooked window overhead as it swung open, and a woman's face popped out. "Who goes there?" she hollered. "State yer business, or be off with you!" The woman's marble eyes peered out, searching the street corner below. A heavy silence ensued, followed by the clang of a rusty bolt as her head popped back inside.

The hooded man leered up at the window, then down at the wax girl. Moonlight shone on the lower part of their waxwork faces.

The man raised his arm, drawing a gloved finger across the girl's throat. As if by a conjurer's trick, a knife appeared in his hand.

A flicker of light picked out his jerky arm movements as the blade slashed across the wax girl's throat. Red liquid spurted from the gushing wound.

A peal of bells rose in the distance, and the scene was transformed by a host of gilded mirrors swinging forward from all sides, blinding Katie with flashing, tinfoil glints of fake lightning.

Multiplied by the mirrored slivers, the man's robotic eyes began to glow in duplicate and triplicate as the head he cradled to his chest tilted and jerked, the scene replicating itself over and over in the long mirrors, a seemingly endless card-flip of quivering reflections. Finally, the girl's image split, and she fell to the ground, her glass eyes staring blankly up at the three teenagers.

In the mirror closest to Katie, the hooded man was laughing grotesquely.

The lights went out.

Katie turned and tried to hurry away. But in that instant of darkness she lost her sense of direction and stumbled. Somebody — Toby? — caught her by the elbow. She took a deep breath of musty, damp-smelling air.

The hologram of Mrs. Llewellyn appeared before them in a soap bubble of golden light, her church organ voice rising and falling: "*Such a pity.* Poor Mary Ann Nichols deserved better from life, as did Annie Chapman, 'Dark Annie' as she was called, who died eight days later..."

A green-edged spotlight picked out the face of another girl standing in the gloom a little farther down. Wearing a long, white dress and lace shawl, she looked like a demure bride, her cheeks circled with bright spots of rouge. The hooded man sprang up behind her.

A gas lamp burned murkily overhead.

The hooded man's bloodshot eyes, like dull marbles, seemed to grow round and then shrink, like a beating pulse. He rumpled the girl's hair, making it fluff up in all directions. He dragged his gloved hand across her throat with the edge of a butcher's knife, causing a red gash and a spurt of flame-colored liquid, followed by a gurgle and rattle as of someone gasping for breath. Again came the pungent, cloying scent of cheap perfume as the second victim's face dipped, and appeared, and dipped again, swallowed by the mist.

"Such a pity about Dark Annie." The apple woman's voice radiated out from the diaphanous cocoon of her hologram. "The Ripper snipped off Dark Annie's ears and sent them to the police. Then he saved some of her blood in a ginger beer bottle to write a missive to the newspapers, but it grew thick as glue and he had to use red ink instead.

"After the murder of Dark Annie, all of London, including the Queen, became fixated on these vicious attacks, especially when they began to escalate in brutality. Isn't that right, Doctor Llewellyn?"

"Yes, my dear, quite right. And I should know, because I was the surgeon who officiated at the autopsies of these poor unfortunates." The robotic Doctor Llewellyn could now be seen sitting in a leather armchair just ahead. "Shall I give our guests some clues, Mrs. Llewellyn, to help elucidate the peculiar facts of the case?" He crossed and uncrossed his mechanical legs with a click-clacking, whirring sound.

"Oh, yes, Doctor Llewellyn. Do tell," twinkled Mrs. Llewellyn, smiling like an apple-cheeked fairy godmother in her floating soap bubble.

"Come closer, right this way, and I shall present the clues forthwith."

The teenagers moved along the smoky passage as fans in the ceiling tore blotches and rifts in the fake fog.

"On September thirtieth, in the year 1888, Jack the Ripper committed a double murder. First, Molly Potter in Berner Street, Whitechapel, and then, shortly before midnight, Catherine Eddowes in Mitre Square, Aldgate — both within earshot of police officers. After the double murder of Molly Potter and Catherine Eddowes the habits of East Enders changed overnight. No one dared venture outside after nightfall, so great was their fear of the Ripper. And those unfortunate few who had no choice were instructed by Scotland Yard to walk in pairs. Hark ye, Mrs. Llewellyn, *in pairs.*

"Suddenly Jack the Ripper's butchery was being debated in the House of Commons, as well as in front of every blazing fireplace in all of England." A spurt of fake fire rose in a hearth next to Doctor Llewellyn, rippling cellophane tongues of orange and red.

"Londoners were outraged that in the wealthiest, most powerful nation on earth such savagery was allowed to go unchecked. Newspapers and politicians denounced Scotland Yard for its ineptitude. Roaming mobs of vigilantes and clerical do-gooders took to the streets to hunt down the hideous monster.

"'Who is Jack the Ripper?' was heard on every street corner throughout the land. How was he able to murder and slice up his victims when the entire Metropolitan Police force was patrolling every inch of Whitechapel? And, most troublesome of all, why did the Ripper's victims *never* cry out for help when help was so very close?"

"Oh, look!" the floating Mrs. Llewellyn chirped, bobbing happily now alongside her waxwork husband. "There's Molly Potter! Molly-Dolly is positively bursting with pride, pregnant as she is with her first child. A baby girl, they say, or so it appeared after the infant was ripped from Molly-Dolly's womb —"

"Er, that will do, Mrs. Llewellyn. No need to open up a Pandora's box of horrors, or dwell on the morbid details of these revolting acts of bloodshed, which occurred, after all, a century and a half ago."

"But our guests *do* need to know the facts. After Molly Potter was murdered, Catherine Eddowes was butchered just before midnight that same evening. Then it was Elizabeth Stride's turn, followed by Mary Jane Kelly, so very, very beautiful she was. A Marilyn Monroe look-alike. Then poor Dora Fowler, slashed and eviscerated near the rookery where she sold parrots, and half a block from where her fiancé was hurrying on his way to meet her. And last but not least a young woman from the nobility, the Duke of Twyford's granddaughter, and the most brutal of all the murders. Lady Beatrix Twyford was carved up like a —"

"*Ahem.* Let us leave the dead in peace, shall we, Mrs. Llewellyn?"

"Yes, my love. Quite right. But do tell our guests about the curious incident of the girls' eyeballs! They shan't want to miss *that* historical tidbit."

"Indeed, my love. I almost forgot." The wax man's head bobbed and swiveled like a giant Kewpie doll, his robotic jaws clamping open and shut. "At the time of the murders the assistant deputy of the CID, Scotland Yard, Major Gideon Brown, gave the orders for Dark Annie and Dora Fowler's eyes to be photographed in the hope that their retinas might retain the image of their killer. There was a popular belief during the early years of plate-photography — started by a short-story writer — that when a person died, the last scene he witnessed would be imprinted on his retina. Superstitious rubbish, of course, but these early sepia photographs proved invaluable to Madame Tussauds' present-day team of forensic artists who compiled the wax likenesses of these unfortunate girls."

Katie wrenched her gaze away from the mechanical man and his hologram wife. She'd had enough of this underground labyrinth of death. *More than enough.*

As she scurried toward the flashing exit sign, another waxwork tableau swiveled to life, depicting the double murder of the pregnant Molly Potter and Catherine Eddowes.

Against a backdrop of glaring strobe lights, Katie glanced briefly at Molly Potter's flannel petticoats peeking out from under her swirling skirts, and then at the fur-trimmed cape Catherine Eddowes had actually worn on the night she died, or so the sign said. But Katie wasn't interested. She turned and scooted away. *If I see one more wax statue of a girl being slaughtered…I swear I'll kill someone!*

Katie hurled herself toward the blinking exit sign. She didn't know where Toby and Collin were, but she couldn't wait for them. Her muscles felt jittery; her knees, wobbly. *I've got to get out of here!*

The life-sized double-murder diorama of Molly Potter and Catherine Eddowes was followed by Elizabeth Stride, Mary Jane Kelly, and Dora Fowler. But then came the most horrific disembowelment of them all. The scene was so gruesome, Katie jerked to a halt, stopping dead in her tracks.

Trying hard not to look at the carnage, she kept her eyes focused on the brass plate below, and silently read the inscription:

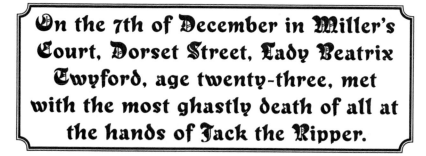

On the 7th of December in Miller's Court, Dorset Street, Lady Beatrix Twyford, age twenty-three, met with the most ghastly death of all at the hands of Jack the Ripper.

An authentic broadsheet announcement, bordered in black, hung nailed to a lamppost:

GROTESQUE MURDER

IN THE EAST-END.

DREADFUL MUTILATION
OF YOUNG WOMAN

Katie tried to avert her eyes. But it was no use. A sepia three-dimensional projection of Dorset Street rose up the wall, shadowed by the needle spire of a church.

Turn The Corner If You Dare!
THIS EXHIBIT IS NOT
FOR THE SQUEAMISH OR FAINT OF HEART.
PROCEED AHEAD TO THE EXIT DOORS
IF YOU WISH TO LEAVE NOW.

Like a candle being snuffed out, the diorama of the dead girl and the sepia 3-D projection went dark, leaving only the faint, filmy essence of smoke in its place.

As if pulled by an invisible force, Katie stumbled around the dark corner, even as the bright exit sign blinked and beckoned and then disappeared behind her.

Katie inched down the narrow passageway, peering into the gloom ahead. Ghostly images and projections mixed with the stifling uneasiness in the air. *Turn back, now!* her inner voice pleaded as she trudged over a rickety drawbridge toward a narrow, little house, passing a horse trough and crooked pilings. The bridge was reinforced with wooden cross-boards that groaned underfoot.

A gust of cool air from a ceiling fan brought with it the smell of mud and the less pleasant odor of sewage as Katie approached the stone house. At right angles to the front door were a rusty iron bell and a metal plate with "No. 13 Miller's Court" hammered into it.

Peering through the first set of barred windows, Katie could just make out an assortment of dustbins and brooms, a water tap and sink. She saw no wax forms or faces, but heard a suggestion of a noise, like someone pacing up and down on the wooden floor.

Katie moved to the next window, which had two broken panes. The jagged edges of the glass looked real. She reached out her hand. The museum would never use real glass. It must be plastic or acrylic painted with a glimmering sheen to mimic real glass, Katie thought.

Sweeping her gaze through the iron bars, Katie willed her eyes to adjust to the dim light inside, which flickered, curled eerily, then shrank away. When the murky light finally held steady, Katie gasped in horror and withdrew her outstretched hand so quickly the jagged glass caught on her index finger, slicing it open.

What the — ? She raised her finger to her mouth and tasted her own blood.

With great effort she forced herself to move back to the window, waiting as the light winked on and off three times rapidly: a pause, another flash, then a longer pause until it held fast, illuminating the room in a murky glow. She took a deep breath, silently chiding herself for being squeamish. This wasn't real after all, even if they did use broken glass.

The room was roughly twelve feet square with brick walls and a wooden floor, obviously painted to look authentic. The door on the far side was padlocked. To the left of the window Katie was peering through stood a fireplace with a large painting of an angel hovering above the bow of a boat. Firelight crackled inside the iron grating, glowing strong, dying away, then growing strong again, as if on a pulsating timer. Next to the padlocked door was an open china cupboard revealing speckled teacups and saucers piled one atop the other, and on the lowest shelf, a hunk of bread, a tub of butter, two spoons, and a broken wine glass. Katie forced her gaze to the brass bed jutting out from the corner. The sheets had been ripped off and lay tangled and bloodstained at the foot of the bed.

Upon the blood-soaked mattress lay a raw mass of what looked like human flesh. The wax girl lay on her back, entirely naked. Her throat had been cut from ear to ear. Her nose had been cut off, and the face slashed until the features were unrecognizable. The stomach and abdomen gaped open, with the organs removed and placed on the girl's right thigh.

Bloodstains splashed the wall and the ceiling. Laid out on the table beside the bed was the final horror. Like pieces of a nauseating jigsaw puzzle, mounds of flesh, presumably meant to look like the victim's breasts, lay symmetrically arranged alongside a quivering heart and what looked like kidneys. There were even little bits of flesh hanging from the picture-frame nails above the fireplace.

"T'was more the work of the devil than a man!" boomed Dr. Llewellyn's robotic voice, though he was nowhere to be seen. "Not even an insane butcher could have created such carnage. Her uterus was cut out and mailed to Scotland Yard." The mechanical voice echoed and bounced off the walls in surround sound.

"On the very day that the Lord Mayor's procession wound through the City of London on its way to the Law Courts in the Strand, Jack the Ripper struck for the last and deadliest time at number thirteen Miller's Court, a lodging house on Dorset Street, shaded beneath the steeple of Christ Church."

In the distance, Katie heard the sound of bloodhounds barking.

"As the Lord Mayor's carriage approached Fleet Street from St. Paul's, Lady Beatrix Twyford, the only victim hailing from the ranks of the peerage, died an excruciatingly torturous..."

Katie had stopped listening.

She turned and ran.

And even when spasms of pain traveled up her legs, she didn't stop sprinting until she crashed through a pair of swinging exit doors into a solarium, lit by sunshine and fluorescent lights, where dozens of people stood milling about in front of a souvenir shop showcasing a glistening array of Jack the Ripper memorabilia: guidebooks, puzzles, tiny wax dolls, china figurines, glittering ornaments, and trinkets of all kinds paying homage to the most famous murderer in the annals of British history.

Katie gave a silent prayer of thanks that she was out of the ghoulish Chamber of Horrors and in the bright sanity of this outer room where people were murmuring kudos for the "spot-on" Jack the Ripper exhibit.

In the next twenty-four hours, Katie would vehemently regret her hasty retreat. Had she known what was about to happen, she would have paid infinitely closer attention to even the most minute details involving the murders.

Chapter Four

Halfpence and Farthings
say the Bells of St. Martin's

THE SENSATION OF HAVING RISEN from the black depths of weirdness into the bright light of sanity rushed over Katie with such relief she felt unsteady on her feet. Nothing in this sunlit solarium could hurt her. No death, no squirting fake blood, nothing macabre or ghoulish.

A tangy nip of peppermint swept past Katie as a young girl wearing high-heeled combat boots and earrings the size of Hula-Hoops pushed past in a rush to get to the souvenir shop. And as the girl scooted across the threshold, a tinkling of bells rang out.

The store, with its carved wooden sign, "The Old Curiosity Shop" was right out of Dickens.

"*Katie!*" boomed a familiar voice from behind her. "*Where the bleedin' hell 'ave you been? What happened to you?*"

Katie swiveled round just in time to see Toby come charging through the exit doors.

He strode toward her, his duster coat rippling out behind him like a vampire's cape. "You gave us a right good scare!" he chided. "One minute you were with us and the next, *poof!* Gone. Collin's in there running around like a chicken with its 'ead cut off looking for you."

Toby's eyes weren't hard or mocking, but quizzical, as they swept over her face. "Dunno how you got past me, Katie. I really don't. I was ahead of you the whole time."

Katie managed a weak smile. "I sort of...had enough...of all that...death." But when she caught the glint of sympathy in his eyes, she took a deep breath and countered more assertively: "The whole scene was, like, *totally* getting on my nerves, dude." But she couldn't keep the quaver out of her voice.

"Can't say's I blame you. Bleedin' harsh in there, 'specially that last bit where the twist 'n' swirl's uterus was ripped out and mailed to the police." He fixed her with another long stare. "*Hold on! Steady!*" He put a hand gently on her shoulder.

Katie glanced down. Her hands were shaking, and she could feel her teeth begin to chatter, though it wasn't cold. Just the opposite. It felt like a furnace in here. *What was it about that last victim that had bothered her...other than the fact that the girl had been butchered? Something about* — But Katie couldn't grasp whatever it was.

"Let's go, luv," Toby urged. "You could use a hot cuppa. There's a god-awful tea shop 'round about here somewhere with soupy little biscuits, but it'll do the trick."

Taking her lightly by the elbow, he steered Katie past The Old Curiosity Shop, navigating a wide swath around the still-thrumming tambourine doors, toward a bank of stainless-steel elevators gleaming in the distance like a row of side-by-side refrigerators.

Moving in the direction of the elevators, up a small set of stairs, they came to an arched doorway bracketed on either side by candelabras with a dozen fake candle stubs resting in electric sockets. Toby motioned to the archway.

"That's the last of the Ripper exhibition, in there. A rogues' gallery of possible suspects. We'll skip it." He nudged her forward.

"You mean there's *more*?" Katie gasped. Dull light from the fake candle stubs turned the ivory of Toby's shirt beneath his duster coat a dingy grey.

Katie shuddered. The last thing she wanted to do was to see more waxwork images of death and dying. Her face must have shown what she felt, because Toby repeated, "It's just a summing up, with clues to who the Ripper was. We'll steer clear of it." He winked. "Promise."

Ahead of them, skirting the right-hand wall, stood a Victorian-style bench with wrought-iron armrests. Katie broke free and made a beeline for it. Plunking herself down on the narrow wooden seat, she squeezed her eyes shut and felt the *thump-thud* of her heartbeat crashing against her ribcage. An instant later she could hear her own little dry gasps of breathing, but was helpless to do anything about it. *What's wrong with me?*

"Going to be sick, then?" Toby asked bluntly. When he sank down next to her, his duster coat billowed out, then settled with a rippling-ribbon effect across his splayed knees.

Katie folded her arms over her chest and pressed hard trying to stop the shivering. Toby, unlike Collin, seemed gifted with infinite patience. Katie could barely hear his low voice with its quirky Cockney accent: "No rush, luv. We've got all the time in the bleedin' world."

With his head thrown back, and his heavy-lidded eyes half-closed, Toby actually appeared to be savoring the musty, mothball-scented museum air. Katie stared past his shoulder to the arched entrance of the last Ripper exhibit, and watched as the fake candle flames flickered against the far wall. In the fragmented half-light, from the corner of her eye, she could see the outline of Toby's strong face with its square jaw and cliffhanger cheekbones.

Minutes later, like a runner breaking an easy stride, Toby ended the silence. "Look, Katie," he said, making an exaggerated gesture as if striking a match and lighting an invisible cigarette, "for what it's bloody worth, I know what you're going through." He blew imaginary smoke rings at the ceiling.

"You don't know!" Trembling shook her words as Katie clenched and unclenched her fists. She hated when people told her they knew just how she felt. *Nobody knows.* "You can't possibly know what it's like to lose both parents in a nanosecond. To have a family one day, and none the next. . ." Why was she telling him this? Katie never talked about her parents.

She pounded the bench slowly with her fists and exhaled in a ragged, shuddering way as if Toby's nonexistent smoke rings had penetrated deep into her lungs. She didn't really mind the uncontrollable shivering, as familiar as rain since her parents' car accident. What Katie hated were the platitudes, those empty, shallow words of pity masquerading as sympathy. "Time heals all wounds," or "This too shall pass," or, worst of all, "I know what you're going through."

No one can feel someone else's pain, Katie thought. *At least not deep down inside where it counts.*

Closing her eyes again, Katie concentrated on the voices all around her — *human voices* — of museum patrons and the sound of their clumping footsteps as they scurried in and out of the archway to the Ripper finale. But such was the trick of echoes in the surrounding hallway that the noises seemed to bounce off the walls and echo softly in her ears from a spot just behind her.

"I *do* know what you're going through," Toby said evenly. "I lost m'dad last year, right about this time. He fell off a frickin' scaffolding, painting a house. Still have me mum, though. She makes lace for a fancy dressmaker. So you're right, I don't know what it's like to lose both —"

Katie's eyes flew open. "Have you ever snorkeled?"

He raised a dark eyebrow. "You mean with fins and a mask?" He shook his head.

She stared past him and said, "My sister and I used to snorkel on Cape Cod, and there was this one time we dove under the water and stayed down too long. . .and I felt. . .a weird. . .sort of. . .panic. . . that I wouldn't. . .make it to the surface. *That's what it feels like!* As if

I'm swimming upward toward the blue sky and fresh air, but I'm not going to make it."

"You'll make it."

"What if I don't?"

"Rubbish," he answered heavily, with a faint inflection that even to think such a thing was daft. "After my old man died, I thought I wouldn't mind being brown bread, too. Took stupid risks..." His gaze slid to the floor. "Still do. It's not easy, Katie. You can't bring 'em back." He snuffed out the imaginary cigarette on the seat between them.

"I never told this to anyone, but when m'dad died I came here..." A strange smile twisted his lips. "Well, not here, but the Victoria and Albert, where the London Stone was on display at the time. I thought —"

Katie gasped and drew back. An odd chill surged up her spine. It was as if Toby could read her thoughts. He met her startled gaze and shot up off the bench.

"Cor, Katie! Not you, too!" He blinked down at her and began to pace. "You're not here for the Ripper exhibit: You're here because of the bleedin' London Stone! Ah, Katie." He shook his head, his voice compassionate but disapproving. "And I thought *I* was the only one with a bleedin' screw loose." Then more kindly, "You can't bring 'em back, Katie, no matter what the legend of the Stone says."

"I'm not trying to bring them back! I just want to make it better. Easier. That's all I'm asking. I just want things to be semi-normal again." What Katie didn't say was that she didn't want to be split down the middle, with most of her life in London with Grandma Cleaves and only summer vacation with her sister in LA. "I know I can't undo the past, but I want the future to be different. I want my sister and my grandmother to get along. I want us to be a family again."

But if Katie were being honest with herself, she would have admitted that Toby was right. She *did* want to undo the past. Rewrite history. *I never got to say good-bye to my parents!*

Katie pushed herself up off the bench and a little away from Toby.

A moment later Collin stuck his head out of the arched door across the way. Flickering light from the fake candles in the candelabras on either side of the entrance made Collin's red hair look sickly orange, like tomato soup gone bad, and brought his freckles, straining against the pale skin across his animated face, into high relief.

Collin's eyes fixed on Katie from under their red brows, then turned to Toby with a sort of eager pounce as he loped across the tiled floor toward them.

"You're missing *everything!*" he crowed excitedly, grabbing Katie's arm. "This last bit of the exhibit is fantastic! The best. Come on! You've *got* to see this! I think I've figured out who Jack the Ripper was!"

"Right," Toby laughed. "That'd be a good Turkish bath, mate. You and ten thousand others before you have tried...and failed."

Collin's fingers tightened around Katie's arm. The wide grin eased off his face and was replaced by a frown. "Bet ya ten quid."

"No way to know for sure, mate. So you can keep your speckled hen squid."

Katie, holding back a smile, wriggled her arm free. "Speckled hen" must mean ten; "squid" was quid. And she was pretty sure that "Turkish bath" meant laugh. She liked the sound of Toby's Cockney voice and was getting used to his rhyming slang.

Collin looked slightly hurt, or maybe angry. His eyes narrowed and then flashed at her. She had expected her cousin to say, *"Dammit, where have you been?"* when he finally found her, but Collin was too wrapped up in trying to figure out Jack the Ripper's identity to give a thought to where Katie had wandered off to, or why.

"Okay. It's like this —" Collin said rapidly, moving his hand back and forth as if brushing away an annoying fly. "I know *you* already know all this," he said to Toby. "But it's new to me." He swiveled his eyes back to Katie. *You take a stab at it, Miss Smarty Pants,* his voice implied. "Here's the problem, or puzzle, as they refer to it in there. From September of 1888 to December of that same year, when Jack the Ripper was murdering girls, no one, *absolutely no one,* was out walking the streets of London at night. The police were on every corner of Whitechapel. The pubs were deserted. Only those who *had* to make their living at night, or ply their trade, dared go out at night. Police were giving free escorts to those who had to walk home alone. And everyone, *especially girls*, were being told to walk in pairs, day or night, for protection. Therefore, the Ripper had to be someone people trusted or at least were used to seeing on the street. I think Jack the Ripper was a policeman! Had to be. Stands to reason."

"That's one theory." Toby nodded, amusement sparking his dark eyes. "Another is that good ol' Jack was a woman. Victorians refused to believe that Jack the Ripper could possibly be a twist 'n' swirl due to the old-fashioned notion that the weaker sex was incapable of brutal violence" — he winked at Katie — "so the supposition that *he* was a *she* is a much later theory. But Jill the Ripper might have been a midwife, due to his or her intimate knowledge of evisceration."

"Or a man *dressed* as a woman," Katie put in, getting caught up in the excitement. "If women were being asked to walk in pairs, and a girl saw another female walking up ahead of her in the dark, she'd probably call out to the other and be totally relieved when the first agreed to walk with her."

"Right! Good one, Katie," Toby said. "*Cross-dresser Jack!* That would explain why none of the girls put up a fight, as if they were all caught unawares. And, remember, those girls would have been on their guard, especially if they were walking with a man. And East Enders didn't trust peelers. Hated policemen, in fact. So I'm with you, Katie. It was either a woman or a transvestite." He held up his palm in a high-five, and this time Katie raised her fist for him to bump.

"Come on!" Collin pivoted around.

Katie watched her cousin trot across the hall and dart back toward the archway. Redheads have a tendency to look either very young, or wrinkly and old, like little gnomes. Collin, though almost eighteen, looked impossibly young. And his shirt, a violent purple striped pattern (a gift from his mother, of course) didn't help matters. It only added to the overall impression of Collin as young and dorky rather than intellectual and sophisticated, which is how he liked to think of himself.

Toby was studying Katie from under his dark brows, an amused expression spreading over his face. *"Ahem!* That wasn't so bad, now, was it?"

Katie grabbed his elbow. "Okay, okay," she said in a pacifying tone. "Lead on."

"Where to, *ma petite?"* He grinned. "The London Stone? The godawful Rosy Lee tea shop with its shepherd's plaid, er, bad tea? Or the bleedin' Ripper finale?"

"Jacques le Ripper, *mon petit gars."*

Chapter Five

Pancakes and Fritters
say the Bells of St Peter's

KATIE THRUST HER HEAD into the long exhibition room. Behind her came the sound of heavy footsteps as a crowd of kids pushed forward to see the final Ripper exhibit. Katie and Toby let them pass and then slipped in behind the smallest boy at the end.

The long gallery was illuminated by low-hanging chandeliers that held dozens of electric candles, with great gobs of fake wax dripping down. It was a very big room, with black-and-white glazed floor tiles and two rows of faux marble pillars — spaced about eight feet apart — going to the back of the room where a wide Plexiglas staircase, in a direct line from where Katie and Toby stood, ascended to an open balcony above.

Set into the two side walls stretched a row of arched niches displaying waxwork figures, seven on either side. At the rear, to the right of the staircase as one faced it, was a "Ladies" restroom door with a cameo of Queen Victoria.

Extending down the middle of the room, between the marble pillars, ran a long, flat, glass-topped display case with Jack the Ripper memorabilia. Nestled in velvet in the end of the display case closest to Katie lay a set of old keys, a worn notecase, a watch and chain, fragments of a jar or bottle, and loose coins stamped "Britannia."

No eerie unreality here, Katie thought with relief. No waxwork dead bodies or eviscerated girls; nothing grotesque to catch the eye. The waxwork figures, positioned in the arched niches down the right- and left-hand walls, didn't move or jump out at you. It was just an ordinary gallery exhibit.

"I can handle this," she assured herself, but her breathing quickened when she glanced down the row of seven victims, looming large and lifelike along the left-hand wall, unnatural smiles plastered on their wax faces, eyes scornful as if mocking their impending fates. Katie caught a glimpse of a feathered hat, a parasol, the flounce of a petticoat on the first girl, Mary Ann Nichols, before averting her eyes and fastening them on Collin in a throng of kids, his bright red head sticking out from the crowd like a roasted yam in a pot of other, bland vegetables.

To their right, a low-hanging chandelier threw wagon wheels of light in front of the first Jack the Ripper suspect with a sign that read

Who was Jack the Ripper!

How did he manage to walk the streets of Whitechapel unimpeded when the whole of the metropolitan police force was standing guard on every corner?

Was he a supernatural phantom who could materialize at will!

Or a flesh-and-blood man bent on harrowing destruction!

Katie heard a click and tumble sound like a lock being turned, coming from the first suspect. Katie moved hesitantly forward, Toby at her side.

Take a guess!
What sort of man could walk the streets of London and not look out of place? What manner of individual would have been above suspicion?
Could Jack the Ripper have been a minister!
. . . The Right Honourable Jack!

Standing on a pedestal, the waxwork figure showed a tall, lean man with a white clerical collar round his neck. The wheel of light from above caught the wax bulge of his Adam's apple in a long, thin neck like a turkey's. Red blotches in his cheeks extended to the tip of his long nose, with eyeglasses drawn low on the bridge. Clutched in knobby fingers was a gilt-clasped Bible.

The next sign read

Or was Jack the Ripper a physician!
. . . Doctor Jack!

This next statue showed a man with a shiny bald head, a too-red face, large nose, and flabby jowls swelling over the turned-up collar of his long black coat. Wax fingers, sprouting hair from the knuckles, clutched a leather medical bag, and he had crinkled, suspicious-looking eyes.

The next sign asked if Jack might have been an aristocrat:

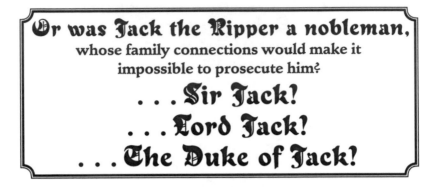

Or was Jack the Ripper a nobleman,
whose family connections would make it
impossible to prosecute him?
. . . Sir Jack!
. . . Lord Jack!
. . . The Duke of Jack!

This wax figure was of a short, barrel-chested man wearing an ermine-trimmed cloak and velvet sash, looking very much like the future King of England, Prince Edward.

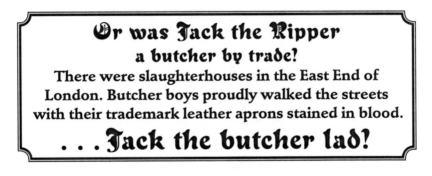

Or was Jack the Ripper
a butcher by trade?
There were slaughterhouses in the East End of
London. Butcher boys proudly walked the streets
with their trademark leather aprons stained in blood.
. . . Jack the butcher lad!

Here was a young man of about sixteen in knee breeches, a tweed cap perched low on his forehead, and a bloody leather apron around his waist.

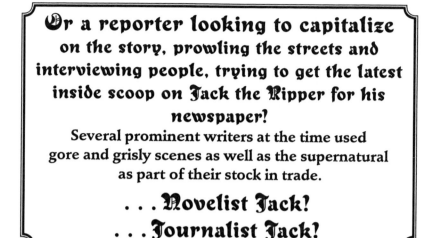

Or a reporter looking to capitalize
on the story, prowling the streets and
interviewing people, trying to get the latest
inside scoop on Jack the Ripper for his
newspaper!
Several prominent writers at the time used
gore and grisly scenes as well as the supernatural
as part of their stock in trade.

. . . Novelist Jack!
. . . Journalist Jack!

This waxwork was of two men: Oscar Wilde, flamboyantly dressed with a red gardenia in his lapel, and Sir Arthur Conan Doyle with deerstalker cap and meerschaum pipe.

Katie jerked to a stop and shook her head. "Give me a break! That's ridiculous! Oscar Wilde as Jack the Ripper? Conan Doyle as Sir Jack? *Puh-leeze!*"

"Bleedin' far-fetched, true enough." Toby smiled. "But the Ripper could easily have been a writer. Bram Stoker was writing blood-sucking scenes of grisly death; Oscar Wilde was into grotesque super-natural death; and Sherlock Holmes was all about solving murder mysteries. *Maybe*" — Toby's smile broadened into an even wider grin — "Jack the Ripper was a psycho ink-slinger doing murder research in the East End."

Katie shot him an incredulous look and scooted past the last waxwork suspect, that of "Constable Jack," depicting a police officer in a crisp blue uniform, brass buttons gleaming, the patent-leather rim of his black helmet sitting high on his head, the leather chin strap tight around his double chin.

As they moved past, Toby pointed to the wooden truncheon, rattle, and bright silver whistle hooked into the belt around Constable Jack's waist.

"I'm done here," Katie said. "We've gone from the grotesque to the ridiculous. They are really grasping at straws here."

"But don't you see?" Toby put in. "People don't like to have their heroes debunked. If you can't stand the thought of the author of Sherlock Holmes being a mass murderer, think how the Victorians must have scoffed at the idea — making it the *perfect* cover for the Ripper. Oh, I'm not saying the Ripper was any of these literary guys. But you can't rule out that he could have been a local hero . . . an East End writer . . . or actor . . . a musician . . . a performer the people knew and loved. Remember, they would have been much more gullible back then."

"How so?"

"A stage actor who played the white knight on stage would remain that way in the minds of young, impressionable girls. *We* know that actors aren't who they portray on the screen, but we're often just as smitten. Back then if a girl had paid a farthing to see a theatrical play, she might easily fall in love with the leading man. Then, if she saw him on the street, she'd never dream he wasn't the stage hero she'd fallen in love with."

"Good point. But how many young girls were in love with Oscar Wilde, do you think?"

"Plenty of boys; dunno how many girls." Toby winked at her.

Katie laughed. "I'm out of here. I'll just go find Collin and tell him I'm done. I'll meet you guys at the London Stone exhibit."

"I'll come, too."

But when they went to find Collin, their search brought them to the left-hand wall. Katie moved quickly down the line of waxwork girls, hardly daring to look at them, starting with Mary Ann Nichols, then Dark Annie, and the twin silhouette of a pregnant Molly Potter standing next to Catherine Eddowes on the same platform because they'd been murdered on the same night, then Elizabeth Stride, followed by Mary Jane Kelly and Dora Fowler. They reached the last Ripper victim, Lady Beatrix Twyford.

In frustration, Katie hurried past, wrenching her eyes away so as not to even glance at this last waxwork girl. She was halfway to the rear of the room, intent on mounting the Plexiglas staircase, when she heard Toby's rumbling voice.

"*H'mf!* Would you look at that? This bleedin' one is the spittin' image of the twist 'n' swirl from the Metro Chicks. Can they do that, d'ya think? Just steal someone's likeness and put it on a wax dummy? Bet the bloke that created her has a thing for the Metro Chicks' lead singer."

Katie heard Collin's voice: "Confound it! What are you talking about?"

Katie spun around and looped back.

"Look!" Toby pointed. "Burn me alive if that isn't the spitting image of the lead singer, Courtney, in the Metro Chicks. Same boat race. I should know. She's bleedin' peasy. Got a bit of a thing fer her m'self. I *dream* about that face."

"Peasy?" Collin's forehead wrinkled up.

"Peas in the pot, mate. Hot. You too, eh?"

Katie drew closer.

"Are you daft?" sputtered Collin, his blue eyes fixed on the wax-work girl. "I'm not *hot* for my own, er — for Courtney! Looks nothing like her. Not the same face at all." Collin inclined his head and continued to study the wax figure while tugging at his lower lip with thumb and forefinger, a nervous gesture Aunt Pru was always after him about.

"Hair color's different, for sure." Toby's eyes moved slowly up and down the wax girl's form, and he seemed to be holding back a smile. "But I swear they used the singer's face when they did this wax model. Look — "

Katie wedged herself between the two boys to get a better look. Her mind was racing. At the edges of her consciousness something was niggling. She raised her gaze to the wax girl's face, and the realization struck Katie like a blow. She let out a gasp.

Then, in a dry, barely audible voice, "That's not Courtney…*that's Lady Beatrix!*"

"Of course, it's Lady Beatrix, birdbrain," grumbled Collin. "Like the sign says." He pointed to the inscription on the pedestal: "Lady Beatrix Twyford. 1865–1888."

"No. I mean *that's* the girl in the portrait. The one Grandma Cleaves found in the attic and hung over my mantelpiece."

Part II:

The London
Stone

Chapter Six

Two Sticks and an Apple
say the Bells of Whitechapel

TWENTY MINUTES LATER, her grandmother's expression *"Beware of what you wish for"* hammered in Katie's brain.

"Katie!" She heard Toby's voice from the doorway of the atrium where she was standing alone.

She glanced over her shoulder at Toby, then back at the London Stone. For a good while now, Katie had been staring at the London Stone, a large boulder, balanced on top of what appeared to be an old, crumbling wishing well. The rocks at the base of the well were blackish-brown and set in dark concrete, in contrast to the London Stone, which was a bright whitish-grey. Leading up to the Stone from the entrance was a broad, squishy line of footprints tracked across a long mat, like an Oscar-night red carpet.

Toby strode toward her. "Beware of pots and dishes . . ." he said in a dead-serious voice, reaching out his hand to stop her from touching the Stone.

Katie jerked back her hand. It wasn't possible to touch the Stone, nestled on top of the well, because it was encased in a prickly, wire-mesh cage. What had startled Katie were the words "pots and dishes."

Please don't let "pots and dishes" mean wishes, Katie thought, peering at Toby, who seemed to have an uncanny ability to read her mind.

"Huh?" Collin sputtered, stumbling through the doorway, following close on Toby's heels. "Pots and dishes? Er... ya mean bitches?"

"Just an expression, mate. 'Beware of what you wish for, because it might —'"

"'Come true,'" Katie finished his sentence.

Toby's eyes fastened on Katie's and didn't waver.

Collin tugged on his lower lip with his thumb and forefinger. "You don't... really... believe the legend, right? I mean... you weren't going to try —"

Katie flinched. "Of course not."

Collin was pinching his lip out so far that Katie wanted to swat his hand from his mouth, like Aunt Pru always did, but resisted. It was a nervous habit. Collin couldn't help it.

"Of *course,* I don't believe in the legend," Katie answered, inching around the London Stone, which appeared from this angle to be rising up out of the well. No muddy footprints straggled around the back of the well, and as she followed it around, she ran her hand over the small, waist-high rocks jutting out just below its rim, rough and flinty against her palm like the boundary walls surrounding Grandma Cleaves's garden.

As she came to the back, Katie heard a weird sort of thrashing sound and glanced over her shoulder. Behind her was a solid, cinder-block wall.

"It's a rum thing about this bleedin' Stone," said Toby, following her around the well. His voice was jovial and light, but there were deep furrows in his forehead. "Legend has it that those who believe, *truly believe,* can rewrite history. Change the past."

Katie nodded. "Most historians think the Stone was part of a pre-Roman stone circle."

"Like Stonehenge," Collin muttered, tugging at his lip so that the word Stonehenge came out sounding like *sternage*. "Thousands of people flock to Stonehenge at the summer solstice. I've seen it on the telly. They do all those weird dances and chanting."

Toby frowned. "The London Stone has nothing to do with Neolithic stone circles. It's the stone of Brutus, part of a Druid altar. *That's* what historians believe."

"So it was used for . . . sacrificial stuff?" Collin's red brows rose. "Cool!"

"Or creepy," Katie said. "But you're wrong." Katie glanced at Toby. She had done a lot of research on the London Stone. The only thing that historians *did* agree on was the fact that the Stone had resided in London as far back as written records existed, along with the fable — or curse — that if the Stone were ever to leave London, the city would instantly cease to exist.

"Sign over there says it *could* be the stone King Arthur drew his sword from." Collin let go of his lip and puffed out his freckled cheeks.

Toby's eyes fastened on Katie with an odd watchfulness.

Katie took a step closer to the Stone, and the room suddenly filled with darting light. Shadows chased one another around the Stone — *not unusual*, Katie thought. This was Madame Tussauds, after all, known for its weird special effects. But what was that strange smell? Like peanut butter and smoky cheese, so strong it was as if someone had opened a jar of Skippy peanut butter and placed it directly under her nose.

"What's that smell?"

"What smell?"

"Like stinky cheese and peanut butter. What's in your pocket, Collin?" Much to Collin's chagrin, Aunt Pru often tucked cheese sandwiches into his pockets, "lest the darling boy starve."

Collin yanked out a smushed box of Milk Duds. "These? S'all I got. I swear." He tossed the box to Katie and she caught it in midair.

Expelling her breath, she reached inside and tugged out two chocolate Milk Duds. She popped one into her mouth, savoring the chewy caramel, then Frisbeed the box back to Collin.

"Katie," Toby said, so close to her ear it made her jump. When she glanced up, she saw that he was standing at least three feet away. Then she heard a sound as if someone had just kicked a tin can and it was rattling its way across the tiled floor, near the strip of red carpet. But when she looked down, there was nothing.

She peered into the corners of the room, then over her shoulder. No tin cans.

More special effects, Katie wondered?

"Katie," Toby repeated, the sound of her name pounding so loudly in her ears, she clamped her hands over them.

"Stop shouting!"

"Not shouting, Katie." Toby looked at her oddly, then lowered his voice to a whisper. "Did you ever read 'The Raven's Claw'?"

Katie darted behind the London Stone, effectively muffling the booming sound of his voice.

"It's a short story." Toby's words pursued her, bouncing loudly off the cinder-block walls. "It's one of those gothic horror stories written around the time of Edgar Allan Poe, 'bout a bloke who gets three wishes if he rubs this shriveled-up raven's claw. But what happens after he gets his first wish is so freakin' awful, he spends his last two wishes trying to undo the first."

Perplexed, Katie popped her head back around the London Stone. "Meaning...?"

"If you interfere with fate, Katie, you do so at your own peril." Toby's voice was back to normal, but it had been so piercingly loud just the moment before that it left a ringing void against her eardrums.

"And...this...is relevant...because...?" she managed to squeak out, though her head was throbbing now, her ears ringing.

"When m'dad died, I used to pray for some kind of über miracle that would bring 'im back. But then I'd reread 'The Raven's Claw' and realized that even if I could change the past, I shouldn't. I'd only be messing with the balance of the cosmos. What's meant to be is meant to be."

"You don't really believe that, do you?" Katie whacked the prickly wire surrounding the London Stone. It thrummed like a giant gerbil cage. "I wouldn't care if I messed up the fate of the whole world, the entire cosmos. I'd give anything to have my parents back. *Anything!* I'd sell my soul to the devil —" But in truth, Katie knew she wasn't going to wish for her parents to be alive again. She merely wanted to —

"Beware of what you wish for, Katie, it might come —"

"Oh shut up. *Just shut up!*" Katie flew round to the back of the stone again, and without thinking, began wriggling her fingers through a small hole, the size of a Milk Dud, in the wire mesh. *How dare he tell me what to do! What a stupid jerk.*

Katie hadn't come here to wish for the impossible. If she could have one wish, *just one*, it wouldn't be something metaphysically impossible. She'd never intended to hope for anything totally unobtainable. All Katie wanted to ask for was one simple little thing. *To have my sister in my life again.*

She tugged angrily at the tear in the wire mesh, widening it. *I don't just want to see my sister for a week or two every summer. I want her in my life!*

Katie squeezed her eyes shut trying to picture her sister, but only managed to conjure up a shapeless image without a face. Last year Grandma Cleaves had argued with Courtney about the "lewd" lyrics in her songs, the "unwholesome" metal studs in her body, and the "ridiculous" tattoos snaking up and down her arms. Now they weren't speaking. *I just want Courtney back in my life. I want Grandma Cleaves and Courtney and me to be a family. I lost my parents. I want my sister back! Is that too much to ask?*

Wriggling and poking at the hole, Katie thought about the wax-work girl downstairs who resembled Courtney, the black velvet ribbon fastened round her neck, the delicate cameo hanging in the hollow of her throat.

Katie glanced down at the widening hole, large enough now to plunge several fingers into. She wriggled them around until her knuckles poked through the hole, and a moment later she plunged her entire hand in.

The tangled wire gave a little at first, then clamped shut around her wrist, like a prickly metal bracelet. *Now I've done it,* Katie thought, trying to wrench her hand free. But it stuck fast. Making a tight fist, she drove her arm in further, then tried to yank it back out again. But each time she swung back, the surrounding mesh circled her arm more tightly, pulling her in.

Frustrated, she hurled her full weight against the cage. Instead of loosening her arm, she managed only to plaster her cheek against the upper portion of the chicken wire, with her hip and thigh pressed tight to the rough side stones of the well.

If she had a little Vaseline, she could slide her arm out.

Behind her she heard Collin wheezing. The air had a different odor now, like the damp smell of wet stones. With her cheek pressed against the tangle of mesh wires, she tried to call out to her cousin but stopped when she noticed that the rocks surrounding the lip of the well were crusted in green slime, sticky against her hip and thigh.

Okay, this is crazy, Katie thought, opening and shutting her fingers on the inside of the wire cage. She tugged her neck back like a turtle, trying to peer around. Where were Collin and Toby?

The London Stone had a barely visible crack just beyond the wire casing. Katie wriggled her fingers until her index finger was touching the small, smooth fissure. When she poked her finger into it, she was reminded of that finger-plunger game she used to play with Courtney when they were kids. At the thought of her sister, laughter bubbled up from her throat with an hysterical edge. Her mind flashed to Beatrix Twyford, who had died such a horrible death. *If only I could go back in time, I'd solve the Jack the Ripper mystery and save Lady Beatrix Twyford!*

A deafening explosion sent shockwaves through her body. A fierce white heat seared through her, as if she were on fire. She tried with all her might to wrench her hand back. Shadows darted around the Stone, then around her head. She rattled the cage with her free hand. She was in agony. Someone must have set off a bomb...and she was trapped!

Her grandmother's words came to her, reverberating in her mind with a melodic cadence. *"Beware of what you wish for..."*

Chapter Seven

Maids in White Aprons say the Bells of St. Katherine's

MINUTES LATER, with the palm of her right hand still pressed firmly against the London Stone, and her index finger embedded in the pitted hole, the gut-wrenching feeling of something exploding inside Katie was gone, along with the painful fire-hot sensation.

Taking a deep breath, she glanced around. Something wasn't right. The light was peculiar. And what was that brick wall doing in front of her? She blinked. The London Stone was protruding from a wall. *A brick wall.* Some sort of curved, iron grate surrounded it instead of wire mesh, and it was sticking out of *a brick wall!*

Hand still firmly on the stone, Katie craned her neck and looked up. A church spire soared high into the sky. A church? Where was she?

She shook her head. This multimedia stuff was so real! Must be another hologram. But the air smelled like outdoors. And the fast-moving clouds scudding overhead looked *real*. And what was that brick-dust smell?

The gravestones in the courtyard were a nice touch, Katie thought. Just the sort of background scenery Madame Tussauds would go in for. She twisted and tugged her finger until she was able to wriggle it out of the pitted indentation, then slid her arm out of the metal grating and reached her hand up to her throat. Something was choking her. A satiny ribbon of some sort was tied under her chin. *What the. . .?*

She touched her head. A pinwheel of a hat sat balanced on her head. Katie took a giant step backward, and the heel of her boot caught in the velvety material swirling round her ankles.

Really, this is too weird, Katie thought. Then the toe of her boot — *her boot* — caught in the hem of her dress. . .*her dress?* What dress? She hadn't been wearing a dress. The only long dress Katie owned was her mother's old prom dress. And she *definitely* hadn't been wearing the prom dress.

"Okay," she said aloud. "What's going on?" She took another step, got tangled in the flounces of the skirt, and fell backward "ass over teakettle," as the English liked to say. From the ground she looked up to see Collin looming over her. Relief surged through her at the sight of his flame-red hair and freckled cheeks, replaced instantly by a seething anger.

"What's going on, Collin?! Is this some kind of a stupid joke?"

"T'ain't no rum 'n' coke, Miss Katherine." It was Toby peering down at her, sunlight splashing across his handsome features. But what was wrong with his nose? Had he broken it? It was crooked, and there was a slight bump in the middle, as if he'd been in a fight. Toby reached down and offered Katie his hand. He was wearing old-fashioned clothes.

"Ha ha. Very funny. How'd you do it?" Katie demanded. "How'd you pull it off?"

"Pull what off, miss?" Toby gently gripped her wrists and tugged her to her feet. But when his dark eyes met hers, they weren't sparkling with amusement. No glimmer of a smile lurked at the corners of his mouth. Instead, his face was full of worried concern.

"Okay, guys. Cut it out. Enough already. This isn't funny anymore. It's mean. A stupid, mean, dumb joke. And you gave yourself away, Toby, when you said 'rum and coke.' There was no such thing as Coca-Cola in the olden days. So cut it out. I assume you want me to believe we are actually back in Victorian England? Ha ha, double-ha."

"What's co-ca-co-la?" Toby asked, a curious inflection in his voice. He threw Collin a quizzical look, then said to Katie, "Rum and coke, miss. Rum as in the stuff you drink, and coke as in a coal fire." He turned to Collin. "Your cousin must have gotten a walloping crack on the noggin when she fell arse over teakettle. It's addled her wits."

"Where are we?" Katie demanded.

Collin, his red hair parted with razor precision and slicked flat across his forehead, stared at her, mouth open. "The steps of St. Swithin's church, where else? I think Toby's right, Katherine. When you fell, you hit your head and—"

"What year is this?" Katie glared at him.

A splotch of color rose up Collin's neck above his stiff winged collar. "Why, it's the year of our lord eighteen-hundred and eighty-eight. God's eyeballs, Katherine. What's gotten into you?"

"And we're in London?" Katie asked. "Queen Victoria's London?"

When Collin nodded, Katie froze. For a terrifying moment she thought she might actually *be* in the nineteenth century. But the very next instant she knew it was impossible. This was all a hoax, another hologram or three-dimensional projection, all part of the multimedia Chamber of Horrors exhibit at Madame Tussauds. Katie laughed as she remembered the sign:

> **Come see the psychopathic mass murderer Jack the Ripper and the disemboweled bodies of his victims. The most terrifying sights and sounds in human history are ready to haunt your steps and reach out cold, dead hands toward your flesh as you move through the Chamber . . .**

The sign had also said that real actors would "come alive" during the presentation.

Okay. So Collin and Toby were part of the Jack the Ripper exhibit and hadn't told her. They were being paid as actors during their school break. But enough was enough.

Katie turned back to the stone anchored waist high in the outside wall of the church. There must have been some sort of spring-loaded button in the Stone that transported her to a different exhibit room, like one of those rides into the future at Disneyland.

Just then she caught sight of a daisy in a grassy patch below, and bending over, yanked it from the ground. It was obviously fake, but a bit of earth clung to the root stem, and the petals frittered away when she plucked at them. *So they planted some real flowers. Big deal. Anyone can plant —*

At the sound of someone calling her name, Katie glanced up and stared in amazement at the sight of two people trotting down the wide steps of the stone church. It was a young woman and a young man — both in their twenties, Katie guessed. The man wore one of those white dog collars, so he must be acting the part of a minister.

But it was the young woman who caught Katie's attention. With features similar to Courtney's, she looked strikingly like the wax figure positioned at the end of the row of Ripper victims. *Lady Beatrix Twyford.* And the dress she was wearing was an exact duplicate of the one in the portrait hanging over Katie's mantelpiece! Pale blue with embroidered rosebuds, a pink sash at the waist. *And there was the same black velvet ribbon circling her neck, pinned dead center with an oval cameo!* The only difference here was that this young woman striding toward Katie was *alive!*

Her hair wasn't the faded, pale-straw color as in the portrait, but a vibrant coppery yellow, with glints of auburn. And her face was just as striking, but without the arrogance. The same beauty mark, like a painted dot, glimmered above her upper lip.

The young woman with the coppery hair was almost level with Katie, a shimmering vision of rippling skirts and ribbons, and as she glided closer, Katie could see clearly that there was no anger or accusation in her dark eyes — so dark a blue they were almost black.

"Lady Beatrix —" Toby glanced over his shoulder. "Your cousin took a right nasty tumble."

"Bea!" Collin sputtered. "Katherine's talking nonsense."

Katie swiveled around to face the London Stone, her back to the others. Her pulse was racing. She wedged her hand back through the metal bars and jammed her finger into the pitted hole. Instantly, her head felt like it was exploding. She felt as if she were falling. . . down. . . down. . . down into a black, swirling hole that choked the air out of her lungs, suffocating her *as if she were being buried alive!*

Gasping and gulping great, heaping lungfuls of air, Katie opened her eyes to bright, fluorescent lights. In front of her was the London Stone, encased in wire mesh and balanced atop the crumbling stone well. The rocks at the base of the well were the same blackish-brown color, set in concrete. And the same broad, squishy line of footprints was tracked across the mat leading up to the London Stone.

Katie glanced across the room. Just outside the door was the sign pointing the way to the Beatlemania gallery, and another directing visitors to the Princess Diana room.

She closed her eyes and for a dizzying moment relief pulsed through her veins as palpable as the feeling of falling had been moments before. She was back! She looked over her shoulder and saw Toby standing stiffly, awkwardly, inertly.

Inertly?

"Toby?" she called out tentatively, leaving her finger embedded in the stone. Some instinct warned her that if she removed her finger she might never return to that other place...*that other world!*

Toby gave a slight movement, as if he heard her but was powerless to speak. His expression didn't change — he looked puzzled, bewildered, almost frightened.

"Collin...?" Katie whispered. Collin was standing just behind Toby.

In the silence, both boys appeared frozen, molded in wax like the figures in the Chamber of Horrors, eyes curiously blank.

The realization hit home. The significance of what had just happened struck Katie like a physical blow. She felt her balance begin to give and her feet stagger out from under her. She let out a gasp and held on to the Stone, gripping it with her fingertips, trying to keep her index finger firmly planted in the hole.

Her mind flashed on an image of Lady Beatrix, and a wave of vertigo shook her. She thought about Jack the Ripper's mutilated victims and about her parents. "I couldn't save my mother and father..." she said softly. *But if this is real, and I can go back to the nineteenth century, maybe...just maybe...I can save Lady Beatrix Twyford!*

If she waited another minute, Katie knew she would lose her nerve. Before she could change her mind, she thrust her index finger deeper into the stone, jabbing her fingernail painfully against something hard at the back of the indented fissure. Then she twisted and turned her finger, rubbing her knuckles almost raw against the outer portion of the stone, until finally she felt the fire-hot searing sensation tingle through her finger and shoot up her arm, pulsing and throbbing as if with its own heartbeat.

She was falling again, unable to breathe, down a dark, swirling shaft. Down, down, down as nausea rose up her throat, tasting of rust and lemon juice.

As suddenly as it began, the falling sensation ceased, and she felt the pinwheel hat squashed on top of her head, its satiny bow pinching the skin under her chin.

She yanked her finger out of the hole, held her breath, and made herself count slowly to ten. *One Mississippi, two Mississippi*. . . When she got to *ten Mississippi*, she lost her nerve. She opened her eyes and blinked around. She was once again outside, and the London Stone was protruding from a wall. *A brick wall!* She'd done it. She'd traveled back in time! And now she was going to save Lady Beatrix Twyford from Jack the Ripper. How difficult could it be, after all? With her superior twenty-first–century knowledge of science and crime scene investigation, learned from *CSI* reruns, how hard could this be?

Katie craned her neck and looked up. The spire of St. Swithin's soared high into the sky. It was a glorious sight. She was in another century. *Another world! Queen Victoria's London! And I'm going to catch Jack the Ripper!*

Chapter Eight

Pokers and Tongs
say the Bells of St. John's

TEN MINUTES LATER, Lady Beatrix and the Reverend H. P. Pinker were sitting with Collin, Toby, and Katie in a horse-drawn carriage that rattled through the misty streets of London. When they left St. Swithin's and the London Stone, Katie had watched in astonishment as the coachman — a bone-thin man dressed head to toe in yellow livery — brought the carriage with its gold emblem to the curbstone. She had gawked, speechless, as he thrust his whip into the whip-socket, dropped his reins, and jumped down from the carriage to open the door for them.

Even now, as the four-wheel carriage clip-clopped toward the West End, Katie felt dazed and in awe. Like the proverbial kid in a candy store, she couldn't stop blinking around, trying to take it all in. Arching her neck out the carriage window she could see the needle-thin spires of Parliament peeking up over the dusky outline of chimneys. On every corner, vendors hawked their wares. To the east, an omnibus crowded with passengers sailed past, drawn by a team of six horses gleaming with sweat.

Katie felt butterflies rise and fall and rise again in her stomach. She sank back into the soft, tufted leather of the jumpseat, taking in great gulps of air that smelled oddly of low tide — like mud and worms and snails and jellyfish, a briny, sulfurous odor.

Can I do this? Can I actually pull this off? Katie wondered. These people sitting next to her in the jiggling carriage thought Katie was their American cousin, newly arrived three days ago from Boston! Katie was from Boston, all right, but a Boston so far into the future it would probably not be recognizable. Except for Beacon Hill. Her home on Beacon Hill was in the historic district. A beautiful, narrow, red-brick townhouse built during the Civil War. But that house was no longer *her* house. She lived with Grandma Cleaves in London. If only her parents were still alive, if only —

No! I can't think about that. I have to concentrate!

Katie took another deep breath and studied Lady Beatrix. Beatrix looked happy and carefree and so strikingly similar to Courtney, it made Katie's insides tighten. Lady Beatrix didn't have Courtney's *exact* face, but it was eerily similar, especially the eyes: a dark, penetrating blue against luminous whites.

Shifting in her seat, Lady Beatrix smoothed out the folds of her sealskin cloak, and Katie noticed that her neck, above the collar of the fur cloak, seemed almost too slender for the weight of her blonde hair, piled high in back and falling in heavy ringlets to her shoulders.

Katie's mind flashed to the portrait of Lady Beatrix over her mantel. The artist had captured a certain likeness, but hadn't conveyed Beatrix's golden-blonde coloring or charm, the sparkle in her eyes, the laugh lines around her mouth. Those dark blue eyes were staring at Katie with interest, and Katie quickly glanced away. She felt like an impostor, a fake. She was being deceitful. *But she had to be!* Beatrix's life depended on it.

But can I really change the past? Katie wondered, a prickle of apprehension tingling up her spine. *And if I can. . .does that mean the future will change as well?* She remembered reading that if time travel really existed, a person might inadvertently stop herself from being born by interfering with a chance encounter between her great-great-grandparents, resulting in her own instantaneous death. *Don't be silly,* Katie told herself. *I'm here. I'm alive. I can't make myself not be born . . . right?*

She wouldn't think about that now, Katie told herself. The London Stone had transported her back in time for a reason. *To stop Jack the Ripper!*

Katie dragged her attention back to the others. Lady Beatrix, with her golden curls and sealskin cloak, was sitting next to the Reverend H. P. Pinker, a baby-faced, roly-poly, affable young man of twenty-four, whose nickname when he was playmates with Lady Beatrix growing up — Katie had learned — was "Stinker Pinker." Collin still called him this, which seemed odd to Katie, given that he was a minister, newly ordained. From the moony, hound-dog look on Pinker's face when he gazed at Lady Beatrix, Katie knew he was in love with her.

Next to the Reverend Pinker sat Collin, his red hair slicked back from his temples, his black frock coat giving him the appearance of a somber funeral director. And then there was Toby, who refused to look Katie in the eye. He seemed to be brooding or bracing himself for something.

The horses whinnied as they swung into a wide driveway, and the carriage jostled to a shivering halt. Katie thrust her head out the window to see what was happening. A high wall of rough stone rose up in front of them, pierced by iron gates. From a guardhouse just inside the wall emerged a squat little man in knee breeches and gaiters. He opened the gate and stood at attention. A loud *crack!* snapped from the coachman's whip, and the carriage wheeled briskly down the broad drive beneath a canopy of tree branches full of lush, gold foliage.

Something felt oddly familiar.

With a jolt of recognition, Katie let out a yelp, bumping her head on the top of the window frame. The grand façade coming into view—a massive oblong of smooth stone—was that of the very building she and her grandmother lived in! It was a condominium complex in the twenty-first century, with a parking garage instead of this sweeping front lawn. Katie's grandmother owned the western wing to the left as one approached, but the modern building had no glass conservatory, or gargoyles on the parapet of the roof, or battlement tower on each corner of the house rising up into the sky, giving the place—at once so familiar, yet so unfamiliar—a medieval eeriness.

As the horses trotted on, stopping beneath a porte-cochere along the side of the house, Katie could see that the cobbled pathway, which didn't exist in her own century, continued into a courtyard with stables beyond.

Collin and Toby jumped out of the carriage before the top-hatted coachman had time to step down and open the door. Collin raced ahead, bounding up the granite steps. Toby strode to the front of the carriage to quiet the horses, which were shifting and prancing in place.

"Thank you, Mr. Parker," Beatrix said brightly to the coachman when they had all emerged from the glossy black carriage. "I shan't need you again today. But tomorrow, at seven o'clock in the evening, would you be so kind as to arrange for the larger brougham? We shall all attend the new play *Dr Jekyll and Mr Hyde* at the Lyceum Theatre."

"Very good, m'lady."

When the carriage rolled away toward the stables, Katie clutched her hands to her stomach. How in the world was she going to pull this off? Her legs were quivering, her palms sweating, and her heart racing. *Why was she here, of all places?* What did it mean?

"Make haste, make haste!" Reverend Pinker cried, scurrying to Katie's side. "I promised your godfather we'd have you home in plenty of time for tea. Mustn't keep him waiting."

"My . . . g-godfather . . . ?" Katie stammered.

"The Duke of Twyford. He hasn't seen you since you were christened. Come along."

"B-but —"

"Katherine!" Collin called impatiently from the top step. "The guv'nor hates to be kept waiting. He made a special trip in from Bovey Castle, our country seat in Devon, just to see you. Come on!"

Okay, how do I address a duke? Katie wondered. *Do I curtsy?* She vaguely recalled that a duke was addressed as "my lord" or "your lordship," but wasn't sure. As she climbed the steps, a glow of gaslight shone from either side of the door, flanked by stone lions. A portly, middle-aged butler swung open the door, and they proceeded into an entrance hall. The black-and-white tiled floor spanned out in all directions like a giant chess board, but instead of chess pieces, there stood several suits of armor in stands against the walls.

I can do this. I can do this. I can do this! Katie told herself as the butler reached for Lady Beatrix's sealskin cloak. How difficult could it be to pretend to be an American girl visiting her British godfather in a house that had been in Katie's family for generations...which meant that Katie was related to these people, right? A great-great-grand-daughter, yet to be born? Is that who she was?

"Toby?" Katie whispered, hanging back as the others ambled ahead through an arched doorway bracketed by giant potted ferns. "What do I call the Duke? Do I curtsy when I meet him?"

Toby shot her an odd look, then bent low and whispered, "You drop a curtsy, miss. Sir Godfrey likes to be called 'guv'nor' or 'sir.' He fair flies into a rage if you address him as 'm'lord.'"

Still, Katie hung back. Her legs were shaking uncontrollably. It was one thing to vow to catch Jack the Ripper and another thing altogether to impersonate someone from a different century.

Seeing her falter, Toby's expression softened. He said in a coaxing voice, "Not to worry, luv. Mr. Oscar Wilde will be joining you for tea. He's a great wit. Lady Beatrix invited him because he always amuses the guv'nor. Come along, now. The guv'nor hates —"

"Oscar Wilde? *The* Oscar Wilde...I mean, er...the writer?"

"Heard of him, 'ave you?" Toby gently propelled Katie forward by the elbow.

"Of course I've heard of him! Who hasn't—" She stopped. "I mean, er, I think so, yes." Katie couldn't be sure if Oscar Wilde was famous in the year 1888. When exactly had he written *The Importance of Being Earnest?* She took a deep breath. *Well, this will be interesting,* she told herself. *I'm about to have tea with a nineteenth-century celebrity, a duke, and a future Jack the Ripper victim!*

And just this morning, when Katie awoke in her bedroom at Grandma Cleaves's house—*in this very house, or a portion of it*— she had bemoaned the fact that her life was boring, colorless, and uneventful.

"Toby?" Katie swallowed hard. "Have you ever heard of...um, that is to say, is there anyone by the name of...what I mean is...do you know anything about...Jack the Ripper?"

"Who, miss?"

"Jack the—" Katie glanced down. She had grabbed Toby's sleeve and was twisting it in a viselike grip. She didn't know whose face looked more astonished, hers or Toby's, but a thought had just occurred to her. At Madame Tussauds, a waxwork figure had borne this inscription:

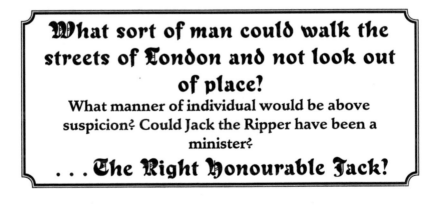

What sort of man could walk the streets of London and not look out of place?
What manner of individual would be above suspicion? Could Jack the Ripper have been a minister?
...The Right Honourable Jack!

That's it! That's why I'm here, Katie told herself. The Reverend Pinker must be Jack the Ripper! The wax statue at Madame Tussauds had shown an elderly minister with a white clerical collar, a bulging Adam's apple, and red blotches in his cheeks extending to the tip of his long nose. But he looked nothing like Lady Beatrix's childhood friend. And besides, the Reverend H. P. Pinker was in love with Beatrix. He wouldn't slash her to ribbons. A less likely candidate for a serial killer, Katie couldn't imagine. Still...

"Miss Katherine?" Toby fastened his dark eyes on hers, then glanced away, but not before Katie saw doubt and puzzlement reflected in them. And something else. Fear?

Chapter Nine

Kettles and Pans
say the Bells of St. Anne's

GAS LAMPS ON THE OAK-PANELED WALLS threw flickering shadows across Katie's face as Toby led her down a hallway papered with blue wisteria against a background of green ivy. In the front entrance hall, the butler turned to Toby and announced that Lord Twyford wished to see Miss Katherine in his study.

"I'll take her, Stebbins," Toby said.

"Very good, Master Tobias." The butler gave a curt nod.

Katie bit back a bubble of laughter. Tobias was such an old-fashioned name. But of course, this *was* the olden days. She smiled at Toby, the corners of her mouth twitching from the effort not to laugh.

Toby shot her a dark look and turned away. Who was *she* to be mocking him? *The duke's godchild, that's who,* Toby reminded himself.

"This way, miss," Toby grunted, a hard edge to his voice as he led Katie past the drawing room where the others were gathered for tea, and along a doglegged hallway hung with portraits of ancestors. Passing the dining room on their left and a music room to the right, they came to the library — a long, lofty room with an iron balcony circling above, accessed by a corkscrew staircase.

Katie glanced around the library trying to get her bearings. Were they at the front of the house or the back? The entire far wall, soaring two stories high, was filled with books, the top section reached by a giant ladder anchored on brass rollers. In the middle of this wall, at floor level, ran a wide archway through the bookshelves.

"Where are we?" Katie asked, turning in a full circle to take in the vastness of the room.

"The library," Toby answered testily.

"I know this is the library." *Duh.* "But what side of the house are we on? East, west, north, south?" The long windows on either side were draped in a gauzy fabric that let light stream in, but filtered the view to the outside.

"This is the western wing, miss. I thought Stebbins gave you the grand tour when you arrived."

Katie bit down on her lower lip. "He might have. . .but I. . . er. . .don't remember." she rubbed the back of her head as if it still hurt.

"Shall I fetch the doctor — ?" The gruff edge in his voice was gone, replaced by genuine concern.

"No! I mean, that won't be necessary. You see, well, I sometimes forget things. . .I was born with it. . .er. . .this forgetfulness. It comes and goes. It's nothing. But if I do happen to forget something. . . important. . .will you help me, Toby?"

Seeing him hesitate, she quickly added, "I wasn't laughing at you just now. I was laughing at your name. I'm sorry if I offended —"

"W'at's wrong wiff my name?" Toby sputtered. Whenever he got flustered, his Cockney accent grew thick. He was usually careful not to let it slip.

"Where I come from, it's not a name you hear very often."

"In the States? I thought it was a right common name." Toby narrowed his eyes and studied her closely. "You pulling m'leg, miss?"

She shook her head. "I've never met anyone named Tobias. It's sort of" — Katie thought for a minute. She remembered reading that if you lie, you should keep as close to the truth as possible — "unusual. It's an old-fashioned name in Boston. The only other Tobias I ever met was a dog."

He raised a dubious eyebrow.

"Look, Toby," Katie pushed on, tucking a strand of hair behind her ears. "If I act strange or say anything odd. . .will you correct me? I don't want to rouse anyone's suspicions." *And if the Reverend Pinker turns out to be Jack the Ripper, I'll need your help.*

"Suspicions? What about, miss?" A nerve twitched beside Toby's cheekbone.

"Well. . .that I'm not who I appear to be. That I'm not some sort of aristocratic girl who knows what she's doing. I don't want to make mistakes. If my manners or something I say sound out of place —"

"Needn't worry 'bout that, miss. Everyone here thinks you Yanks are an ill-bred lot who don't know the first thing about manners. You're all a bunch of Wild-West cowboys as far as we're concerned."

It was Katie's turn to peer at him doubtfully. Surely Toby was pulling *her* leg. "Just promise you'll help me, if I need it. That's all I ask."

Toby felt instantly sorry for the girl. He knew how it felt to be seated at a formal dinner table and stumble over which fork to use. The Twyford household boasted ten types of forks, each with a different set of prongs. There were your basic fish, meat, and dessert forks, as well as a five-pronged sardine fork, a long-pronged pickle fork, a two-pronged snail fork similar to the three-pronged oyster fork, and a fruit fork, a knife-edged pastry fork, and even an ice-cream fork shaped like a spoon. God 'elp you if you used the wrong one. "Right-o, Miss Katherine. I shall endeavor to do m'best."

He motioned her through the archway of books into a billiard room where stained-glass windows cast a kaleidoscope of colors onto a green-covered billiard table. Wedged between a stand of gleaming suits of armor at the other end of the room stood a narrow, iron-studded door.

Toby strode past the ancient armor and heaved open the door. "Guv'nor's chambers are through here, miss. I'm a bit out of favor with the old gent at present. Likely as not he'd fly into a fair tiger's cage if he spied me —"

"Tiger's cage?"

"Rage. So I'll just practice m'rail shots and wait fer y' here. Though truth to tell, the old Rob Roy is all bluff and bluster."

"Rob Roy?"

"The old boy. He's all bark and no bite. He'll put on airs and graces, to be sure. But he's not such a bag of sand — grand — as yer might be expecting. Nasty bark he has to be sure, but no bite. The duke is an old softie at heart." Holding the door open with one hand, Toby reached for a cue stick with the other. "Just remember to curtsy." He winked reassuringly.

Katie nodded her thanks and hastened through the door but was surprised to find herself standing at the foot of a long greenhouse, or rather, a conservatory, with an arched roof rising overhead like a glass bubble and catching twinkling glints of late afternoon sunlight. Long rows of potted plants in pebbled trays formed aisles extending to the back. Katie stepped down several stone stairs until she was fully submerged among the tropical foliage, and when the flickering sunlight overhead grew steady, she could just make out a glass-paneled door at the end of a row of potted orchids.

Brushing past a small tree with tiny orange fruit, Katie hurried to the glass door which was slightly ajar, but paused with her hand on the white porcelain knob when she heard voices on the other side — *angry voices.*

Not wanting to eavesdrop, she released the knob and stepped away, then halted abruptly. She was here to stop Jack the Ripper. She was *supposed* to eavesdrop. And anything else necessary to save Lady Beatrix Twyford. She was here for a reason. And *that* reason did not include being polite and on her best behavior.

With this thought firmly in mind, Katie inched forward and cupped her ear to the glass.

"Blast it, Major Brown!" boomed an elderly voice. "You have the effrontery to ask me such a thing?"

"I do, sir," shot back a younger man's voice, polite but firm.

Katie wiggled closer, peering through the crack in the door jamb, but could make out only a fraction of a fireplace on the opposite wall, flames blazing in the hearth.

"Beatrix is my granddaughter! And need I remind you, her forebears were kings, princes, noblemen. You can't honestly believe I would consent to her marriage to a *commoner*? Her parents would turn over in their graves, and our family would be the laughing stock of the peerage. Now, if you held a title, even a lowly one, and were the *Commissioner* of Scotland Yard, say . . . or even Chief Constable . . . rather than a mere assistant deputy . . . *that* would be a different kettle of fish. But as I foresee neither a knighthood, nor a commission in your future —"

"Grandfather!" came Lady Beatrix's voice, clearly distraught. "We're in love. Surely that counts for —"

Katie's eyebrows shot up. Lady Beatrix was in the duke's study.

"It counts for nothing, my girl, nothing." The duke drew in a wheezing breath. "And *you*, Major Brown. Damn your eyes! You have the audacity to ask me such a thing and bring my granddaughter with you? No self-respecting gentleman asks for the hand of a man's granddaughter and brings her along with him. Only a toady —"

"Grandfather! Stop! Gideon . . . I mean, Major Brown, was dead set against it, but I insisted. You know how apoplectic you get. It isn't good for your health! And I wanted you to understand how in love I am. I've accepted his proposal."

"Humph! I've a good mind to take you over my knee. Bah! You don't know the first thing about love. And it is *I* who shall tell *you* to whom you will become affianced! You're a disobedient, young flit of a girl barely out of the schoolroom. I should send you back to —"

Lady Beatrix began to sob, slowly at first, then long, heart-wrenching, gulping sobs. "I-I lost my parents when their carriage overturned. Please don't let me lose the person who's most dear to me."

"There, there, m'girl. There, there," the duke's voice softened considerably. "This won't do. Won't do at all. Run along now. Major Brown and I need to have a little talk. That's my good girl. Never could deny you anything," he muttered. "Run along now."

"T-thank you, Grandfather," Lady Beatrix whispered. Katie heard what sounded like the young woman planting loud kisses on her grandfather's cheeks, followed by the soft patter of footsteps drawing close.

Katie ducked behind an almond shrub and, crouching low, peered through a clump of prickly leaves just as the glass-paneled door swung open. Katie had expected to see Lady Beatrix's face tear-stained and full of anguish, but saw only a joyful look of triumph. No tears, just a secret smile playing on her beautiful face. Lady Beatrix obviously knew how to handle her grumpy grandfather.

Halfway down the center aisle, Beatrix stopped and glanced over her shoulder as if wrestling with her own desire to turn back and eavesdrop. But clearly thinking better of it, she swiveled around and strode gracefully past a tray of strawberry plants and out the iron-studded door at the other end. When she was gone, Katie scooted from behind the shrub and once again pressed her ear to the beveled glass.

"Look here!" she heard the duke roar. "This is untenable. When I was Home Secretary you distinguished yourself, to be sure. The Bellmont business got nasty. You handled it well. You showed yourself to have the makings of a true gentleman. But what you're asking now is not the mark of a gentleman, but of a —"

"And how, Sir Godfrey" — Major Brown cut him off — "does one summarize *in true gentlemanly terms*, the necessity of resorting to murder —"

"Damn and blast you to hell! Are you threatening me?" shouted the duke. "Do I detect a subtle implication that if I thwart your request for my granddaughter's hand in marriage, you plan to expose me with the Bellmont affair?"

"Certainly not. The idea never crossed my —"

"Nor shall it. *Ever.* Am I correct, Major Brown?" It was an order, not a request.

"On my honor, Lord Twyford. I know my duty to Queen and country, *and to you*, Sir. Surely you know that by now."

"I commissioned you in the name of Her Majesty! You killed one of England's most notorious enemies and, aside from the House of Lords being forever in your debt, you earned your position as assistant deputy of Scotland Yard — handed to you on a silver platter. Now, my boy, pay heed. There is a position in the War Office at Whitechapel, Director of Covert Operations. I can put your name forward in exchange for dropping this absurd notion of marrying —"

"Never."

"And if I cut my granddaughter off without a penny? God's teeth, man! What will you do then? Condemn her to live in a rat hole on a policeman's salary? Where's the pride in that, Major Brown, eh?"

"I love your granddaughter with all my heart. I'd lay down my life for her. But no matter the outcome, let me be clear, Sir Godfrey. I will not be fobbed off with a promise of a directorship. I've made my way thus far on my wits, my fortitude, and my integrity. I've done my duty to my country and shall continue to do so. But I *will not* be bribed."

"Here's a deal for you then, eh?" came the duke's querulous voice. "Come back when you have risen in the ranks. I'll take nothing less than your becoming deputy head of CID, or better yet, Commissioner of Scotland Yard, before I consider your request for my granddaughter's hand in marriage."

"Very good, m'lord. But I want your promise in return that you will not hinder my efforts in any way. If you give me *your* word as a *gentleman*, you shall have mine in return. I shall not ask for Lady Beatrix's hand again until I've risen to the topmost ranks of Scotland Yard, or" — he lowered his voice — "if our sovereign queen should deem to knight me for my...services."

"You do that, son. You do that. But mind, it won't be easy. You'll have to achieve something mighty spectacular. Mighty spectacular indeed."

"I intend to, Sir Godfrey."

"So we have a deal, then, eh, m'lad? You're an ambitious, talented young man with a bright future. I admire self-made men such as yourself. Now then, I could use a spot of brandy. Let's drink on it, shall we?"

A minute later, Katie heard the clink of glasses followed by sounds as if the two were hurriedly swallowing their drinks.

"You may go now, Major Brown," said the duke. "And tell Stebbins to send along my godchild, Miss Katherine, if you please. I drove in from the country just to see her. Fetch the child for me, there's a good lad."

Katie raced down the center aisle of plants, nearly knocking over a pot of lavender. When she reached the iron-studded door at the far end, she turned full around, smoothed out her billowing skirts, and attempted to settle a complacent smile on her face just as Major Brown came charging through the glass door looking like an angry bear caught in a trap.

Seeing her, he skidded to a halt. He looked nothing like what Katie had envisioned. In a ruggedly handsome face anchored on a thick neck above broad shoulders, his green eyes fastened on Katie's.

"A pleasure to meet you again, Miss Katherine." An ironic smile twitched at the corners of his lips. "Sir Godfrey is expecting you. But you're looking quite flushed. I trust nothing is amiss?"

Sunlight, glinting through the glass dome overhead, highlighted the powerful, almost sinister angles of his jaw and cheekbones, and made the chestnut gleam of his hair appear several shades lighter than his moustache.

"No. Nothing's wrong," Katie said breezily, though she could feel the power of his cat-green eyes boring into her like heat piercing her skin. She flinched and pushed past. *He knows I was listening*, she told herself. *Or he suspects.*

When Katie eased open the door to the duke's study, the words "murder" and "England's most notorious enemy" pounded in her head. It was clear from the conversation she'd just overheard that Major Brown had killed someone *with* the duke's knowledge and consent, and quite possibly the Queen's.

Sir Godfrey, the Duke of Twyford, was gazing out the window. He gulped down a large snifter-full of amber liquid, then a second, and a third, giving Katie time to scan the room.

The ceiling of the duke's study was high, with big windows over-looking a garden. In the center of the room stood a broad desk littered with papers, pipes, ink jars, quills, keys, cigars, banknotes, and loose coins. Around the walls, above the wainscoting, ran a line of medieval weapons — spears, war clubs, and devil masks — as well as big game trophies. Over the fireplace, where a steady blaze glowed, was a rhinoceros head, its marble eyes reflecting light from the flickering flames. Perched on either side of the chimney shelf sat two stuffed birds, a vulture and an eagle.

Katie gave a little gasp of recognition. The vulture and eagle were the same ones collecting dust in an old trunk in Grandma Cleaves's attic. Bald in patches and moth-eaten, they had been toys for Katie and Courtney when they were younger.

When the duke swiveled around to face her, bitterness flared so intensely in his watery blue eyes, and his jowly, wrinkled face held such a sour expression, Katie forgot to curtsy.

"So it's you," he wheezed. "Spitting image of your mother." He lowered his great bulk into a leather chair by the fire and motioned for her to take the seat opposite.

Katie stepped over a pile of open ledgers on the floor covered in tobacco ash and sank into the massive club chair, the seat cushion of which sagged almost to the floor.

"Sinkhole of a chair, eh? Bloody nuisance." The duke snatched up a black cigar from a side table and began examining it end to end. He bit off the tip, and with a loud grunt, spat it into the fireplace. "Do y'know the difference between a hyena and a police bobby?" he poked the unlit cigar in her direction.

Katie kept her gaze fully directed on the duke and shook her head.

"Humph!" He glowered. "The hyena has the more exalted moral character. Which is why" — he raised a clenched fist — "that son-of-a-sloth will *never* marry my granddaughter, not whilst there's an ounce of breath left in me! What d'you say to that, eh?" He clamped watery blue eyes on Katie, as if daring her to contradict him.

"Major Brown will roast in *hell* before I allow him to marry my granddaughter. I'll foil his every move, thwart him at every turn, that's what I'll do."

"But you gave your word —" Katie blurted, then dug her fingernails into the leather armrests of the chair. "Er...um...I mean..."

"Don't gibber, girl! I detest gibbering. Doesn't amount to a tinker's curse what I promised the sorry son of —" During the thunderclap of silence, they stared at each other. "I told you that, did I?" he demanded suspiciously, and when Katie nodded, he made a face as though smelling a rotten egg. "Bah. I talk too much. Means nothing."

He rose and poured himself another drink from the crystal decanter by the window. "The unctuous blighter hasn't a pauper's chance in hell of rising in the CID. He'd have to solve an unsolvable case or catch a notorious criminal. What are the odds of that, m'girl, eh?" He ran the bulbous stopper of the decanter across his grey-whiskered chin.

"But we mustn't underestimate Major Gideon Brown, no indeed," the duke continued, brandishing the decanter above his head like a torch. "Tenacious as a bulldog and methodical to a fault — *don't I know it!*" He swung the bottle back down and poured another drink. "Odds are, Major Brown is plotting a course of action as we speak. But we'll beat him at his own game, eh?"

In one gulp, the duke drained his brandy snifter, ending with a noise that sounded like "*Haaaaaa-ah!*" as if he'd just chugged a foot-long stein of beer. Then he hurled the crystal glass into the fireplace where it crashed and crackled causing Katie to jump out of her seat.

"God's teeth! I'll not bungle this one!" the duke roared, as the fire embers sputtered and sizzled, lapping up droplets of brandy. "Send Collin to me at once...no, send Toby. I've a dark suspicion that *Toby's* my man."

Part III:

Jack the Ripper Strikes

Chapter Ten

Murder in Buck's Row.
August 31, 1888.

Seventeen-year-old Georgie Cross had a round, clean-shaven, good-natured face that flushed with a strawberry rash whenever he got excited. He was wearing knee breeches and a ragged white shirt beneath his porter's smock, and his hobnailed boots made loud clumping sounds against the cobblestones. It was early evening, and as Georgie ambled into Buck's Row on his way to Spitalfields Market, he found himself joyfully whistling the tune of "Auprès de ma Blonde," the French marching song—his knees stepping high along with the rousing melody.

Georgie fisted his hand and pounded it to his heart like a Roman soldier pledging allegiance. Georgie was in love. *Again.* But this time it was *true love*. Dark eyed, dimple-cheeked, buxom Cecilia, a dancer at the Veux Music Hall, wasn't a bit like his last twist 'n' swirl, Monique. No, Cecilia was going to be his one and only true love forever.

Georgie couldn't read or write, but he was a great one for stories. He remembered them all in his head, and right now he was remembering that odd little fable about a wizard — or was it a warlock? — named Zeus, who, at the beginning of time, when all humans were born with two legs, two arms, and one head with two faces, decided to cut everyone down the middle and scatter their cleaved parts across the universe. Then he commanded all future generations to go out and search for their rightful other halves to make them whole again.

It was a story Georgie had loved hearing his mother recite ever since he was a wee nipper. And Cecilia — Georgie felt it down to the tips of his toes — was his true other half, his twin flame. She just didn't know it yet.

Georgie flushed scarlet thinking about Cecilia's long, shapely bacon and eggs, and her beautiful dark mince pies.

Those ebony eyes of hers made the blood rush to his head when she chanced to favor him with a smile. True, she wasn't the type of girl his mum would approve of. She wore far too much paint on her face. But Cecilia was a can-can dancer after all. She needed to rouge her cheeks and paint her eyes and smile encouragingly at the toffs at the dance hall in order to get an extra sovereign here and there. No harm in that. Underneath all the powder and dross, Georgie felt sure Cecilia was as demure as a saint. And those ruby lips...

But thinking of Cecilia's luscious red lips reminded Georgie unhappily of all the crates full of ripe fruit and vegetables he would soon be straining to load and unload well into the night, stacking them in the market stalls so as to be ready before dawn.

With a heavy sigh, he glanced around. Buck's Row was dimly lit, with only a few sputtering gas lamps casting flickering shadows into the gutters. The full moon overhead made the street appear brighter, illuminating Berber's Slaughterhouse across the way in a pale, amber glow.

A cat yowled in the distance.

Georgie gave an involuntary shudder, not at the high-pitched cat wail, but at the slaughterhouse. As he approached, he couldn't help but scrunch up his nose at the stench. He caught sight of Johnny Brisbane standing in front of the slaughterhouse with a group of butcher lads in blood-smeared leather aprons. Johnny Brisbane was Georgie's mother's cousin's brother-in-law. He owned the East End Butcher shop called The Cut, near Petticoat Alley, but got his meat here at the slaughterhouse, hauling great hulking carcasses across town to The Cut. Georgie's mum had wanted Georgie to apprentice with Johnny.

"Ta!" Georgie waved, as more boys in bloody aprons came piling out of the slaughterhouse through large wooden stable doors, with giant crossbeams. The butcher lads were gulping in deep breaths of fresh air, trying to fill their lungs after being inside where it reeked of dead flesh. As hard as Georgie's job was, Georgie could never be a butcher, not with the crying sounds of the dying animals and the stench. *Never.* The mere thought turned his stomach.

He was sorry that he had come this way. Buck's Row made him uneasy. It had no crime because a constable box stood just around the corner, but Georgie always gave the slaughterhouse a wide berth just the same, as did most everyone else in the East End.

He quickened his pace and continued humming "Auprès de ma Blonde," but a nervous wobble rose in his voice. This whole street gave him a bit of the old gooseberry light — fright — that he used to feel as a young nipper on goblin day.

A flash of silver caught his eye. Something brownish, like a pile of oilcloth, lay crumpled near the curbstone. An old coat, mayhaps?

"Let's have a look-see," Georgie murmured. Might be something of value, fallen off a tradesman's cart. Anything lost on the roadside could be claimed as salvage. Last month Georgie had found a broken spindle chair at the side of the road. He'd mended the peg leg, patched the straw seat with a dock hook and twine, and gave it to his mum, who was right pleased.

"Top-drawer, Georgie," Ma had proudly pronounced when he presented it to her. He'd always been clever with his hands. Maybe this bundle in the road was another top-drawer find, a discarded coat or burlap blanket he could patch up and give to his sister.

Full of high hopes and whistling contentedly again, Georgie approached the protruding heap, then realized with a jolt that it wasn't an old coat or a canvas oilcloth, but a girl.

"Must be ill, poor thing." But as he circled the prone figure, his legs went taut, and he felt suddenly nervous, like a stiff-legged dog sensing trouble.

"Oi, then. What's wrong wiff yer, lass?" he said loudly. When the girl didn't respond, he hollered over his shoulder to the butcher boys half a block away.

"Here! Give us a hand, mates! Some poor chit's gone lost her footing."

Bending closer, Georgie could see that the girl's clothes were in disarray and her bonnet lay in the gutter next to something shiny. Born to a life of scarcity, Georgie plucked the silver object from the gutter and slipped it into his pocket. It was a pair of silver opera glasses, but he was too worried about the girl to give the treasure — as treasure it surely was — much thought. A portion of his brain registered that it would fetch a good price at Pickwick's Pawnshop. But his conscious brain remained focused on the girl...something was wrong. But Georgie had been mistaken before. Ma said often enough that when it came to twist 'n' swirls, Georgie didn't have the sense he was born with.

Johnny Brisbane came trotting down the street. When he reached Georgie, he glanced down and said, "Trollop's drunk as a skunk, I s'pect."

"Or fainted," said Georgie.

Together they leaned over for a closer look. Georgie touched the girl's cheek. It was warm. *Thanks be*, he thought, but when he lifted both of her hands, they fell back down, curiously limp.

"God's fish, Georgie! She's copped it!" cried Brisbane.

"Don't say that! She's warm as a toasted crumpet."

"Deader 'n a haddock, don't I know it. I works in a bleedin' butcher shop, and I say she's copped it, right good."

"No! No! Can't be. I think I can hear her breathing, only it's ever so faint. Come on, Johnny. Let's get her on her feet."

Brisbane backed away. "Not me. I ain't touching her." He crossed himself. "I tells you she's brown bread. Brown bread!"

"She's not! She can't be," Georgie insisted, touching the girl's cheek again, and as he did so the scarf across her neck fluttered slightly revealing the corner of an open gash. With a shudder, Georgie flicked the rest of the scarf away and stared down at a glob of blackish blood oozing from a great gaping wound across her throat.

"Blimey! Look at that!" cried Johnny Brisbane. "Her throat's been chived from ear to ear!"

A scarlet flush crept up Georgie's neck, suffusing his cheeks in a bright strawberry rash. He rose up hollering, and didn't stop shouting and waving his arms until he'd reached the corner of Buck's Row and Bradley Street, where he flagged down Police Constable Misen of H-Division, Whitechapel.

Too late he remembered the glittery opera glasses in his pocket. Did they belong to the dead girl?

Chapter Eleven

Old Father Baldpate
say the Death Bells of Aldgate

EARLIER THAT SAME EVENING, an hour before Mary Ann Nichols
was murdered in Bucks Row, Whitechapel, the air was crisp, cool, and
alive with fog swirls along the gaslit Strand as the horses clopped
toward the Lyceum Theatre. Inside the carriage, Katie glanced at Toby
sitting across from her on the leather seat, looking miserably uncomfortable in formal evening attire. He kept running his index finger
along the inside of his winged collar, pinched together round his neck
by a wide silk tie, above a tight-fitting frock coat. He reminded Katie
of an usher at a funeral. *A handsome usher.*

Next to Toby, Collin looked less glum, but equally stiff in a
black dinner jacket, with a monocle dangling foppishly (and foolishly,
Katie thought) from a cord around his neck. Collin's hair, slicked back
with oil, made him look like a red-haired seal rising from the water's
depths, wet and glistening. Between Toby and Collin sat the Reverend

Pinker in dog collar and tail coat, staring over, not through, a pair of gold-rimmed spectacles.

Lady Beatrix, hands folded in her lap, wearing an orange-and-blue gown, a single large diamond pinned at her throat, appeared radiant and happy on Katie's right, with Oscar Wilde in velvet smoking jacket, knee-breeches, and patent-leather boots on Katie's left. The men all wore silk top hats, and flowers poked from the lapel button-holes of their jackets. Oscar Wilde's flowers were large, flamboyant, and a deep scarlet color.

A jangle of harness bells rang out as the coach clattered to a stop in front of the Lyceum Theatre. Katie heard the distinct *crack!* of a horse whip and craned her neck to get a view out the open window. Dozens of carriage lamps, burning bright, flickered on the sides of the cabs and coaches lined up in front of the theater. Horses whinnied. Amidst the crush of people thronging toward the entrance doors, Katie felt tension in the air and could see anticipation on almost every face.

The opening night of *Dr Jekyll and Mr Hyde* was obviously a big event, Katie thought. She'd seen reruns of the famous story on TV, but this was different. This was the real thing. She wondered if Robert Louis Stevenson had written it as a play first or as a novel. She couldn't remember. But she did know that the gothic horror story was going to be a great success and would someday — a century or so in the future — even become a Broadway musical.

The footman, dressed in purple and yellow livery, jumped down to the curb, clicked the latch, and swung the carriage door open. Katie gathered up the folds of her velvet gown in her right hand, while awkwardly clutching an enormous ostrich feather fan and a satin purse in the other, and attempted to climb out of the jiggling carriage with grace. With the footman's help, she eased first one foot, then the other, down the wooden carriage steps, but the train of her gown kept getting tangled around her ankles.

"Dexter." Lady Beatrix turned to the footman when they were all standing on the curb. "We shan't stay long after the final curtain call. We're expected at the Thespian Club for dinner."

"Very good, m'lady," Dexter answered with a sweeping bow, elbows rigid by his side, reminding Katie of a parrot whose wings had been clipped.

Katie took a deep breath. Yesterday she'd been in the twenty-first century. Today she was in Victorian London, and would stay here until Jack the Ripper was caught. That was her mission. She could go home anytime, she told herself. But first she had to save Beatrix Twyford.

She took another deep breath, and glanced around. The night air smelled of horse sweat, clashing with warring perfumes wafting from all the ladies who swept past. Across the cobblestone street, the gleaming white theater with its giant columns rose like a Greek temple beneath a bright full moon ringed with mist. Katie remembered something about Jack the Ripper slashing his victims around the time of a full moon, and gave an involuntary shudder.

She took a tentative step, trying hard not to stumble, but the bulky opera cape weighed her down, and her hair, piled high in coils above her head and woven with thick strands of pearls, felt as cumbersome as a beehive helmet. If it hadn't been for Agnes, Beatrix's lady's maid, Katie would never have been able to dress herself. Wriggling into her gown had been more complicated than getting into a fancy prom dress. The silk gloves alone, reaching past her elbows, were fastened with twenty tiny pearl buttons each. And then there were the flounces of beaded material draped over the horsehair bustle in the back that had to be snapped, pinned, and tugged into place like a jigsaw puzzle.

Grandma Cleaves always told Katie to wear sensible shoes. *Forget sensible shoes.* This century didn't know from sensible anything! In the past (or was it the future?) when Katie was writing a research paper on nineteenth-century costumes, she had admired the romantic pictures of women in long, billowing gowns. But the reality was different. It wasn't romantic at all. *Just a total pain!* Hard to stand up and impossible to walk. And it took hours to dress! The heavily boned corset was a torture device. The inside had actual bones — *bones!* — and metal wire strips to cinch her waist and hold the shape of the dress in place. When she was finally dressed, powdered, and misted with perfume, Katie had made a promise to herself. She would never *ever* complain about wearing her bulky ski parka when it was cold. The heavy opera cape made her ski parka feel like air.

Katie tugged at the lower half of her gown, trying to untangle it from around her calves. Her gaze swiveled to Lady Beatrix standing to her right. *I'll just imitate Beatrix. If that doesn't work, they'll have to carry me into the theater!*

Lady Beatrix, with a dexterous sweep of her right arm, gathered up the folds of her train over her wrist and began gliding effortlessly toward the marble steps. *Damn. How does she do it?* Katie wondered. *It looks so easy!* But it wasn't. Katie felt as if the velvet gown would swallow her up and make her lose her balance like one of those roly-poly dolls that wiggled and jiggled from cars' rear windows. She lurched, jerked, and stumbled forward.

Noting her distress, Oscar deftly grasped Katie by the elbow, pinching the folds of her gown between his fingers and Katie's wrist, making it appear as if Katie herself were clutching the material, and guided her up the moonlit marble steps. At the same instant, Toby flanked her other side, positioning himself in such a way that if Katie tottered, he and Oscar, between them, could straighten her up.

Silhouetted against the shimmering light from the enormous gas jets flaring up on either side of the pillared theater doors, Toby watched Katie from the corner of his eye. *Cor blimey, what's wrong with the girl?* he wondered. When she first arrived from America, Toby had thought that Miss Katherine, with her amber-eyed beauty, flawless complexion, and glossy chestnut hair, was the most graceful creature in all of London. Now the girl was tottering as if punch-drunk. She seemed awkward, hesitant, unsure of herself.

Toby's heart gave a great leap in his chest. *She must have hurt herself when she took that tumble yesterday in front of the London Stone.* Two days ago, Miss Katherine hadn't paid him the least notice, but yesterday after she'd fallen, her eyes seemed constantly to seek him out, intently peering at him beneath their long, dark lashes. And in the library she had asked him, no, begged him, to correct her if she acted strange or forgot which fork to use. He watched as her lips pressed together in a baffling sort of determination, as if she were willing herself to walk without wobbling. She glanced up, and her gaze burned into him.

Toby drew a sharp breath and staggered back, distancing himself from her, allowing Mr. Wilde to escort her through the arched doorway. Toby was accustomed to girls' sidelong glances at him, but to actually stare like this? He didn't know what to make of it. Proper young ladies didn't look a bloke full in the eye. Barmaids, tavern girls, dance-hall chits, perhaps. But not high-born, well-bred girls. It simply wasn't done. Perhaps it was because she was from bricks and pates — the States. That must be it. Yanks were a different kettle of fish.

No sooner had Toby stepped away from Katie than Collin sprang forward and took his place at her side.

Toby watched them all move forward in the dusky twinkle of the gas lamps and again felt his heart thud in his chest. Yesterday morning, before visiting the London Stone, the girl had seemed cold and petulant, with a smooth, porcelain hardness to her skin. The lip salve on her mouth had stood out like a bruise. Now he could swear the girl wore no salve, yet her mouth was the color of rose petals.

Stop it! Miss Katherine is as far from my reach as the moon from the sun, Toby chided himself. She was a rich American heiress sent to London to find a suitable husband. One with a title! An earl, a viscount, a baron. Not the illegitimate son of a Cockney lacemaker. Toby's brown-bread father, to be sure, was the youngest brother of the Duke, but Toby could never inherit a title or land because he'd been born on the wrong side of the blanket. The Duke of Twyford, out of loyalty to his dead brother, afforded Toby a certain stature in the household. Not quite a servant, nor quite a family member. Toby was given an education of sorts, and the job of companion to Collin. His latest task was to make sure Collin didn't get into any more trouble with dance hall girls, or rack up any more gambling debts.

Katie peered back over her shoulder, a tight little smile twisting round her lips. She shrugged her shoulders as if to say, *I feel as out of place as you do, Toby.*

He tore his eyes away. The Duke would boil him in oil if he overstepped himself with this American twist 'n' swirl, who also happened to be the Duke's godchild. *The guv'nor would cut me into pieces and feed me to the dogs. And rightly so,* Toby thought. *No, I'll not be going near the chit, no matter how often she makes simmering-stew eyes at me. Not in this lifetime. Not in a hundred years!*

Katie and the others waited in line behind a gaggle of elderly ladies decked in sparkling diamond tiaras, accompanied by a red-faced, portly man adorned with medals and ribbons.

Oscar whispered in Katie's ear: "Overdressed dowagers and a tedious cabinet minister. Peacocks in everything but beauty and brains." With his free hand he tapped impatiently at the toe of his patent-leather boot with his ebony cane.

Minutes later they advanced into the crowded lobby, festooned with framed posters of upcoming productions of *Macbeth*, *Othello*, and *The Duchess de la Vallière*. Katie noted that each man, upon entering the lobby, instantly snatched off his silk top hat and tucked it under his arm. She swiveled around, seeking out Toby, and when she caught sight of him passing the ticket-seller's window, he stopped midstride, studied her quizzically for a moment, then darted off into the crowd.

"The Lyceum is more crowded than usual, even for opening night," the Reverend Pinker commented, glancing over his gold-rimmed spectacles.

Oscar continued his tap-tap-tapping. "Oh, look!" he twittered in a low theatrical voice. "There's Princess Sophia of Karlsruhe!"

"Where?" Katie asked, eager to see what a princess looked like.

Oscar nodded in the direction of the princess. "That plump woman in purple plumage with tiny black eyes and those wonderful emeralds!" He lowered his voice. "She'll be talking interminable bad

French during intermission and laughing immodestly at everything that is said to her."

"Oscar! *Hush, do,*" Lady Beatrix chided in a soft whisper, the glitter of the diamond pinned to her throat matched the glittering laughter in her eyes. "She'll hear you."

"My darling Lady Beatrix. When will you ever learn...there is only one thing in the world worse than being talked about, and that is *not* being talked about." Oscar shot her a mischievous grin.

At the top of the grand staircase, an usher in red velveteen escorted them into a private salon where blue flames crackled in a fire grate flanked by stone gargoyles. The walls of the long gallery were embedded with mosaic tiles, and the ceiling, inlaid with thousands of tiny square mirrors, made the polished floor sparkle and dance.

"Ah. The Byzantine Room," Oscar said, cocking an eyebrow around the salon. "No doubt, we're to imagine ourselves in an El Greco painting," he harrumphed. "But it's a sham, and not a good one at that. All paste and mirrors."

Crossing the room, they proceeded into a narrow hall and stepped through a curtained archway that opened into an ornate private box with plush seats, four on one side of the aisle, four on the other. *This is wonderful!* Katie thought, leaning over the padded rail and looking directly down onto the stage. A domed ceiling overhead, painted in bright popsicle colors, showed winged cherubs and wood nymphs leaping over the proscenium arch.

Katie gave a great sigh. She'd never seen such an opulent theater in her life. It was dreamlike and breathtaking. She'd been to plays with her grandmother, but never like this.

Noticing that the others were settling into their seats, Katie unclasped her cape and, careful not to upset the bustle — like a camel hump — at the back of her gown, sank into the seat between Collin, fiddling with his dangling monocle, and Oscar Wilde, smoothing the folds of his velvet knee-breeches.

Lady Beatrix, with the grace of a ballet dancer, lowered herself into the seat across the aisle. She looked beautiful and serene in her orange-and-blue gown, the single, large diamond sparkling at her throat. The Reverend Pinker plunked himself down next to Lady Beatrix and proceeded to read the playbill.

Katie took a deep breath. The air wasn't musty, like in the old London theaters she was used to, but crisp and clean with a hint of fresh paint and lemon polish.

Oscar drew out a pair of opera glasses from his waistcoat and thrust them into Katie's gloved hands. "Take a gander over there, *ma chère.*"

"Where? What should I be looking at?" Katie asked, raising the binocular-like glasses to her eyes. She swept them toward the stage, but the curtain was drawn and the orchestra pit, hidden behind large ferns.

Oscar raised an eyebrow, reached for the glasses and plunked them snugly against his eye sockets. "There is no dearth of opportunity here, young lady. One comes to the theater to spy and to be spied upon. Surely you didn't think we were here for the literary enlightenment and pedantic posturing of an underpaid playwright? Tut-tut, how very *American* of you. Look there, second balcony below, an unsuspecting peeress — lovely in pink brocade and pearls — chatting affably with that notorious rascal —" He swiveled around to the left like a sea captain sighting land. "Ho-ho! And there's poor Lady Fermor who doesn't care a whit for music, but is very fond of musicians. And over there is Lady Windermere. When she married the Duke of Mandeville he had eleven castles, and not a single house fit to live in. Now, his grace has twelve houses, and not a single castle. There's Monsieur de Koloff, the Russian Ambassador, who has gout and keeps a second wife in Bayswater. And in the royal box, my dearest, darling Lillie Langtry, looking wonderfully munificent with her grand ivory bosom, large, forget-me-not eyes, and those luscious coils of golden hair — not straw-colored hair, mind you, but the golden red that is woven into sunbeams and hidden in amber. She has the face of a saint, but the fascination of a sinner, *n'est-ce pas?*" He thrust the glasses back into Katie's hands. "You must see the world for yourself, *ma chère.*"

Katie stared at him. Did everyone in this century talk like this, or was it just Oscar Wilde? She raised the opera glasses and scanned the crowd. All around her the flash of satin and the sparkle of glittering jewelry caught the winking light from the gaslit chandeliers.

"Who's that bald guy — er, I mean, gentleman, in the box next to ours?" Katie whispered. The man looked familiar. His bald head was shining like the dome of St. Paul's, rising above thick shoulders draped in a ruby-red sash.

"That's His Royal Highness, the —"

" — King?" Katie sputtered.

"Are you daft?" Collin cut in. "That's the Prince Regent. The Prince of Wales. He won't inherit the throne until his mother, the Queen, dies."

Of course, Katie muttered to herself. There wasn't a king during Victoria's reign. The Queen's husband was Prince Albert. *Get your head out of the clouds,* Katie chastised herself. *Pay attention, and stay focused!*

After the shock of seeing the future King Edward VII up close and personal and looking more . . . well, *real,* than his waxwork replica at Madame Tussauds, it took Katie several minutes before she realized that Toby was not sitting with them.

Was that him in the gallery far below, in the wings off to the left? She raised her glasses and searched the crowd, but with no luck.

Chapter Twelve

You Owe Me Ten Shillings
say the Bells of St. Helen's

KATIE SCANNED THE CROWDED THEATER. "Where's Toby?"

"Dunno." Collin shrugged, the gleam of gaslight from the wall jets making his face appear ghostly pale.

"Mr. Wilde? Do you know where Toby is?"

"My dear girl, you must call me Oscar. I insist," said Oscar. "As to Master Tobias, the dear boy could be here, he could be there. He could be anywhere. Such is the insouciance of youth!"

"Reverend Pinker? Have you seen—" But H. P. Pinker was busying himself looking through his own opera glasses as if fascinated with the winged cherubs carved overhead in the proscenium arch.

Just then, a short man with a thick body and almost no neck—but sporting a profusion of side whiskers and a brown, feathery beard—appeared through the curtained archway and strode down the aisle. When he caught sight of Oscar, he stopped short.

Oscar scowled at the man, then kicked moodily at the balcony footrail. Katie heard him curse under his breath. The whiskered man's beard spread fanwise over his collar with what appeared to be bristling indignation. He pivoted, and bowing low, spoke to Lady Beatrix, but the words seemed wrung out of him almost against his will.

"Lady...Beatrix...an honor...as...always. I brought you a little something. A playbill signed by the playwright, Mr. Robert Louis Stevenson, with my compliments." He gave a curt nod and handed Beatrix the playbill.

"How very kind of you, Mr. Stoker. Let me introduce you to my friends. This is the Reverend H. P. Pinker who runs the East End Charity Mission for Widows and Orphans. Rev. Pinker, this is Mr. Bram Stoker, the theater manager."

"A pleasure, Mr. Stoker. A pleasure indeed. A lovely theater. Quite outstanding, I must say. The recent renovations do you credit."

"Thank you, sir. The pleasure is all mine." Stoker shook Pinker's hand vigorously. "I am familiar with your good works. If I, or the theater, can assist you at any time with your charitable endeavors, please do not hesitate to ask."

"*Omigod!* That's Bram Stoker. He wrote *Dracula!*" Katie gasped.

"*Dracula?*" Collin looked confused.

"You know! Count Dracula, the vamp—" Katie bit back her words. *Dracula* must not have been written yet. *Damn, damn, double-damn. I have to be more careful,* Katie told herself. But it was hard. She had fallen into a rhythm with the people in this century. And Collin looked so much like her own cousin, Katie kept forgetting which was which.

Oscar gawked at her. "Certainly not!" he sputtered. "I mean to say, to be sure it *is* Bram Stoker. But he's no more a writer than a flea. His last endeavor, *The Primrose Path,* was an abysmal failure. And *Dracula,* you say? As in Vladimir the Impaler?" Oscar's lips curled in disdain. "The man doesn't have it in him to write a decent grocery list, let alone—" He drew in a sharp breath and jumped to his feet.

"*Ahem!*" Oscar wagged his finger in Mr. Stoker's direction. "You're not writing anything gothic and ghoulish per chance, are you, old boy? It's a morbid fancy if you are. The reading public won't go in for folklore about vampires." The two men's eyes met, and for a moment there was silence.

"How could you possibly know?" Stoker's voice was a husky croak.

The Reverend H. P. Pinker dropped his opera glasses with a loud *clunk!*

Bristling like a porcupine, all quivers and whiskers, Stoker picked them up. It appeared that he might hurl them at Oscar. His grey-gloved hand shook with rage.

"My advice to you, old boy," Oscar said cheerily, "is stick to what you do best — managing a theater. For pity's sake, leave the scribbling to us who scribble for our livelihood." He sniffed at the flower in his lapel. "Every jack-a-napes and his great aunt believe they can put pen to paper and write novels with the abandonment of a whoremonger. The world is a stage, but the play is badly cast, I fear."

"Oscar, please!" Lady Beatrix implored.

"You, sir, are mistaken. I have been doing some little research . . . er . . . on . . . European folktales, to be sure. And vampires in particular. But how on earth did you . . . ?" Bram Stoker stroked his fanlike beard. "Only my wife knows . . ." His voice trailed away. He looked devastated.

"Ah. And how is your dear, sweet Florence? Give her my regards. Perhaps it was *she* who told me you were meandering down the supernatural primrose path," Oscar said with all the vitriolic acerbity of a poison arrow aimed straight for the heart.

Bram Stoker sputtered indignantly: "Y-you haven't spoken to my wife. You wouldn't dare!"

"Daren't I?" Oscar's left eyebrow shot up.

"My wife and I have no secrets from each other."

"Ah! I am sorry to hear that. It has always been my contention that the proper basis for marriage is mutual misdirection."

A shudder passed through Bram Stoker, and his bushy beard twitched convulsively, then he turned on his heels and darted down the aisle, disappearing through the curtained archway.

"Oscar. You are a beast!" Beatrix chided. "I won't have you acting like a truculent schoolboy whilst a guest in my grandfather's box. Go apologize to the man at once. The fact that you were his wife's former suitor is no excuse. And when *did* you last see Florence?"

"*Spurned* suitor. I fled Ireland when she accepted that pitiful excuse for a man, and I haven't clamped eyes on her since. Very well, I'll apologize. I *was* rather monstrous." Oscar smiled in mock contrition. "Everyone knows that Mr. Stoker is so desperate to be a writer he'd stab his own mother in the heart just to inscribe an epigram on the poor woman's tombstone."

Katie laughed out loud. The history books didn't lie. Oscar Wilde *was* witty and snarky. But he was wrong about Bram Stoker's writing abilities. *Dracula* would be the bestselling horror novel of all time, with a gazillion knock-off movies and vampire books all thanks to Bram Stoker who started it all. *And a good thing, too,* Katie thought, *because I love the TV series* True Blood.

Oscar Wilde leaned over to Katie and said in a stage whisper: "Did you notice the perspiration bursting out across Mr. Stoker's forehead like noxious dew? And that stony face? So like marble in its melancholy? Vampires indeed. No one will read such drivel. What next, *ma cherie?* Werewolves? Witches? Wizards? All cultivating their supernatural proclivities at my alma mater, Oxford College?"

"Or an English boarding school," Katie said. She grinned, thinking of Hogwarts.

"How droll! Vampires at Eton." Oscar roared with laughter, but sprang to his feet when Lady Beatrix demanded he leave at once and make amends.

"Go with him, Pinker, do," Lady Beatrix implored Reverend Pinker. "Make sure Oscar gives the poor man a proper apology."

Pinker nodded, and a moment later he was propelling Oscar Wilde down the aisle and out the archway at the rear.

A bell chimed. Then chimed again. The play was about to begin.

Ushers in velvet uniforms scurried about the theater turning down gas jets in brass sconces. A bellboy dressed all in blue with gold braid at his shoulders strutted across the stage in front of the curtain, holding a large sign for all to read:

STRANGE
CASE OF
DR JEKYLL AND
MR HYDE
♪ ACT I ♪

The orchestra struck up something in a minor key, and when the red curtain began slowly to rise, the chandelier suspended high above flickered and went dim.

"Beatrix. Lend me your opera glasses," Collin whispered.

"I don't have them," she whispered back.

"I can't bloody well see without them. Deuce-it-all." Collin snapped his fingers as if a thought had just occurred to him. "I remember now. You gave them to Major Brown."

"Did I? I thought Reverend Pinker was holding them for me."

"No. I distinctly recall you gave them to Major Brown."

"Well, then. He'll bring them later. He's joining us after the second act."

"Where is Stink Pink? Why hasn't he returned?" Collin demanded, craning his neck around. "He's got a pair. I saw him using them."

"Shh." Beatrix put a gloved finger to her lips just as a dozen drums, reeds, horns, and xylophones rang out all at once.

Katie clasped the armrests of her chair and peered down at the stage. Her heart was pounding. *This is amazing! I'm about to see the first-ever, opening night of* Dr Jekyll and Mr Hyde. *How crazy is this?* Her stomach tightened. She could almost feel the jangle of musical notes from the orchestra rising inside her along with the swell of anticipation from the crowd.

"I can't see without opera glasses! I'm nearsighted as a church mouse. That blighter Major Brown botches everything."

"Hush, Collie," Lady Beatrix whispered. "Your vision is fine. Mr. Whistler says you have the eye of a true artist. An eye for detail. So stop this foolishness."

"My own sister knows naught about me," Collin grumbled. "I can't see in the dark. No one can."

Collin whispered something to Katie, but she ignored him as she stared down at the stage. The view from the Duke's private box was amazing. Grandma Cleaves often took Katie to the National Theater, but their seats were never this good. Last month they saw the musical *Backbeat* about the Beatles, and when Katie had texted Courtney to tell her how fabulous the songs were, her sister texted back: "Poor you. Grandma Cleaves hates music. Did she ruin it for you?"

Courtney and Grandma Cleaves are like oil and vinegar, thought Katie. *They don't mix.*

Katie tugged her thoughts back to the present. The velvet curtain had risen fully above the stage now, revealing an English sitting room. An actor with a long, lean jaw hastened across the stage to thunderous applause. So thunderous that the backdrop scenery — painted to resemble a wall, with a real door but fake windows — wobbled slightly.

He must be famous, Katie thought, judging by the still roaring crowd. There were no movie stars in this century, she reminded herself. Stage actors were the mega celebrities here. Katie's eyes grew wide with excitement. She loved historical novels and old plays. Loved acting them out in her bedroom. But Courtney was the showbiz type — the true actress in the family.

When the clapping finally died down, the actor strode to a writing desk at the front of the stage, near the footlights. "*I thought it was madness!*" he boomed out, flinging a sheaf of papers onto the desk. "*But if anyone can help, it will be Dr. Lanyon. He is Henry Jekyll's oldest friend. I shall go to Lanyon's house immediately.*"

A solemn-faced butler shuffled forward. "*Very good, Sir. Your coat, Sir.*"

A doorbell chimed from somewhere off stage. "*Now who the devil can that be?*" intoned the actor, stroking his long, lean jaw, and then in exaggerated surprise: "*Why! It's Dr. Lanyon. The very person I meant to consult! Come in. Come in.*"

"Katherine!" Collin hissed. "Did you bring opera glasses? I can't see their faces! Blast it all. How can I watch the play?"

"You have *ears* don't you?" Lady Beatrix whispered angrily from across the aisle. "You don't need to see. Just listen."

Katie nudged Collin's elbow and pointed to the monocle dangling from a black ribbon around Collin's neck. She'd never seen a real monocle before today, only in the movies. She assumed that the circular lens was a sort of magnifying glass.

Collin stared down at the monocle and let out the same exaggerated gasp of surprise as the actor had just exhibited on stage. Scooping up the lens, Collin plunked it into the folds of his left eye and leaned over the padded handrail, peering down at the people below like a jeweler examining rare gems. He was bending so far over the railing, it was no surprise to Katie when the monocle popped out of his eye. She watched it sail outward on its black ribbon, only to swing back and thump him on the chest.

Collin yelped and cried out: "Pinker's down there. I saw him. Near the orchestra." He turned and shouted in Katie's ear. "Quick as a wink I'll go fetch Stink Pink." And with that, he leapt up and hurried away through the darkness.

Katie bit back laughter. *Quick as a wink I'll fetch Stink Pink.* Collin was a comedian. Whether or not he meant to be, he was funny—and quite endearing, unlike her own, twenty-first-century cousin Collin who was serious and pedantic. Katie drew in a breath. The word "pedantic" was on her vocab quiz this week.

But my vocab quiz is thousands of days and millions of minutes into the future.

Chapter Thirteen

Mary Ann Nichols, Ripper Victim no. 1

LONDON HOSPITAL TO THE SOUTH was an indistinguishable blur in the swirling fog as the police surgeon's carriage turned into Buck's Row. Dr. Ralph Llewellyn, a thin man with a drooping moustache, drooping eyes, and an underhung jaw like a basset hound's, had been sitting in the carriage, ready to jump out, make a cursory examination of the girl's body, and return home as quickly as possible. He was thoroughly annoyed at having been roused from his sleep to attend to a corpse in the foggy East End. It could easily have waited until morning.

So when the four-wheeler shuddered to a halt on the curbside near the dead girl, Dr. Llewellyn flung open the carriage door and stepped down gingerly. Leaning heavily on his cane, he clumped quickly across the dark street. His left foot, particularly his big toe, was riddled with gout, and it throbbed painfully. All he wanted to do was get back home and climb into bed with a hot brandy.

Peevishly, he looked around. He didn't like being in this area of Spitalfields with its slaughterhouses and damnable foul stench. True, some sections of London were far worse, full of thieves, vagabonds, and beggars, but even so, Dr. Llewellyn did not take kindly to being near slaughterhouses that reeked of fetid odors. The girl should have had the decency to die somewhere well lit and clean.

Moving closer to the body, he glanced with disgust at the curiosity seekers who had begun to gather, along with the newspaper reporters. Why, oh why, was the world riddled with news reporters? *They've got to sell papers,* he told himself, but it was thoroughly distasteful all the same.

Dr. Llewellyn knew he should order the police constables to erect screens around the body so that he could proceed with his examination in privacy. But as he didn't intend to stay long, he decided against it. Let the onlookers have their sport. It was only some parlor maid or shop girl, after all. What did her privacy matter? The sooner he was rid of this whole business and back in his warm bed, the better.

He advanced toward the body. From the look of the girl's clothing, the rusty-colored coat with seven large brass buttons, her black stockings and worn brown boots, Dr. Llewellyn deduced that the victim was just another female from the lower orders, not worth bothering about, especially at this hour. She and her ilk were like barn swallows: Shoot ten out of the sky and twenty more took their places. Common, foul little things, thruppence a dozen.

He knelt down. He had a good memory, especially for small details, so he didn't bother with his notepad and pencil. The girl was lying on her back with her legs straight out, as though she had been formally laid out, not as if she'd fallen into a heap. Her throat had been cut from ear to ear, completely severing the carotid arteries, but only a small pool of blood had collected in the street from the throat wound. "Not more than would fill two wineglasses," Dr. Llewellyn muttered to himself. He always measured blood loss in terms of wineglasses, beer steins, and gin tumblers. Perhaps, given the paucity of blood, the girl had been murdered elsewhere and her body carted here to Buck's Row.

A comb and a small looking glass were in her coat pocket, but nothing that might identify her. He opened her mouth to check her teeth and gums. The girl's upper teeth were crooked, but strong and white with no sign of decay, indicating she was fairly young. Tooth rot told a lot about a victim's age and general health. Her gums were healthy as well, but two teeth from her lower jaw were missing. He placed her age as somewhere between seventeen and twenty-one, and speculated to the constable leaning over his shoulder that she might be one of the many milliner's assistants who trolled the Haymarket trying to pick up a few farthings by flirting with the lads — and then something had gone terribly wrong.

"'Twas a blessing she died young, saving her from a life of poverty and destitution...or worse," Dr. Llewellyn muttered more to himself than to the constable.

"Right you are, sir," Constable Jones nodded in agreement. "Once the likes of her gets a taste of the extra ready, it's only a matter of time before she becomes a full-fledged Whitechapel whore using her earnings to buy gin and Lord knows what else."

"True enough, Constable. True enough," Dr. Llewellyn agreed. In no time at all she'd be aged beyond her years. Drunk and brawling, she'd look like an ugly hag before her twenty-fifth birthday. 'Twas a blessing she died young.

Dr. Llewellyn called over his shoulder to the sergeant on duty, who was holding back the crowd of onlookers. "My job is finished. Take the body to the mortuary, Sergeant."

"Yes, sir. Right away, sir."

Dr. Llewellyn returned the comb and looking glass to the girl's coat pocket. He was in such a hurry to get back to his warm bed and even warmer brandy that he left before the body had been taken away, which was against procedure. But it was a foggy night, so no one would blame him. Except, of course, the assistant deputy CID of Scotland Yard, Major Gideon Brown. Major Brown was a stickler for protocol and demanded that corpses, *all corpses*, be treated with respect. Young fool. The very idea was ludicrous. *I've done all that I can here.* Silly girl probably provoked her lover and had it coming. Most of these girls deserved their fate. It was unfortunate, but there it was. Nothing more to be done.

Later, police surgeon Dr. Ralph Llewellyn would curse himself for making critical oversights that might cost him his job. Had he lifted up the girl's dress and two flannel petticoats, he would have made a startling discovery. The girl had been disemboweled, a condition her tightly laced stays served partly to conceal. Dr. Llewellyn justified this oversight by telling himself that anyone in his position would have done the same. The death had not impressed him as anything more than a lovers' altercation. True, it wasn't every day that a girl had her throat cut, but this girl was a member of that trivial class not worth exerting extra time, effort, or grievance over.

Still later, however, when Dr. Llewellyn was pressed by reporters and almost sacked by Major Gideon Brown, he would regret his hastiness and amend his impressions: "I have seen many terrible cases," he would tell the pressmen solemnly, "but none so brutal as the murder of that poor young girl. An innocent dove struck down in the flower of her youth. A senseless tragedy."

But for now, climbing back into his curtained carriage, Dr. Llewellyn didn't give the body of Mary Ann Nichols a second thought.

Chapter Fourteen

When Will You Pay Me say the Bells of Old Bailey

AFTER THE CURTAIN FELL to thunderous applause and a standing ovation, the spectators in the private boxes drifted down the hall into the Byzantine Room to await their carriages. The rest of the theater crowd — those not in private boxes — began pouring down the grand staircase into the lower lobby.

In the Byzantine Room Katie came face to face once again with Major Gideon Brown. During the last act of *Dr Jekyll and Mr Hyde* he had entered the duke's box and slipped quietly into the seat next to Lady Beatrix. Collin, who had returned only moments before, caught sight of Major Brown across the dark aisle and began kicking moodily at the balcony footrail.

"Bloke's a blighter *and a commoner*," Collin had hissed to Katie. "He's got no business seeking out my sister's company. The duke will put a stop to it, by god. And if he doesn't," Collin said with unsmiling satisfaction, "*I will.*"

Katie didn't know whether to feel sorry for Gideon Brown, a victim of class prejudice, or wary of him. He was an assassin, and in Katie's book that made him a suspect. Though how or why he could be Jack the Ripper wasn't clear to her. The Ripper might, after all, be just some homicidal lunatic having nothing whatsoever to do with the Twyford family. On the other hand, Lady Beatrix was to be his last victim, so the odds were high that there was a connection.

Just before the final curtain fell, wheezing and out of breath, the bulge of his Adam's apple moving rapidly up and down above his clerical collar, Reverend Pinker had slumped down into the empty seat next to Katie. He'd missed most of the play, as had Oscar Wilde, who gave his excuses to Lady Beatrix that it was far easier to gauge the audience's reaction to the play while trolling the back of the theater.

Now, standing in the sparkling Byzantine Room all aglitter with mirrored ceiling tiles and plush sofas, Katie shook Major Brown's extended hand. Shaking hands was different in this century. You kept your gloves on and held your hand aloft, and the gentleman either bent and gave the air above your hand a slight peck, or he shook it and quickly stepped back. Major Brown took Katie's hand but held it a moment too long. "A pleasure, once again, Miss Katherine," he said, his eyes never leaving her face.

"The pleasure is all mine," Katie said agreeably, though her pulse was racing and the high lace collar of her dress was itching her badly. She didn't trust Major Brown, and not because he had a powerful, almost pompous air about him, or because he had killed an enemy of the crown on some secret mission. It was something else...something about the penetrating way he looked at her with those cat-green eyes.

Major Brown was speaking to Lady Beatrix now, and the hard set of his mouth, Katie noted, had softened considerably until his eyes fastened on something across the room. Katie followed his gaze. The white cuff of Reverend Pinker's sleeve, where it fell just below his black waistcoat, was dappled with something red, like splatters of paint.

Swaying slightly from the cumbersome weight of her gown, Katie moved in for a closer look and stopped dead in her tracks. Reverend Pinker's sleeve was flecked with blood.

From the door at the far end of the room an usher in a blue velveteen uniform cried out, "The Duke of Twyford's carriage, if you please!"

With a swoosh of long skirts and the clack of men's boots on the marble floor, Katie followed the others out of the Byzantine Room, into the hall, and down the grand staircase to the main lobby. Katie caught sight of Toby in a throng of people at the bottom of the stairs. He was chatting with a girl selling peanuts — in small brown bags tied with string — from a box at her waist that was attached to a cord around her neck.

"Peanuts!" cried the girl, slanting her eyes flirtatiously at Toby. "Get 'em whilst they's hot! Nice 'n' hot! Here you go, luv, want some peanuts?" she thrust a bag under Katie's nose as Katie approached. "Hot as a chimney pipe, they is!" The girl elbowed Toby playfully in the ribs, and when he gave the girl a wink back, Katie felt a pang of irritation and a strong impulse to kick him.

Another girl, this one selling oranges, pushed through the crowd and sidled up to Reverend Pinker. "Ev'ning, Reverend. Did yer get m'message?"

"Molly, please. Not here, not now. Talk to me at the Charity Mission tomorrow." The red blotches in Pinker's cheeks, which usually extended to the tip of his long nose, now suffused his entire face like crimson clouds.

"But I don't *wants* to talk to yer at the mission! What I *wants* to know is did you get me bleedin' message what I gave the gentleman in your box to give to you —"

"Trouble?" Major Brown stepped between the two.

"No trouble a'tall, guv." The girl smiled sweetly. "Just seeing if the gent 'ere would be wantin' some oranges. Blood red, they is. Sweet and juicy."

"I think not," Collin cut in, sweeping the orange seller aside with a none-too-gentle nudge.

Moments later Katie found herself standing with the others outside the white-pillared entrance of the Lyceum Theatre. Reverend Pinker, she observed, was perspiring even though the night air was cool, and a crisp breeze fluttered the awning over the carriage park where the duke's coach was drawing up.

A group of newspaper boys swooped out of the darkness, waving sheets of newsprint and shouting, *"Murder! Murder in Whitechapel! Read all about it!"*

Katie gasped. The smell of ink, not yet dry, permeated the air as the boys waved papers above their heads.

"Murdered girl! Sliced from ear to ear! Read all about it!"

The cries punctured the night with something evil and tragic and ugly. Katie had been expecting something like this, but even so it sent a chill up her spine. But was it the Ripper?

"Unidentified girl murdered in Whitechapel!"

Major Gideon Brown thrust his hand in his pocket, drew out a coin, held it out to a newsboy, and snatched up a single sheet of newsprint. He scanned it quickly and made his apologies. "Beatrix," he said breathlessly and then changed it to the more formal "Lady Beatrix" when he caught Katie watching him. "Forgive me, but I shan't be able to join you at the dinner party. You must go without me. I'll fetch a cab."

Out of the mist a tall, hawk-faced police officer came hurrying forward. He exchanged several words with Major Brown, and fumbled in a breast pocket for his notepad. "Dunno her name, sir. We 'aven't got much information yet."

Major Brown, clutching tight to the handle of his military swagger stick, said curtly, "Come with me, Constable Jarvis."

Toby stepped forward. "I'll fetch you a cab, Major. What shall I tell the driver?"

"The Bow Street Morgue. There's a good lad."

"Gideon," Lady Beatrix protested, tendrils of blond curls fluttering across the silk rosebuds fastened into her upswept hairdo. "There's no need for a hansom. We'll take you to Bow Street. But surely, darling, this can wait until..." Her voice was lost on the wind.

"No, you go on without me. I'll join you later." He leaned over and settled Beatrix's fur cloak more securely around her shoulders. "Pinker?" He turned to Reverend Pinker and in a commanding voice asked, "You'll see Lady Beatrix safely home after the party if I'm detained?" Then he stopped, noting Pinker's bright red face and the fact that he was sweating profusely. "You all right, man?"

"Fine. Yes. Fine," stammered Pinker, running a knobby finger round the inside of his clerical collar. "I'll see everyone home. Indeed, yes. Of course, of course. My pleasure."

"Major," Toby said, drawing himself up. "May I go with you?" He hastily tucked in his shirt and adjusted his frock coat, which was several sizes too small for his muscular shoulders. When Major Brown nodded, Collin told Katie in a contemptuous voice that Major Gideon Brown was mentoring Toby. "It was Beatrix's idea," Collin admitted grudgingly. "Toby wants to become an officer in the CID at Scotland Yard."

Katie's heart pounded hard against her ribs. "*Toby!*" she cried, improvising. "My fan! I dropped it over there—" She pointed toward the theater door, and when he darted back to look for it, she followed close on his heels. "I-I need a favor," she stammered, steadying herself against a white column. "I need to..." But how was she to ask him? "I need to know if the dead girl's name is...Mary Ann Nichols."

Toby's dark eyes regarded her coolly, then flashed with revulsion when she explained that she needed him to be her "eyes and ears" at the morgue. He drove a clenched fist into his palm, spun her around, and marched her back to the others waiting by the curb. The look on his face suggested that he thought she was insane.

A minute later, Katie stood dejectedly watching as Toby, Major Brown, and Police Constable Jarvis climbed into a hansom cab and sailed away into the darkness. Listening to the receding clatter of horses' hooves and the raucous hooting of carriage horns, Katie began to seethe with anger. How dare Toby dismiss her as if she were some addle-brained nitwit of a girl from the nineteenth century!

Chapter Fifteen

The Mortuary

THE BOW STREET MORTUARY was situated in the basement of a narrow building three blocks away from the Bow Street Police Station. There were two corpses in the back courtyard awaiting burial.

When Major Brown took in the sight of the cadavers in the courtyard, he wondered if it had been wise to bring Toby along after all. The two corpses, laid out on concrete slabs, had been a bluish-purple color only yesterday, but were now so covered in lime dust they looked chalk-white, like a pair of apparitions. Twin coffins, made of splintered pine, lay stacked one atop the other in a sea of stiff mud beneath the overhang of the mortuary roof.

Major Gideon Brown had given his word to his fiancée, Lady Beatrix, that he would mentor Toby, and by God he was glad to do so. The boy was a decent, hardworking lad determined to become a police officer, and if he passed his end-year examinations with honors, Gideon would pave the way for him to become a constable, then a sergeant, and so on up the ranks. Toby reminded Gideon of himself at that age. They both had Cockney antecedents, both were from the East End, and both were considered outsiders in "good" society. And by virtue of merit — *not bloody social rank* — both could, as the former Prime Minister Benjamin Disraeli maintained, rise to the top despite humble beginnings.

Now, as Major Brown, Toby, and Constable Jarvis moved past the ghost-white cadavers, they instinctively held their breath. Dead bodies were usually preserved in ice, but by summer's end ice was in short supply, and lime dust had to suffice.

Gagging from the odor of decomposing flesh and the acrid smell of lime, Major Brown took out a key attached to his gold watch chain, jiggled it in the door lock, and hurriedly swung open the rear door to the morgue. Toby and Constable Jarvis crowded in close behind. When the door slammed shut, effectively blocking out the stench, Major Brown tugged a lantern from a wooden peg set close into the wall and adjusted its flame. The oil lamp threw uncertain light into the gloom ahead, and a minute later they were hastening down a set of damp stone steps.

Ducking through a narrow doorway, they moved into a vast, stone-block room with bars on the only two windows at street height, just above eye level. The glass panes were grimy with soot, and what little ventilation the room afforded came from a crack at the top of the right-hand window.

In the dim light, the mortuary looked to Toby like a medieval torture chamber: cramped, spare, with sharp-looking instruments skirting the walls. In the center of the floor stood three trestle tables topped with stone slabs. Laid out on the one nearest the half-open window was the body of a dead girl, fully clothed.

A police officer standing in the far corner scrambled to brighten the room. He lit the largest of the oil lamps hanging from the ceiling. The elongated flame sputtered and jumped, emitting grey smoke that swirled upward into the still air, making the room look larger than it was.

Glancing from Major Brown's rigid face to Constable Jarvis's thin, twitching one, Toby watched Major Brown stride toward the dead girl, his black boots crunching across the gravel floor.

"Where's Police Surgeon Dr. Llewellyn?" Major Brown barked at the officer fiddling with a second lantern.

The man swung around so fast, splinters of light slashed across the girl's body. "Dunno, sir." The officer lifted dull eyes first to the dead girl, then to Major Brown.

"He ought to be here," Brown fumed. "Go fetch him at once. No! I shall need you, Sergeant...McKenzie, is it?"

"Yes, sir. McKenzie, sir." The lantern light silhouetted McKenzie's wide girth against the back wall, making it rise and shrink and rise again in zigzag patterns.

"Right then, Sergeant McKenzie. Send Officer Webster to fetch Dr. Llewellyn. Where is Webster?"

"Gone 'ome, sir."

Major Brown swung around to Jarvis. "Police Constable, bring Llewellyn here at once. I don't care if you have to drag him out of bed in his nightshirt. Do it now!"

Jarvis, a tall, thin man whose angular shoulders stuck up from his navy-blue uniform, scrambled across the room and ducked back out through the narrow doorway.

Toby watched as the veins in Major Brown's temples began to bulge. Major Brown had a reputation for not suffering fools gladly. He was known for giving his all to every endeavor and expecting the same from subordinates. So it was not by luck, Toby knew, that Major Gideon Brown had risen quickly in the ranks to become the youngest assistant deputy CID of Scotland Yard.

"All right, Sergeant McKenzie." Major Brown's voice was deceptively neutral. "Who is she? What do we know about her?"

"Don't know nuffin'," admitted McKenzie, a heavy-jowled, broad-nosed man, whose skin was faintly plum-colored.

Major Brown drew in a sharp breath. "Read me your report, Sergeant."

"Report, sir?"

"Surely Dr. Llewellyn didn't release the body without giving you a detailed report?"

"Ahhh . . . no, sir. He's got a good memory, sir. He'll be here in the morning. I'm sure he'll make out his report then. Or dictate it to me."

"There are rules, protocols, and procedures, Sergeant McKenzie." Major Brown's face looked hard and contemptuous. "And as it appears none have been followed," he said, stripping off his white theater gloves, "it is therefore up to us. Hand me that leather apron and put one on yourself."

"But, *sir!* I never . . . that is to say, I just take notes. I'm handy at note taking, s'why I was assigned — "

"Well, then, you are now assigned to assist me, Sergeant McKenzie. This girl's body has not been examined and we can't wait for that mongrel dog, Llewellyn, to grace us with his presence. If rigor mortis sets in we won't learn anything this poor girl has to tell us, will we?"

"Tell us? What do you mean? It won't tell us nuffin', sir. It's dead as a doornail. Beggin' yer pardon, sir."

"Toby." Major Brown turned. "Grab that notepad over there and take down exactly what I tell you."

Toby scooped up a pad and pencil from a copper-lined shelf next to a coal stove in the corner.

"'oo's he?" McKenzie pointed a plump finger at Toby.

"He's the lad who will assist us with note taking until Dr. Llewellyn arrives. In the meantime, look lively, Sergeant. What exactly *do* we know about this girl?"

McKenzie fumbled through a bundle of papers. "We knows the corpse was lying on its back with its legs straight out, near the gutter in Buck's Row."

"Sergeant McKenzie, forthwith you will call the deceased either by her name, which we don't know, or by her gender, which we do."

"Sir?"

"She. This is a female cadaver, correct?"

"Yes, sir. I thinks so, sir. Wait a bit! Could be one of them pretty boys what dresses up as — but, no, says here, it's a girl 'bout twenty years of age."

"The girl, whom we shall call Polly Jones, as we do not know her name, was found lying on her back with her legs straight out near a gutter in Buck's Row. Was the location of the body closer to Bakers Row or Brady Street? Northeast corner or northwest?"

"Don't rightly know, sir. I wasn't there, now, was I? Sergeant Folly and Police Constable Merriman was there."

"And where *are* Sergeant Folly and Constable Merriman?"

"Gone 'ome, sir."

"Why is that, Sergeant McKenzie?" Major Brown's voice was low and even, but Toby could hear an undercurrent of simmering rage.

"On account of Dr. Llewellyn says that the remains of the chi... er, the deceased, was not worth bothering over, seeing as she was probably just some Whitechapel whore. Can't say's I disagree, sir. No cause for keeping good men from their warm beds just because a worthless strumpet decides to go an 'ave herself chived. She'll still be 'ere in the morning, sir. Little Miss Polly ain't going nowhere."

"I see. Thank you, Sergeant McKenzie." Again, Toby noted that Major Brown's voice was deceptively calm, but if Toby had to wager, he'd guess that Sergeant McKenzie, along with Police Surgeon Dr. Llewellyn, would both be out of a job in the morning.

"So? We have no accounting of where in the street the body lay, only that her legs were straight and she was found lying on her back? Do we know who found her, Sergeant?"

"H'm. T'is here somewhere, sir," McKenzie wheezed, leafing through his papers. "A market porter lad...by the name of..."

Toby glanced over McKenzie's shoulder, scanning the pages. "Would that be Georgie Cross?" Toby asked, reading an underlined name. Toby knew Georgie Cross. They'd attended Charity Grammar School together.

"That's 'im! The very one! Georgie Cross."

"Did anyone get Mr. Cross's address, Sergeant?"

"Don't need his address, sir. We knows where 'e works as a market porter."

"I see. Yes. That *is* helpful," Brown said, but the irony in his voice seemed lost on McKenzie, who continued.

"Remember, sir, what I told you? It's only a Whitechapel whore. Hundreds same as her. We can't be runnin' round bothering ourselves with the likes of whores, now can we? It would be —"

"*What*, Sergeant McKenzie?"

"Beneaff our dignity, sir. That's what Dr. Llewellyn tells us. We take extra special care wiff them what matters, and not wiff them what don't."

"I see. I do indeed." It was the first time Major Brown did not address Sergeant McKenzie by his name or rank. Toby wondered if the poor man would even last until tomorrow. He had an idea Major Brown would dismiss him before the night was through. Luckily, Sergeant McKenzie seemed blissfully unaware he was tottering on the brink.

"Toby? Ready, lad? Let's begin." Major Brown reached for a measuring rod dangling from a metal hook. "Please take note: Polly Jones is five feet two, dark-brown hair, unblemished complexion. There are two teeth missing from her lower left jaw. Her throat has been cut from ear to ear. She is wearing a brownish — or is that a reddish? — colored ulster with seven large brass buttons, and underneath the ulster is a yellow linsey-woolsey dress, two flannel petticoats, one of which has the embroidered initials "M. N." She has on black woolen stockings and brown leather boots. There is a comb and a looking glass in Miss Jones's pocket. I'm going to lift the petticoats to determine...*Good Lord!*" Major Brown dropped the girl's skirts and took a step backward, almost stumbling.

"What is it?" Toby glanced up, pencil poised in midair.

"Sir?" McKenzie puffed out his blue-veined cheeks.

Major Gideon Brown swallowed hard and instantly made a show of composing himself. "I think...perhaps...it would be judicious for us to wait for Police Surgeon Llewellyn after all." He took several deep breaths. "In my regiment in India I assisted in several field autopsies, but I've never seen anything. . ." His voice sounded strange and hoarse. "No need to come any closer, lad." His green eyes contemplated Toby. "Just take down what I say. And steel yourself not to look."

Brown continued in a low, grim voice: "The unidentified female, whom we are calling Polly Jones, and whom I believe to be between the ages of fifteen and twenty-five, has been. . .disemboweled." He mopped his brow with his sleeve. "Polly Jones is wearing a pair of close-ribbed brown stays which are, in part, holding in her entrails." He swiveled around.

"McKenzie, the cutting shears, if you please. Sergeant McKenzie!"

McKenzie was taking in great hulking gasps of air. The color had drained from his face and he looked ready to faint.

Toby stepped to the wall, unhooked the cutting shears, and handed them to Major Brown who with great precision proceeded to cut away the girl's clothing. When he was done, he took out his pocket watch and counted the minutes until Police Surgeon Llewellyn arrived.

Two hours later the dingy mortuary with its low ceiling and dank smelling air was filled to overflowing with police officers. Dr. Ralph Llewellyn, after being severely reprimanded by Major Brown, was just finishing up the last of the autopsy.

"In the lower left part of the abdomen there is a gash that runs in a jagged line almost as far as the diaphragm," he dictated to Sergeant McKenzie, who was hastily scribbling it down in Toby's notepad. "The perforation exposes both her large and small intestines, and the lower quadrant of the stomach."

Toby stood in the shadows trying to ignore the stiffening tension behind his eyelids and in his joints. Street lamps still burned outside, but already Toby could hear the faint stirrings of the city, the clatter of milk carts rumbling past. He could smell dawn in the air.

Toby knew he should feel sickened at the sight of the poor dead girl, but he felt only numb as if her death weren't real. He'd felt this same reaction before. Once when his grandmother had passed away — though he wasn't allowed to call her "Grandmother" or claim kinship. She'd been laid out in the parlor of Twyford Manor, and it had been an afterthought on the Duke's part, letting Toby view the remains of the Marchioness of Drumville. And then there was Elsie, his baby sister, whom he'd found dead in her cradle from an infected rat bite on a morning similar to this one. A morning full of promise, with dawn mist in the air and the clatter of milk carts rumbling down the street.

"It's a deep gash, completely cutting through tissue," Dr. Llewellyn droned on, enunciating in a falsely pompous, upper-class voice. "There are several other incisions running across the abdomen, with three or four of the cuts perforating downward on the right side." He raised his eyes and spoke directly to Major Brown. "Due to the severity of the wounds, I would speculate that the weapon was a long-bladed knife, moderately sharp, and used with great violence. Wouldn't you agree, Major Brown?"

When Major Brown didn't answer, Dr. Llewellyn eyed him with seething contempt. What did the blighter mean by rousing him from his slumber a second time in one night, and for a Whitechapel whore! The very idea. Trying to make a name for himself, no doubt. Well, he, Dr. Ralph Llewellyn, was far senior to this young upstart. He'd have a talk with the Commissioner in the morning. Still and all, Dr. Llewellyn knew he'd have to tread carefully. The girl had been brutally attacked, and he'd missed all the signs. So he'd finish the autopsy and cozy up to this young fathead. What choice did he have? He'd tell Major Brown that Mrs. Llewellyn was sick with palsy, otherwise he would never have been so preoccupied and neglectful. The lie ought to suffice, with the double delight that Mrs. Llewellyn was in the pink of health.

"Dr. Llewellyn?" snapped Major Brown.

Dr. Llewellyn fiddled with a flap of skin on the girl's abdomen, snipped out a piece of intestine, dropped it into a glass jar filled with alcohol that would later be mixed with formaldehyde, and raised his gaze to meet Major Brown's.

"Does this remind you of anything, doctor?" Major Brown demanded. "Anything at all?"

Bristling with resentment, Dr. Llewellyn made a prodigious show of stifling a yawn. "There's been a report of several West End cats being eviscerated. Perhaps —"

"Anything else?" Major Brown cut him off and cast a frosty gaze around the room. "Would anyone like to hazard a guess?"

But no one spoke, whether because they were afraid to further provoke Major Brown's ire, or because they simply didn't know, Toby wasn't sure.

"Well, gentlemen," Major Brown continued in a steely voice. "It reminds *me* of the 'Feckless Fay' case last December on Boxing day. 'Feckless Fay' lost her life as the result of a wrong decision. The girl took a shortcut home through a dark alley. Could this be the work of the same man?"

Toby was glad that Major Brown was creating an uproar. It was far easier to concentrate on the undercurrents swirling around the dark, mildewed mortuary than to think about the poor creature lying dead on a stone slab, being prodded over by the likes of Dr. Llewellyn.

Death had its indignities, but this. . .this was almost worse, Toby thought, watching Dr. Llewellyn cut up, examine, and dissect the girl like an insect under a microscope. It was the ultimate degradation. Far better to have drowned in the Thames than to be examined under a magnifying glass by this arrogant old fool with his brandy breath and his sharp-nosed, buffoonish face.

At the sound of footsteps, Toby swiveled around just as Police Constable Jarvis burst into the room. "Sir, I done what you asked! I found 'er name! It's Mary Ann Nichols." He hunched over trying to catch his breath.

When Jarvis straightened up, he gasped out, "She's been living with her father and stepmother. Stepmother runs the Stag's Leap Boarding House. The girl is nineteen and helps prepare meals for the lodgers. When not helping her stepmother, she does a bit of work making lace doilies for a few extra shillings. She's got a boyfriend, Willy Makepeace, a printer's machinist in Old Kent Road...goes by the name Mad Willy. Neighbors say he beat her somefin' awful last week on account of she was steppin' out wiff someone else. Her father was heard saying if Mad Willy went near his daughter ever again he'd chop him up into mince pies, on account of Willy done loosened several of Mary Ann's teeth. I've got two men making the rounds lookin' for Willy Makepeace. His mother says her little Willy wouldn't hurt a fly. But like I says, neighbors told me he fair flew into a rage last week and beat Mary Ann somefin' awful."

"Good work, Constable Jarvis! Excellent!" Major Brown clapped him heartily on the shoulder.

"So 'er name isn't Polly?" rumbled Sergeant McKenzie drawing himself up and rubbing his chin.

Dr. Llewellyn sauntered across the room, his face blandly incurious. He reached for his silk hat hanging from an iron hook by the door, and brushed it with his sleeve while peering about the room. "My work here is finished. Our victim, it appears, is not a Whitechapel whore after all, but a rooming house serving wench. Mary Ann Nobody. Tut, tut."

Toby wrenched his gaze from Dr. Llewellyn's face to Mary Ann Nichols's yellow-tinged cadaverous one. *Miss Katherine knows the dead girl*, he thought. *Outside the theater she said she needed to know if the dead girl's name was Mary Ann Nichols! But how can that be? How was it possible that Miss Katherine would know the name of the victim? She's only just arrived from America. Mary Ann Nichols and Miss Katherine were from two different worlds. Two different classes. Did Miss Katherine know the killer? Had she overheard someone threatening to murder Mary Ann?*

Toby determined then and there to find out. In the words of Major Brown, he didn't care if he had to drag Miss Katherine out of bed in her nightdress. He was going to get answers.

Chapter Sixteen

When I Grow Rich
say the Bells of Shoreditch

IT WAS WELL AFTER MIDNIGHT when Katie tiptoed barefoot down the thickly carpeted hall, past the descending grand staircase, on her way to Collin's bedroom. She was dressed in a high-necked granny nightgown beneath a frou-frou sort of robe that Agnes, the ladies' maid, called a "wrapper," made of yards and yards of silky material cinched around her waist with an enormous velvet sash.

Katie felt like a wobbly birthday present all wrapped up with a big fat bow as she crept along the corridor passing several ancestral portraits, including the present Duke of Twyford, who frowned loftily down at her from his giant, ormolu picture frame. In the portrait, the duke was younger and looked less formidable, almost. . .comical. A crown of flaming red hair spiked up from his head and fanned out from his chin like wine-stained porcupine quills.

"The curse of the Twyfords," Grandma Cleaves had jokingly dubbed the redheaded gene that ran rampant in every generation.

Approaching Collin's door, Katie knocked softly, then turned the porcelain knob and slipped inside. She tried to close the door quietly behind her, but it slammed shut with a thunderclap *bang*.

Startled, Collin dropped the book he'd been holding. It fell to the floor with a resounding *thwack* that mingled with the echoing *bang* of the door. Dueling loud noises in the soundless night.

"God's eyeballs, Katherine!" Collin cried incredulously. "You can't come barging into a fellow's room at *this* hour! It's not done. Simply not done." Collin tightened the felt belt around his dark-green bed robe. "I don't know *what* they teach you in America, but here —"

"Collin —" Katie jerked her head toward Collin's manservant. "Get rid of him, Collie," she whispered. "We need to talk." Luckily for Katie, everyone in England, or at least here in the Twyford household, thought Americans were a nation of raucous heathens, so Katie was forgiven for not having the manners of a "well-brought-up" English girl.

The manservant, an elderly man with bushy eyebrows, looked extremely put out, but said, "Very well, young master," when Collin dismissed him. Before leaving, however, he shuffled slowly across the room and hoisted up a wicker laundry basket at the foot of the wardrobe. "I shall see what can be done about your waistcoat, Master Collin," he said in a voice as dry as dust.

"Never mind the waistcoat, Jeffries. Give it to the deserving poor. The blood will never come out, and you know it. You also know I can't abide tainted garments. Gruesome business." He visibly shivered. "And Tinker and Lady Jane Grey?"

"In the basement, Master Collin."

"Good. Don't let them out until. . .well, until dead cats stop showing up on our doorstep. Bloody nuisance. If I find the lunatic who did it, I'll carve him up myself."

Jeffries clucked his tongue, nodded, and sent a portentous glance in Katie's direction. "Shall I return in *precisely* five minutes, young sir, with ginger biscuits and warm milk?" He tapped a bony finger at the side of his long nose as if in secret code.

"No, Jeffries. That will be all, thank you."

When Jeffries left, a disapproving frown on his wrinkled face, Katie hastened to the middle of the room. "Collin? How does Toby come and go as he pleases? Is there a side entrance? A servants' entrance? You said he has a room over the carriage house in the stable block."

Collin acted as if he hadn't heard her. There was a candle burning on the bedside table, another atop a desk strewn with books, ink jars, and an assortment of bugs caught in amber. The anatomy textbook Collin had dropped lay splayed open on the floor, spine up, like a miniature pup tent.

Collin scooped up the anatomy book and moved across the room, his dark-green robe flapping around his ankles over a purple plaid nightshirt, which dragged along the floor. A matching plaid handkerchief embroidered with the Twyford crest sprouted out of the robe's breast pocket. Katie wondered if a plaid stocking cap with a little tasseled ball might complete Collin's nighttime attire. She'd seen similar outfits in pen-and-ink sketches of Ebenezer Scrooge. She glanced over to the four-poster bed. There, on the topmost pillow, laid out in a perfect triangle below the swagged canopy, was a purple plaid nightcap minus the tasseled ball.

Trying hard not to laugh, Katie swiveled her gaze back to Collin who was clumping across the floor, his slippers slapping noisily against the polished oak floorboards. She watched as he flung the anatomy textbook onto the desk. Back home, in her own century, that exact desk with its inlaid leather blotter would stand in a corner of her grandmother's library. And this room would be a guest room, the paneled walls a muddy brown, not this rich golden hue with its highly polished sheen. And the fig-leaf wallpaper on the opposite wall would be replaced by a yellow daffodil pattern.

A raspy noise pulled Katie's thoughts back to the present. Collin had just struck a match and was lighting several candles on his bureau, illuminating a framed picture of his sister as a young girl of about ten or eleven. The younger Lady Beatrix looked strikingly like Courtney at that age.

Collin repositioned the picture so it wouldn't be scorched by the candles and then thudded across the room to the fireplace. When he reached up to brighten the gas jets on either side of the mirrored chimneypiece, Katie caught a glimpse of his reflection in the looking glass. In the sputtering gas light Collin's freckled skin had a smoky, shadowy quality, like a bruise. His tight-lipped mouth looked more mischievous than humorless above the velvet collar of his robe. And the expression behind the icy-blue eyes staring back at her in the mirror was almost...predatory.

She felt a prickle of apprehension and swiveled her gaze away. Katie knew from Grandma Cleaves that in every generation since the nineteenth century there had been a Collin in the Twyford family, as well as a Prudence, like her Aunt Pru. This boy leering at her in the mirror, a glint of red peach fuzz stretching across his chin, was probably Grandma Cleaves's great-great-grandfather.

Turning full around, his back to the fireplace now, Collin laughed awkwardly. He had been staring at her in the mirror with something *other* than cousinly affection, and she much preferred her own Collin's indifference. He usually treated her as if she were an insignificant fly in the ointment of his life.

Katie glanced at the four-poster bed looming against the far wall. Carved into the headboard, below the canopy, was the family coat of arms: a unicorn leaping over a large stone. *That's my bed!* Or it would be, with a different canopy, more than a hundred years into the future.

At the sight of the flying unicorn Katie felt a pang of nostalgia — not for her old bed, but for her father, and how he used to recite the old English nursery rhyme: *If wishes were unicorns...maidens would ride.*

Katie felt suddenly queasy. Her parents — *who haven't even been born yet* — would die in a car crash on their way to Logan Airport to pick up Collin. Katie reached out a hand to steady herself against a high-backed chair by the desk. *Why am I here?* she wondered, blinking around. *Why this house? This century? This room? This bed?*

"Not feeling well, Katherine?" Collin swooped in next to her and caught her outstretched arm, but the physical nearness of the boy who looked like her cousin but wasn't, in a room she knew from a future century, with furniture she had a connection to, made her stomach muscles clench. It was as if something in this room were warning her, *Turn back. Go home. Run!*

"C-collin. Maybe I shouldn't be here. Maybe I was wrong. I should go home. I don't belong here." *But what about Jack the Ripper? He's going to murder Lady Beatrix. Can I save her? Can I actually stop a psychopathic serial killer?* Katie blinked around the room as if seeing it in a new light. *What am I doing here? What was I thinking?*

"God's fish, Katherine! Of course you don't belong here — in my bedchamber!"

God's fish? Katie let out a strangled laugh. Her nerves were twitching like a fish on a hook, but not *God's* hook. More like the devil's. She plunked herself onto the desk chair, and absently leafed through pages of the anatomy book. A scribbled notation here, another in the margin there, a splatter of ink, blue-black against white parchment.

"I vow, Katherine. You Americans have a strange sense of humor. You vex me, you do." Collin's voice was hoarse. Katie realized she was still laughing — a soft, crazy sound — as she flipped through the pages of the textbook.

Collin began to pace the floor, finally settling in a tufted armchair by the fire.

An image of Courtney playing her electric guitar flashed into Katie's mind, along with another image of a waxwork Lady Beatrix being eviscerated. "I can't go home," she whispered. "At least not yet."

"But you must, Katherine! You simply must." Collin nodded his head vigorously. "If staying here means gallivanting at all hours of the night and entering a chap's room unannounced and, er, in a state of undress . . ." He drummed his fingers across his knees. "Then, yes. You should return home posthaste. A proper young lady does not enter a young man's bedchamber in nothing but her dressing gown unless...I suppose...she's married to the chap."

"I'd hardly call this a state of undress," Katie muttered, tugging at the lace collar of the granny nightgown. There wasn't an inch of her body that wasn't covered. "I've got more clothing on right now than I've ever worn in my entire life, even in the dead of winter. But that's not important. What's important is why am I here? I mean *really here?* Right now, in this house? In this—"

Katie was about to say "century," but stopped herself. *Am I really here to save Lady Beatrix from Jack the Ripper? Or for a different reason?* The London Stone hadn't exactly sent her traveling back in time with a roadmap or a set of instructions.

"You're upset, Katherine, and I don't know why. But for what it's worth, I'm sorry. Truly. Did you have a bad dream? Is that why you came tromping into my bedchamber at this ungodly hour? It happens to me all the time. Not young ladies barging into my bedchamber. Not that. No. I get terrible nightmares. Headaches, too. Beatrix has some excellent remedies. If you like, I can have her mix one of her potions. It'll lift your spirits without purging your bowels, word of honor." Collin held up his hand like a boy scout. "So why don't you trot on back to bed, and I'll have Jeffries send for Beatrix. I guarantee things will look brighter in the morning. Things always look better in the morning. That's my credo."

"Mine, too, usually. But this isn't usual, Collin. And it's *not* about nightmares." *Not sleeping ones, anyway,* Katie thought, blinking at this boy sitting across from her. With his dark red hair hanging low over his ears, and a few trailing curls skirting his left eye, he looked less priggish than her cousin Collin back home, whose orangey-red hair was cut short above his ears, accentuating slightly myopic eyes. This Collin's mouth was broad and wide. Her own cousin's was thinner, more compressed. She lifted her gaze. Collin was gawking at her. Too late she realized he'd caught her studying his mouth.

"God's teeth, Katherine!" Collin slapped his forehead with the palm of his hand. "I'm thicker than molasses, with the brains of a tom turkey! I *know* what this is all about!" He snapped his fingers and shot her a look as if a lamp light had just gone off in his head.

"I've got it!" He beamed. "I know why you're here. I mean *really here!* Right now. In my room. You fancy me, don't you? That's it, isn't it? You've a mind to pitch into the matrimonial cart with me before Prudence Farthington gets a toehold." Collin jumped out of his chair. "The Duke is always going on about our bloodline being six hundred years old. He wants an heir and makes no bones about it. But look here, Katherine. For what it's worth, I'm a good fellow, a decent chap who knows his place in society and duty to his family — knows it only too well — but I wouldn't say I'm exceptional. The girls usually fancy Toby." He stopped pacing and blinked at her owlishly, the light of revelation still burning in his eyes.

"Doubtless you see the advantages of marrying a peer of the realm. How many American girls get to garner the favors of a future duke, eh? But, God's whiskers, Katherine, this is *rawther* sudden. And truth to tell, Prudence has taken quite a shine to me. Don't know why, but there it is, and the Governor's hot as toast for it. Like I said, he's desperate for an heir. And to top it off, the Earl of Farthington has pots of money. Good old Prudence will have me neat as ninepence if I play my cards right. That's what the Duke says.

"But wait-ho, Katherine! Why *are* you here tonight? I mean, why exactly? Do you want me to spirit you away like the heroine of one of those romance novels you young ladies are so fond of? A page out of Mrs. Radcliffe's book, eh? *The Mysteries of Udolpho?* Is that it? The Duke told us you were here to find a titled husband. Don't misunderstand, Katherine. I find you very attractive, I do. Who wouldn't? A fellow would be lucky to have half as pretty a wife — if a somewhat less sharp-tongued one. Hell's bells, I've half a mind to cry quits with Prudence this instant! Give her my compliments, tell her I'm not good enough for her. She'll get over me, eh? So let's have a kiss on it, shall we? Dive into the courtship waters, and see if we want to come up for air?"

Collin moved toward Katie with a jaunty swagger. He knelt down in front of her chair and for the briefest of moments their eyes locked: Katie's, in horrified disbelief; Collin's, in a lascivious rapture, especially when his gaze fell to her lips. He puckered up his own and leaned in for the all-important, seal-the-deal kiss.

"Are you nuts?" Katie leaped out of her chair. "Jeez, Collin! I wouldn't kiss you if you were the last man on earth! Ugh! It would be like kissing...my grandfather!"

Collin froze. Baffled, he opened his mouth to speak, but managed only to sputter out a sound between a squawk and a squeal.

"G-*grandfather!*" he finally roared. "As bad as all that?"

His lips were no longer puckered, but pinched in a sour-lemon expression. "Good Lord, Katherine, no need to be so inflexibly honest. Less candor and a simple 'no, thank you' ought to have sufficed, oughtn't it?" Collin awkwardly stood up. "I am not unaware that young ladies don't usually go in for redheaded blokes...but a chap doesn't want to hear he's no prize in the connubial bullring. Henry the Eighth was a bleedin' redhead, and he had six wives."

"It isn't that," Katie assured him.

"You can take your feminine favors and go to the devil for all I care!" A bitterness almost beyond description passed over Collin's freckled face. "You're all the same, you and your ilk! One Jenny-Jump-Up is just like another. That's what the Duke says. I'm a blundering fool. A dunderhead!"

With a stab of guilt at having wounded his pride, Katie reached out her hand but drew back at the sound of something scraping just outside the windows. She swung around and listened. It was louder now. A clumping, thudding noise of footfalls approaching along the roof, then a faint tapping as of fingers on glass.

"Quick!" Collin cried. "It's Toby. He mustn't find you here! You've got to go. Now."

"No!" Katie sputtered. "I need to talk to Toby."

The desperate, pleading look Collin shot her tugged at her emotions. She needed to ask Toby about the dead girl in the morgue, but Collin's face looked so pained, almost scared, that she nodded and hurried in the direction where he was frantically pointing.

"In there! Yes, there. Hide!" He jabbed his finger repeatedly at a small, arched doorway on the far side of the four-poster bed. "And stay put!" he hissed.

Why? Why hide? Katie wondered as she scooted through the narrow opening into a small alcove just a few feet below the level of Collin's bedroom. The space would be a bathroom in the next century.

Half hidden from sight now, she watched Collin spring to the far window. Throwing open the velvet drapes, he unhooked the bolt. A moment later the window leading out onto the shingled roof was flung open. First one black boot sidled over the sill. Then the rest of Toby's dark figure emerged.

Looking like the Grim Reaper, Toby stamped his feet and closed the window with a hollow slam, which billowed the tasseled curtains on either side. "I can stay only a minute," came his deep voice from beneath a hooded cloak as he strode across the room and spread his hands to the fire.

In the silence that followed, Katie glanced back over her shoulder and scanned the future bathroom. Instead of a white porcelain sink, bathtub, and linen closet that ran the length of the opposite wall, the small room was made up as a sort of artist's garret with canvases, jars of paint, pots of glue, and charcoal drawings filling every available space. Dozens of caricatures — beady-eyed politicians, crooked-nosed bandits, sour-faced schoolmasters — stared out at Katie from thick sheets of paper tacked to the walls.

Hanging from the window wall were five familiar faces painted in whimsical colors: Katie's own, Major Brown's, the Reverend Pinker's, Queen Victoria's, and Napoleon Bonaparte's, all with cartoon features.

Katie turned and quietly moved down the steps for a closer look. Candles burning in a line across the windowsill threw flickering light onto the exaggerated faces, which rose in humorous parody

above long necks attached to animal torsos. Katie's own grinning likeness was joined to a pink caterpillar body. And despite the over-arched
brows and four-inch eyelashes, her eyes had a softness and appeal to
them which made Katie smile.

Next to Katie's comical face, the Reverend Pinker's horsy one
looked almost three-dimensional, with one eye partly shut and the
other peering out from saucer-sized spectacles. Major Brown's caricature looked like a vicious Rottweiler with a cringing, sinister leer.

In the corner, clamped to a wooden easel was a large canvas
half-covered with a splattered drop cloth. Katie stepped closer and
flipped up the cloth. The canvas beneath showed the beginnings of
a portrait of Lady Beatrix, the right side of her face drawn only in
pencil, the left side outlined in colored chalk. But it was definitely the
soon-to-be oil painting of Beatrix that would hang in Katie's room
back home in the twenty-first century. Had Katie never set eyes on
Beatrix's portrait to begin with, she would never have recognized
her as one of the waxwork victims at Madamn Tussauds. And *never*
would have wished herself back into the past, hoping to catch Jack the
Ripper.

Katie swiveled sideways and her foot kicked against a metal
waste bin with a chalkboard balanced on top. Chalk, eraser, and slate
clattered to the floor, and the wastebasket rolled noisily.

Footsteps.

"*Ahem!*" Katie heard Collin clearing his throat just outside
the door. "You see — *h'mf* — confound it, Toby, I've. . .er. . .got. . .
a. . .visitor!"

"Bloody hell! What are *you* doing here?" Toby glared from the
top of the stair risers at Katie as she scrambled to right the chalkboard and dustbin. "What the devil's going on?" he thundered.

Collin raised his hands in a "don't shoot" gesture. "It wasn't me,
I swear!" he yelped. "I didn't lure her here. I thought she wanted to be
my. . .um. . .carving knife. But I was wrong. Don't give me that look,
Toby. She's daft! Bats in the belfry! A bun short of a dozen, I swear it!"

"Is that like a french fry short of a Happy Meal?" Katie blurted out, momentarily forgetting what century she was in.

"What?" Both boys gaped at her.

Katie shook her head. "Never mind. What's a carving knife?"

"Wife," Collin said, glancing sheepishly down at his feet.

Toby exploded down the steps, his dark boots stomping like Darth Vader's — which, like McDonald's, was an icon far in the future. "I don't care if you're as daft as a barn owl, Miss Lennox. Answer me this," he demanded. "How is it that you are acquainted with Mary Ann Nichols?"

"*Are* acquainted?" Kate shot back, stalling for time. Did that mean Mary Ann Nichols was still alive? Jack the Ripper hadn't struck yet?

"Cor blimey, answer the question!"

"I *told* you," Collin yelped, "all her teacups aren't in the upstairs cupboard." Collin tapped his temples to indicate that Katie didn't have all her marbles.

"Let me repeat the question," Toby said slowly, enunciating each word as if talking to a small child. "*How do you know Miss Mary Ann Nichols?*"

"I don't."

"How *did* you know her?"

"I didn't."

"After the play this evening, you asked me — no, begged me — to find out if the murdered girl at the morgue was Mary Ann Nichols." The urgency in Toby's voice was growing.

"Mary Ann who?" Collin chimed in.

"Is she the murdered girl?" Katie asked, trying to keep her voice casual.

"You tell me."

"I wasn't at the mortuary," Katie countered.

"What do you know *of* her?" Toby lowered his voice and it had a razor sharp edge to it.

Katie's heart thudded. Her mind raced. What should she say? What *could* she say? *Well, Toby, it's like this: I know all about Mary Ann Nichols because I went to a Jack the Ripper exhibit at Madame Tussauds more than a hundred years from now!*

"Collin?" Katie spun around. "Did you do these drawings? They're really, really good," Katie choked out, as if she'd never seen such incredible caricatures before.

"You think so?" Collin's face brightened.

"Absolutely. They're fabulous. And that portrait of Lady Beatrix?"

"That's not mine. I'm hiding it for Beatrix. She's sitting for an American chappie named Whistler. Do you know him? James Whistler? It's a surprise for the Duke's seventy-fifth birthday."

"Whistler?" Katie gasped. "*Whistler* is painting Beatrix's portrait? That exact one?" she pointed. "Wow. He didn't sign it! Er...I mean... um...he *hasn't* signed it yet. And, well, anyway, your work is every bit as good as his," Katie lied. If Whistler had painted the portrait of Beatrix hanging in Katie's room, then it was worth a fortune. And it had been sitting in Grandma Cleaves's attic collecting dust for who knows how many years!

Toby eyed Katie with chilling hostility.

Collin grinned. "Mr. Whistler says I've got to study anatomical drawings of muscle and tendons, the whole musculature, like Leonardo da Vinci's *Vitruvian Man*. I'm good with heads, but can't seem to manage bod —"

"Enough!" Toby bellowed. "I want answers, Miss Lennox, or I'll march you down to the Bow Street station myself. Better yet, I'll go fetch Major Brown and bring him here."

"You'd best answer him, Katie." Collin nodded vigorously. "Major Brown is a rotter, make no mistake. By gad, you don't want to be dragooned by the likes of him. There's nothing to fear from us. I'll see no harm comes to you. Tell us about this Nichols girl. Let's have no more prevaricating." Collin had pitched his voice low to sound firm, but it came out more querulous than convincing. "Well?" he insisted. "Tell us what you know this instant!"

When she'd avoided Toby's fierce gaze for as long as she could, Katie raised her chin and announced, "I didn't know Mary Ann. I never met her. Never spoke to her. But I was fairly certain that she was going to be murdered."

"Why didn't you tell me this earlier? Or report it to the authorities?" Toby flung at her. His cape was muddy, and the bowler hat that had been jammed on the back of his head at the theater was missing. Locks of dark hair hung down around his shoulders. "Well?" He drove a gloved fist into his palm, and then, as if with sudden inspiration, he let himself smile.

Drawing off his muddy gloves, Toby reached inside his cloak and drew out a pocket watch. "It is now twenty-five minutes past two. You have precisely five minutes to elaborate in regards to how you could possibly know Mary Ann Nichols would be murdered. I suggest frankness, Miss Katherine. And if I am not satisfied by your account" — his smile grew tighter — "I assure you, I shall wring your neck and beat you to a bloody pulp, *and then* I shall march you down to the Bow Street Police Station."

"Wait, ho! See here!" squealed Collin, jabbing his finger in the air. "You mustn't talk to Katherine like that. This won't do, Toby. Won't do at all. I know the Governor set you the task of watching over me so I don't get into any more foolish . . . er . . . scrapes. But dash it all, it is now I who will have to rein *you* in, old chap. Make sure you don't make a hash of things. Threatening to beat a young lady to a bloody pulp, indeed! Can't have that, Toby. You'll have to apologize. By Jove, I don't care if Katherine slit this poor girl's throat or a dozen like her. I can't allow you to threaten a guest under the Twyford roof, particularly one who *happens* to be the Duke's goddaughter."

"And I don't care if she's God's own lamb to the slaughter. She's got three minutes." The candles burning in a line across the windowsill threw undulating tongue-flames upward into the raftered ceiling.

"Okay," Katie said, trying to sound bold. "I'll tell you everything I know. But I guarantee you will *not* believe a word of it."

"Two minutes, forty-one seconds." Toby's big shoulders grew rigid as his eyes narrowed.

"First," Katie said, holding up her hand, "you have to swear that what I'm going to tell you stays between the three of us. Just us. Promise?"

"No. You want a jellied eel, you'll have to talk to the magistrate."

"Jellied — ?"

"*Deal!*" Collin said in a stage whisper.

"Then my lips are sealed," Katie said. "No jellied eel, no deal."

Collin let out a sound resembling, "*Ugggh!*" then leaned over, cupped his hand to his mouth and whispered in Katie's ear: "You just said, 'No deal, no deal.'"

"What's it to be, Miss Lennox?" Toby demanded.

"No jellied eel. I won't tell you a thing unless you promise it stays between us."

Toby grabbed her wrist, yanked her up the stairs, and tugged her skidding and squirming back into Collin's room. "Tell me now, or I'm dragging you out of this house and taking you directly to Major Brown's lodgings, dressed in your chemise and night-pinnings if need be."

"Surely not, Toby! You can't take Katherine to that bruiser's house in a state of undress! She'll be the laughing stock of . . . of her entire country! A state of undress, indeed. What will the Duke say when he hears about this?"

Toby strode to the window, Katie in tow. With his free hand he snapped open the window, and the curtains billowed in the blustering wind.

"See here, Toby!" Collin squawked. "You can't do this! She'll catch her death of cold. It's not decent! She'll break her neck on the rooftop, she'll —"

"He's bluffing," Katie said between gritted teeth, hoping it was true.

Maintaining a firm grip on Katie's wrist, Toby slouched out of his Grim Reaper cape and threw it around her shoulders. Then he hoisted her in a fireman's carry over his shoulder and pitched himself halfway out the window. Katie could feel the sting of cold air.

"Okay. Okay!" she cried. "You win. I'll tell you."

Toby slogged back into the room and dropped her unceremoniously into the armchair by the fire. Behind them, Collin scrambled to fasten the window as another gust of air made the logs in the fireplace sputter and sizzle.

An uneasy expression pinched around Toby's mouth as he gripped both of the chair's arms and leaned forward with his face menacingly close to Katie's. "I'm listening."

Staring up into his dark eyes, Katie could feel her heart beating heavily. She took a deep breath and let it out slowly. "I know about Mary Ann Nichols...because...I'm clairvoyant. Psychic. Telepathic. I can see into the future. Sometimes. Not always. There. Are you satisfied?"

Toby regarded her with skepticism, then his strong jaw relaxed, and the squint lines around his eyes deepened into amusement. "It doesn't take a bleedin' Oxford scholar to figure out that you're either an incredibly good actress or completely deranged."

"None of the above," Katie muttered, folding her arms firmly across her chest.

"Above what?" yelped Collin, clearly puzzled.

Katie stared at him. "None of the above" was probably an expression used to fill out computer forms. "None of those choices," she quickly amended.

"Prove it," Toby said. The hostile gleam in his dark eyes had returned. "Lock the grady moore, Collin," he instructed without taking his eyes off Katie.

Collin scrambled across the floor and shot the bolt in the door.

"This is the last jellied eel you're likely to get from me, Miss Katherine. Prove that you are indeed a hocus-pocus mind reader, or I'm going to take you over my knee and wallop the living pony and trap out of you."

"Okay. That's it, buster!" Katie sprang to her feet. "Have you ever heard of women's liberation? You lay a hand on me and I'll karate chop you in the solar plexus so hard you won't sit down for a week! Take *that* jellied eel and shove it up your —"

"April in Paris?" Toby raised an amused eyebrow.

"If that means —"

"Arse!" Collin squealed.

"Then yes, Toby," Katie said, breathing hard. "You can shove it up your April in Paris!"

Toby leaned closer. His lips brushed across her cheek making her shiver as he whispered softly in her ear, "I'm assuming that women's liberation has something to do with John Stuart Mill and the suffragette movement. But it's of no consequence. If you prove that you're clairvoyant, you can wallop me in the solar plexus as hard as you want. Otherwise, make no mistake, I'm marching your April in Paris to Major Brown's lodgings, and he can handle this as he sees fit. That's a right fair jellied eel, Miss Katherine, now isn't it?"

Chapter Seventeen

Pray When Will That Be?
say the Bells of Stepney

"Okay, Toby. Close your eyes and conjure up a picture of the dead girl," Katie instructed.

Toby stared at her, his gaze never wavering from her face, but Collin squeezed his eyes tightly shut.

Katie closed her own eyes and pretended deep concentration. "I see. . .a girl. . .whose throat has. . .been slit. . .but there's more. She's been eviscerated. Disemboweled." Katie opened her eyes. "Am I correct?"

"Jumping Jehoshaphat!" Collin cried, striking his fists together. "Katherine, you're a mind reader! That's *exactly* what I was thinking! A naked girl all cut up to ribbons. Blood everywhere! Lots and lots of blood. Toby! Katherine is a blooming mind reader! God's truth! She read my mind. She did!"

Katie looked at Collin. "I didn't read *your* mind, Collin. You weren't *at* the morgue. I was picking up Toby's thoughts."

"No. No. You were picking up mine! Lord love a duck! That's *exactly* what I was thinking! Exactly, Katherine!"

"Before we go any further," Katie said, "may I ask a favor of both of you? At home everyone calls me Katie to avoid confusing me with my aunt Katherine, so I'm not used to being called Katherine. You are both welcome to call me Katie."

Just then, one of the candles on the desk spluttered and puffed out.

Katie cast her mind back, trying to dredge up details about the first victim from the Madame Tussauds Jack the Ripper exhibit. "There wasn't a lot of blood was there, Toby? The police officer who found her, or maybe it was a doctor or coroner or undertaker — whoever it was, didn't pick up on the fact that Mary Ann Nichols was disemboweled because...because...I'm not sure exactly...Maybe her clothing was covering it up. Am I right?"

Collin gestured with his arms. "I tell you, in *my* mind I saw lots of blood! And I was thinking about that cat! Did you see a cat, Katherine?" And then as though defending a point, Collin said eagerly. "You did, didn't you? I knew it."

Katie looked at Toby's scowling face. "Words can't describe the horror of it, or accurately convey what happened to that poor girl. And it's horrible talking about her like this. But am I right, Toby? Do we have a deal?"

Toby remained mute, but Katie charged on. "The reason you can't tell Major Brown or any other policeman is because the person who did this — *and who will kill more girls if we don't stop him* — might be a police officer."

"Major Brown!" Collin whooped. "It's him, isn't it? He's a bad lot. I've known it all along. I hate that blighter. I've always hated him. Now the Governor will *have* to put a stop to his involvement with Beatrix. I've been right about Major Bumble-Brain from the start. If only people would listen to me —"

"Major Brown is *not* the culprit." Toby's eyes were cold, his voice hard as steel. "Major Gideon Brown would no more kill an innocent girl than you or I could fly to the moon or travel through time. He's an honorable, decent man. To accuse him is an unjust, wicked—"

"But it's true! It has to be. Katherine saw it in her visions. She's clairvoyant! A soothsayer!"

"No, Collin. That's not what I said and not what I saw."

"But—"

"I *said* it's a possibility that the killer is a police officer. Whoever's doing this will continue, and it's going to get worse. The killer will be someone who can walk the streets of London undetected. Someone above suspicion...like a police officer, a minister, a doctor...someone you wouldn't expect. A woman for instance, or—"

"A woman!" Collin bristled, his eyes bulging out like the stuffed trout hanging over his desk. "*Never!* The gentler sex couldn't perpetrate such a dastardly—"

"Or a man dressed as a woman. Any number of people, Collin. The point is, the killer has to be caught before he murders more innocent girls, *especially his last victim*. We've got to stop him. *We have to find him*."

"Just gaze into your crystal ball, Katherine. Dash it all, *you're* the clairvoyant one." Collin stumped over and flopped himself into the armchair by the fire. "You need to tell *us* who this blighter is."

"It's not like that, Collin. I don't have a crystal ball. I only know that he'll strike again. And the papers will call him Jack the Ripper."

"Surely you can conjure this killer up in your mind and"— Collin snapped his fingers.—"*Poof!* He'll come to you. Close your eyes and give it a try—"

"No, I can't."

"But *mightn't* this Jack-of-all-Trades killer just pop into your mind when you least expect it?"

"No. That's not how...er...my gift works."

Collin scratched his chin. "If you can't predict who the killer is, how do you know there *will* be more murders? You have a gift, as you call it. I'll accept that. But if you can't tell us the identity of this Jack-of-Hearts killer, how can we trust that your visions are, er, trustworthy?

You said you wanted to return home, Katherine. Are you afraid of this rum bloke, is that it? You're having nightmares about him, and that's why you crept into my room like a sleepwalker?"

"No. I mean, yes. I mean, no. I'm not having nightmares. Well, I am sort of . . . having nightmares," she ended lamely.

"Toby, old boy? What are you thinking?" Collin asked from his slouched position in the chair. "You're awfully quiet. Not still contemplating hauling Katherine off to prison, are you?"

"I'm thinking that Miss Lennox might not be a mind reader after all. Perhaps she knows the killer. Perhaps the *killer* gave her all this information."

"Killer? How? When? The only person she's been with is *me*. You don't think I'm the killer? Shall I confess, then?" Collin said almost eagerly. "There's a jellied eel for you. I confess. It was me. I killed that poor girl and . . . the cat, too. My blimey motive would be, er . . . er . . ." He stuck his neck in and out of his robe's collar like a turtle. "*Hmmm*, what motive? I hate women, that's it! All women. I'm a misogynist through and through so I went to the East End, found a lusty wench and —" he drew his finger across his throat.

"I'm not accusing you of anything, Collin," Toby said quietly.

"Well, *that's* a first." Collin grinned, then turned to Katie and said in a conspiratorial whisper, "I'm always in the soup with Toby *or* my grandfather."

"I don't believe in hocus-pocus," Toby said, glancing from Katie to Collin and back again. He shook his head. Like most Cockneys, he had a superstitious bent, yet he scoffed at people who were ruled by portents and bad omens. And as for predicting the future, that would mean that man did not have free will. Toby definitely did not believe that one's life was set in stone and everything was preordained.

"So, Miss Katherine," Toby pronounced his words slowly, his eyes never wavering from hers. "If you *can* foresee the future, and I say *if* because I don't believe such a thing is possible. But *if* it were possible, and we could catch this phantom killer and stop other girls from being butchered, does that mean the future — as you foresee it — is changeable and not set in stone?"

Set in stone. At the mention of the familiar phrase, Katie thought about the London Stone. *Nothing is set in stone,* she thought. *Or maybe everything is! Maybe time is a continual loop with the past, present, and future on a circular continuum.*

"I don't know, Toby," Katie answered. "I just don't know. If you'd asked me that question several days ago I'd have said the future hasn't happened so it can't possibly unfold in any predictable fashion — every decision, every action a person makes, or a thousand people make, can trigger another action or reaction, and therefore the future hasn't happened and can't be predicted. But now I'm not so sure. Maybe the future, like the past, has already happened. Maybe we can travel back and forth through time —"

"And *maybe* man will fly to the moon," Collin scoffed, rolling his eyes.

"And walk on it," Katie said, holding back a smile.

"And I'm a monkey's uncle," Collin mocked.

"Maybe you are…or descended from one." Katie sighed. In the next century Collin and Toby would face a barrage of new inventions and modern technology. Telephones, airplanes, automobiles, electric lighting, phonographs, radios, refrigeration, flush toilets, vaccines. If they lived long enough, they would also see two world wars, rocket ships, computers, medical advances.

"So, what number am I thinking of?" Collin demanded, squeezing his eyes shut again. "It's between one and ten."

The gas jets on either side of the mantel threw spangles of light across his scrunched-up face.

"I can't read minds, Collin. I can only see images…sometimes. Blurry images. Pictures in my head. That's all."

Collin sprang from the chair and thrust out his open hand. A strange, almost wild expression had settled on his face. "Read my palm, then," he insisted. "What's in my future? Am I to have a long, happy life like the old gypsy in Hyde Park tells me whenever I cross her palm with a heaping lot of chinking coins? Better yet, am I going to come face to face with this Ripper-Van-Winkle bloke?"

"Collin. I can't read palms. I'm not a fortune-teller."

"Dashed useless then, aren't you?" Collin blinked myopically down at his open palm, but when he glanced up, he was grinning. "It's all right, Katherine. We're going to help you. We're going to track down this Jackass the Slasher."

"Jack the Ripper."

"Him, too. Isn't that right, Toby?"

Toby's eyes had never left Katie's. "I'm going to need something more tangible," he answered in a heavy, unemotional voice.

"More tangible? More tangible than a dead girl?" sputtered Collin.

Chapter Eighteen

I Do Not Know
say the Great Bells of Bow

IN FRONT OF THEM, the stone church showed pinpoints of flickering light through its stained-glass windows. High above, fast-moving clouds whirled across the sky with such dizzying speed it made the church steeple appear to be in motion and the clouds, stationary.

Katie had spotted the churchyard with its moss-covered headstones long before the four-wheeler slid into the shadows at the curbside. And it would have been a pleasant enough ride from Twyford Manor through the cobbled streets of London had Toby not scowled at her the whole time.

Katie thought about the jellied eel she had made with Toby. If her plan worked, it would be nothing short of a miracle. Her spirits lightened just thinking about it. But as she climbed out of the swaying carriage, drops of condensation fell from the coach's roof ledge and splattered her face. Collin laughed when she looked up at him sputtering.

He adroitly avoided the drips by leaping onto the ground, with Toby following close behind.

With an exaggerated flourish of gallantry, Collin offered Katie his pocket handkerchief, but she wiped her face with the sleeve of her velvet jacket instead and scurried on down the brick path.

A man in clerical robes walked with absentminded briskness toward a group of people huddled near a gravestone in the far corner of the churchyard. A small boy dressed all in black stared thoughtfully down at the newly turned earth, a bouquet of violets clutched in his tiny hands.

As Katie and Toby strode along the path, Collin hung back, swirling and jabbing his umbrella in the air like a sword. "Those winged cherubs, there," he said, poking at a carved angel on a headstone, "seem dreadfully solemn, don't you think? I ought to be a stone mason. I'd teach these somber blighters a thing or two. See that one over there? Instead of a skeleton holding a scythe, I'd have a mermaid strumming a lyre."

Katie bit back a smile.

"This place positively *reeks* of death and bereavement," Collin chortled. "Needs to be livened up, I tell you! Death isn't half as bad as it's made out to be. Dying is all part of the game, don't you see? All part of life. The flip side of the coin. Heads you win, tails you lose. We're all going to come a cropper sooner or later. We're all going to throw tails on the coin of life."

Collin grinned and tapped his chin. "The profundity of my insights often astounds even me. The coin of life. . .like the fountain of youth, or good versus evil. It's all one and the same, don't you know? Mustn't wax maudlin over the inevitable, eh?"

As Collin jabbed his sword-stick umbrella around the churchyard, Katie glanced at Toby, whose dark eyes stared back at her with cold skepticism. With his boxer's nose and the thin scar slashed across his cheekbone, Toby's face reflected an angry disdain. She didn't blame him. Not after last night. Not after what she'd promised. And yet. . .if her plan worked, Toby would have to honor his end of the bargain. It was a risk, but she might be able to pull it off. If not — as Collin had so aptly put it last night — Katie would be in the soup.

Well, here goes, she thought. *Nothing ventured, nothing gained. But once ventured, she could lose everything . . .*

❖

As they crossed the churchyard toward the iron gate leading to the London Stone, Toby stared at Katie and felt a jolt in his gut.

Last night had been long and frustrating for Toby, and he was not blessed with a patient nature. He knew he should have informed Major Brown right away that Katie knew intimate details about the dead girl's murder, yet he had kept quiet. Something about this American twist 'n' swirl knocked him totally off balance. He had known her for only a few days, but already she had the ability to tie his emotions in knots. That she had this unearthly hold over him wasn't an easy admission for Toby to make. He prided himself on his ability to keep his emotions in check. But the viselike grip she held him in had happened so suddenly, so overwhelmingly, Toby hadn't realized that his feelings for someone — *anyone* — could be so explosive, so all-consuming. He'd been furious when he caught her in Collin's bedchamber last night, but had masked his emotions by being overly harsh with her. Yet he knew, without a shadow of a doubt, that he had to steel himself against the clasp she wielded over him. He was determined not to make the same ill-fated mistake as his mother, who had fallen in love above her station — and his father, who had fallen in lust below his. Keeping a level head was an attribute that Toby held as dear as life itself.

Toby noted that Katie's face was ghostly pale, outlined against the harsh grey of the large stone. Legend had it that the London Stone could grant three wishes for those who were pure of heart. But legend also claimed that the stone was the very one that King Arthur had pulled his sword from.

Toby watched as a spray of damp curls fell across Katie's forehead. When she looked at him it was with an expression of fear, and the gut-wrenching spark in those eyes seemed to glaze over, as if she were about to swoon. He reached his hand out to steady her.

Clutching her arm, Toby thought about the jellied eel he had made with her, and the message he'd left in the stuffed vulture in the Duke's study. He laughed at the lunacy of it. There was no denying that the girl tugged at his heartstrings like none other. Why else would he have agreed to such foolishness?

She might be an accomplice to a murder. She might be any number of things. But of one thing Toby was sure: *He must never show the girl what he felt about her or she'd possess a power over him that would destroy him.* He knew this as surely as he knew she was no more clairvoyant than he was. Less so, probably, for he came from a long line of fortune-tellers and soothsayers. His own mother was the seventh child of a seventh child and possessed second sight. This girl was gifted, but not with second sight. Toby would stake his life on it. In a manner of speaking, he already had. If by twelve noon she could not tell him what he'd written on the parchment he put into the stuffed vulture, which he'd then sewn shut again, Toby would cease doing Katie's bidding. If, on the other hand, she succeeded, Toby vowed he'd follow her anywhere. *Even to hell and back.*

They reached the London Stone, whose opening was dubbed "The Raven's Claw" because it was jagged and uneven and just wide enough for a claw or a small finger. He watched as Katie's gloved hand closed around the spikes of the grating around the London Stone. Then she peeled off one of her kid gloves and poked her hand through the bars. A moment later she was jabbing her index finger into the Raven's Claw fissure, and for an instant Toby's world exploded. A kaleidoscope of colors flashed across his eyes, and he felt that all the air in his body was being sucked out of him. A deafening explosion rang out. Thunderbolts of light flashed around the Stone, then pierced his eyes. A red-hot poker of pain ran up his arm. He had no choice but to let go of Katie's arm. Then he heard a faint whisper of a voice: *Beware of what you wish for . . .*

Part IV:

Katie Seeks
Proof

Chapter Nineteen

Best to Come Home
say the Bells of Winterloam

Katie heard the explosion and then felt it. It was so loud that when the noise finally died away, it left a ringing against her eardrums like a high-pitched tuning fork.

Her head throbbed. She yanked hard to free her arm from the grip of the iron grating surrounding the London Stone, but like a steel trap at the mouth of a cage, the wire mesh clamped painfully around her arm, digging into her flesh and cutting off her circulation. The pain was unbearable. She took a deep breath and hurled her body backward to pull free of the iron jaws. *Beware of what you wish for...* echoed in her brain.

I want to go home! I need to go home! she wished with all her might. *Take me back to Madame Tussauds in the twenty-first century,* she begged as if the Stone had ears and could grant her wish.

Another deafening explosion sent new shockwaves through her body. White-hot heat seared her arm. Shadows darted around the

Stone, then around her head, blurring her vision. She was falling, down, down, down into the rabbit-hole abyss of blackness, and a moment later it was over.

The pain was gone. Bright light flooded the room. The room? Had she made it? Was she back in Madame Tussauds? Katie squinted her eyes and tried to peer around, but the light was blinding. And what was that smell? Peanut butter? Chocolate? And something antiseptic, like the disinfectant used in hospitals ... or museums.

Wax museums.

Katie forced herself to open her eyes.

"Katie," came Toby's voice so close to her ear it made her jump. She glanced down. Her hand and arm were free. And the velvet jacket she'd been wearing was gone. She felt blissfully light and unencumbered by petticoats and heavy clothing. She was wearing a T-shirt and jeans. "*Katie,*" Toby repeated. *But which Toby was it,* Katie wondered.

She heard a sound as if someone had just kicked a tin can across a tiled floor, and it rattled and thrummed somewhere near her feet. But when she looked down, there was nothing near her sneakered feet. *Sneakers!* The joy of wearing high-tops surged through her, almost overwhelming her with happiness. With her free hand she reached up. Gone was the cloche bonnet with the enormous satin bow tied under her chin.

"Katie!" came Toby's voice so loudly this time she had to clamp her hands over her ears.

"Stop shouting!" she cried, feeling a wave of nausea. But she also felt light as air without the layers of bulky clothing—the overskirt, the underskirt, the petticoats, the flounced bustle.

"Not shouting, Katie." Toby looked at her oddly, then lowered his voice to a whisper. "You crossed over, didn't you, Katie? The Stone is a portal, and you did it, didn't you?"

Katie swallowed hard and nodded. The boy towering over her, with his strong dimpled chin and crooked smile playing around the corners of his wide mouth, didn't have a boxer's broken nose or a scar slashed across his cheek. And this boy was a good deal taller than the one she'd left in the churchyard, but they looked so similar. "How . . . long . . . have . . . I . . . been . . . gone?" she managed to choke out.

"You haven't been gone. That's just it. That's the way it works."

"How do you know?" Katie asked, her voice still weak.

"Because I made it happen, too. Last year. After my father died. The Stone was being exhibited in the Victoria and Albert, not here. But there's something you need to know, Katie. Something very important."

Katie grabbed his arm. "Can I get back? Can I *go* back?"

He nodded. "But only three times. Then it's over. You can't do it again. But it's more complicated than just going back and forth . . . it's about changing the past and—"

"Stop!" Katie put up her hand. She felt another overwhelming sensation of queasiness rising from the pit of her stomach and up her throat. "Wait," she managed to gasp out. She took several deep breaths until the room around her, with its disinfectant smell, stopped spinning.

"I-I wondered about changing the past," she managed to pant out, still doubled over and breathing in great gulps of air.

"You'll be okay, Katie. Just breathe slowly. I know you're reeling. I've been there. It's awful. Just give yourself a minute." Toby—*the twenty-first century Toby*—did something that made her straighten slowly back up. He began rubbing her back in small circles the way her mom did when Katie was little and had the wind knocked out of her.

Breathing in odd, heavy bursts now, Katie told him she'd traveled back to Victorian England during the time of Jack the Ripper.

"But I have so many questions," she said. "What I need to know is . . . can I . . . change the past?" Painfully, Katie pulled her arm out of the wire-mesh cage surrounding the Stone.

"Okay. Here's the deal—" the other Toby said.

"Don't you mean, jellied eel?" Katie shot back under her breath, trying for levity. If she didn't make a joke, she'd start to cry.

As it was, she had to blink back tears.

"Exactly," Toby said. The fluorescent lights in the ceiling panels illuminated his wide grin as he loomed over her. "But it's not a jellied eel you're going to like —"

"Try me. I need to know everything. I need to know *why* this happened. *How* this happened. And. . .can I change the past?" She asked plaintively, running a hand over the top of her hatless head, feeling normal hair — not woven with strands of pearls, or twisted into a high knot, or braided so tightly to her skull as to cause migraines.

"Can I change the past?" Katie repeated.

She felt a cold tremble running through her body when Toby said simply, "You can change small things, inconsequential things. But you can't alter history. At least I couldn't. *And I tried.* But there's something you have to know," he continued in a distressed voice. "Something crucial."

"I'm all ears," Katie told him, but turned her back on him as she scooped up her backpack in the corner where she'd left it. *I've got to get back to Grandma Cleaves's house!* "You can tell me *everything* on our way to my grandmother's. There's something I've got to do. Where's Collin?"

"Last I saw him he was heading for the Rock 'n' Roll Hall of Fame. He wanted to get a picture of himself standing next to Neil Diamond."

"Neil Diamond! Puh-leeze!"

"What?"

"Neil Diamond? He's ancient."

"Collin said it's for his mother. Neil Diamond's her favorite singer."

Katie nodded and smiled. "I forgot. Aunt Pru loves all those old-fogey singers."

"Hey. You're from Boston. I thought 'Sweet Caroline' was the Red Sox anthem?"

Katie grinned. She threw her arms around Toby's neck and squeezed so hard she almost couldn't breathe herself. "I'm home, I'm home, I'm home! And I love 'Sweet Caroline.'"

"Yeah. And my favorite group, Courtney and the Metro Chicks, does a wicked spoof on that song."

I know, Katie thought. *I helped write it!* "Let's go," she whispered, starting to get all choked up again.

"What about Collin?"

"No time. We've got to get back to my grandmother's house. I'll explain on the way. And you can fill me in on everything you know about the London Stone. And, by the way, where did you go when you traveled back in time?"

"Scotland. Eighteen fifty-five."

"How come? I mean, why then?"

"I went back to the time of Madeleine Smith. She killed her lover with arsenic. . .or was accused of killing her lover. I thought I knew how she did it. I'd been doing research on the case. It's a sort of unsolved murder. Famous case. I thought I had it all figured out. But I didn't. I was way off base."

"Did you meet any of your ancestors?"

"Yup. Madeleine Smith's doomed lover for one."

Katie met his gaze. "So does the London Stone just take people back to famous murder mysteries?"

"No. It does more than that. It grants your innermost wish. That's why I told you beware of what you wish for, because it might —"

"Come true. I remember. But the wish I wished for can't come true." *I want to say goodbye to my parents!* "So no worries."

"There's one other thing you need to know, Katie. It took me a long time to figure it out. The short story, 'The Raven's Claw,' is what made me realize —"

Toby stopped midstride and took a deep breath. "The most important thing you need to know is that your last wish will be to undo the others."

"What? That doesn't make sense."

"Whoever wrote 'The Raven's Claw' must have gone back in time himself using the London Stone. The short story is a parable, a warning. The protagonist in the story strokes the Raven's Claw, and is granted three wishes. But what happens is so horrific that he uses his last wish to undo the others."

Chapter Twenty

Do Not Tarry
say the Bells of St. Garrily

"But, Toby!" Katie cried. "The past has already happened. It's part of the stream of history. What I need to know is, can I stop Jack the Ripper? Can I save any of his victims?"

Toby had accelerated his stride, fairly pulling her along behind him down the Plexiglas staircase and through a crowd of tourists to the ticket window. He inquired as to the policy for reentry once they'd left the museum. A woman behind the counter wearing cat's-eye reading glasses nodded and told them to hold out the backs of their hands, which she marked with a rubber stamp. "And keep your ticket stubs, just in case. Museum closes at five sharp tonight."

Toby hustled Katie toward the entrance doors. "You can change small things, but not big things. That's my best guess." They were passing the lavatories.

"Wait! Omigod, a real bathroom!"

Toby chuckled. "I know, I know. I had the same reaction. Chamber pots and outhouses are the pits."

And they stink, Katie was about to say. She looked longingly at the "Women" sign over the restroom door. She thought about hot water. *Hot running water.* She shook her head. "It's okay. I'll wait till I get home." The thought of a real bathroom brought a shudder of unexpected pleasure. She turned to Toby, who was grinning ear to ear.

"The first time I came back," he said, his eyes sparkling, "I took the longest hot shower on record. I just stood forever under the spigots relishing the jets of water. Who would have thought?" He laughed. "Some of the things we take totally for granted are the greatest gifts on earth, like showers — and flush toilets!"

Now it was Katie who was tugging Toby along with her through the revolving doors, and a moment later, they were headed down Marylebone Road to the Baker Street tube station.

"We don't have much time." He grew serious.

"What do you mean?"

"You're going to start to feel as if you're fading in and out," he said, glancing at his watch, "in a little over an hour. Then you either go back to Victorian England, or you stay here. The museum closes at five. It's now three-thirty."

"And if I choose...to stay?" Katie felt her mouth go dry.

"Then it's over. You can never go back in time to the same place again. You only have a two-hour window...give or take. I'm betting you'll go back. Actually, I know you will."

"And you know this because...?"

"Because that's what I did."

When they were outside the museum, Katie glanced back over her shoulder. It was so different here. Space-age street lamps soared overhead like giant propellers, and the asphalt streets, gummed with grime, held no hint of nineteenth-century cobblestones.

As they loped off down the street, crossing walkways painted Day-Glo orange, Katie was struck by the deafening noise and sputtering rumble of modern trucks and cars sweeping past, the belching gas fumes, and most striking of all, the dull cinderblock buildings on every corner. Gone were the stone gargoyles on overhanging ledges, intricately carved woodwork, and cobbled walkways; gone, too, the profusion of scrolled ironwork gates and the flower sellers on every corner.

Katie sighed. There was a roundness to the nineteenth century that the twenty-first lacked. Arched doorways, oval windows, circular pillars were all missing here. And the balloon-like dome over Madame Tussauds with its "JUMP THE Q" sign in bold mustard yellow against a lipstick-red background, looked like an inflated, fake planetarium crayoned against the sky by a five-year-old.

Though this century is modern, Katie thought, *with sophisticated technology, the architecture looks so . . . chunky . . . and heavy . . . as if someone threw cement blocks together and piled them high.*

"Okay," Toby said. "Tell me everything. Start at the beginning." Katie nodded, and as they hurried to her grandmother's home, she told Toby all that had happened to her, ending with Toby — the other Toby — hiding a message in the stuffed vulture.

When they arrived at Twyford House Condominiums, Grandma Cleaves wasn't home. Because it was Wednesday, her grandmother would be at the Charity Mission in the East End doing volunteer work.

Moving quickly through the front vestibule, Katie pressed the code and turned the key in the lock of number 211 and motioned Toby to follow.

Inside her grandmother's place, they hurried past the coat closet (a "cloak closet" in the olden days) and descended several steps into the oak-paneled foyer. Katie stopped and blinked around. Down the hall, spanning out to the left, was an octagonal room called the "morning room" at Twyford Manor, but here it was used as a sort of den and dining room combination. The library, opening down the hall to Katie's right, was part of the original library. The other half would be part of Mrs. Drumlin's studio apartment.

Glancing through the mullioned windows at the rear of the foyer, Katie caught sight of the car park. There were no remnants of the old carriage house or portico.

Taking a deep breath, Katie led the way up the baronial staircase, past the stained glass window at the landing, and on up into the attic. Just a fraction of the original attic, it smelled strongly of mothballs and dust.

Weaving past boxes of Christmas ornaments, broken toys, trunks full of clothing used for dress-up, and shelves packed with cardboard boxes, Katie brushed past ancient furniture draped in old sheets, giving the cluttered attic a haunted appearance. With Toby following on her heels, Katie deftly picked her way through the clutter. But even with Toby close behind, Katie couldn't help the jumpy feeling in the pit of her stomach.

A dim hanging bulb cast a shadowy glow from the raftered ceiling. This portion of the attic smelled like heat, old paint, wood, glue, and dust. At the far end stretched stacks of chipped teacups and broken pottery. A pile of canvases lay stacked against a workbench. Lining a shelf in the corner under the eaves was a collection of old-fashioned hats, and next to the hats, on either end of the book shelf, perched the moth-eaten eagle and vulture. Bald in patches, the vulture peered down at them with lifeless marble eyes. The eagle's eyes were missing, and most of its feathers, giving it the appearance of a worn and much-loved teddy bear.

Katie reached for the vulture. Mounted on a wooden base carved to resemble a tree branch, the stuffed bird made a clunking sound as it scraped across the metal shelf. It was heavier and more bulky than Katie remembered. She turned to Toby when she finally got it down.

"Got a Swiss Army knife or something?"

"Will a box-cutter do?"

"You carry around a box-cutter?" Katie's eyebrows shot up at the sight of the blade Toby wrenched from the pocket of his duster coat.

He shrugged, looking sheepish. "Never know when it might come in handy."

"Remind me to keep you close whenever I'm in a dark alley." Katie turned back and stuck the box-cutter into the seam at the base of the bird, below the wings. She didn't gingerly pick at the worn thread. She gouged and stabbed at it.

When she'd made a hole the size of a small plum, she wiggled two fingers inside and eased a compression of gauze out, then several wads of stuffing, until her fingers touched something crinkly. She grappled with the bunting, then managed to grab a small, yellowish piece of rolled-up parchment, the outer layer as thin as onionskin, from the bowels of the bird.

Katie scooted to the workbench, sat down, and gingerly smoothed out the small piece of parchment. It had been rolled up like a small scroll, the size of a narrow cigarette. Katie feared it might crumble in her hands, but instead it was so stiff she couldn't manage to uncurl it without tearing it.

There was a canvas apron hanging from a peg on the wall. Toby unhooked it and strode over to the bench. "Here." He spread the canvas apron on the workbench. Toby took the rolled parchment from Katie's trembling hands.

Taking great care, Toby smoothed out the tightly wound parchment. Watching him, Katie had a momentary vision of the other Toby with his silky black hair, fathomless dark eyes, and inscrutable smile. The two boys were different. Yet there were striking similarities. They both had dark complexions, angled jaws, and smooth-as-silk black hair.

"Can you make out the words?" Toby asked, peering down at the ancient writing.

Katie leaned over and squinted, trying to read the words, but the ink had seeped into the paper over the decades and was splotchy and smudged.

"I think it says, 'My sister's pet name was Tuppence.'"

"On the other hand," Toby maintained, "It might say, 'My sister's pet's name was Tuppence.'" His glance lifted to hers. "Maybe his sister had a pet cat or dog named Tuppence."

Katie nodded. "But look here. The next sentence reads, 'Because of me, she died.'" Katie cocked her head sideways. "Does that mean the pet died or the sister?"

"Dunno. The sister, I think. But why write this? The dude's not Jack the Ripper, is he?"

Katie swallowed hard. "I don't think so. No. Not possible. I mean, it's unlikely."

But was it? she wondered. *Could Toby be Jack the Ripper? Or Collin, for that matter? Or even the Duke?*

Chapter Twenty-one

Do Not Go Home say the Bells beneath the Great Dome

TEN MINUTES LATER they were back downstairs heading out the door.

"Hold on!" Katie sputtered. "I just thought of something—"

She raced down the hall to the library. There was an old Bible in the library that listed all the births and deaths in her grandmother's family going back generations. Katie never went near the dusty old tome because it listed her parents' deaths. Both deaths had been carefully recorded in her grandmother's spidery handwriting. It had so upset Katie, Grandma Cleaves had taken to hiding the heavy leather-bound book or at least wedging it unobtrusively among the bookshelves.

"What?" Toby asked, tromping noisily behind.

"Help me look for the family Bible. It's leathery and old, with a huge gold clasp that looks like a buckle," Katie said, tugging him along with her into the library where afternoon sunlight was pouring into the room through floor-to-ceiling windows, making the rows upon rows of bookshelves sparkle and seem to dance.

Katie blinked around, shading her eyes from the dazzling light. The room was half the size of its nineteenth-century counterpart, yet it still looked massive. Katie remembered seeing her father perched on top of the tall, wheeled ladder that ran on brass rails around the book-crammed shelves, his arms laden with leather volumes. She remembered watching him climb midway down and when he caught sight of her peering up at him, he had laughed and called out, "Look, Kit-Kat! A veritable feast for a book-lover such as myself!" Then he climbed down several more rungs and held out a small book to her. "You'll like this one. Same author as *Kidnapped*. Remember when I read that to you and Courtney? You hid under the covers and begged me to stop reading. Well . . ." he chuckled from his perch on the middle rung of the library ladder. "This one's scarier. But of course you're older now."

She remembered reaching up for the book. Remembered the kindness in his eyes. They had been visiting Grandma Cleaves during a school vacation. The slender volume her father handed to her was by Robert Louis Stevenson. *Strange Case of Dr Jekyll and Mr Hyde.*

Katie had forgotten.

Dad gave it to me the summer before he died. How could I forget he gave it to me? After the double funerals everything had become a blur for Katie. And when she moved to London to live with Grandma Cleaves she had tried hard not to think back on the life she had once shared with her sister and her mom and her dad. It was far easier to lose herself in a book than to remember who had given it to her.

Katie felt the sting of tears. "My dad loved this room," she said out loud. She shook her head trying to banish the memory of how happy her dad looked that afternoon, sunlight bathing him in a golden glow. Her heart caught in her throat. *I wish my parents were alive. If Collin's plane hadn't been delayed . . .* Her parents had died on the way to the airport to pick up Collin. They had waited an extra fifteen minutes because his plane was delayed. If her mom and dad had driven to the airport on schedule, they would have missed the truck that overturned in the Sumner Tunnel, causing their car to crash. "If only they hadn't died —"

If wishes were unicorns, maidens would ride.

That was one of her father's favorite sayings.

"Hey!" Toby called out. "Is that it? Over there?" He pointed to the oak table against the far windows; as he strode across the room toward it, he stepped into the same golden, dazzling light that had engulfed her father that day so many years ago. The light spilled over Toby's shoulders like a shimmering golden cape, enveloping him and swirling out behind him onto the floor.

Katie saw where he was pointing. She dashed over to the table and tugged out the leather-bound Bible from under a stack of dictionaries. But the leather-bound book with its gold clasp was so heavy it fell from her grip and clunked against the surface of the table. She yanked it open and thumbed through the pages, then ran her finger down a column of dates. Her heart pounded. She couldn't believe what she was reading. She blinked. Then blinked again. "So young. He died so young," she gasped.

"Who?"

"Collin Chesterfield Twyford, the third. The nineteenth-century Collin. Here's his birth date, and here — ! Wait a sec. It says he married Prudence Farthington in eighteen hundred and eighty-nine . . . at the age of eighteen. That's awfully young, isn't it?" She glanced up at Toby.

Toby shrugged. "They married young in those days."

"But look here! It's so tragic. He died several months later on September 12. Drowned in a peat bog on the moors in Devon, near Bovey Castle, the Duke's country seat. He was so young." Katie stared hard at the old-fashioned script, with its curlicues and flourishes, hoping she had misread it. She pointed to the next sentence and stepped away. Toby moved forward.

"Hmmm," he said, looking perplexed. "Seems like my namesake was with him when he died. Says here Tobias Becket" — Toby glanced up — "did you know that Becket is my last name? Anyway, Tobias

Becket pulled Collin's body out of the bog. Horrible way to die. It's like quicksand." He blinked at Katie, then back down at the page. "Says here that Tobias Becket, trusted family friend, accompanied Collin on a hunting expedition on the moors. Collin lost his footing and. . .drowned in the peat bog. He was buried in Dartmoor at the castle. Oh, no —" Toby groaned. "He died just after his son and heir, Collin the fourth, was born."

"This is awful!" Katie cried. "How can I go back knowing that Collin has less than a year to live? Maybe I can warn him. Maybe —"

"No, don't. You can't. I mean. . .you shouldn't."

"Who says I shouldn't? I'm going to warn him. *And Toby.* I'll make Toby promise to keep Collin off the moors. Or better yet, stop them both from going to the castle at all."

"Katie." Toby took both her wrists in his hands.

She tugged back.

He held fast. "These people — these other boys, Collin and Tobias — have been dead a very long time. You can change little things in the past, but not big ones. And I thought you told me you wanted to save Beatrix Twyford? What's it say about Lady Beatrix in the family book?"

"I forgot to look."

Katie ran her index finger down the page. "There's only one entry. Nothing about Jack the Ripper or how she died. Just the date. November ninth, in the year eighteen eighty-eight."

"Which is odd," Toby said. He cupped his large hand over hers and ran it down the page as if guiding a computer mouse. "Each of these other entries list the person's place of interment and cause of death: apoplexy, scarlet fever, brain fever, consumption, old age, infected wisdom teeth. Not much advanced medicine in those days. This entry here says the fifth Duke of Twyford died a lingering death from gout in 1842 at the advanced age of fifty. Didn't know you could die of gout. But I do know that fifty was considered ancient."

"That would be the Duke's father or grandfather." Katie's mind flashed on an image of the guv'nor, with his large domed head, watery blue eyes, and multiple chins. The poor man would lose Beatrix and Collin all within a year. It would probably kill him. He wouldn't need gout to do that for him. He'd die of sorrow.

"So what does this other Toby look like? Not as handsome as me, eh?"

Katie blinked at him. "Toby looks like you. . .or, rather, you look like your ancestor," she said, and quickly changed the subject, not wanting to think about how handsome they both were. "Why does Collin have to die so young? It's not fair. It's bad enough Beatrix gets slaughtered. . .but Collin, so shortly after?"

"At least the Duke gets an heir. Collin Twyford the fourth. And obviously Toby has kids, too, cuz I'm here." Toby grinned.

Katie *definitely* didn't want to think about the other Toby having a girlfriend or a wife. . .and children. She stared down at the page once again. *But the Duke will have an heir.* Collin had a son before he died. She read the dates and chuckled. "What a goose."

"Who?"

"Collin. He married Prudence after he got her pregnant. The baby was born just weeks before Collin's accident. At least that's something. He got to see his son before —" But Katie couldn't say it. *Why, oh why, does everyone in my family die violent deaths?* Katie took a deep breath. *That's not true,* she told herself. In her own family her parents were the only ones to have had an accident, as far as Katie knew. But Collin and Beatrix felt like her family. She fisted away a tear and thumped the leather-bound Bible shut. *I have to get back to the nineteenth century!* "Maybe. . .just maybe I can change history. Save Beatrix *and* Collin!"

"Don't count on it. The most you *might* be able to do is discover the identity of Jack the Ripper, which is pretty cool. But don't count on —"

Katie wasn't listening. She sped out of the library and veered down the hall to the kitchen. She needed to call Courtney. Just to hear her voice. Katie's own cell phone, nestled in her backpack, rarely got reception at her grandmother's house. The stone walls were too thick.

Hurrying into the kitchen, Katie snapped up the land-line phone on the butcher-block counter next to the microwave, hit the speed-dial button for her sister's number, and waited impatiently until Courtney's voice message pounded in her ear: *"Yo! Dudes and dudettes! Leave a message at the beep and I'll get back to you as soon as I am able. . ."* this last was sung to the tune of a Beatles song.

"Hey, Court! It's me," Katie all but shouted into the phone. "I just wanted to say. . .um. . .I miss you. Call me. *Please, Courtney.* It's important. I'm heading back to Madame Tussauds. I'll be on my cell phone for the next half hour. *Call me! Call me! Call me!*"

Katie dropped the receiver into its cradle, and the *thunking* sound of plastic hitting plastic reverberated through the kitchen. A sound not heard where she was headed.

Chapter Twenty-two

Secrets to Tell, tolls the Tyburn Vestry Bell

An hour later Katie was standing in the rain-soaked churchyard of St. Swithin's, a swirl of mist rising up from the ground as she splayed her fingers against the surface of the London Stone and took deep, shuddering breaths until the vertigo sensation of tumbling through time and space started to wear off, and she could just make out Collin in the distance, jabbing his umbrella at a moss-covered headstone.

She closed her eyes. Right before hurling through time, in the 21st century, Katie had raced into the Jack the Ripper exhibit to memorize the names of his victims, the dates and places in London where they were murdered, all in the year 1888.

1. **August 31, Mary Ann Nichols, Buck's Row**
2. **September 10, Dark Annie, Hanbury St.**
3. **September 30, Molly Potter, Berner St.**
4. **September 30, Catherine Eddowes, Mitre Square**

5. **October 3, Elizabeth Stride, All Hallows Field by Traitors' Gate**

6. **November 9, Mary Jane Kelly, Wareham Rd.**

7. **December 1, Dora Fowler, Birdcage Alley, near Clavell St.**

8. **December 7, Lady Beatrix Twyford, Miller's Court, Dorset St.**

Next to her, Toby was bending low, whispering into her ear. His presence, looming over her (so soon after being with the other Toby), was unnerving. Almost menacing. Katie pulled her shawl tightly around her shoulders. The high lace collar of her dress was soaked with perspiration or mist. Katie couldn't be sure which.

"Let's have it, lass," Toby demanded in a mocking tone. His coat, thin and black and several sizes too big, hung on him like a loose cape. "If you are truly clairvoyant, as you insist that you are, surely it ought to be an easy thing to tell me what is written on the parchment, sewn into the guv'nor's stuffed vulture?"

Toby inwardly smiled, then outwardly grimaced. He knew, as surely as he knew his own name, that Katie could not comply. How could she? There wasn't a person alive who knew the pet name he had called his sister. His baby sister who died of an infected rat bite. Toby shuddered just thinking about little Emma. The gangrene that had set in. Her contorted, bloated body. Three years old. He had called her Tuppence. Her tiny face always so trusting, so adoring. Even up to the last minute of her life, when the fever had taken hold and the puncture wound on her arm had swelled to the size and color of a red beet, bursting its skin, Emma had blinked up at him with wild, yet trusting grey eyes.

Toby was breathing hard now. He tried to slow his breathing, but a chill, having nothing to do with the mist-soaked air, prickled down his spine. His secret was safe, surely? Katie would not, *could not*, know about Emma. He had never shared his inconsolable grief with anyone. So sure was he that Katie was a charlatan that he had recklessly written down the name of endearment he had used for Emma. *Tuppence.*

After penning her special name, along with a cryptic missive, Toby had sewn the rolled-up parchment inside the Duke's stuffed vulture and, after replacing the bird on the fireplace mantel, had locked the study door behind him. Then he escorted Katie to the London Stone at her request. At no time could Katie have sneaked back into the Duke's study, even if she'd had a mind to. Toby had given her no opportunity. He had stayed by her side from the moment he had locked the Duke's door. "I'm sticking to you like plaster-paste," he had informed her. And he had done precisely that.

Aside from a bit of weirdness for a split second when Katie had poked her finger at the London Stone — and the light surrounding her splintered, momentarily blinding him — the girl never left his field of vision. He had watched her as closely as the Duke's vulture must have watched its prey before it had been stuffed and mounted and showcased.

A little smile twitched at the corner of Toby's lips now as he studied Katie standing in a puddle of mud. In a matter of moments he would be free and clear of the silly chit. He would deliver her to Major Brown's doorstep and be done with her. He had upheld his end of the bargain. Good riddance. She meant nothing more to him than a stray, bedraggled, soaking wet kitten — which is precisely what she looked like right now.

Katie glanced sideways at Toby. He was gnashing his teeth. She wanted to laugh. Not because he was glaring at her, but because to the best of her knowledge she had never used the word "gnash" before. But that was exactly what Toby was doing. His face was grim, and he was staring at her with an angry sort of intentness. Glowering at her. *And* gnashing his teeth. The sound like stone against stone, achingly audible.

I should put him out of his misery and just tell him what he wrote. But will that cause him more misery?

"You're going to hate me," Katie said with conviction. She wasn't sure why, but she knew it as surely as she could feel the grey blanket of mist rise up like gas from the wet ground. *Toby's going to be very, very angry.*

"*Phhfft*," Toby shot back contemptuously. "Do you put such a high value on your ability to make a bloke dance to your tune? You have no more power to make me hate or *love* you than you have of throwing a thunderbolt at Mt. Vesuvius."

A long peal of thunder exploded in the sky.

Katie jumped.

Toby clamped a protective arm around her shoulders just as a gust of chilly air whirled in at them, and a moment later the skies opened to a roar of driving rain.

"*Tuppence!*" Katie shouted above the din of sluicing rain. "Your sister's name was Tuppence," she shouted, feeling the thrum of raindrops, slashing down hard. "Or she had a pet named Tuppence. A dog or a cat maybe. And it died. Because of you." But this last was drowned out by another clap of thunder.

Katie blinked at Toby's ashen face. He looked, for a split second, as if she had driven a thunderbolt into his heart.

In the distance came the thud of heavy church doors closing shut against the rain, followed by the clang of church bells. Had Katie been truly psychic, the sound of driving rain, the booming bells, the banging of heavy doors...and the far-off crash of thunder might have alerted her to the dangers that lay ahead. The foreboding in the air was as thick and ominous as a shroud.

But Katie could think of nothing and no one except Toby, and the expression of pain burning deep in his eyes.

Chapter Twenty-three

Let Us Now Go
say the Bells of Le Bow

TWO DAYS LATER it was sunny and bright with no hint of rain in the air.

"Tell me *again* why I'm in this *stupid* disguise," Katie fumed as the horse-drawn carriage carrying her, Toby, and Collin pulled away from the mews behind Twyford Manor.

The date was September 2, 1888. It was Saturday morning and the three teenagers were on their way to Whitechapel to attend the murder inquest of Mary Ann Nichols, which made Katie happy. But the disguise — the boys had made her dress as an old woman — made her miserable. Stickpins jabbed into her head, holding the black widow's bonnet in place, and the corded ribbon under her chin was tied so tightly, she felt as if she were being strangled. A wiry veil dangled down from the bonnet's brim, covering her face like a beekeeper's helmet.

Sitting in the forward-facing seat of the carriage, Katie angrily punched at the enormous patchwork skirt that billowed like a giant mushroom over mounds of itchy wool underskirts. She tugged at the frumpy jacket which was bursting at the seams across her shoulder blades where Toby had wedged a throw pillow to give the appearance of a hump.

And the odor! The mushroomy stench of moth-eaten wool was so pungent it made her gag, as if whole colonies of dead insects had been decaying in the scratchy fabric.

To make matters worse, Toby and Collin had the audacity to look pleased.

"God's whiskers, Katherine!" Collin's red eyebrows shot up. "We couldn't allow you to go as yourself, now could we? Respectable young ladies do not attend murder inquests! The Duke would have our heads on a silver platter if he discovered we escorted you to an inquest in the East End. Bad enough in the West End, but in *Whitechapel?* He'll boil us in oil if he finds out."

"This has nothing to do with the Duke, and you know it," Katie harrumphed, plucking at the layers of moth-eaten clothing. "You two idiots made me wear these stupid clothes on purpose!"

"Now why would we do that?" Collin wrinkled his brow.

"To torture me!"

"This is the thanks we get then, is it, lass?" Toby clenched every muscle in his face not to burst out laughing. Katie looked a fright. They'd been successful in disguising her as an ugly, old crone. And a hunchback one at that. But if he showed any sign of amusement at her bedraggled, old lady appearance, there'd be no end to her railing and fuming. Yet the effort to keep an impassive face cost Toby a painful side stitch. He *had* made her wear raggedy, uncomfortable clothing deliberately. And rightly so. She had tricked him into giving his word not to tell Major Brown what she knew about the murdered girl. And worse, into promising to help her investigate a phantom killer named Jack. How Katie had pulled it off, he still didn't know. But he would get to the bottom of it. Katie was no more clairvoyant than a spoke in the wheel of this carriage. And yet . . .

"Why couldn't I go dressed as a boy?" Katie demanded. "Why an old woman? This isn't fair! A grizzly bear costume would be more comfortable than this ridiculous outfit!"

"Wouldn't complain were I you, Mistress Kate," Toby countered. "It was *you* who made the jellied eel to keep Major Brown in the dark. 'Tis folly for a lass to attend a murder inquest. T'aint ladylike, my poppet." Toby put a heavy emphasis on the last two words. He would honor his end of the bargain, but he didn't have to make it easy for her. Making her miserable took some of the sting out of being duped. When she had told him what he had written on the parchment hidden in the Duke's stuffed vulture, it was as if a poisonous serpent had reared up and dug its fangs into his soul.

"I'm not your poppet. Whatever that is," Katie fumed as the carriage bounced and shimmied over uneven cobblestones. Ever since she told him what was written on the message inside the Duke's stuffed bird, Toby had been treating her in a haughty, condescending manner. It was driving her crazy. She glanced down at her moth-eaten skirt, mended in patches. Toby had insisted she wear extra woolen petticoats beneath the already oversized skirt, which, combined with the Hunchback of Notre Dame jacket, made her feel like a trussed-up sausage ready to burst. She was hot and itchy, and droplets of sweat were beading across her nose; the wiry veil hanging down, prickly as thorns, was secured so tightly round her throat, she couldn't scratch her face without gouging her skin.

"You look like a mongrel pup with that hang-dog boat race of yours," Toby said, chuckling despite himself. "A caged mongrel pup beneath that fishnet veil." But his voice was gentle when he said, "Look here, Miss Katherine. Collin is right. We couldn't let you go as yourself, now could we? Half o' bloomin' London will be there, and I'll not have 'em gawking at"—he was about to say *your impossibly pretty face*— "the Duke's goddaughter. As if you were first prize at a ring toss. Come now, lass. My old granny's bag of fruit looks right lovely on you."

"Bag of —"

"Suit. And those church pews are comfy, I'd wager?" He pointed at Katie's shoes.

Katie glanced down at the soft leather shoes and conceded the point. "They are definitely more comfortable than anything else I've worn in this—" she was about to say century, but quickly amended it to "country."

Toby shook his head. "You ham shanks are an odd lot."

"We *Yanks* aren't half as odd as you...you...what rhymes with Brits? Nit-wits? No one here knows anything about comfy shoes." Her favorite red high-top sneakers were waiting for her a century or so into the future.

"Katherine!" Collin looked aghast. "Proper young ladies do not go around berating their host countries. I do not know what they teach you in the United States of America, but here in England young ladies are taught proper manners. There's a reason the sun never sets on the British Empire. A very good reason. We are a nation of advanced intellect and superior contrivances, such as shoes! I'll have you know our cobblers are the finest in the world."

"Without a Brussels sprout." Toby shot Katie a mocking smile. "Without a *doubt*, my poppet." He winked at her and felt a spark of perverse satisfaction when she let out a howling curse.

"Most unladylike," Toby tsked, feigning disapproval. But in truth, it was one of the things he fancied about Katie. She could swear like soup and gravy without even blushing, and her brazen way of looking him in the eye with both a challenge and a hint of vulnerability just about did him in.

Toby tore his eyes from Katie's veiled ones. It unnerved him, this attraction he felt for her. It was dangerous. *She* was dangerous. And not because she claimed to have the power to foresee the future. There wasn't a Cockney alive that did not believe in soothsaying. It wasn't Katie's self-proclaimed ability to see the future that disturbed him, but her power to read his own secrets that unnerved him. And the feeling that he was being pulled toward her . . . as if she were reeling him in. A hapless fish on a taut line.

Watching now as Katie fussed and plucked at her frumpy clothing, sitting in the carriage seat across from him, Toby told himself that he'd been right to disguise her as a hobbled old crone. She could no more go to a murder inquest looking like the Queen of the May than he could go dressed as the Prince of Wales. And since he couldn't very well make her invisible, the old funeral dress, the veiled hat, and the hump sprouting from her shoulders were just the thing. *It's for her own good*, Toby assured himself.

But the truth of the matter went deeper. The protectiveness he felt toward her was out of all proportion to his designated role as general dogsbody to the Twyfords. True, he couldn't stand the thought of others gawking at her beautiful face as they had at the Lyceum Theatre, but this was deeper than mere jealousy or attraction. There was something powerful drawing him to her. Something otherworldly. He knew he had to protect her but didn't know why. And he knew just as surely that whatever attraction he felt for her, whatever bound them, was a gossamer thread that would need to be severed. His feelings for her could not be acted upon. *And not because she's the goddaughter of a Duke, and I'm the illegitimate son of a Cockney lacemaker.* There was something more, something almost preternatural being played out here. *But what? And for what purpose?*

Staring at her, Toby was not aware that he was scowling when he said to Collin, "Oughtn't to have let her talk us into this, Collin. It's a sad business when you and I allow ourselves to be bullied by a mere chit of a ham shank barely out of the schoolroom."

"Bullied?" Katie clamped angry eyes on him. "We had a deal, remember? A jellied eel."

"Toby's right, Katherine!" Collin nodded vigorously, his Adam's apple shooting up and down his freckled neck like a pinball. "You are barely out of the nursery. You haven't even had a season, nor been presented at court! You have *no* business attending a murder inquest."

"A mere babe in the woods," Toby taunted, pleased when Katie pulled a face at him behind her wiry veil.

"A babe in the woods who is going to catch the most notorious murderer in the annals of British history!" cried Katie indignantly. But by the dark look Toby shot her, she knew she'd said too much. "Er...I mean...I had another...a...er...premonition."

Katie took a deep breath. She needed to be on her guard. She couldn't let their condescending attitudes get under her skin, prickling her like the yards of itchy wool she was swaddled in. It wasn't their fault they were born into a century where girls were considered inferior. But even so, their chauvinist attitudes — *especially Toby's* — would try the patience of a saint. And Katie was no saint.

Wanting to think about anything other than her itchy, smelly, lumpy clothes and the two infuriating boys sitting across from her, Katie threw open the carriage window. She hooked her elbow over the edge and stuck her veiled head out. The morning breeze felt blissfully cool as it raked through the fishnet veil against her hot cheeks. And even though these frumpy clothes Toby had made her wear were as prickly as hedge thorns, she had to admit it was a fairly good — if pug-ugly — disguise. But next time, Katie vowed, she'd go dressed as a boy.

Up and down the street, pushcart vendors shouted their wares. *"Knives! Get yer knives sharpened here!"* And *"Strawberries! Fresh, ripe strawberries!"*

There, on the corner, was a costermonger pulling a wheelbarrow filled with turnips. And up ahead, an omnibus clattered to a stop at the curb to pick up passengers. In no time at all, Katie forgot her irritation and smiled at the nineteenth-century scenes that were unfolding before her eyes.

Chapter Twenty-four

The Death Inquest

The Coroner's Court for the death inquest of Mary Ann Nichols was being held at the Working Lads Institute in Whitechapel Road. Outside the brick building an excited crowd had gathered. It was Saturday morning, September 2. A cool breeze ruffled the black garments of the people standing in line waiting to be admitted.

A block away, the Duke's carriage disgorged the three teenagers, who hastened past a row of hansom cabs lining the curb. The horses chomped feed from nosebags tied around their necks.

"What's that?" Katie asked, jerking to a halt as a giant bicycle came barreling down the street toward them. Powered by a man pedaling furiously, the odd vehicle had a single front wheel and two enormous rear wheels. A yellow-striped awning with fringe shaded the driver's face from the sun. Katie laughed. The contraption reminded her of the paddle boats shaped like swans in the Boston Public Garden's lagoon.

Collin frowned at her. "It's a velocipede, of course."

Toby, too, shot her a curious look, so Katie hastened to add, "We don't have centipedes...er...velocipedes...back home."

"Odd," Toby said, his voice low. "They were invented in the United States. Your President Cleveland rides one. Not a week goes by when a photograph of him pedaling a velocipede doesn't make front-page news."

Kate shrugged and charged forward. *So Grover Cleveland is president of the United States right now*, she thought. But for the life of her, Katie couldn't remember anything about President Cleveland except that he summered on Cape Cod.

Drawing closer to the front entrance of the Working Lads Institute, Katie noted that there were two separate lines of people queuing up outside the front doors.

"Looks to be a lot of ticketed folk waiting to be accommodated, to say nothing of the public," Toby motioned to the two lines. "Far more than would regularly show up at an inquest. But the victim's death was unusual, and the victim was female. Let's hope Major Brown is as good as his word. We're to find the constable on duty and give him our names. Wait here." Toby exchanged glances with Collin and lowered his voice, "Don't let our twist 'n' swirl out of your sight."

Before disappearing into the crowd, Toby turned to Katie. "Remember, luv. You're supposed to be a feeble old woman, so squiggle your eyes and don't forget to limp. I brought along this curried egg so you'd smell like an old person." He slipped something into Katie's pocket, winked at her, and scooted away through the crowd.

Katie reached into her pocket. If it was a curried egg, she was going to smush it in Toby's face when he returned. But when she tugged it out, it was nothing more than a small, round sachet tied on top with string. "What is this?" She wrinkled her nose at the rotten egg smell and held it out for Collin's inspection.

"A camphor baglet. Don't you have those in America? They're used in wardrobes to kill moth larvae. It's what old clothes always smell like." Collin, too, wrinkled his nose at the pungent camphor odor.

Just then, Toby darted back through the crowd, followed by a blue uniformed police officer with a droopy moustache.

"Ma'am," the officer nodded politely to Katie, believing her to be an elderly matron. "Name's Grub, ma'am. Officer Grub. I'll be taking you in along wi' me, orders o' Major Brown. Better take my arm," he suggested. "It's a densely packed crowd today."

Katie clutched Officer Grub's proffered elbow and, remembering to hobble, followed his lead through the throng of people waiting in line, all of them staring expectantly at the entrance door.

"Make way! Make way!" Officer Grub shouted, waving his wooden truncheon. Katie thought of the children's picture book *Make Way for Ducklings* and chuckled. Remembering that a murder inquest was no laughing matter, Katie pursed her lips primly.

And yet, Katie thought, glancing over her shoulder at the people queuing up all the way around the block. All these people were technically dead...*or will be by the time I return.* Long dead. So whether she laughed or not, it really didn't matter. Nothing matters here because it's already happened! Expressions like "make way" and contraptions like velocipedes were distant memories in the twenty-first century. If Katie managed to save Beatrice or any of the other Ripper victims, they would all still be dead for decades when Katie returned home. And Collin? Could she save him, too?

The other Toby, from the twenty-first century, had told her that she could change small things, tweak the past here and there, but she couldn't drastically change the future. And even if she were to change the past, the ultimate outcome of major world events would not change one bit.

But if that's the case, why did I return to this century? Why bother to catch Jack the Ripper at all? And yet she was here. No amount of logic could have dissuaded Katie from returning. She was here for a reason. She felt sure of that. The fissure in the ancient rock that was the London Stone had enabled her to travel back in time. There was a reason the Stone had sent her here. But what reason and why, she wasn't sure.

Katie took a deep breath and told herself she had to stay focused. She scanned the expectant crowd, and realized with a jolt that Officer Grub was speaking to her.

"Beggin' your pardon, ma'am, but it's not a nice crowd, not by any manner of means. Step lively. There's a bit o' mud. There yer go." The front doors parted at the sound of his commanding voice and the sight of his blue uniform. Once through the doors, Officer Grub marched them through a courtyard along a narrow, stone-flagged path, up a set of stairs, and through another set of doors into a raftered room that stood bleached in sunlight. Black-clad men in silk top hats were talking in subdued tones at the back of the room. The hushed but excited atmosphere reminded Katie of the Lyceum Theatre just before the curtain went up.

Officer Grub led them down the center aisle to an empty bench fitted against a whitewashed wall, several rows back from a semi-circular raised platform. Hunkered at angles on this platform stood a trestle table, a wooden podium, and two Windsor-back chairs. As Katie sank down onto the bench facing the podium, Toby and Collin settled beside her, wedging her tightly between themselves like human shields.

Katie squirmed in an effort to negotiate some elbow room between the boys, but gave up and glanced around. The temporary courtroom was a big room with long, arched windows along an upper gallery running halfway around the room, like in a church. Katie half expected to hear an organ ring out, or a choir burst forth in song. Instead, a bell clanged, doors flew open overhead, and a swarm of people rushed forward pushing and shoving.

At the sound of their stampeding feet, Toby, too, glanced up and watched the trample of people elbowing one another for empty seats until the balcony was crammed to capacity. Their faces belonged to every class of people, young, old, rich, poor — and all united, Toby thought with a twinge of irritation, in their bloodlust and morbid curiosity. They were here to take in every last gory detail of a young girl's brutal murder.

Squished in between the two boys, Katie was thinking similar thoughts, only with a different perspective. In her own world, courtroom TV, crime dramas, and CSI shows were primetime hits. Katie had watched endless reruns of the famous Casey Anthony murder trial, so she understood the inquisitive faces peering down from the gallery above. *People are drawn to murder no matter what century they live in,* Katie told herself.

From a distance came the sound of a second wave of pattering feet, followed by a full-blown mad dash as the back doors banged open and a new horde of people stormed into the room, hastily snatching up every available seat.

Katie craned her neck around. Was that Reverend Pinker plunking himself down on a seat in the back row?

Collin nudged Katie to get her attention. "Here comes the jury."

Katie swiveled back around, facing forward. With the courtroom crammed to overflowing, the smell of sweat wafting through the air was so pungent Katie had to remind herself that deodorant hadn't been invented yet. Most people bathed only once a week.

"And over there, next to the coroner's platform," Toby said, pointing to a roped-off area, "are the witnesses."

Katie looked across the room to where Toby was pointing. Huddled together behind a rope partition stood several people peering around nervously and shuffling from foot to foot. Katie's gaze was drawn to a girl of about nineteen, who stood in the front and looked very self-satisfied. Of all the witnesses she alone appeared to be relishing the excitement. And she had obviously taken great care with her appearance. Her shiny auburn hair was done up on the crown of her head in a dramatic mound of curls braided with paper flowers and butterflies. There was something familiar about her. . . .

Katie tugged at Toby's sleeve to ask why the witnesses hadn't been given chairs. Standing tethered behind the rope partition they looked more like convicts about to be herded off to the docks.

Toby, having anticipated her question (though wrongly) answered, "Yes, pet. That auburn-haired girl is well pleased with herself, happy to be the center of attention. What the witnesses say here today, what they look like, what they wear, will be chronicled in newspapers all across London. See that table . . ." — He pointed to where several men sat perched on stools, busily sketching. — "Those are pen and ink artists. And that lot over there are journalists."

Oscar Wilde sat in the midst of the journalists, pencil and notebook at the ready, a floppy scarlet neckerchief billowing at his throat. Katie put her gloved hand up to wave, but Toby crunched her fingers between his own and placed her hand back on her lap. She was supposed to be incognito.

"And that's the witness stand, I'd wager," Collin said, motioning to what looked like a prisoner's box.

Next to the witness stand police officers wearing bowler hats instead of helmets stood at attention. Messenger boys in knee breeches and tweed caps stood poised by the side doors ready to rush the news copy to Fleet Street.

"Over there are the constables of H-Division, Whitechapel," Toby announced proudly. "And here comes Major Brown."

Major Gideon Brown strode toward the coroner's platform and stood facing the crowd, tall, erect, and looking very polished in his dress uniform. He glanced neither to the right nor left but straight ahead at full attention.

"Why are they having a trial when there's no defendant?" Katie asked, speaking loudly to be heard over the din. The decibel level in the room was deafening. "Or do they have a defendant?" she shouted, blinking around, confused. "Who's on trial here, anyway?"

"Are you daft, Katie?" Collin hollered into her left ear, making her yelp in pain and clamp a hand to her ear. "This is an inquest, not a trial."

"Yes," Katie muttered, massaging her still-ringing ear. "But why is there a jury —" She stopped midsentence. For now, she would just have to watch and listen. Both boys were staring at her as if she didn't have all her tea cups in the upstairs cupboard.

A minute later a hush fell over the room.

"*Gentlemen of the jury!*" A clerk strode to the podium and gaveled for order with a large brass mallet. "*The coroner!*"

A tall, lean totem-pole of a man in a pinstripe tailcoat marched to the podium, and the jury of fourteen — all men — stood up, swaying a little, then sat down again. The smell of ink mingled with the acrid odor of perspiration in the air. Sunlight dusted every corner of the room, and the shuffling of papers and nervous clearing of throats could be heard throughout.

"*Oyez!*" The court clerk bellowed to the jury.

Toby leaned over and explained to Katie that "*Oyez*" was the Norman-French summons to order that went back a thousand years.

"*Oyez!*" The clerk repeated. "You good men of the jury have been summoned here this day on the second of September in the year of our lord eighteen hundred and eighty-eight to inquire for our sovereign Lady the Queen of England, when, how, and by what means Mary Ann Nichols came to her untimely death. We hope to obtain such evidence today as will lead to the apprehension of the miscreant responsible." The room was so quiet that a dropped pin could have been heard in the far reaches of the vast room.

A formal roll call and a swearing-in of jurymen came next, then a quick exchange between the coroner and the court officer.

"Everything is in order, Coroner Baxter," the clerk pronounced, his side whiskers bristling like a peahen. "The jury has viewed the mortal remains of Mary Ann Nichols. Therefore, Coroner Baxter, I recommend that we proceed forthwith."

Not the faintest rustle of a skirt, nor flapping of a fan, nor nervous clearing of a throat could be heard as Coroner Baxter stepped forward, and in a no-nonsense voice called the first witness.

Police Constable Neil.

Constable Neil, the first police officer to arrive at the murder scene, lumbered up to the stand, helmet in hand, his face sorrowful and jowly like a bulldog's. After taking his oath to queen and country, he told the coroner that the body of Mary Ann Nichols was discovered in Buck's Row, Whitechapel. He indicated the location by tapping his large forefinger on a fold-out street map.

"And this is the precise location, Police Constable Neil, where the body of Mary Ann Nichols was discovered?" Coroner Baxter asked in a deceptively mild tone.

"Tha's right, sir. The body was lyin' in the gutter —"

"In the gutter, Constable Neil?" The coroner asked, looking down at the notes on his desk. "Let me see. Here it is. I think I understood that the body was found face up near the curb on the sidewalk. *Not in the gutter.*"

"It be the gutter, sir. Sure enough. Not more'n fifty feet from Spits Alley, right in front of Mrs. Green's lodging house."

There arose a quick discussion as to the exact location, and whether or not the body of Mary Ann Nichols lay in the gutter or on the walkway next to the curb. "A distinction of some importance to be sure, wouldn't you agree, Constable Neil?" demanded Coroner Baxter.

"A distinction without much difference," Collin whispered testily. "At this rate we'll be here all day." Collin rolled his eyes and sighed.

"Baxter's just giving the people a show for their money," Toby whispered back. "He courts the limelight more than most, but he's a shrewd coroner, make no mistake."

"Now tell us as precisely as you can, Constable Neil, what happened *after* you arrived at Buck's Row and found the body of Mary Ann Nichols."

"Well, sir. I didn't find the body on me own. I was led to the spot by Georgie Cross, the market porter boy. It was him what directed me to the dead girl. Georgie thought the girl done fainted. But after I inspected her and saw that 'er throat was cut, I knew she be dead. I thought she committed suicide."

"I take it, then, this is the reason you did *not* investigate the surrounding area or perimeter near the gutter?"

"Not at first, sir, no. Like I said —"

"*Constable Neil!*" The coroner boomed so loudly the rafters seemed to shake. "Had you directed your attention to the surrounding area, mighn't the consequence have been the apprehension of the dead girl's assailant? By not investigating the periphery you gave this man — *who may have been lurking in the shadows* — ample time to slip away undetected, did you not?"

"Could 'ave slipped away undetected long afore I arrived. Like I said in my official report, I did not know she was murdered until the police surgeon arrived, but I did my duty by clearing the area." Constable Neil went on to explain that after he determined that the girl was dead, two night watchmen at the slaughterhouse in Buck's Row stood with him watching over the body as did a crowd of butcher lads from The Cut until the surgeon arrived.

"So you spoke to no one? Interviewed no one except two night watchmen and several butcher boys?" the coroner asked, his voice oozing contempt.

Constable Neil swallowed hard. "No, sir. I mean, yes, sir."

"What is it, man? Yes or no? Speak up!"

"I done knocked on the door of the boarding house cross the street from the gutter where the body was lying and spoke to Mrs. Emma Green who said she did not hear anyone cry out, or sounds of a scuffle, which again made me think the girl done herself in."

Scowling over silver-rimmed eyeglasses that sat low on his long, crooked nose, Coroner Baxter stared first at Constable Neil, then down at his leather ledger. "And you took this scanty information to indicate that the girl had taken her own life? 'Tis a pity and a folly you did not search the area, Constable."

Police Constable Neil was sweating. He took out a large handkerchief and mopped his bulldog brow.

"Describe for us, Constable Neil, the condition of the body and the approximate time whence you came upon it."

Constable Neil did so and then grumbled about it being hard to see the dead girl as there were no street lamps in the vicinity, nor stars out, nor moonlight.

"We understand it was a dark and foggy night, Constable Neil. But it would please this court to understand more thoroughly why you came to the conclusion of suicide when clearly—"

"Well, sir," Neil interrupted. "'Tis a hard lot these girls 'ave, right enough. And I 'aven't never in all my years of being a police bobby — *and a right good 'un at that*—come across a girl wiff 'er throat cut afore. So I says to myself, Albert. The poor girl's done chived 'erself!"

A titter of laughter went through the packed room. Even several members of the jury smiled.

The coroner gave Constable Neil a sharp look from over his silver spectacles. After a mild rumbling as if to clear his throat and a bout of coughing into his fist, Constable Neil continued, only less dramatically this time, as he chronicled what steps he had taken when he came upon the dead girl.

"Tell me, Constable Neil. Was there any blood on Georgie Cross's clothing?"

"No, sir."

"Did you search his pockets for a knife or sharp instrument?"

"No, sir."

"Why is that, Constable Neil?"

"Why is what, sir?"

"Why on earth, man, didn't you ascertain whether or not the person who *claimed* to have stumbled upon the girl was, in fact, her killer? Surely you've gleaned some measure of deductive intuition in your *many* years of being a police constable?"

"But Georgie Cross didn'a kill 'er! He found 'er! He came running to get me! Why would he do that if he done killed her? Not likely, sir. And Georgie Cross is not one to chive a girl, not him. I knows Georgie since he was a wee nipper. Be madness to fink it be Georgie."

"Yes, yes, Constable. Everyone in the East End of London, to be sure, is related to someone else's Great Aunt Fanny, twice removed. But that does *not*, by any stretch of the imagination, presuppose that Georgie Cross, or anyone else of your acquaintance, is *not* a cold, hard-hearted, vicious criminal."

When Constable Neil, his face pasty grey, his beefy hands shaking as if with violent tremors, finally stepped down from the witness box, a stirring of excitement ran through the room as the next witness was called to the stand.

Georgie Cross.

But Georgie didn't come forward. He wasn't among the witnesses standing ill at ease behind the roped-off area on the other side of the coroner's platform.

Coroner Baxter raised grey caterpillar eyebrows above his silver spectacles and bellowed at his clerk demanding to know what had become of the crown's most important witness. "*Find him!*" Baxter shouted. "Find him at once. I don't care if he's attending his own mother's funeral, bring him here this instant!" Several officers scurried from the room.

Minutes later, a butcher boy by the name of Tommy Bunting stumbled forward looking unnerved and miserable. He was wearing the rough-cut sackcloth and apron of his trade, and when he answered the coroner's questions, his knuckles showed white as they gripped the railing in front of him.

"If you please, Thomas Bunting, would you tell the jury how you came to discover the body of Mary Ann Nichols in Buck's Row?"

Not much older than sixteen, the boy explained that it was Georgie Cross, not he, Tommy Bunting, who discovered the body. "I comes runnin' to the spot where the dead girl lays after I hears Georgie hollering fer help. I dinna ken she be dead, leastways not right away. I thought she might 'ave fainted."

"So, Master Bunting? You did not notice the girl's throat was cut or that she had other injuries?"

"No, sir."

"Was there no one with Georgie Cross when he first came upon the girl lying in the gutter? No butcher boys perchance?"

"No, sir. None of us lads were wiff Georgie. We come a' running to see what the commotion was after Georgie started shouting for help."

"If no one saw Georgie Cross stumble upon the dead girl, isn't it possible that Georgie Cross might have been the perpetrator?"

"The what, sir?"

"The person responsible for killing Mary Ann Nichols."

"The one 'oo chived her? Not Georgie, sir! Not 'im. He couldn' squash a spider, not Georgie. Don't got it in him. Can't stomach the sight of blood."

"And how do you know this?"

"Cuz he holds 'is breath when 'e comes round to the slaughter-house. Most folks can't stomach butcher blood, the smell of it, the squealing noise them animals make when we slaughts 'em. But Georgie can't abide it a'tall. Goes green 'round the gills, does Georgie. T'aint likely you can chiv a girl when you can't stomach blood, now can you?"

"Can't you?"

"Don't reckon so, no, sir."

"But a butcher lad would have no compunction, is that what you're saying?"

"'Ave no what, sir?"

"By your own admission, a butcher lad would have no difficulty slitting the throat of girl as easily as . . . a calf, or a sheep, or a pig."

"Didn't say that, sir. What I said was —"

"Answer my question, Master Bunting. In terms of sheer strength, technical know-how, and the ability to 'stomach' the sight of blood, a butcher lad, or anyone else associated with the slaughter-house trade, would not be squeamish about, nor have difficulty, slicing the throat of a young girl."

"Don't reckon no one I know would go around chiving a girl's throat. Not like a dumb animal what's for eating. Not the same, now, is it?"

"Did any of the butcher boys who came running when Georgie Cross *allegedly* stumbled upon the body, have blood on them?"

"Blood, sir?"

"You heard me, Master Bunting."

"Well o' course we did."

"We?"

"We all had our leather aprons on. We're butcher lads, now, ain't we? Butcher lads wear butcher aprons. Aprons 'ave blood sure as the sky is blue. T'wouldn't be no butcher lad wiffout a bloody apron."

Several other butcher boys answered in a similar manner. Then Mrs. Emma Green was called to the stand. Mrs. Green was a woman of sixty-odd with a doughy face, a red-veined nose, and the hint of a dark line above her top lip. She was clutching a tartan shawl round her shoulders and was nervously weaving the fringe between her fingers.

"I was awake at the time," Mrs. Green began, her voice high pitched and anxious. "I couldn't sleep. And like I told the officer gentleman who spoke afore the butcher lads just now," she pointed a tangled-with-fringe finger at Constable Neil, who smiled weakly back at her. "If that poor girl had screamed, I would have heard her. It was a warm night, and my windows were open —"

"But it was dark and foggy, isn't that correct, Mrs. Green?"

"Yes, sir. Dark and foggy, but ever so warm. Warm and misty-like. My bedroom window faces the street. When I can't sleep, I sit by the front window and knit a bit. I was sitting there most of the evening, and I didn't hear nothing."

"And you are quite positive you did not doze off, or leave to brew a cup of tea, perhaps?"

"No, sir. I did not, sir. If that poor girl had cried out for help, I would have heard her."

"Indicating, perhaps, that Mary Ann Nichols knew her assailant and was not in mortal fear at the time of her death. You've been most helpful, Mrs. Green."

An eager stir of excitement whirled around the courtroom as Mrs. Green stepped down from the witness box and the saucy-looking girl with shiny auburn hair was conducted to the stand.

This girl has a keen sense of drama, Katie thought, watching her sashay forward. The previous witnesses had all looked ill at ease, especially Constable Neil, who had left the witness box with the pained look of a hunted animal. But this girl seemed positively cheerful as she stepped jauntily into the witness box, the gleam of anticipation unmistakable in her dark, expressive eyes.

"Dora Fowler," the clerk announced.

Omigod! Katie gasped and involuntarily gripped Toby's knee, then quickly let go. *Dora Fowler was going to be the Ripper's seventh victim!*

Toby shot her a look.

Although Dora couldn't know it, she would soon take center stage in a murder case that would rock the whole of London, and in no time at all, the entire world. Dora, settling herself into the witness box with a great flourish, seemed to sense, with the keen instinct of a terrier sniffing the air, that more blood was in the air. *She just doesn't know it's her own!*

From the witness box, Dora Fowler smiled coquettishly at her captive audience and, after repeating the solemn words of the oath, began her testimony. Gaining confidence as she went along, Dora proceeded to describe, at length and with many gestures, the last time she had seen Mary Ann Nichols alive.

The coroner was very kind and very gentle when questioning Dora, but even so, the people in the packed courtroom seemed to collectively lean forward, anticipating something juicy. They were not to be disappointed.

Several minutes into Dora's recitation — which Katie felt sure was well rehearsed — Dora sputtered, "I think I may have saw him! Him what done it!" she exclaimed breathlessly. "I shall never forget my last conversation wiff my dearest friend in all the world — no, not till my dying day!" Dora glanced around, pleased with the ripple of intense interest running through the room.

"Am I to understand, Miss Fowler, that Mary Ann Nichols was with a man when she had her last conversation with you?" The coroner looked puzzled. "You did not mention this in your statement to the police."

"Well, o' course not. When the officer was askin' me all those questions about poor Mary Ann, wasn't I in a state? I shed so many tears I wasn't thinkin' straight, now, was I? But I tells you. I saw him!" In a dramatic stroke of inspiration, Dora began twisting and untwisting her handkerchief and sniffling loudly until one large tear zigzagged down her plump cheek.

"All right, Miss Fowler. Let us start at the beginning," said the coroner patiently. "Who was this man?"

"Dunno, sir. I just knows what he looked like. Didn' ask his name."

"Are we to understand that you *believe* you saw the individual who may have committed this terrible crime? Can you describe him for us?"

"He was tall, and ever so thin, and looked like a gent. And he was carrying a black bag, like what a doctor lugs about when he trots off to visit sick people."

"A leather satchel?"

"Tha's it!"

"Describe this satchel."

"It were made of pigskin or the like, wiff a brass key lock on the strap, you know the sort, sir. What all them doctors carry, but the handles were ever so worn. I could see finger marks on the handle as if he was gripping it right hard." Dora was on a roll.

"This is all new to us, Miss Fowler," said the coroner patiently. "Let's begin again. This gentleman that you saw with Mary Ann Nichols the night she died, what sort of clothes was he wearing?"

"He was wearing a gentleman's clothing. A black hat on his head. And a heavy black coat, wiff a woolen scarf round his neck. I remembers everythink very particular because I thought it was odd him wearing such a heavy coat and scarf when it was a fair warm day, wiff the sun shining and all. I had a queer feeling that maybe he was a preacher, and the scarf was covering up his collar, or such like —"

"You said it was night time when last you spoke with the deceased. Now you tell us the sun was shining? I must say, Miss Fowler, there are several contradictions in your statement."

"I saw him several times! Once during the day. Once at night afore poor Mary Ann was chived! In and out of the Grey Goose Tavern they was. Seen 'em together several times all day long!"

"Several times?" The coroner sounded dubious. "You are under the Queen's oath, Miss Fowler."

"And don't I knows it!"

Another titter ran around the room.

"And you took this man to be in what trade?"

"A gentleman's trade, to be sure. Tall and mean he was, though. Didn't have the face of a gent, more like the face of a bricklayer, and full of scars it was, too."

"Again, Miss Fowler. I must remind you that you told Constable Neil that the last time you saw Mary Ann Nichols alive was the week prior."

"I never said that!" she cried out passionately. "I said the last time I had a proper sit-down chat wiff me best friend, Mary Ann, was a week afore. But I seen her and talked to her on the day she got chived. I swear to the almighty, or he can strike me down as I sit here. What I fink, sir, is you had better have a talkin' to wiff your officers from Scotland Yard 'oo mixed up my words! That fat one, there" — she pointed across the room to Constable Neil — "talked to me just like the bloke from the *London Star*, 'oo wrote down my words in his paper, sayin' I said things I never said. Said if I gave him a full accounting, he'd pay me right proper. But I'm not one to be making a profit from the death of my poor girl Mary Ann. Not me. I wouldn't take a farthing. Though I did let 'im stand me solid for a warm gin at the public-house, just like I dids with that officer bloke —" Again she pointed to Constable Neil, who flushed bright scarlet.

A peal of raucous laughter rang out, though it was quickly suppressed when Coroner Baxter gaveled for order. "In the future," he said severely, glancing over his glasses around the room, "the good citizens of Whitechapel here today shall refrain from making noise of any kind whilst I address my witness!" He turned back to Dora, his grey fuzzy eyebrows arched in displeasure. "Have you anything further to add, Miss Fowler?"

Dora was losing credibility with the coroner as well as with the good citizens of Whitechapel. As if sensing a shift in tactics was in order, she raised a clenched fist in the air and tilted her chin defiantly. "'Course Mad Willy was lurking in the background. I done seen him skulkin' about in the shadows."

"Mad Willy?"

"Yes, sir! Mad Willy, her man!"

"Er. . .um. . .let me see," the coroner thumbed through his notes. "That would be William Makepeace? Her boyfriend? But you said nothing about William Makepeace being present on the day that Mary Ann died. Mr. Makepeace has an alibi—"

"I said nothink because Mad Willy's a mean 'un, sir. He's the one what fisted her in the mouth. Popped poor Mary Ann a good one when he heard she was steppin' out wiff another man. And didn't Mary Ann herself tell me that her new fancy gent was going to do right by 'er? And now. . ." she clutched her hands theatrically to her heart. "And now. . .poor Mary Ann be brown bread 'n' butter!" She wailed and began sobbing loudly into her balled up handkerchief.

Another stir of excitement went round the room.

"That will be all, Miss Fowler. Seeing as the witness is upset and has apparently begun to contradict herself due to her obvious distress, we shall ask this witness to leave the stand in order that she might collect herself."

Dora rose, faced the jury, and in a small but confident voice declared that Mad Willy "must'a done it!"

The coroner told Dora to step down at once.

Several news runners standing by the exit doors dashed out in order to get Dora's testimony into the papers by the afternoon deadline. It appeared from the look of frustration on Coroner Baxter's face that he was not giving credence to Dora's sworn evidence. The next witness was much more credible.

Katie leaned forward when Jeffrey Nichols, printer's machinist and father of the deceased, took the witness stand. Mr. Nichols was very pale with a full beard and moustache threaded with grey, and he was wearing mourning clothes: a tall silk hat, black frock coat, black tie, and trousers of a dark material. The clothes, Toby told Katie later, must have been hired for the occasion. A printer's machinist couldn't afford expensive mourning attire. East Enders hired suits for weddings and funerals.

"My daughter was given to foolish pride, God forgive her, but she didn't deserve such a fate. Prettiest and kindest of all me nine children, and unlike her mother, my little girl was not going down the path to ruin. Mary Ann's mother was much given to drink afore she run off with that Spitalfields tinker."

In his rambling testimony to his daughter's character, Mr. Nichols took every opportunity to belittle and blame his wife who had abandoned him because she was besotted in equal measure by the gin bottle and the tinker's man. "Had the missus been home tending to her god-given duties, my poor little Mary Ann wouldn't have been given to foolish pride, thinkin' herself above 'er class. Steppin' out with gents on a regular basis. She be full of foolish pride, but there was no harm in her, no harm a'tall."

Jeffrey Nichols began sobbing, and Katie felt sure that his tears, unlike Dora's, were in earnest.

Toby leaned over and whispered, "It's time to leave."

"What? Now? But —" Katie sputtered.

"Yes, right now. Major Brown's been staring at your boat race for a full five minutes. He's on to us, I'll wager. We'd best scapa flow."

"Scapa — ?"

"Go."

Chapter Twenty-five

Oranges and Apples
say the Bells of Whitechapel

OUTSIDE THE WORKING LADS INSTITUTE, Katie scurried behind Toby as they all hurriedly strode toward the carriage stand. It wasn't easy to walk fast with her long, billowing skirt rustling over the multi-tiered underskirts and with the pillow-padded hump on her back. As they swept along, Katie tried hard to remember exactly what she had read on the plaque under the waxwork figure of Dora Fowler at Madame Tussauds. *On December 1, in Birdcage Alley off Hosier Lane, within earshot of two police officers and just half a block from where her fiancé was hurrying to meet her, Dora Fowler would become Jack the Ripper's seventh victim.* Dora Fowler was famed for her talking parrots, which she trained and sold at the bird market on Clavell Street. She would be murdered six days before Lady Beatrix.

"He'll strike close to midnight," Katie said more to herself than to Collin and Toby. "And if we don't stop him" — she glanced up at the two boys, her words muffled behind her thick veil — "Dora Fowler will die in Birdcage Alley off Hosier Lane, where she sells parakeets and parrots, on her way to meet her fiancé. Her wounds will be even more brutal than Mary Ann Nichols's. We've either got to stop him dead in his tracks or warn Dora and keep her away from Birdcage Alley." Katie shuddered just thinking about it. Was it possible to change history? Could Dora actually be saved? Was forewarned, forearmed? Or would another girl have to die in Dora's place? *You can tweak the small things, Katie, but not the big ones.* Toby Becket's words rang in her ears. Words he had spoken to Katie in the twenty-first century.

When they slowed down at the curb, Collin shot Katie an annoyed look and in a mock-Cockney accent chortled: "I'm bleedin' fed up wiff all this talk of Jack the Slasher! You're giving me fair goosepimples." In his own voice, he said, "You can't be serious! Your visions tell you that this bloke will murder again? How is that possible? No one would cut up a girl a second time. Why would they? For what purpose? You heard Dora Fowler. She as good as said that the boy-friend, Mad Willy, did it. Why would he strike again? Surely these prophecies of yours might be wrong? And if you know that Dora Fowler is going to be murdered, you must have an inkling as to who the killer is. These clairvoyant visions of yours seem to be very selective. Mightn't you wake up tonight, snap your fingers, and *thwack!* the slasher's name will come to you?"

"Ripper. His name is. . .or, will be. . .Jack the Ripper. That's what the world. . .er, the newspapers are going to start calling him after he murders his next victim."

"So in your dreams this ne'er-do-well killer has a nickname, but no identity?" Collin persisted. "That seems odd, don't you think? And at the inquest no one referred to anybody named Jack. Are you sure about all this, Katherine? Absolutely sure —"

"Yes! Yes! A gazillion times, yes! I could have psychic visions until doomsday, but I still won't be able to tell you who Jack the Ripper is. That's why you've got to help me. Why we need to do this together."

"Like the three musketeers!" Collin shouted, punching his fist wildly in the air. "One for all, and all for one."

"Gawd help us." Toby rolled his eyes.

"But look here. Are you absolutely sure you can't conjure this bloke up in your mind's eye? Try it again. Go on, squeeze your eyes shut, and give it a whirl."

"Damn it, Collin!" Katie exploded. "How many times must I tell you? I don't know who the Ripper is. No one will ever know unless we expose him . . . or her."

Collin looked dejected and a little apprehensive. "You mustn't swear, Katie. How many times must I tell you that? It's simply not done. Not acceptable in polite society. Not whilst you're a guest in the Twyford household." Collin jabbed his umbrella at a crack in the walkway and sighed heavily. "Maybe you could conduct a séance tonight. Or try now. Close your eyes and concentrate. Who knows . . .?" he muttered, shrugging his shoulders heavily.

"Grrrrr." Kate made a noise deep in her throat, then unhooked her heavy veil and swept it backward over the crown of her black bonnet. She scrunched up her face and closed her eyes as if in deep concentration. She counted slowly. *One-Mississippi, two-Mississippi, three-Mississippi.* When she reached ten-Mississippi, she kept her eyes tightly shut, but said in a cackling, other-worldly voice: "The . . . only . . . vision . . . I see . . . before me" — her eyes flew open — "is *you!*"

Collin stepped back, startled.

"*Boo!*" she shouted.

Collin turned white.

Katie laughed. "The only faces I saw when I closed my eyes were yours and Toby's. Unless you two are in cahoots as cold-blooded murderers, you'll have to take my word for it that I haven't got a clue who the real killer is."

A flush of crimson spread across Collin's cheekbones and long, freckled nose.

"*That's not bleedin' funny!*" Collin bellowed.

Toby stepped between the two and glared at Katie. "If *indeed* you possess the gift of inner sight," he said through clenched teeth, "you'll be struck down cold if you abuse it, or use it to frighten others.

That's what Cockneys believe. Making fun of others using clairvoyance is like dangling a dead fish in a bloke's face — do it once too often and you'll end up tugging fish scales out of that thick skull of yours."

Toby strode off down the street. Katie realized, as she watched the color flood back into Collin's face, that being thought of as clairvoyant in an age where superstitions ran rampant, provoked a nerve-racking fear in Collin, and maybe Toby, too. People were still jailed here for practicing witchcraft. Katie would have to tread more carefully. Her sense of humor was definitely not appreciated.

As Collin was still looking queasy, Katie gently touched his arm, but when she did so, he visibly flinched. She immediately told him she was sorry. "I was only kidding around, Collin. Of course, I didn't see your face or Toby's. And I promise you, I can't now, nor will I ever be able to conjure up the identity of the killer. Once I have a vision about something, I can't have another," she assured him, making it all up.

Collin grunted. "Is that like once you've had typhoid fever, you can never get it again?" he asked, furling and unfurling his umbrella and moving slowly down the brick lane.

"I don't know anything about typhoid." The only thing Katie could remember about the disease was something about a woman named Typhoid Mary who infected dozens of people in New York City.

"But I do know this," Katie continued, taking his elbow and scurrying alongside him, trying to match him stride for stride and failing miserably in her cumbersome skirt. "Jack the Ripper will strike again unless we stop him. And if we don't find out who he is, no one else on the planet will ever discover his real identity. He'll go down in history as the most notorious, unidentified killer in British history."

"Are you telling me that this mystery man can continue to slit throats all over London and the police will never catch him?"

Katie nodded and apologized again for having spooked him.

"You didn't frighten me, Katie, *you startled the living daylights out of me!*" Collin was laughing. "Whatever possessed you?"

"Gallows humor, I guess. But honestly, Collin, why in the world would you think I thought you were the killer?" Katie inclined her head, then it was her turn to be startled.

"Not me," Collin whispered. "I know *I'm* not this Ripper bloke." He lowered his voice even more, "I thought you meant . . . Toby."

"What?" Katie gasped. She raised her eyes and stared at Toby's retreating back as he stepped off the curb and strode across the cobbled street.

"Toby has a way with the girls. Especially East End girls. Of *course*, I know Toby didn't do it. But when you pointed your finger at me . . . for half an instant I thought . . ." his voice drifted away. "You are haunting my thoughts with all your mumbo-jumbo supernatural visions. What if you're right? What if these other girls are murdered by the same person? I tell you, Katie, it half scares me to death. I couldn't sleep last night. I woke up in a fair sweat. I wish it was me. I wish I *was* the killer so I could tell you no other girls will die. But that's not going to happen, is it? These other girls you mentioned, and Dora Fowler, are going to die, aren't they?"

"Not if we can stop Jack the Ripper."

"That's it, then. We can't let Jack the Ripper slice up Dora Fowler or anyone else."

Katie nodded as together they stepped off the curb. "Toby! Wait-ho!" Collin called out, tap-tapping the cobbled road in front of him with his umbrella as if it were a blind man's cane. "Hold still. What's your hurry?"

Toby slowed down and when they finally caught up with him, Collin asked why he was in such a dashed-darn hurry. Toby's voice was stiff with emotion when he answered.

"I want to find Georgie Cross before the bluebottles drag him in front of a magistrate and lock him behind bars for a crime he didn't commit."

"What's a bluebottle?" Katie asked.

"A large buzzing blowfly," Collin explained, "that lays its eggs in decaying plants and animal matter. It's also the name of a blue cornflower. But, in this case, it's the Cockney name for the police."

"Because of the blue uniforms they wear?"

"No. Because Cockneys don't trust the police. It's a derogatory term."

"I don't get it. Why would calling a police officer a blue fly be derogatory?"

Toby shot Katie a sour look. "Because they cluster around criminals like bluebottle flies around a festering sore."

Chapter Twenty-six

No. 29 Hanbury Street,
site of the second murder

THE LONG LINE OF ATTACHED row houses on Hanbury Street, where Georgie Cross lived with his grandmother, rose up into the London sky like a steep, pockmarked cliff. Bird droppings and loose bricks gave the once beautiful eighteenth-century facades an air of nineteenth-century neglect.

And though the pilasters flanking the front doors showed decay, and the ornamental fretwork had long since been cut up for firewood, the Cockneys who lived on Hanbury were hardworking and respectable. At No. 29, in the middle of the street, the stoop had been newly scrubbed and the front door glistened with a fresh coat of shiny black paint. The heavy bronze doorknocker was so highly polished it glinted in the afternoon sun.

It was half-past three in the afternoon when Toby, Collin, and Katie began wending their way down Hanbury, leaving the Duke's carriage parked two blocks away on Brick Lane. All along the street dozens of children were jumping rope, tossing jacks, and playing hop-the-stone, their gleeful cries filling the air. The girls wore starched, white pinafores; the boys, knickers and paddle-boat jackets. And though their clothes showed patches and mending, none of the children were barefoot or wore rags, except for one boy with a deformed leg, who hobbled with a wooden crutch.

Around the communal water pump, resting on chairs brought outdoors for an afternoon of minding the children, sat a cluster of elderly matrons smoking pipes, knitting, and occasionally smiling indulgently at their charges, their heads covered with frilly white bonnets.

Most of the women who lived on Hanbury Street worked out of their front parlors gluing matchboxes, sewing bundles of artificial flowers, or making pennyworth sachets, called sweet lavender pillows. Others took in needlework and laundry.

But at No. 29, Mrs. Amelia Richardson, Georgie Cross's grand-mother, was one of the lucky few who ran a thriving packing-case business. On any given day, including Sunday, cardboard boxes spilled out from her front parlor into the hallway, past the kitchen, and out into the tiny backyard, reached by a narrow set of steps. It would be here, in this recessed back garden, flanked left and right by neighboring fences, that the body of Annie Chapman, known as Dark Annie, would be discovered on the eighth of September.

Georgie Cross's grandmother would be the first to spot the dead girl. Gazing down from her second-story window, Mrs. Amelia Richardson would see what looked in the predawn light to be nothing more than a bundle of dirty rags against the dark patch of paving stones below.

Annie Chapman's body would be artfully arranged and carefully laid out. In terms of sheer brutality, Annie Chapman's evisceration would far surpass that of Mary Ann Nichols. The young woman's neck would be so severely severed that the killer, in a bizarre attempt to hold the head in place, would tie an embroidered handkerchief with the initials "CCT" around the victim's neck, securing it to the flesh above her clavicle with a large, rusty safety pin, and to the back of her skull, near the left earlobe with an onyx hatpin.

As Toby, Collin, and Katie approached the shiny brass door-knocker of No. 29 Hanbury, they were each lost in their own thoughts. Toby was thinking about Georgie Cross and how best to approach Georgie's grandmother to discover his whereabouts; Katie was thinking that somewhere here along Hanbury Street, Dark Annie would die at the hands of Jack the Ripper; and Collin, feeling moisture prickle across his forehead, was wondering where the devil he'd put his handkerchief.

"I'm always losing things," Collin muttered under his breath, pat-ting down his vest and greatcoat, searching for the pocket square with the family coat of arms — a unicorn leaping over a large stone — and embroidered with his initials, "CCT," for Collin Chesterfield Twyford, so he could mop his brow.

"Oh, bother," Collin chortled. But there were two dozen more at home. His manservant, Jeffries, would fetch him a new one when they returned to Twyford Manor.

Chapter Twenty-seven

Cobblestones and Daisies
say the Bells of St. Maisy's

"Okay," Toby said, turning to Katie as he reached for the door-knocker of No. 29 Hanbury. "Yesterday when Collin and I were here, Collin did not come in. I think it best if you both stay outside. Keep an eye out for the peelers."

When Katie protested, both Toby and Collin shot her scornful looks.

"You can't go in there, Katie." Collin made a face. "If Georgie's grandmother spies you up close she'll know in an instant you're not a frumpy old lady. How are we going to explain that, eh? How do we tell her you're —"

"Not the real McCoy?" Katie made a face.

"The real what? No, indeed. I was going to say you're not the genuine article."

Toby frowned at Katie. "Real McCoy? Cockneys say 'real MacKay' or 'real Magee.'"

"It's, er. . . .a cowboy expression," Katie improvised, thinking she'd heard it on a TV Western.

"Well, whether or not you're the real McCoy, MacKay, or Magee," Toby said. "You're *not* my great-aunt Mildred or m'little old granny. So stay put. That's an order."

Toby turned and rapped on the doorknocker.

Collin clamped on to Katie's elbow as an extra measure of protection against the possibility that she might charge through the door. He scrunched up his face again, and Katie thought he looked like a red-headed monkey about to scratch his head.

But when Mrs. Amelia Richardson swung open the door, Katie stayed put. Toby swept off his hat, mumbled his apologies for the intrusion, and asked if he could speak to her. Georgie's grandmother gave him a curt nod and beckoned him inside.

Stepping over the threshold and closing the door behind, Toby glanced around. Mrs. Richardson's front hallway was immaculately clean and well lit. He followed her into the front parlor where dozens of cardboard boxes were piled in corners and stacked along the walls in towering rows according to size. Glue pots and box cutters, set out on long tables by the front windows, had an orderliness to them; and the red damask curtains, tied to one side of these long windows, allowed bright, slanting wedges of afternoon sunlight to spill over the shoulders of two women sitting on stools, assembling boxes. The girl closest to Toby, wearing faded green velvet, raised her glue brush and smiled at him.

"Is Georgie here, then, Mrs. Richardson? Or have the peelers carted 'im off?" Toby asked, reverting to a thick Cockney accent. He jiggled a few coins in his pocket — an unwritten Cockney gesture that indicated he wasn't here to beg, borrow, or steal.

"Georgie's not home, m'lad, as well you know," Mrs. Richardson said, leading the way into a tiny sitting room that held a row of framed black-and-white silhouettes above the fireplace.

Hands on hips, Mrs. Richardson turned to Toby. "The bluebottles come and went, but they wouldn't 'ave found my Georgie, not for all the tea in China, no thanks to you, Mr. Tobias Becket! If it weren't that I knew your grandmother since we were wee sprites, and she having been married to her third husband, me own dear cousin, underfootman to your grandfather — God rest their souls — I wouldn't be givin' you the time of day, now, would I?"

"What's this, Mrs. R? You've known me longer than me own father, who spent as little time with me as a pork chop in a fishmonger's window! What're you on about? Where's Georgie, and why would I know he's not here? And why am I getting the royal codswollop welcome, Mrs. R? What's happened since yesterday?"

"I'll tell you what, m'boy! After you left yesterday, John Davies, who rents out me third floor, overheard someone shouting at Georgie. This other bloke be wanting Georgie to do right. To give somefink over to the police. Now what might that be, eh?" she gave Toby the fish eye, employed by East End grandmothers far and wide as the don't-you-be-lying-to-me look. "And who else but you, Tobias Becket, be wantin' to muck round with them bluebottles?"

Toby shook his head. Cockneys were law-abiding for the most part, but deeply distrusted police officers, who were easily bribed. "'T'wern't me, Mrs. R. I swear it. I wouldn't rat out Georgie to them bluebottles. On me honor, may God strike me dead if that ain't the truth."

Mrs. Richardson wasn't wearing a frilly white cap like the grandmothers sitting outside around the water pump. Her grey hair was pulled severely off her face in a tight bun with no adornments; and like Katie, she was dressed head to toe in black. But unlike Katie's, Georgie's grandmother's face showed a webbing of deep wrinkles around her mouth and eyes as if etched with a straight razor.

"You best be tellin' the truth, Master Tobias, for all your high-and-mighty bloodfolk relations with the Duke of Twyford, who can kiss my rump. Who else but you would be demanding that my Georgie hand over somefink to the peelers, eh? And none but you has a voice like a bleedin' toff when it suits him, but can talk like a Cockney easy as pumping water.

"Answer me wiff the truth, boy, or your dead granny will rise from her saintly grave and haunt you for the miserable, lying, harmful boy that you are!"

It took several minutes and much remonstration on Toby's part to convince Mrs. Richardson that he wasn't the one who had been arguing with Georgie yesterday. At long last, after Mrs. Richardson grudgingly admitted that she never truly believed Toby would harm her Georgie, she explained in a rambling monologue that George and this mystery man must have come to fisticuffs because there was an obvious scuffle. "George got his head bashed against the kitchen hearth, and I found him bleeding and moaning on the floor. Wasn't barely conscious, my poor Georgie. Great, fat lump rising on his pate." She made a hand gesture indicating how large the lump on his head was. After she learned that Georgie was being summoned to testify at the murder inquest, she had spirited him away to a secret place.

"He was running a fever and moaning ever so much, poor lad. I wasn't about to let 'em throw him into prison or worse, Bedlam Hospital. You're as good as dead already when you enter one of them hospital jails. And you know right well my Georgie wouldn't harm a flea, much less a defenseless girl. That brown-bread girl who got chived must have been a strumpet right fair, and got what was coming to her. More's the reason Georgie shouldn't be mixed up in this business. It will all quiet down. You'll see. Such a fuss about a girl who was no better than she ought to be."

"Mary Ann Nichols weren't no strumpet, Mrs. R. I'd stake my life on it."

"Mary Ann Nichols was a swinging door, sure as I'm standing here."

"So where's Georgie, mum?" Toby tried to steer the subject away from the murdered girl who was obviously guilty of being a whore in Mrs. Richardson's eyes.

"Georgie's in a safe place. Being nursed back to health. I ain't saying where. Hummph." She crossed her arms over her voluminous chest.

"Does he have a raspberry tart, then? Did she take him somewhere? The bluebottles will track him down, Mrs. R. Tell me where he's hiding and I'll help him, God's truth."

"He's safe with a friend of mine, not a raspberry tart. He's sick with the fever. My friend has potions. She'll fix him. He'll be up and about in no time. But if I find the coward that whacked my Georgie on the head. . ." She clamped her lips together, and no matter how hard Toby tried to convince her to tell him where Georgie was hiding, Mrs. Richardson wouldn't budge. Toby tried a different approach.

"Mrs. R, there be a friend of Mary Ann Nichols at the inquest who said she saw Mary Ann's killer. Didn't get a good look at his boat race, but would recognize his clothing" — Toby was stretching the truth here — "and said she took notice of the church pews and billy goat he be wearing. The police will come back, Mrs. R, demandin' to see the tips and toes Georgie be wearing that night. Them lot's probably outside right now, ready to pound on this here door. If you don't want Georgie thrown into a flowery dell, you'd best give me over his clothes or the bluebottles be all over 'em like flies on butter. We gots t'hurry, Mrs. R."

Mrs. Richardson frowned. She didn't want her grandson thrown into a flowery dell — a prison cell — so she grudgingly nodded, on the condition that Toby promise to return them when all the fuss had died down. When Toby agreed, Mrs. Richardson clumped wearily up the stairs to fetch the clothes Georgie Cross had been wearing the night Mary Ann Nichols was murdered.

"Don't forget the church pews, Mrs. R!" Toby hollered up the stairs after her.

Georgie's shoes.

Chapter Twenty-eight

Fisticuffs and Sore Feet say the Bells along Fleet Street

A SIX-MINUTE WALK down Hanbury and around the corner brought the three teenagers to the waiting carriage. The coachman sat dozing on the bench overhead, snoring loudly. Inside the carriage, Toby and Collin settled into the leather seat across from Katie, their backs to the coachman. Ladies always faced forward in carriage compartments due to their delicate constitutions.

Toby signaled the driver by rapping on the roof with Collin's umbrella, and a moment later, the carriage lurched forward down the street, joining the procession of horse-drawn vehicles sweeping west toward The Strand.

"Got your pocketknife handy, mate?" Toby asked Collin. "Left mine at home in case I was searched at the inquest."

As the four-wheeler rumbled along, Toby opened the rucksack Mrs. Richardson had given him for safekeeping and made a careful inspection of Georgie's shirt, waistcoat, and cap. Then his boots.

"Every Cockney within earshot of the bells of St. Mary Le Bow hides a bit of the ready in his daisy roots," Toby explained, turning over the worn boots. "Me mum, er, *my* mother," he corrected himself, "kept her baptism certificate in the heel of her roots."

Collin handed Toby his pearl-handled pocketknife.

Toby snapped it open and slipped the three-inch blade gently between the heel and welt of the boot. He gave a slight flick of his wrist and the heel cantilevered outward like a Chinese puzzle box.

Nestled inside were three bright copper pennies.

Katie leaned closer. The boots looked like her favorite Doc Martens back home, but with a cuff of canvas folded over the top, tied with rawhide laces. Nails rimmed the sole from heel to toe. They even smelled like Doc Martens. A blend of saddle leather and wet dog.

Toby did the same flick of the wrist with the sharp blade, and the heel of the left boot slipped outward. This time Toby pulled out a ticket stub.

"What is it?" Katie asked, eyebrows raised.

"Pawnbroker's stub. Looks like we hit the jackpot."

"I say! Good show, old boy!" cried Collin. "But, er . . . how does this help us . . . exactly?"

"We know two things," Toby answered, his voice low. "First: The person who pummeled Georgie near to death in Mrs. Richardson's kitchen yesterday wasn't a bleedin' Cockney or he'd have checked his roots. Second: Whatever we find at the pawnshop is probably connected to the murder of Mary Ann Nichols. Something Georgie found on or near the dead girl, more 'n likely. Some sort of evidence, perhaps. And if Georgie pawned it, it must be valuable, else he'd have left it alone. Not like Georgie to steal from the dead. I'll bet you a touch me on the knob, it's shepherd plaid."

"Huh?" Katie blinked at him.

"Bet you a bob — a shilling — it's shepherd plaid. Bad. Whatever we find is not going to be good."

"But if Georgie Cross is a thief," Collin harrumphed, "stands to reason he's a murderer as well. We should let the police do their work.

When they find Georgie, they'll chuck him into Newgate Prison and throw away the key. Has it coming, I'd say."

"Just cuz he bloody nipped something, doesn't make him a criminal."

Collin bristled. "Yes, it does!"

"Not in my book, mate. Finders keepers, losers weepers. Cockneys are bound by different rules of honor."

Collin's eyebrows shot up like little red pup tents. "If the boot fits, might as well wear it. This boy, Georgie, stole something from Mary Ann Nichols and murdered her to get it."

Katie glanced out the carriage window. The pawn ticket might provide a clue like Toby said, but they still had to find Jack the Ripper before he attacked Dora Fowler, Lady Beatrix, and the others.

"Where to next?" Collin asked. "To the pawnbroker's? That would be a ruddy adventure! Never been to a pawnshop."

Toby scowled. "That's because you've never been down and out, mate, or you'd be as familiar with 'me uncle's store' as you are with caviar and oysters."

"Your uncle owns a pawn shop?" Collin asked, incredulously.

"It's just an expression, Collin. Everyone calls pawn shops 'me uncle's store' like it's all in the family and whatnot."

"Really? What fun!" Collin rubbed his hands together like a gleeful kid on his first excursion to see lions at the zoo. He pounded the ceiling of the coach with his umbrella handle, slid open the trap door, and shouted directions to Stebbins, the driver. "Move on, man! Move on! We've work afoot!"

Katie laughed.

"What?" Collin caught her eye.

"You sound like Sherlock Holmes."

"Sherlock who? Oh yes, right. Dr. Doyle's story about a detective, wasn't it?"

Katie remembered that *A Study in Scarlet*, the first Sherlock Holmes story, had only just come out.

"Right-oh," Collin said. "Onward and upward to the pawn shop."

Toby stared at Katie, his dark eyes intense. "Have you read *A Study in Scarlet* by Dr. Doyle?"

"Of course! It's one of my favorites. I love all — " Kate stopped in midsentence. "It's one of my favorite short stories."

"Mine, too." Toby's eyes bore into hers.

Katie smiled. She couldn't help herself. "I predict that Sir Arthur Conan Doyle will write many more stories . . . all bestsellers . . . for years to come."

"*Sir* Conan Doyle?" Collin said incredulously. "The bloody fool hasn't been knighted. Not that I'm aware of. His wife, Touie, and Beatrix are chums."

"But he *will* be knighted, won't he?" Toby blinked at Katie.

"Are *you* bloody clairvoyant, too?" Collin glanced from one to the other.

"If the . . . boot fits . . . wear it," Katie said, staring back at Toby with unwavering, twinkling eyes.

Toby tore his eyes from hers. *Bloody hell!* he thought to himself. Katie's laugh was magical, her smile like golden sunshine. The girl was a menace. He folded his arms across his chest, and scowled at the scenery passing by outside the carriage window.

Crack! went the coachman's whip as the four-wheeler barreled steadily east toward Billingsgate. Toby tried hard not to think about the American girl sitting across from him. He lowered his window and continued staring morosely out as they jounced along cobbled streets heading for Pudding Lane where the Great Fire of London had started two centuries before.

Crack! went the coachman's whip a second time as the carriage rattled through the mist along Thames Street, passing warehouses and sugar refineries, until the road divided. The carriage skittered to a halt in front of a bustling market street full of secondhand shops.

Katie craned her neck out the opposite window, mesmerized by what she saw. The street opening up before her was the image of Diagon Alley from Harry Potter, with the same crowded, bustling air. That could be the Leaky Cauldron over there; the Owl Emporium across the street; Gringotts Bank up ahead. Katie smiled, happy just to be here. It felt as if she were in a movie. Any minute magical creatures would stare back at her.

Instead, when they descended from the jiggling carriage and hastened down the busy cobbled street, Katie saw shop windows displaying fishing rods, bird cages, blankets, bottle openers, pots, pans, knives.

Across the street a plump woman, bundled up in several shawls, cried out: "Penn'orth of needles! Get yer penn'orth of needles right here! H'penworth of buttons, farthingworth of thread! Step right up!"

They moved past a linen-draper and haberdashery, and Katie was over the moon. It looked exactly like Madam Malkin's Clothing Shop for Wizards! Katie wondered if J. K. Rowling had traveled back in time as well. Is this where she got her ideas for all the magical shops in Diagon Alley?

Katie tugged at Toby's sleeve. "Where are we? What's this place called?"

"Billingsgate Market."

Katie felt disappointed.

"What's the name of the street?" she persisted.

"No proper name. It's called Diagonal Alley by folks around here, on account of it's a diagonal to the Market Square and the quay —"

"I knew it!" Katie made a fist and punched the air. "Rowling must have studied olden-day Victorian photographs."

"Olden day?"

"Er, I mean present-day, black-and-white photographs."

Collin scratched his chin. "What other types of photographical picture images would there be?"

"Perhaps some day there'll be photographs taken that show vivid colors. The green of your waistcoat, Collin. The deep blue of the sky."

The two boys stared at her.

As they walked farther along, the lane narrowed considerably and Collin managed to step in a saucer-size mound of dung.

"Bloody hell!" he cried, tugging his patent leather shoe from the muck with a squishy sound. "I say, Toby, this is rawther an unfashionable destination, don't you think?"

"You were expecting moneylenders to put up shop in Grosvenor Square?"

"Well, rich people have to pawn their goods, too, I shouldn't wonder," Collin chortled, scraping his sodden shoe against the cobbled stones at the curb. "*Especially* after a bad round at the races."

Minutes later they passed the customs-house quay and emerged in front of a market square that loomed like a crumbling Roman coliseum, all heavy puddingstone and cracked archways leading down a long thoroughfare of secondhand stores.

Collin jabbed his umbrella into the air. "I say, I don't much care for these coarse, cheap shops."

"*Disce aut dicede,*" Toby muttered in Latin.

"Learn or depart?" Collin asked.

"More like shut up or leave," Toby answered.

"To that I say, *Jedem das Seine*. To each his own. I'll stick with my posh West End shops, you can have this assortment of . . . of . . . rabble."

"It's a deal, mate, if you'll just hold your gob. There's thieves aplenty in the side alleys. You'll be spotted for a proper toff with loads of the ready, make no mistake. Keep your voice down."

The winding lanes were narrowing, making it impossible for carriages to pass. The only horse Katie could see was a bone-thin mare tied to a post up ahead. Branching left and right were pathways and shadowed alleys filled with children playing, dogs barking. And everywhere bells could be heard jangling against the door jambs of secondhand shops selling old clothes, old jewelry, and other wares of all kinds.

Katie took a deep breath.

From the hay and straw market to the east came the pungent smell of alfalfa and clover and fresh-cut grass. The biggest difference between her century and this one was the smell of horse dung and hay. She blinked and glanced around.

Reflecting off shop windows, scattered glints of sunshine threw brilliant colors of fractured light on an amazing array of tangled fishing rods, crooked birdcages, faded blankets, bent corkscrews, old doll houses, and jars full of mismatched buttons. In the milliner's window on the corner, bolts of crimson silk glistened with a lustrous, blood-red sheen.

Crisscrossing the busy, narrow street scurried all manner of dock workers, oyster-boatmen, market porter lads, serving maids, shop girls, paupers, and common people. Lean-to sheds were piled high with coal; wheelbarrows brimmed with potatoes and oysters; and tea dens reeked of fried fish and grease-soaked chips. Outside the Boar's Head tavern, a man in an ankle-length leather apron stood hunched over a kettle-drum cauldron, spearing sausages that sizzled in the fire-flame depths, luring passersby with its strong, smoky aroma.

Katie's stomach growled.

"Fancy a bit o' beef stew or hot eel soup?" Toby asked.

The thought of eel soup made Katie's insides lurch, but she was so hungry, she hastily nodded and pointed to a stall where potatoes lay roasting on red-hot coals in a stone pit.

Toby scooted across the lane.

Katie could hear him haggling over the price, and a moment later, Toby returned with three piping-hot potatoes wrapped in newspaper. They sat down on a cobbled stoop below a scrawny tree and unwrapped their prizes. The potatoes had been smile-sliced end to end, the mouthlike opening brimming with melted cheese and grilled onions.

"Potato pasties for your pleasure." Toby gave a little nod.

Collin glanced down at his lunch, wrapped in days-old newspaper, scowled gloomily, and set it on the hump of a bulging tree root. But Katie, knowing that the burnt-toast smell of the baked potato would eventually lure him in, decided to hasten things up by making exaggerated "mmmmmm-goood" sounds as if she'd never tasted anything so delicious in her life. And the potatoes *were* delicious. In no time at all, Collin succumbed. He snatched up his steaming potato in its ink-smeared newspaper, blew on it several times, and began devouring it with gusto.

"Why is this place so distressingly unfashionable?" Collin quipped between heaping mouthfuls. "Who knew such rabbit warrens of bare-knuckled life existed?"

Toby responded with exasperation. "Let's just follow Sancho's advice and not look a gift horse in the mouth, shall we, mate?"

Katie wasn't sure if Toby was referring to the potatoes or the pawn ticket.

"'Twasn't Sancho's advice at all, old sod," Collin harrumphed with an air of absolute certainty. "It was Byron's." He made a pompous show of dusting crumbs from his shirtfront.

Toby rolled his eyes at Katie and said to Collin, "Byron wrote a poem *about* Sancho."

Collin jumped to his feet, sputtering with anger at being corrected by Toby. "As for a gift horse, if you think we've been given a golden egg in the form of a claim ticket stolen off a dead girl, I'll bet you a farthing your gift horse will turn out to be nothing more than a decrepit old nag."

Toby tugged out the claim stub and waved it in the air. "*This* gift horse could turn out to be of champion stallion lineage and will land us over the finish line and into the winner's circle! What say you to *that*, Mr. Doubting Thomas?"

"I say, don't call me a Doubting Thomas unless you care to wake up in the middle of next week with your head bashed in." He made a fist.

Katie gulped down the last of her potato.

"Toby, apologize," Katie ordered, trying hard not to laugh. "Promise never to call Collin a Doubting Tom ever again." She crumpled the newsprint into a tight ball and cuffed Collin playfully on the shoulder. Then, for no reason she could think of, she hooked first one elbow around Toby's neck, the other around Collin's, and hugged them both.

The two boys froze. Hugging boys in public, Katie knew, was not done by proper young ladies in Victorian England. But here, in this back lane, far from curious eyes, Katie couldn't help herself. She laughed happily and released her grip, and they both sprang away from her like coiled springs...or, she thought wryly, hot potatoes.

Chapter Twenty-nine

Three Bells and Three Whistles
say the Golden Bells of Thistles

TEN MINUTES LATER THEY WERE bending low, descending the
down-under stoop of the Thrice Whistle pawnshop. Toby heaved his
shoulder against the door, and as it swung open, a jangle of bells rang
out below the sign of three golden balls, the insignia of all pawnshops.

Katie had envisioned the pawnshop as being a dark, dusty place
where a gnarled old man — like Fagin — would be hunched behind a
wooden counter sorting his money while robbing customers of their
family heirlooms. Instead, the shop was a long and bright, bustling
place with a balconied second floor under a cheerful arched roof. At
the ends of the room enormous fires crackled beneath identical hooded fireplaces. Oil lamps dangled from the rafters, and high up on the
walls, cross-slits for windows shed bands of light onto the wooden
floor below. It reminded Katie of a thriving department store.

A long glass case, framed in wood, acted as a giant counter,
spanning the room end to end, stopping short of the dueling fireplaces

with their stump-sized logs. Behind this display counter, half a dozen men, wearing checkered vests and plaid trousers, stood ready to help the long lines of customers. At the rear of the pawnshop, stretching up to the balconied second floor, rose shelf upon shelf of glistening and polished wares. Every shelf was labeled; every item, numbered and accessed by wooden ladders on roller-wheels that squeaked across the floor when summoned by rope pulleys.

Beneath the glass countertop lay a sparkling array of jewelry, pinned like butterflies on long swaths of blue velvet. At the far end of the counter, Katie saw hundreds, maybe thousands, of wedding bands and row upon row of eyeglasses, watches, cufflinks, necklaces, bracelets, and brooches.

On the shelves along the far wall could be seen clocks and vases, teapots and kettles, flatirons, pewter mugs, top hats, and an endless procession of porcelain figurines, everything from milkmaids to the queens and kings of England. The higher the shelf, the bigger the item: ship models, busts of famous philosophers, leather suitcases, musical instruments. From one rafter, near the left-facing fireplace, hung a stuffed rhinoceros.

"Cool!" Katie blurted, glancing around.

Toby eyed her curiously. "You cold, luv?" he asked, raising his hand to catch the attention of a pawn clerk he knew.

"No. Sorry. Just an expression," Katie mumbled. But the shop *was* cool. It reminded Katie of an old-fashioned general store and an Aladdin's cave rolled into one.

"What's this?" Collin asked, poking his umbrella tip into a tall bin the size of a pickle barrel.

Toby took a place in line near the left-hand fireplace and glanced over his shoulder. "Looks to be sacks of ladies' hair."

The floor of the pawnshop was crowded with boxes and barrels filled to the brim with toy soldiers, umbrellas, buttons, shawls, books, and tools.

Katie moved next to Collin and peered into side-by-side barrels. The first held ribbon-bound blond hair; the second, handfuls of darker tresses, some braided and knotted, others balled into spidery webs.

"*Gross*," Katie muttered.

"Not sold by the gross, Katie," Toby swiveled his gaze to meet hers. "More likely by the bundle."

"Why?" Collin asked, his voice like a hiccough, a deep wrinkle forming between his brows. "Why would someone sell their hair?"

"For wigs, and braids, and bun clusters," Toby explained. "Ask your sister. She's sure to possess elaborate 'hair adornments' sold by wigmakers and worn at the opera and fancy balls."

"Never," Collin bristled, joining Toby at the back of the line. "Beatrix would never . . . buy . . . hair. *False hair*. Who knew you could sell it? What will they think of next? Selling one's underdrawers?"

"Yes," Toby said with tight-lipped annoyance. "People pledge their Eddie Grundies all the time. There's a warehouse back there filled with clothing: daisy roots, church pews, billy goats, hand racquets, Peckham ryes. Boots, shoes, coats, jackets, ties; and yes, lots of early doors, pairs of underdrawers. People don't pawn their Eddie Grundies for a lark, Collin. Often it's a toss-up between food on the table or a warm winter coat. Everything glistens on the shelves here, but a pawnshop isn't a charitable guild."

Collin returned Toby's exasperated stare. "But it's a bit like a bank, now, isn't it? A pawnbroker lends you money and uses your property as security, rather like the lowest common denominator of a bank. The fact that there are people who would stoop to such depths as to pawn their nether garments," Collin said with a shiver, "makes me grieve for all mankind." He kicked at a barrel filled with umbrellas, and they clinked and shuffled against one another.

"Hoy!" shouted a checkered-vested clerk no older than Collin. "Don't touch the merchandise, my young friend. This ain't no red 'n' yella sample shop."

"Red and yella?" Katie whispered to Toby.

"Umbrella," Toby answered, then turned back to Collin. "Until you've lived in the church pews of the poor, Collin, don't sermonize. But look around, it's not just the poor who are hocking their goods. Notice the family crest on those soup spoons?" He nodded to a felt-lined case farther down the counter.

Collin and Katie peered at the contents.

"By Gad! I know that coat of arms!" Collin sputtered.

"Pipe down," Toby said softly, but with an edge to his voice.

In the line next to them now, two little girls aged about eight and ten were hoisting a music box and Punch and Judy puppets onto the counter.

"Please, Mama," wailed the smaller of the two.

The mother, a slim woman in her twenties, with level, somber eyes in a heart-shaped face, nodded to her daughter and placed a woolen shawl and a rattle-clapper alongside the music box. "Mustn't fuss, my lamb. Papa will be home soon, I'm right sure of it." She sighed and swept back a strand of light-brown hair caught under the tilt of her worsted bonnet. With a determined set to her mouth, she reached into her pocket and pulled out two brooches—enamel minia-tures—painted with baby faces, younger versions of her daughters.

Katie drew in a sharp breath. It was wrenching to see this family hock their treasured possessions. Katie touched the strand of pearls around her neck. On her bureau at the Duke's house sat a jewelry box full of pendants, necklaces, brooches, earrings. Each morning Agnes chose appropriate pieces and pinned, clasped, and fastened them on.

Katie reached into the small reticule that dangled from her wrist.

"I tell you, Toby, that's the Buckleys of Buckingshire's coat of arms! They would *never* pawn their silver. Must be stolen! Filched! We shall demand the lot of them back. Surely this shop doesn't com-merce in stolen property? We'll set this matter right. Follow me."

Toby grabbed a fistful of Collin's jacket and yanked him back-ward, reining him in by the scruff of his collar like a frisky pup. "You'll do no such thing. Likely as not, the Marquis of Buckingshire is down on his gambling luck and sent a servant round to pawn the family plate. No doubt he fully intends to redeem the soup spoons in due course."

"I should think so! He's a nobleman. A peer of the realm!" Collin sputtered, the ginger fuzz of his moustache glinting in the cross-slit light from the window above. "Imagine foregoing one's soup course!" Collin harrumphed indignantly, smoothing down his lapels. "Sir Buckley's family must have soup come winter. Imagine Christmas pudding and no soup!"

Toby made a sound in his nose like a snorting bull. "The Cockneys have a saying about the three golden balls hanging over pawnshops. The sign means, *two to one you won't get your goods back.* And here's another laugh for you. Saint Nick is the Patron Saint of Pawnbrokers. So, best watch out, Collin. If you pawn your Adam and ants" — he turned to Katie — "pants," then swiveled back to Collin — "they'll nick off yer Mars and Venus —" He stopped in midsentence and glanced sheepishly at Katie. "Er, your candlewick. Sorry, luv. Not acceptable talk in front of the fair sex."

Mars and Venus probably meant penis, Katie decided. But what was a Candlewick?

"By Gad!" Collin cried, balling up his fists. "The Buckleys shall get their soup spoons back, or my name isn't Collin Chesterfield Twyford, the third. Sunday luncheon devoid of soup is like...er...rhubarb pie without crust...*unthinkable.*"

"In the words of Marie Antoinette —"

"Let them eat cake," Katie's voice joined Toby's, who peered at her as if he couldn't quite figure out who she was and where she came from.

Katie smiled. *I come from a kingdom by the sea...far, far away.*

At the front of the line now, Toby held up the pawn ticket.

"Give it here," said a gap-toothed, young clerk in a vest two sizes too big, patterned like a large chessboard. Toby extended the pawn stub, and the young man snatched it up and scurried to the far corner through a curtain of beads that plinked and pinged like rain on a tin roof.

In the next line over, the brown-bonneted mother reluctantly twisted off a ring from her left hand. "This too, sur. If you please, sur."

"Your wedding band, mum?" An older, grave-faced clerk enquired.

"Yussir." The woman's voice was quick and determined, but her head was bowed in defeat as she handed over the ring.

A moment later, when several coins were exchanged, Katie couldn't stand it any longer. She scooted around Collin, past Toby, and positioned herself next to the young mother.

"How much to redeem the miniatures?" Katie asked.

Before the dour-faced clerk could answer, Katie reached into her reticule and tugged out a fistful of coins. The money system in this century was different from that of the twenty-first. If she held out the coins, Katie hoped the clerk would take what he needed.

"Is it enough?" Katie asked, her voice composed, but her heart thumping wildly.

A pair of glum, unwinking eyes stared at her. "More 'n' enough, madam."

The clerk's outstretched fingers opened and closed like the mouth of a snapping turtle as he snatched up six coins from Katie's outstretched palm. "This will redeem the *en-tire* lot with interest, save for the ring." He slid the gold wedding band onto his gnarled pinkie and wagged it in the air. "Let's see. . ." he continued with exaggerated interest as he clamped a magnifying eyeglass onto his eye and made a great show of peering at the inside of the ring. "Upon my word. I see a wedding date engraved here and a wife's name. Lizzy. Eighteen eighty-one."

"How much?" Katie insisted.

"Madam?"

"What did you buy it for?"

"Oi. We don't buy nothink, mum. We loan money in exchange for personal property."

"How much to get it back?"

"Let me see. . .the amount needed to redeem this here *item*" — He pronounced it *eye-tom*. — "be one pound, eight shillings, plus 'alf a crown added for interest."

"You'd charge interest? Even though you've had it less than a minute?"

"But o' course."

"And if she never returns to reclaim it?" Katie demanded.

"My uncle keeps the ring and sells it."

The grave-faced clerk snatched the rest of the coins from Katie's outstretched palm, and with an unctuous smile and serpentine flourish, presented the young mother with the ring.

"Bless you, mum," cried the woman, turning to Katie. "Me 'usband's a dockworker and ever so kind and generous he is. But 'e's gone missing. Never done a bunk afore, not me Alfred — " She stopped. "May the angels bless you, mum. I ain't never going to forget you. This 'ere is Lizzy, same as me, and me little one is Meg-o-mine. Say 'ow do you do, Meggie, Lizzy. This fine lady saved your dollies like a right proper saint. Give 'er a curtsy and we'll be on our way." The young mother glanced nervously around as if she feared reprisal.

Just then, the young clerk in the oversized vest strode back through the beaded curtain and set a roll of gauze on the glass surface in front of Toby, who slowly unraveled the flimsy cloth.

"That there's a true gem." The young clerk grinned, showing gapped teeth. "Crusted wiff rubies and wee diamonds. Them's real awright. We done checked. So, if you be wanting this property of yours redeemed, at twenty percent interest, that will be — "

But Katie wasn't listening. Stunned, she stared down at a pair of rose gold opera glasses, the binoculars of which were studded with tiny rubies like red stars. In the mother-of-pearl handle glinted the diamond initials "BFT." *Beatrix Fairbairn Twyford.*

Chapter Thirty

Pasties and Perch
say the Bells of Fenchurch

OUTSIDE THE PAWNSHOP Collin blinked rapidly and straightened up almost as if he were recovering from a punch in the face. His hands were shaking; his voice, unsteady.

"Major Brown killed that girl!" Collin sputtered. "He was the last person to hold Beatrix's opera glasses. And he tried to blame me!"

"Don't jump to conclusions, Collin," Katie shot back. "Reverend Pinker claims *he* had the opera glasses."

"I tell you! I saw Major Brown tuck the opera glasses in his breast pocket. When Beatrix asked for them, he blamed me. Said I had them. I never even touched them, let alone pocketed them. This is proof *positive* that Major Brown is the murderer! He killed Mary Ann Nichols, and in his haste to get away, dropped the opera glasses. He's a blighter, I tell you. I've been saying it all along, but no one listens. They think I'm jealous of Brown. But blast it! I've known from the beginning he's a bad lot. Only the Duke believes me. By god, they'll all believe me now." Collin's red eyebrows shot up and down in his scowling face.

Toby stared sharply at Collin, but said nothing. A clock in a distant tower began striking the hour.

Katie took a deep breath. *Collin might be right*, she thought. If Major Brown was in possession of Beatrix's opera glasses when he killed Mary Ann Nichols, he could easily have dropped them in the struggle.

A movement from the bakery shop across the way caught Katie's eye. She would not have noticed at all, thinking about Collin's accusation, had it not been for the impression that someone was watching them. A head jerked back out of sight. Which reminded Katie of something.

"Wait!" Katie snapped her fingers. "Reverend Pinker had specks of blood on his sleeve at the theater. I distinctly remember it!"

Smoky sunlight streamed across the door of the bakery across the street.

"Katie! Are you cracked?" Collin spoke sharply. "Stinker Pinker couldn't hurt a fly, let alone kill a girl. I've known him my whole life. He doesn't have it in him. He's incapable of deceit. Honest to the core." Collin rapped his umbrella on the curb.

"There was blood on his cuffs at the theater, Collin. I definitely saw it." Katie turned to Toby. "You're too quiet. What's going on? What are you thinking?"

But Toby's face was emotionless.

"You can't deny it, Toby!" Collin moved closer, whacking his umbrella high in the air and letting it land with a thump on Toby's shoulder. "The facts are the facts. I tell you, Major Brown was the last person to handle those opera glasses and he blamed their loss on me! And unless you bloody well think I did it, he's our man. He's a dark horse and always has been, but everyone thinks he's the bloody King of Spades. I know everyone laughs at me behind my back, Toby, don't deny it. I've made mistakes and am not always on the mark. But

I'm right about this. No matter how often you champion the blighter, you'll eventually come to realize, Major Brown is our man."

Toby was silent, but his eyes betrayed a dull anger. After a long pause he flicked the umbrella off his shoulder.

"We'll have to bow and arrow it. Pool our sticks and stones to get Beatrix's opera glasses out of hock." Toby swooped off his cap and tossed it on a stoop. "Everything of value into the pot." He nodded to the tweed cap.

For the next five minutes they pooled their possessions. Katie unclasped her pearls and placed them into the hat. Collin dipped his hands into his pockets and fished out some loose coins and his pen knife and placed them in the cap. Toby piled more coins and several banknotes he kept in the heel of his boots into the mix and then snatched up the cap. "T'won't be enough," he said, jiggling the tweed cap as if weighing it on a scale. "Collin? What else have you got?"

Collin glared at Toby, then at Katie. "Katie, this is your fault. You had no business giving that witless Lizzy woman money for those damn miniatures. She'll only come back and hock the lot of it again next week. Drove her husband away is my guess. It was a waste of good money. We wouldn't be in this fix if you hadn't given it all away. And don't ask me to hock my underdrawers. I won't do it. The opera glasses can rot in hell for all I care. That was a foolish, foolish thing to do, giving a complete stranger your hard-earned coins."

Toby gave a curt nod of agreement.

"Not you, too." Katie shot Toby a disappointed glance, then turned back to Collin.

"I didn't earn those coins, Collin. The Duke gave them to me for pocket money. I know you're upset, or you wouldn't be saying such things."

"Blasted right, I'm upset. In my book charity begins at home. You can't just throw good money at every Tom, Dick, and Horatio who goes begging. I'm not completely heartless, Katie. That woman's plight touched me as well, but where the lower classes are concerned it's just one big endless pit. Your coins are a tiny drop in an endless ocean of poverty." Collin let his umbrella clatter to the pavement. He untied his cravat, shrugged out of his greatcoat, and handed over his gold watch with its gold fob chain to Toby, along with his pearl tie pin, cravat, and greatcoat. "There. Take it all. Take the blasted lot."

❖

HE CLOCK IN THE DISTANT WATCHTOWER was striking the half hour when Toby finally exited the pawnshop, clutching tight to the newly redeemed opera glasses, his face grim. With the collar of his coat turned up, he motioned to the others, and strode down the street in a westerly direction.

Behind him, Collin and Katie had to scramble to keep up. A block from the pawnshop, Katie glanced over her shoulder. The narrow, twisty lane looked vaguely sinister with its sagging iron grates, quivering shop awnings, and brick walkways choked with weeds.

They were moving fast, rounding corners now, passing shop after shop. Katie had to stop to catch her breath. Constricted by corsets, as well as the fake hump between her shoulders, Katie felt a trickle of perspiration run down her neck. Her hand closed on a spiky rail in front of a tea shop.

She took several deep breaths. The veil shrouding her face strained against her cheek bones, the black ribbon at her throat felt as constricting as a noose. She tugged at it, and then, in a moment of panic, clawed at the knot until it ripped and unraveled in her fingers like shredded cabbage.

"It's all right, Katie." Coatless Collin, sleeves flapping like swan wings, was at her side in a flash. "You mustn't fret. We can turn Queen's evidence against Major Brown! They'll believe us. They'll have to. Just don't jabber on about any hocus-pocus portents, or we'll really be in the soup.

"*The soup*. I forgot about the Buckingshire soup spoons! I'll return at first light and redeem the lot. Sir Buckley deserves our charitable services as much as that wretched mother and her witless brats!

Come on, now," he coaxed. "Let's be off. Cook promised licorice twists and gingerbread for tea. Pinker is joining us. Mustn't tarry. Come along. There's our coach rounding the corner."

Katie glanced up.

In a *whoosh* of dust and dirt, the Duke's carriage scraped in at the curb across the street.

"Mind the muck!" Collin directed, tugging at Katie's arm.

In several strides Toby was in front of the coach, unhooking the carriage steps, letting them clatter to the curbstone.

"Ho, there!" cried a portly man in a porkpie hat, exiting the Queen Anne Pub to their right. He hobbled over to Katie, belched, and the air smelled of whiskey. "I seen you coming down the street. That was a right fine thing you did at the Thrice Whistle, mum." He took off his hat, shaped like a shovel, and bowed low in front of Katie.

"I knows Lizzy Stride since she was a little kipper." The man motioned to the height of his calf. "Gots her faults, does Lizzie, but she be a good girl. Shame 'bout her boiler house, Alfred. Alfred's not one to do a bunk. Somefink bad must've happened. Alfred's a dockworker. Might've tumbled into the Thames. Can't swim, not Alfred. That's what might o' gone wrong. Poor sod." The man belched and stumbled away.

"Wait!" Katie cried, running after him. "Was that woman in the pawn shop Elizabeth Stride?"

"Course it be. Little Lizzy. Busy Lizzy. Tha's her."

Katie clasped her hands to her mouth. She felt queasy. Elizabeth Stride was one of the Ripper victims. *What's going on?* Katie wondered. *Why am I meeting the victims?* Was it coincidence that Elizabeth Stride was in line next to them at the pawnshop? Katie had been warned that she couldn't change history. But she had to try to stop that poor woman from being slaughtered.

"I *can* change history," Katie whispered, vehemently. "I have to!"

"What's that, Katie? What are you mumbling about?" Collin was again at her side. "You're shaking. Katie. It's all right. Not to fret. We'll return the opera glasses to Beatrix and confront Major Brown.

We'll have him behind bars tonight or my name isn't Collin Chesterfield Twyford, the third."

A prison wagon rumbled past.

"Look there, Katie! See that van filled with felons? *That* will be Major Gideon Brown heading off to gaol, or my name isn't—"

But Katie wasn't listening. She hurried over to Toby. "That woman. The mother, Lizzie, at the pawnshop. She...she..."

"Another Jack Sprat victim, eh?" Collin swooped up from behind, his shirtsleeves waving, his umbrella jabbing the air. "I say, Katie, old girl," he continued in a disbelieving voice. "Is every woman you meet going to be sliced to ribbons? Surely no one is *that* clairvoyant. I mean...well, that is to say. If they all die...er...well, I mean, if your prophecies come true, mayhaps they die *because* you've met them, not vice versa."

"Huh?" Katie shook her head. "What's that supposed to mean?"

"Maybe they die because you've foretold it, *not* the other way around."

"But I've already told you the names of Jack the Ripper's victims. I knew Elizabeth Stride was going to be murdered before I ever met her. Not vice versa. If the girls I keep meeting die because of me, that would mean I had a hand in their deaths. I'd be responsible. That's just not the case here."

Katie shuddered. She wrapped her arms around her waist. *Could it be possible? Could Collin actually be right? Do these women die because I've gone back in time? Or did I go back in time because they died?* Katie closed her eyes and took several deep breaths. *No. I'm not responsible for their deaths.*

"Katie," Toby said so softly that Katie flicked open her eyes to see if it was truly him speaking. She leaned toward him, swaying slightly.

He took her by the elbow. And when he whispered in her ear, his voice was so low, it sent goosebumps up her spine. "You never mentioned Lizzy Stride. She wasn't on your death list."

"But of course she was!" Katie tugged her arm away.

"Toby's right, Katie," Collin stepped in. "I'm good with names. You said that after Mary Ann Nichols's death, this Jack-of-All-Slashers would attack a woman named Dark Annie, then a double murder on the same night of Molly Potter who is with child and Catherine Eddowes. And then a stunningly beautiful girl, you said, named Mary Jane Kelly...and then Dora Fowler from the inquest...and finally, you told us there would be one last victim. The way you looked at me when you said 'one last victim' sent shivers through me. I thought maybe you were implying that *Beatrix* was on that list. Stuff and nonsense, of course. Beatrix isn't some brash street girl to be slaughtered for her sins. But be that as it may, Katie, I do not recall any mention of an Elizabeth, or even a Lizzy, on your Jackknife list."

Katie swallowed hard and turned to Toby. "Elizabeth Stride gets murdered on October Third. She's the victim after the double murder of Molly Potter and Catherine Eddowes. It's hard to keep them all straight. But I *know* I told you about her."

Toby shook his head and with deceptive mildness, said, "No, Katie. You never breathed a word about Elizabeth Stride." He tipped his cap and strode off in the opposite direction from the waiting carriage.

"Where are you going?" Katie shouted.

"Tower of London," he called over his shoulder.

"Why?" Katie persisted, hurrying after him.

"Need a lump of ice."

"A lump of—"

"Advice."

"I'll come with you."

"No. Just me, alone."

"But *why* the Tower of London?" Katie asked, resigned to the fact that she couldn't stop him.

"Traitors' Gate."

"Traitors' Gate?"

"There's someone there I need to see."

"Who?"

For the first time since leaving the pawnshop, the frown eased off Toby's face, replaced by a half-smile.

"A traitor."

Chapter Thirty-one

Butchers and Beefeaters
say the Bells of St. Peter's

THREE DAYS LATER. September 5, 1888

The East End butcher barn, called The Cut, was a crooked warehouse in a stable-like building with a peaked roof that soared into the cloudless London sky.

Inside, slabs of meat dangled from dozens of steel hooks hung from the ceiling: There were sides of beef, pork, and mutton.

Katie felt queasy as the swaying carcasses overhead caught the light in shadowy reflections. The glistening sheen of animal flesh made the carcasses look as if they'd been polished with mahogany wax.

Holding her breath against the foul stench, Katie peered down at her boots covered in sawdust and speckled with blood from the dripping raw meat. *There's no refrigeration here*, she had to remind herself. Unable to hold her breath a second longer, Katie took a deep gulp of acrid air and tried hard not to gag. She thrust her hands deep into her pockets and wiggled them about. She was dressed head to toe as a beggar boy: battered hobnail boots, ripped knee-breeches, and a torn sailor jacket. Scrunched low on her head sat a woolen cap.

Toby had plastered an eye patch over Katie's left eye, and it felt as if her eyelid were swollen and inflamed under the itchy scrap of wool. Toby had insisted on the patch, as well as grime on her face.

"We'll just put a little ankle and foot on your nose," Toby had informed her not half an hour ago.

"What's ankle and foot?" Katie asked.

"Soot. We've got to disguise those twist 'n' swirl pink cheeks of yours. Or . . . I *could* knock out one of your teeth," he said with a mischievous gleam in his eye. "Blimey, pet. No larkin' about this time. Remember," he continued in a thick Cockney accent, "you're me l'ttle, half-wit cooosin."

"You sound like Eliza Doolittle."

"Who?"

"Er . . . no one," Katie shot back. George Bernard Shaw must not have written *Pygmalion* yet.

Toby gave her an odd look. "Whatever you do, Katie lass, don't be smiling with those perfect white teeth of yours. I'd wager there's not a single soul in the whole of Whitechapel that doesn't have crooked teeth. *Or rotting ones.* There's no West End dentists where we're going. So don't be opening that flip-flap of yours — keep it buttoned, or I *will* knock out a few teeth." Toby chuckled as he smeared muck on her face until it dried like hardened clay. She was supposed to be in disguise as his mute, half-blind cousin.

When they arrived at the slaughterhouse, Toby gave another order. Katie was to wait outside in the hansom cab with Collin while Toby questioned the butcher lads who had seen Mary Ann Nichols's body the night she'd been murdered.

Now, standing in bloody sawdust, Katie wished she'd obeyed, and she was glad of the patch shielding her eye from half of the dangling carcasses.

In the corner, Toby was talking to one of the butcher lads who was hoisting half a joint of beef over his shoulder. The boy was nimble, eager, and athletic-looking with a purple scar running from his nose to his upper lip.

"There's a knack to getting it in the right place on your shoulder, mate," said the butcher boy, shifting the weight of the carcass. One of the creature's bloody hooves rested on a knot in the rope wrapped around the boy's leather smock, which extended from his neck to his ankles.

"Oy, there! Mind the hook," another butcher lad shouted as Toby ducked his head below a cow's tail.

"Like I told yer," said the first butcher lad with the purple scar, "we didn' see nuffin'. Not till Georgie Cross came wailin' down the street hollering fer us to help him wiff some tart he thought stumbled in the street. Shame 'twas Mary Ann Nichols. Billy bend-you-round-his-finger was fair sweet on poor Mary Ann afore she started in wiff Mad-Willy."

Toby raised an eyebrow. "Billy bend-you-round? So, Mary Ann liked 'em rough, did she?"

"Naw. Billy-bend is soft when it comes to twist 'n' swirls. Got a gentle spot fer the girls, he does. And Mary Ann did 'im a good turn. She introduced Billy-bend to her friend, Dora Fowler, what sells them birds in Clavell Street Market. You know, the girl wiff them big, beaut'ful mince pies? When Dora bats them mince pies at a bloke, he could fair drop dead on the spot."

"I know Dora Fowler." Toby nodded. "She was at the inquest."

Kate inched closer until she was standing just behind Toby's elbow. The two boys were talking with such thick accents, Katie was having trouble following their conversation.

Toby and the butcher lad continued for several more minutes in what sounded like pig Latin, then Toby nodded, waved, and wheeled around, shoving Katie hard between her shoulder blades as if to say "get a move-on."

Katie stumbled, righted herself, then loped close on Toby's heels, hastening through red-speckled sawdust toward a set of doors leading past a courtyard, and around the corner into the shop front where a butcher-block counter stretched end to end fitted with scales and carving knives. Large joints of meat, similar to those in the slaughter barn, swung from metal hooks behind the counter, but were ticketed at a price per pound. Bluebottle flies circled the glistening meat.

A line of women stood waiting at the counter to buy dinner. Toby pointed out the shop owner, Johnny Brisbane, helping a young woman with a flattened nose at the front of the queue. The woman peered at bits and pieces of hanging meat. After she chose one, Johnny Brisbane slung it to the counter to be weighed, then motioned to one of his butcher boys to cut and whittle it as per his instructions.

Johnny Brisbane turned to the next woman in line. "Here's a loin of pork for one-and-six, Mrs. Bayswater. And I have a nice leg of lamb for the same."

"I knows yer tricks, Johnny. You can do better than that, you being my niece's cousin's husband. Come on now, Johnny, don't be swindling a near relative."

"All right, Mrs. Bayswater, you be pullin' my heartstrings. Four-pence off that loin of pork, fivepence off the leg of lamb. Can't do better 'n that, now can I? You'd have me in the poorhouse if I sell off all my meat so cheap."

A minute later, Toby pulled Johnny Brisbane aside in such a way that didn't allow Katie to listen in.

Shortly after, as they were leaving The Cut, Katie glanced over her shoulder. Brisbane's leather apron was awash with old blood stains as well as bright splatters of new ones. It would be easy, Katie thought, for a butcher lad to cut a girl's throat, then march innocently away from the crime. No one would question his bloody apron.

As the horses began their relaxed trot toward Clavell Street, Toby sat forward in the carriage, arms folded, brows drawn together in a frown.

"You ought not to have been in a slaughterhouse, Katie. It's not a fit place for a proper young lady. We had a deal," he said quietly.

"I know, I know," Katie hedged. "A jellied eel. But today I'm a half-blind, mute, twelve-year-old boy, *remember?*" She tugged off the scratchy eye patch and thrust her head out the window to avoid meeting Toby's stony glare.

The windows of the carriage had been left open, and the seats were still slick with morning dew, so when Katie slid across the wet leather, she could feel the damp soak into her threadbare breeches. A quick glance down the road revealed a string of crooked houses where street noises and the smell of Dijon mustard filled the air.

"A right fair jellied eel," Toby pronounced, and Katie could feel his eyes boring holes into her back.

"The deal," Collin said, "was that *you* promised to do whatever Toby and I told you, and in return we'd *allow* you to accompany us."

With great effort Katie resisted the urge to throw back at him that she'd made the deal with Toby and Toby alone.

"All right. All right," Katie muttered, her elbows dangling out the window as she tried to decide how best to deal with Toby's anger. In Katie's mind, there were only two strategies. The first was to make nice, smile and act contrite; the second, to go on the offensive. But being combative, or even righteously indignant, she felt, was not the way to handle Toby, so she opted for contrition, but not before Collin interjected with a lofty snort:

"You're lucky Toby doesn't wallop you on the spot!" he harrumphed. Almost as an afterthought, he added, "A Twyford would never wallop a girl, of course. And...er...Toby's half Twyford, don't you know."

Katie swung her head back into the carriage and looked into Toby's dark eyes, but instead of seeing anger, she saw amusement. They stared at each other for a long moment.

His voice was soft, almost like a caress, when he said, "Collin's right. I would never hit a twist 'n' swirl. Though truth be told, Katie, you near make me want to amend my gentlemanly ways." He startled her by laughing.

So Toby wasn't mad at her for tagging along after him into the slaughterhouse? His reaction confused her, and she had to tear her gaze from his. Was he taunting her? Mocking her? She stared hard at his chin so she could concentrate. But that only managed to distract her. His chin had a dimple when he smiled, and he was grinning like a Cheshire cat. The dimple was undeniably sexy.

Sexy? Ugh! Katie thought. *The last thing I need right now is to be attracted to a guy I'll never see again!* But Katie couldn't ease the image of hooking up with Toby from her mind. *He's technically dead,* she reminded herself. *Or will be when I travel forward in time again.*

"Okay," she announced, with a nonchalant shrug. "I made an itty-bitty mistake in judgment. I thought — since you were questioning a witness — I should be there. That was our deal. I'd help with the investigation."

Toby smiled.

Katie felt embarrassed but wasn't sure why. She was pretty certain Toby would make her life miserable by making her wear another ridiculous, itchy, uncomfortable disguise, but she forced herself to smile back.

"I'm sorry, Toby," she said, in a syrupy sweet voice. "But this really has to be a fifty-fifty deal. We need to be partners here. I'm your silent partner today because I'm supposed to be blind and mute, but tomorrow — "

"No tomorrow, Katie. All bets are off. Tomorrow you stay home and knit by the fireside. Or perhaps you can do needlework like a proper English lass."

"No way! You can't dictate what I can and can't do. We had a deal. You need me."

"Not any more, pet. You gave us all the information. You said yourself you can't predict the future anymore. Your clairvoyance was a one-shot deal, is how you phrased it."

"So you're telling me I'm history? I'm toast? All because I didn't listen to your Machiavellian, chauvinistic, insufferable edict to stay put in the carriage? What did you think? I was going to faint dead away when I saw a bloody carcass hanging from the rafters?" She was fuming and wondered what Toby would say if she told him she'd watched dozens of gory autopsies on TV crime shows. "You must be kidding me!" She slammed her fists on the damp seat.

"History? Toast?" Collin sputtered in a wheezy voice. "Whatever do you mean, Katie? No matter how you slice a boiled egg, a noun can't *be* another dissimilar noun. A horse can't *be* a tree. A girl can't *be* history. And as for toast, did you mean burnt toast? Or toast with marmalade? Perhaps you meant a crumpet with jam and butter? That would be an apt metaphor *for a girl!* But in the future, if you're going to bandy about metaphors, I would thank you to —"

"Oh, shut up!" Katie shouted her frustration. "What I meant is you can't just diss me, er, dismiss me. I'm the bones of this operation. I'm the most important spoke in this wheel. You need me if we're going to stop Jack the Ripper!"

Collin tugged on his lower lip. "You distinctly told us that your psychic abilities dried up after your initial vision. You swore to me that you could not tell us who this Jack-the-knife is. I grilled you on that point, and you said —"

"Yes. I mean, no. I don't know who the murderer is, and never will, unless we catch him. That's absolutely correct. But that doesn't mean I won't have good ideas — *better ideas* — than you two. Because I . . . er . . . come at it from a different angle. . . a different historical perspective." *You don't know how different!* She took a deep breath to calm down.

"Because you're a twist 'n' swirl or a Yank?" Toby asked in a matter-of-fact voice.

No, because I watch CSI. I'm from the twenty-first century. I'm more logical. More advanced . . . more evolved!

"Kind of. Sort of." Katie groaned, realizing she couldn't explain her reasoning and was only digging herself deeper into a hole. "Look, you guys. You need me because of where I'm from and who I am and what I know about the world that you don't. I'm better equipped to . . . er . . . solve crimes."

"I see. That's logical," Toby said.

"Precisely. By the very nature of where I come from, I'm more logical…less…naïve."

Collin fell backward with a thud of his shoulder blades against the leather seat and clamped his hands theatrically to his heart.

"*Naïve?* God's eyeballs, Katherine! Call a man a gutter snipe, call him a son of a boar, call him a scoundrel, but *never* call a British bloke *naïve!* Might as well call him the village idiot, or a lily-livered coward, or a simpering *girl*. It's beneath an Englishman's dignity!"

"Oh, *puh-leeze!*" Katie harrumphed.

Toby looked amused. "You'll stay in the carriage, Miss Katherine. And this time you will do as you're told. I'll have your promise, pet, or we'll press home and unload you at Twyford Manor where Lady Beatrix and the Duke can play nursemaid to your tantrums."

His face grew serious. "I don't owe you an explanation, but I'll give it to you just the same. I didn't want you in the slaughterhouse for your own safety. I'm responsible for you, and I don't want you harmed. Johnny Brisbane is a dangerous man, capable of great cruelty. He once snapped his own dog's neck, then tore half its hide off with his bare hands because the dog lost in a ratter's fight.

"Give me your promise, lass. You will stay in the carriage when Collin and I talk to Dora Fowler. She's got until the first of December to live, if your visions are trustworthy."

"That's exactly why I need to go!" Katie pleaded, hating the high-pitched wail in her voice.

"That's *exactly* why you're staying here. I don't doubt you believe you're well versed in the vast ways of the criminal world," he chuckled at the absurdity of the statement. "But I *will* have your promise on this." He shot her a hard-as-stone look.

A hollowness filled Katie's chest. Toby's piercing gaze didn't compel her to obey. Quite the opposite. She hated being left out. She was here to catch Jack the Ripper, not obey insufferable orders from an arrogant jerk who had no clue how to track down a serial killer.

"*You'll get my promise when hell freezes over!*" she muttered under her breath.

As it turned out, hell froze over five minutes later.

Chapter Thirty-two

Farthings and Fate
say the Bells of Ludgate

WHEN THE FOUR-WHEELER came to a full stop half a block from Clavell Street, between Charlotte and Commercial Road, the horses shifted, prancing in place, making the carriage sway.

"Let me be blunt as a dull knife, Katie. You will *not* follow us. Give me your word on this, lass." Toby smiled. Or we'll leave you home next time. And don't give me that pouting face. This is a flowery dell of your own making."

"Flowery dell?" Collin raised an eyebrow.

"Prison cell."

"Good one, old chap!" Collin clapped enthusiastically. "Mark my words, Katie. Disobey our orders and you'll be doing needlework in a rose arbor, or some such thing."

"Mustn't paper bag her, Collin," Toby chuckled, then swiveled to Katie. "What's it to be, lass?"

Katie folded her arms across her chest. She had a childish urge to stick her tongue out at both of them, but glared hard at Toby instead, hoping to convey the frosty promise that she wasn't about to back down. Her father's words flashed in her mind. *"When backed into a corner, Kit-Kat, never concede, only negotiate."* Her father had been a litigator before he switched careers to become a classics professor. And he always called her Kit-Kat.

"Okay. Here's the deal." Katie dragged her eyes from Toby's and stared out the window at a toothless man standing on the corner selling canaries from a cage attached to a shepherd's staff. The smell of cider vinegar and horse sweat reached her nostrils and she scrunched up her nose.

"I'll promise," she snapped, "under one condition. When you return, you swear to tell me everything. Every last detail. Whatever Dora tells you, whatever Dora says, whatever Dora does, I want to hear it. A full recounting. Everything. Every last —"

"Even if she bats them beautiful mince pies at me?" Toby teased, sunlight slanting across his face highlighting the scar on his cheek.

Katie wrenched her gaze from his scar and glowered. *"Especially* if she bats her eyes at you." Why had she said that? Katie wondered. "Er...not that I care," she added. "But it might be part of her M.O."

When both boys looked puzzled, Katie quickly explained, *"Modus operandi.* That's Latin for mode of operation —"

"Don't you mean *modi operandi?"* Toby corrected. *"Modes* of operation? Dora Fowler has more than one method of maneuvering. She's got a temptress bag full of tricks at her disposal."

"Whatever." Katie rolled her eyes. "Just report back everything."

Chapter Thirty-three

Gargoyles and Canaries
say the Bells of St. Mary's

RELIEVED TO HAVE KATIE well away from him, Toby accelerated his stride down Clavell Street, Collin barreling along close behind.

With the church spire of St. Mary's to the west and blue sky above, London Hospital rose up in the distance like a grim mausoleum, and Toby could well imagine that on its rooftop consumptive patients were stretched out on cots taking the sun cure, just as his mother had.

The only redeeming feature of the hospital, Toby knew, was its roof on sun-drenched mornings. Otherwise, the pain and poverty inside those stone walls was intensified by fog and rain and bitter cold, with nary a bottle of medicine in sight. It was a beggar's hospital, dismal as a prison, where the poor were shuffled off to die.

Toby stared at the hospital's jagged façade, remembering a freak show performer who was a patient there. Joseph Merrick, nicknamed the Elephant Man, had confided in Toby that his greatest desire was to be taken to a sanatorium for the blind so that he might meet a woman who wouldn't be repulsed by his deformities. Someone who would love him for his watch and chain. His brain.

But was such a thing possible? Toby wondered as he and Collin continued down the street past a shriveled old man with puckered skin begging at the crosswalk. Was it possible to find a girl — a *wife* — who cared only for your mind, not for the accident of your birth or the deformities on your face?

Toby wasn't vain. He cared little for his appearance, hardly giving it a thought. Yet he wondered whether Katie felt repulsed when she looked at him so challengingly, so openly, at the sight of the scar on his cheek, or his pugilist nose. Did she mind that the Duke had called him the son of a whore? Toby pushed such thoughts away. What cared he for Katie's opinion? She was the Duke's goddaughter, not some Cockney lass he had any right to lust after. Toby would never be a gentleman, never be accepted into the society that was her birthright.

He cursed himself for his lack of discipline. He was acting like a besotted schoolboy who alternately wanted to kiss the twist 'n' swirl and strangle her.

At the slaughterhouse, he had wanted the latter. He had seethed with a blind fury when he realized Katie had followed him into the maggot-infested barn. It had taken all his self-restraint not to drag her out kicking and screaming, but that would only have drawn attention to the situation. And one slip of that accursed tongue of hers, one argument from those bee-swollen ruby lips, would have exposed Katie for the girl that she was — a porkpie thrummer with nary a blemish to her skin, nor crooked tooth in her smile.

Damn her eyes! She was the devil's own daughter disguised as an angel sent to torment his every waking moment.

But she had courage, Toby had to admit. Katie wasn't some simpering highborn aristocrat, ready to swoon at sights that might fell a grown man. *Yet she was bloody exasperating!* Determined, too, and hopelessly enthusiastic about tracking down a crazed killer.

Toby fervently wished that Katie were mad. Marbles and conkers. Bonkers as a lunatic at full moon. But if her premonitions were right, if other girls were destined to be butchered by a man named Jack, Toby had to do everything in his power to stop it. Even if that meant spending more time with the most maddening ham shank he'd ever met.

A thought occurred to him. He could easily determine if Katie was daft as a barn owl. Why hadn't he thought of it before? *He'd take her to Traitors' Gate.*

Clavell Street Market, better known as Bird and Feather Alley, wasn't a market at all but a cobbled lane spanning several blocks of brick tenements where stalls of bird sellers stretched all the way to Commercial Road.

Toby and Collin pressed past a man auctioning cockatiels, another selling starlings, still another peddling smelling-salts made from macaw beaks, in little brown bottles.

"Here y'are lad, four a penny." A man so bald his head glistened in the sunlight stepped toward Collin, holding out duck eggs in a leather pouch.

Further along, an old woman in a straw hat with a tame rat on her shoulder claimed to be selling nightingale powder that relieved warts in less than three minutes. Toby tugged Collin along by the sleeve.

They made their way past tier upon tier of cages hung on the brick sidewalls, filled with cockatiels, macaws, ducks, doves, canaries, blackbirds, turkeys, swallows, and screaming parrots. The crooked lane was a cacophony of chirps, warbles, honks, and squawks cleaving the air like a chorus of discordant bells.

Toby glanced around. Although he much preferred this crooked lane of bird sellers to the slaughterhouse, he didn't take pleasure in seeing so many caged creatures.

Not so Collin, who seemed to be immensely enjoying the loud squawking, preening, and bobbing heads of so many birds.

"I say!" Collin beamed. "Rawther like the avian arcade in Regents Park, only tenfold as loud! When we tell Katie what she's missed, she'll be madder than a wet" — He glanced up at the roosters perched high above on the window sills. — "chicken." He laughed. "Jolly good show, this."

Toby threaded through the crowd, making his way toward a middle-aged woman surrounded by parakeets in wicker cages. Mrs. Fowler, Dora's mother, was seated beneath a striped awning, and to Toby she looked like one of her crimson-fronted birds. As she cocked her head and winked, Mrs. Fowler's beaklike nose poked out from a narrow face; and her hair, dyed a garish purple-red, hung in a low swoop across her forehead, dwarfing her features. Next to Mrs. Fowler's, Collin's ginger hair seemed almost subdued.

Toby tipped his cap and asked Mrs. Fowler where her extremely pretty daughter, Dora, could be located. Mrs. Fowler, beaming at the compliment, pointed to a parrot stall a block away. "That's Dora's kit over yonder, across the way from the rhubarb man."

Toby thanked her, and he and Collin shot down the street. The air was so chokingly thick with molting feathers and bird droppings it was hard to breathe. To their left, St. Paul's Cathedral perched like a great broody hen at the top of Cannon Street. Toby chuckled at the image of the most famous landmark in London appearing like a hen. But the images of birds, including that of Mrs. Fowler, were pervasive, the street being chock-full of them. Great ones, small ones, exotic ones, and ordinary ones in all colors of the rainbow.

Shadows bounced off the brick tenement walls behind the bird stalls, swooping overhead like birds of prey. Lengthening his stride, Toby counted seven black-lead boot-scrapers set into the door stoops until he came to the rhubarb-hawk man across the street from Dora's parrot stall.

As they approached, Dora began batting her dark, silky lashes above enormous velvet-brown eyes, the lids of which shimmered with a paint-pot full of pigments, making them appear brilliant and alive, and as colorful as her birds.

At the inquest Dora had worn the merest hint of makeup. Today she had dabbed on too much rouge, lip-salve, and a thick eyebrow penciling that, together with her sparkling eyelids, made her look like a gypsy queen about to dance below a harvest moon.

"Tobias!" Dora squealed, glancing from Toby to Collin and batting her lashes. She made a delicate attempt at clearing her throat, the air was so thick with bird dander.

"'Morning, Dora." Toby grinned.

"A pleasure, I'm sure," Dora continued in a cooing voice, the spongy layers of her hair, beneath her large plumed hat, bobbing up and down. "What brings you to me humble place o' business, Tobias? You being such a grand toff these days. La-di-da. But then, I'm a lady if ever there was one. Saw yer oglin' me at the inquest." She cleared her throat again, then, forgetting ladylike manners, coughed loudly and spat onto the street.

"Come on, now. Rest yer plates of meat." Dora flashed an amiable smile and patted the stool next to her.

With lightning speed, Collin plunked himself onto the stool and stared at Dora like a lovesick calf. Stretching out his lanky legs and clasping his hands behind his head, he gave a half-whistle in appreciation of Dora's beauty. Several caged parrots returned his whistle in kind, but the sound was disgruntled and shrill.

Toby raised an eyebrow at Collin, then began to converse with Dora in a flirtatious tone, trying to wheedle information about Mary Ann Nichols. Behind them, a large parrot in a domed cage made sounds like a purring cat.

Dora extended one gloved hand and placed it on Collin's thigh, but kept her eyes fastened on Toby. "Yer sly as a fox, Tobias. Don't be trying to sweet talk me. Even clever boys like you ain't no match for the likes of me."

Across the street, the rhubarb man sat eating tea biscuits and bawling out the price of his hawks over the heads of the people walking past.

"T'weren't trying to sweet talk you, Dora," Toby laughed.

Just then, a portly man in a bowler hat strolled into Dora's stall. "You got any talking parrots, little lady?" he asked in an American accent.

"Yes, sir! Right here, sir." Dora directed his attention to a scarlet parrot perched in the nearest cage.

"Hello, Polly," Dora sing-songed, waggling a gloved finger at the bird. "And how are you on this here fine morning?"

With the skill of a circus performer, Dora began to bluff the customer by imitating parrot talk. "'joyed me breakfas this mawning. 'joyed me breakfas."

Dora swiveled back to the man. "Pretty Poll says she enjoyed her breakfast."

"Hello. Hello." The bird seemed to squawk, but it was really Dora throwing her voice with the skill of a ventriloquist.

"Listen to Pretty Poll!" Dora cried in feigned amazement. "Pretty Poll? What's yer name? Tell this nice gent yer name."

"Pretty Poll. Pretty Poll," the bird seemed to screech. "Take me home ter the Missus. Pretty Poll! Pretty Poll!"

Toby flashed Dora a wide grin. Dora's voice trick, Toby knew, was made easier due to the large bonnet she wore, the ribbon beneath her chin hiding the warble of muscles up and down her throat. Most Cockneys learned to throw their voices at an early age, but Dora had perfected the art. She barely moved her lips.

"Splendid!" cried the American man. "I'll take her. It's providence that this bird should know that my wife has been after me for a talking bird. The missus wants company. And now she'll have it. How much?"

"Ten bob. Twelve wiff the cage, sir."

"Twelve shillings is a bit steep." He frowned and shook his head.

"Well, sir! She's expensive because she talks. Can't do better than Pretty Poll. Comes direct from deepest Africa. A rare find, she is. And seeing as she's me favorite...if yer promise to treat her kindly, yer can have Polly wiff 'er cage complete for eleven bob. Ain't none of me birds as talkative as Pretty Poll, ain't that right, Poll?" Dora turned to the bird.

"*How d'do, I'm Pretty Poll. Take me 'ome to the missus. Take me home. Take me home.*"

"Delightful!" cried the man, counting out eleven shillings, plus sixpence for seed. "A true bird of paradise." He clasped the cage and ambled away, talking to the bird all the while. "Hello there, Pretty Polly. Say how d'do to daddy. Say hello. Don't be shy."

"Eeeeeekkkkkkkkkkkk!" squawked the parrot all the way down the lane.

Toby roared with laughter and took off his hat to Dora, a true Cockney compliment.

Dora giggled.

Collin rubbed his chin, watching Polly and the man disappear down the street. "You must be sad to see her go. Takes time to train a bird like that. She went cheap at eleven shillings. You'll need to be a shrewder bargainer in the future, Dora."

"Blimey! Not a bit of it!" Dora swatted her hand playfully against Collin's sleeve. "That bird's good for nothink 'cept plucking. Can't say a blessed thing. Dumb as a doorpost. Got six of 'em, I has, what can't say a word." She motioned to her birds. "Me smart one over there I calls Prudence, on account of it's me favorite name."

"Mine, too!" Collin seemed overjoyed at the happy coincidence.

Toby glanced at the stall next to Dora's, stacked with yellow cardboard boxes, each holding a dozen newly hatched chicks. In the stall to the left, Minorcas and Leghorns were selling at seven shillings a box.

Toby took a deep breath. Through a combination of flattery and wheedling, it took him several minutes before he got Dora to open up about the murdered girl.

"Me poor Mary Ann was quite a beauty afore Mad Willy knocked her teeff out." Dora dabbed at her sparkly eyes.

"Why would anyone do such a dreadful thing?" Collin asked, leaning close.

"Mad Willy was jealous, tha's why. Mary Ann was getting her fair share of attention from a gentleman toff at the tavern where she worked. Proper gentleman toff he was, too. Mary Ann liked to crow about it every chance she got." Dora's face darkened. "Tried putting on airs even wiff me, she did." Dora shifted her position on the stool so her thigh was touching Collin's. Then she pitched her voice high in imitation of Mary Ann:

"'Look here, Dora!' says Mary Ann to me, 'ain't I a fine lady now? I got right lovely clothes, a goodly sum of the ready, and me gentleman friend says there's lots more where that comes from.'" The faintest shadow of a smile touched Dora's lips. "Didn't do Mary Ann no good now, did it?"

"A toff, you say?" Toby pressed. "You know his name, don't you?"

"I might and I may and that's really no rum 'n' coke," Dora sing-songed the nursery rhyme. "'sides, this toff didn't want to do the nasty wiff Mary Ann, just wanted to talk wiff 'er. Imagine that! What a lark, getting a bit of money for nothink in return."

Toby produced a shiny coin from his vest pocket.

A glimmer of a smile crossed Dora's lips. "Two more of them bob and I'll tell you right proper."

Toby tugged out one more coin and, flipping it between his fingers, made the pair dance over and under his knuckles. Dora swiped at the coins and pocketed them.

"Toff's name be Oscar Wilde. Mr. Oscar Wilde. Proper toff 'e is, too."

Toby's eyes went round with surprise. "And the tavern where Mary Ann worked, t'was the Fish and Kettle, eh?"

"Not by a long shot. It be the Cock and Bull on Flower 'n' Dean, near Brick Lane."

Toby's face was inscrutable when he asked, "Do you know Dark Annie?"

"Lor'! Course I do. She be my cousin's bag o' strife."

"His wife?"

"Tha's right. Afore Rufus Chapman got chived, Dark Annie was his wife. She's a lucky one. Gets me cousin's soldier's pension, she does. Lives like a princess wiff her very own digs over on Broom Street. Lucky girl."

"Dark Annie...is Annie Chapman?"

"Course she is, Toby! Lord, you're as thick as molasses on a frosty morning."

Chapter Thirty-four

Death Knells and Fate say the Tower Bells of Traitors' Gate

THE TOWER OF LONDON was built by William the Conqueror in the year 1078. Featuring a wide moat, and inner and outer fortress walls, the historic castle had alternately been a royal palace, a prison, and a place of execution. With few exceptions it looked precisely as it did in Katie's own time, including the armory, which held the crown jewels of England.

Katie drew in her breath and stared at the imposing structure, its ramparts gleaming white against the startling grey stones of the battlements. Yesterday Toby and Collin had visited Dora Fowler while Katie sat in the carriage. Today, Toby and Katie were alone. Collin was lunching with Lady Beatrix and Oscar Wilde at the Thespian Club, trying to ascertain why the famous writer had been garnering Mary Ann Nichols's favors before she was brutally murdered.

Toby gestured. "Admission to see the lions in the royal menagerie, behind that gate there" — he pointed — "is the sum of three half-pence, or the supply of a cat or dog."

"A cat or a dog?"

"For feeding the lions, leopards, and lynxes."

"What?" Katie gasped. She was pretty sure there were no animals left behind the castle walls in the twenty-first century, except for the ravens.

"Not to worry, luv. Lady Beatrix is heading the committee for animal welfare. She wants to transport the big cats to the Zoological Society in Regent's Park."

"I hope she's successful." Katie nodded, but couldn't contain a shudder thinking about feeding time.

"So you don't fancy going to the West Tower and paying three half-pence . . . or a dog?" Toby laughed.

"That is not funny." Katie crossed her arms and made a face. "Can we change the subject, please?"

Toby grinned. "Beatrix wants to feed them grain. Imagine! Feeding a lion barley corn and hay! As the guv'nor would say: *Bosh!*"

"Tell me about Traitors' Gate and the Tower," Katie said, hoping to divert the conversation away from lion food.

"Right. Let's see . . . what can I tell a Yank that you wouldn't already know?" He scratched his chin, but there was a spark of humor in his eyes. "Her Majesty doesn't reside in the Tower of London, like in the old days, but the fortress is still owned by the crown. The outer stone wall completely encloses an inner barricade wall, creating a double defense against attack. Should an enemy attack on English soil, the Queen will be dispatched here for protection." Toby cleared his throat. "Prisoners arriving at the Tower were brought by boat along the Thames River, there." He pointed to the gray swath of muddy water rippling against the embankment they were walking upon. "The condemned would first pass under London Bridge, where the severed heads of the recently executed would be displayed on spikes." With a mischievous grin, he made a slashing gesture across his throat. "Think of the shock of seeing those dangling heads, knowing *yours* would soon be one of them."

Toby pointed to a corner tower rising above the muddy moat. "Behind those walls rode kings and knights in shining armor. Lady Jane Grey's ghost is said to prowl the grounds of the inner fortress. Can't you just see the jousting tournaments? Medieval ladies tossing their garters? The blazing torches? The chanting? Cockneys say if you listen closely you can hear the echoes of arrows whizzing past, bugles sounding, and the clank of armor weighing down the horses as they thud across the field. Whenever I'm here I always imagine the prisoners mounting the steps to put their heads upon the chopping block. Anne Boleyn, Sir Thomas More, Queen Catherine Howard."

Toby swiveled his gaze and pointed. "Look there at those slits for windows in the battlement walls. Makes you wonder at all the prisoners who gazed out, praying for their freedom."

Katie blinked up to where Toby was pointing and had an instant, terrifying image of severed heads on metal spikes, like the ones at Madame Tussauds. She pushed the thought away.

They were almost at Traitors' Gate. There was a chill in the air and a mist rising off the river to their right. After the Duke's carriage had dropped them off at Castle Hill, Toby and Katie had walked down to the river and were moving toward Traitors' Gate, the waterway entrance into the Tower of London.

"Cockneys believe that on chilly days a smoky mist creeps up from the river showing the faces of the executed, mouths crying out for help. Then these apparitions dissolve upward into the battlements. The last thing a convicted traitor would see before his head came off was the flight of a *black raven*, sacred bird of the Tower."

"Are you quite done? Because if you're trying to scare me, you're not succeeding. I've been here before, several times. I probably know as much of the history of this place as you do."

"You only arrived in England last week, luv. I was under the impression that this was your first time at the Tower of London."

"No. I mean, yes. What I mean is, I haven't actually been here, *here*. I've read about being here. And...well...there's a small re-creation of the Tower of London outside Boston, and I've been *there*."

"Outside Boston?"

"In Concord, Massachusetts. Right next to the Minuteman reenactment of our Revolutionary War," Katie lied.

Toby shot her a skeptical look. "A re-creation of the Tower of London?"

"It's kind of smaller. Like a doll house, only bigger."

"A doll house of the Tower of London in America? Will wonders never cease. You ham shanks amaze me. Are y' pulling my leg again?" Toby asked, lapsing into his Cockney accent.

"We Yanks amaze ourselves."

"Why replicate the Tower of London?"

Katie shrugged. "For money, I guess. They charge people to see it. Don't look so surprised. Someday we Yanks might even replicate London Bridge...or buy it out from under you."

Toby laughed. "Ham shanks owning London Bridge? When monkeys fly to the moon."

"That, too," Katie muttered under her breath as Toby took her elbow and steered her forward down the gravel path skirting the water.

"I'd best tell you about the Oracle of Traitors' Gate. Her name is Mrs. Traitor." Toby's voice echoed against the lapping waves.

"Mrs. Traitor? At Traitors' Gate? Doesn't that seem a bit —"

"Fanciful?"

"Coincidental?"

"Not a bit of it. Mrs. Fowler, Dora's mum, goes by the name of Fowler because she sells fowl, as did her mum and her mum before her. Her family name is not Fowler, nor is Dora's. It's the way it works. You have your Christian name and your professional name. Lots of the yeoman warders behind these tower walls are known to their mates as "Mr. Yeoman." Same for tailors, potters, sailors, carters, wheelwrights. It's the old way of things. The Oracle of Traitors' Gate has been called

Mrs. Tray, short for Traitor, for so long, no one knows her true name. Rumor has it that her ancestors came here to be executed."

"Why not call her Mrs. Oracle?"

"That would be daft, now, wouldn't it? She's been standing outside Traitors' Gate for her whole life. People cross her palm with silver and she tells them what they want to know."

Toby went on to explain that he had visited Mrs. Tray yesterday to find out who Dark Annie was and where she lived. "Mrs. Tray knows every single Cockney who resides within earshot of the bells of Saint Mary Le Bow. She told me what Dora told me. Dark Annie is Annie Chapman and lives in Shoreditch on a soldier's pension from her late husband. Ten to one that's where Georgie Cross is hiding. I'm paying them a surprise visit tonight."

"I'm coming, too," said Katie, avoiding his eyes.

"Not a chance, lass. And don't argue. Now, about Mrs. Tray. Be polite, don't gawk at her. Even though she's blind, she sees everything. She's a true mystic, a genuine clairvoyant, *not a counterfeit.*" He stared pointedly at Katie who shot him back a "who me?" look.

"Mrs. Tray is the seventh child of a seventh child. Rumor has it her auntie poked out her eyes so people would believe she had 'the gift' and pay good coin for her predictions."

"Now you're pulling *my* leg. You don't honestly mean to tell me that her *own aunt* poked out her —" Katie stopped. She remembered the movie *Slumdog Millionaire* where the child's eyes had been burned with acid the better for him to beg money in the streets.

"That's just rumor, luv. No one knows the truth about old Mrs. Tray. She earns large sums advising Cockneys who come here to Traitors' Gate to ask for advice. She wears rings on every finger worth countless sums, and no one dares rob her because she can put a hex on any man alive."

"No one can hex someone. That's superstitious nonsense."

"T'isn't. But whether she can or not is irrelevant. Cockneys *believe* it to be true. That's all that matters. And there's not a one amongst us that would dispute her predictions."

As they approached Traitors' Gate, Katie saw mist rising off the Thames, shrouding the arched entrance in a blanket of grey vapor. A stone causeway leading up from the river was slick with green moss. Katie shivered. Traitors' Gate was so ancient, but still held something deadly about it. She could almost hear the whispering of sighs and the stamp of long-ago footfalls ringing in the hollow beneath the arch.

She glanced up.

Traitors' Gateway was a long, thick wall of flattened grey stones rising forty feet into the air. The gate itself was an archway of stones set into the wall, the upper reaches curved and funneled like a dark train tunnel. The air was moist and smelled as dank as a wet basement.

Originally, this entrance had been the water gateway into the Tower. The river had flowed under the stone arch so that barges and boats could sail through to moorings on the other side. In this century, heavy reinforcements of oak timbers and vertical bars closed it all off to the public, with the Thames wharf built up beyond, and the vast moat on either side no longer filled with water, but swampy mud. In Katie's own century it would be filled with green grass.

Even in the blurry mist, Katie could see the metal spikes on top of the gate and the iron fence in the distance. No one could enter the Tower from this gate unless ordered by the Queen. Katie took hold of the iron railings, wet with slime, and glanced through the tunnel-like entranceway.

Slow footsteps approached from the wharf, accompanied by shuffling and wheezing. An old woman in a crinoline skirt, black bonnet, and short velvet cape appeared from out of the mist.

"Tobias!" There spread across the woman's face a look of pure delight. "Tobias! Is that you?"

"Yes, ma'am." Toby took off his cap and made a slight bow.

The old woman shuffled closer, rubbing her hands together. Her black cloak, lined in red, gleamed against her jeweled hands. Her face showed a watchful tension as she peered sightless in Katie's direction. As she stepped closer, the sun peeked through the clouds above Traitors' Gate, etching flat shadows of the iron bars onto the ground across their path. Far away and muffled, one of the tower clocks began to toll the hour.

Katie's first impression of the Oracle of Traitors' Gate was one of pity. The old woman was hobbled and sightless, her eyes as misted and foggy as the vapor rising off the river. When she beamed in Toby's direction, the animation in her wrinkled face made her look cheerful and kind-hearted, like a fairy godmother in a Disney movie. Katie half expected a magic wand to appear from the folds of her hooped skirt.

"Tobias?" The woman called out again, her voice like a tinkling bell as she groped the air searching for him.

"Mrs. Tray," Toby said, stepping closer so she could take his arm.

"I knew 'twas you, lad," she chuckled. "You have such a strong presence. There's an aura about you: great blazes of purple and blue as of the wind before a storm. Just like your father. Never did such storm clouds roil around a man as your father, though he be highborn true enough. *Your mum now*, she was a gentle lass . . . I always knew her by the sound a petal makes when it falls to the ground. *God rest her soul.*"

Mrs. Tray patted Toby's arm. "I knew you'd be back. You were troubled yesterday. Tell me what's in your heart, lad, and I'll tell you what's to be."

"There's someone I'd like you to meet, ma'am. She's visiting from America."

Mrs. Tray nodded and the waves of her snow-white hair beneath the black bonnet puffed around her cheeks like fluffy clouds. "Bring her tomorrow, then."

"She's here with me now."

"Who?"

"The lass I'd like you to meet."

There was a long, silent pause. The old woman appeared bewildered, then she leaned closer, scrutinizing Toby's face with earnest, sightless eyes. It was this eager earnestness that made Katie's heart constrict.

"I think not," the Oracle said gently.

"I beg your pardon, ma'am?" Toby's eyebrows shot up. "Would you like us to come back tomorrow?"

Mrs. Tray must have caught something plaintive or worried in Toby's voice, for she lifted and lowered her bejeweled fingers as if feeling something in the air. "Tomorrow, lad. I should very much like to meet your friend. When the Tower clock chimes half after eleven o'clock, bring her here to me. Now, what else can I do for you?"

"The lass is with me. Standing by my side."

"She's not, Tobias." There was the sound of a dog barking in the distance, or perhaps the faint roar of a lion from behind Traitors' Gate.

"Ma'am . . . ?"

"Bring her tomorrow, there's a good lad."

The old woman's words sent a chill up Katie's spine.

"But she's here, Mrs. Tray! Right here. Perhaps you can't sense her because she's not a Cockney. I should have thought of that."

The old woman's sightless eyes flickered around like darting pinwheels as if trying to locate Katie. "Tobias, my son. There is no one here but the two of us. I would sense a third person, see their aura . . . whether they be friend or foe, Cockney or no."

The silence that followed these puzzling words was finally broken by Toby's firm, insistent voice. "Begging your pardon, ma'am, but Miss Katherine is standing next to me, as real as you or I."

"I . . . think . . . not . . . Tobias," the Oracle said softly and with great hesitation.

The color drained so swiftly from Toby's face, Katie reached out to him. She wondered if Mrs. Tray knew the effect she was having on him.

"You think Katherine's not here?" he said doggedly, sharply.

"There's nobody here, Tobias. Nobody at all."

"As I live and breathe, ma'am," Toby sputtered defiantly. "Her name's Katherine and she's alive and present as the moon and the stars."

"Not a bit of it. Whoever she is, she's not real, my lad."

"*Let's go!*" Katie whispered, shrinking back into the shadows.

Toby stood rigid. "Do you mean to make a riddle of this, Mrs. Tray? Are you saying Katherine's not real and never will be to me because of our different stations in life? Or are you saying she's not long for this world?"

"If one be alive or one be dead...yes. Is she very pretty, then? This imaginary friend of yours?"

Toby uttered a small, harsh laugh. "She's not imaginary, ma'am." He turned to Katie. "Say something."

"Hello, Mrs. Tray. It's a pleasure to meet you." Something scraped above on the sloping wall. A raven black as night, with a wing span as wide as an eagle's, flapped noisily.

"I'm from Boston," Katie continued. "I'm visiting the Twyford family. Toby has been kind enough to help me. Show me the sights." Katie babbled on until, with a startled realization, she whispered, "You can't hear me, ma'am, can you?"

"Not feeling well today, Mrs. Tray?" Toby asked, a desperate note in his voice.

"Perfectly well, Tobias. Thank you."

"You really can't see or hear her?" he demanded.

Mrs. Tray's wrinkled lips compressed. "There's nobody with us, Tobias. I promise you, lad. There's no draught. No sense of another human being. We're alone."

Katie had an idea. "Toby? If she can't hear me, try this. Tell her I've recently come from the London Stone. Just do it, Toby. *Mention the London Stone!*"

"Now look here!" Toby bristled. "The two of you are talking gibberish."

"Toby, *please*. Tell her I arrived from...or rather, I've touched the Raven's Claw fissure in the London Stone. I'll explain everything later."

When Toby did so, Mrs. Tray's hands clamped over her heart. "Oh, dear. Oh, dear. Oh, dear!" Her voice rose with shattering loudness, then fell away. "Oh, dear me. Tobias, I feel bound to warn you —"

"Warn me?"

The old woman's eyes, though sightless, gleamed like shards of splintered glass.

"This girl is not who she claims to be. I've encountered this before. Terrible ordeal. Terrible."

"She's an impostor? Is that what you're saying?" Toby's face hardened.

Katie gasped. She hadn't realized she'd been holding her breath. "*Toby, please, let's get out of here!*"

"Mrs. Tray?" Toby asked, blinking suspiciously at Katie. "What do you mean? She's not who she claims to be?"

"She's just not from our world."

Toby sighed. "That's right, ma'am. *Katie's from America.*"

"Not this world, Tobias. Not *our* world." Mrs. Tray's words fell with a heavy, chilling weight.

Toby thrust out his jaw and began to argue. "'Course she's not from our world, Mrs. Tray. She's from across the sea, but that doesn't mean Katie's not alive and present. Just means she's not from here."

The Oracle of Traitors' Gate shook her head. "Not from here. Not from there. Not from anywhere. Mind your step, Tobias. Mind your heart. Protect yourself, my lad. I was very young when first I encountered a person of the Stone. I sense danger, Tobias. Hidden danger darting along my nerves." Her voice quavered.

Katie felt an overwhelming sense of claustrophobia. Flickers of sunlight slanted across the wet stones at the bottom of the Tower wall. Tentacles of light picked out iridescent slime and moss on the rock formations.

In the distance a train whistle shrilled and echoed and died away. Katie had a strong feeling of déjà vu, almost as if she were back inside Madame Tussauds. She glanced up at the vines clinging to the brickwork below the battlements just as a peal of bells rang out, startling her.

"A pity about Dark Annie. Such a horrid way to die," came Mrs. Tray's church organ voice, which sounded to Katie surprisingly like the hologram woman at Madame Tussauds. She peered closer at the old woman. With her white hair tucked under a lace cap and her soft skin wrinkled like an apple, Mrs. Tray was the spitting image of the hologram woman from the museum!

"What did you say, Mrs. Tray?" asked Toby. "Did you say Dark Annie? She's going to die? I asked you about her yesterday. I wanted to know where she lived. Is that why you spoke of her just now?"

Katie grabbed Toby's sleeve and yanked. "Ask her if she knows anyone named Llewellyn. *Mrs. Llewellyn.*" That was the name of the hologram woman.

Toby turned grimly toward the old woman. "My friend from America is asking if you know a woman by the name of Mrs. Llewellyn."

"Gracious me!" cried the Oracle. "How extraordinary! Ask your young friend why she would inquire after Amanda Llewellyn."

Katie said quickly to Toby, "Tell her a woman from my world...er, sort of...looks almost identical to Mrs. Tray. It can't be a coincidence."

"What is she saying, Tobias?" insisted the other, staring in Katie's direction, breathless with wonder as if looking up at the moon. Or through the moon, from the cloudy formations in her sightless eyes.

"Katie says you resemble a woman named Mrs. Llewellyn. She's wondering if it's a coincidence."

"Oh, my, how delightful!" beamed Mrs. Tray. "Amanda Llewellyn is my sister. And do you know, Tobias? It's been years since anyone commented on the resemblance. Oh, this tickles me to no end. Amanda was a great beauty in her day. But, Tobias, is my sister involved in any-thing unsavory? She's married to a bothersome, swaggering man, the police surgeon Dr. Ralph Llewellyn, but still. . .I shouldn't have thought that Amanda would be mixed up with a Stone person. Oh, Tobias! Ask your friend. Is Amanda in any danger?"

Toby blinked several times. "*But you're the bleeding Ora —!*" The fierce defensiveness in his voice died away. "Er, excuse me, ma'am." He swiveled around to glare at Katie. "Answer the question."

Katie shook her head and raised her shoulders up and down. "Dunno. I don't think so."

"There *are* two of you!" Mrs. Tray clapped her hands together. "I feel it now!" She peered at them through foggy eyes. "Yes. It's clear to me. One of you has traveled a great distance to get here. So great a distance I couldn't perceive it at first. Not from our world, to be sure, but here nevertheless."

Toby sighed as if frustrated that they were going around and around in a circle. "Thank you for your time, Mrs. Tray. But I think we'd best be getting on. Good day to you, ma'am."

"Tobias, wait! When people come from the Stone, it's always about death. *Always about murder.*"

"People...from a stone? I don't understand." Toby scratched his temple. "They come *from* a stone? What does that mean? Are you saying Katie's not human? Not real?"

"People — ?" blurted Katie. "How many others?"

"Quite real, I'm sure," answered Mrs. Tray. "They always come here with the intent of doing good deeds, righting despicable wrongs. But often they are misguided. Misaligned, as it were."

"So I should have nothing more to do with the lass?" Toby demanded.

"I can't tell you what to do, Tobias. I can only caution you to tread carefully. Your friend may have good intentions, but the road to the underworld is paved with such intents, *hmm?*"

"I'll cast her out, then. Tell her to go to the devil." Toby's hand closed around one of the spikes of the iron gate.

"Not a bit of it, Tobias. Follow your heart. She is here, but she can change the course of events only with the help of someone from this world. *Our world.* She can't do it herself."

"*This world?* What are you saying? There's another world other than ours?"

"My dear Tobias. There are infinite worlds. Yes. I believe you must help her, because I sense that you *want* to help her. But be cautioned, young Tobias. Beware of what you wish for, *what she wishes for!* In the end it may all come to naught...or perhaps this time destiny *shall* be altered. We can only hope, for the sake of those poor girls —"

"What poor girls?"

"The ones about to be slaughtered."

"So there really is a mad man out there? Someone about to butcher innocent girls?"

"Tobias. Hear me well. I can only know what you know. I can't predict the future. I see what you see, I feel what you feel. Everything I ascertain is because I pick up the feelings, the senses, the ideas from . . . you. Somewhere inside you, you believe that a mad man will begin to slaughter innocent women. I'm discerning this from you as strongly as a vibrating, pulsing heartbeat. And if it's true, I hope that you and this young lady from the London Stone will try to stop the carnage. It's your destiny."

Toby's eyes blazed at the mention of destiny. "Just for clarification, Mrs. Tray. You believe that Katie is an impostor, not of our world, and though she has good intentions, the outcome she wishes to see — that of stopping a man named Jack the Ripper from murdering women — is not altogether possible?"

"Everything is possible, Tobias. Follow your heart. But treat everyone as if they would do you harm."

"*Especially Katie?* Is that what you're saying?"

"People from the Stone mean us no harm, Tobias. I don't believe she would hurt you or anyone else. Stone people rarely do."

"What the deuce are you saying? That she has a heart of stone, perhaps? Is that it? Is that what you're trying to warn me about?"

"A person of the Stone. From the Stone. Through the Stone. She doesn't belong here. She's not real." Mrs. Tray raised her jeweled hands, and the rubies and emeralds winked in the sunlight. "Most men to their credit — or discredit — fall in love with an imaginary someone, rather than a real someone, Tobias. The real is often rather gritty. Stone people *do* have that advantage."

Mrs. Tray whispered something in Toby's ear.

Katie tugged at Toby's sleeve "Toby. Ask Mrs. Tray how many others have been here before me?"

"I won't." Toby shook his head stubbornly. "To do so would be to admit that you're from another planet."

"I promise you, Toby, I'm from *this* planet, just like you. I'm not an alien from Mars. I've traveled a great distance to get here, that's all. The one thing I can tell you, though, with my hand on my heart, is I'm alive. I live and breathe. And I'm real in the here and now."

"That's not *all* you're going to confess to me, lass. When we leave here, you're going to explain yourself. *You're going to tell me everything!* Even if I have to hit the great bloody London Stone over your thick skull, I'll have answers!"

"Oh, dear me. Dear, dear me. Tobias. Such a temper. There shall be no hitting of stones upon anyone's head. Is that clear, young man?"

"Crystal clear, ma'am," Toby said through gritted teeth.

Chapter Thirty-five

Steam Coal and Fame
say the Bells of Mark Lane

"ALL RIGHT THEN," Toby said, a harsh edge to his voice. His mouth was drawn down, his eyes fixed on Katie. "We can walk several miles back to Twyford Manor, or" — his face broke into a twisted, almost devious smile — "we can take the Underground Railway."

From the way Toby was glaring, Katie knew he was challenging her. She remembered reading about the first subway trains in London and how people were frightened to ride them. Was that it? Was Toby trying to scare her into telling him who she was and where she came from?

Katie raised her chin. The last thing she was afraid of was the Metro System. She'd ridden the Tube so often she could almost do it blindfolded. How difficult could it be in this century? If Toby expected her to cower, he was mistaken.

"Let's take the Underground!" she said breezily, and by the surprised look on his face, Katie knew she'd been right. Proper young ladies probably wilted dead away at the thought of traveling below ground. She bit back a smile. Toby was so transparent.

"Are you *sure*, luv?" A hint of disbelief, or was that derision, in his voice?

"Of course." Katie pulled an innocent face.

"Most twist 'n' swirls are afraid to go down into the subterranean bowels of Hades."

"Not me." Katie smiled sweetly. "Won't bother me one bit."

Toby definitely had something up his sleeve. Katie could sense it. But if he was planning on frightening her into revealing what she knew about the London Stone, it wasn't going to work. She'd offer him a portion of the truth. She had to. But as far as she was concerned, Toby was on a need-to-know basis, and he didn't need to know. At least not everything. Mrs. Tray had said that people from the Stone could not change the course of events by themselves. Which was why Katie needed Toby's help. But Katie also knew, with the razor-sharp certainty of a dagger at her throat, that if she told Toby she had traveled back in time, he'd think she was crazy. What's more, he might even try to thwart her efforts to stop Jack the Ripper.

No, Katie couldn't risk it.

After leaving Traitors' Gate, Katie and Toby hiked back along the River Thames, with the southern side of the Bloody Tower on their right. Passing the Warders' Hall, they traversed a wooden bridge over the moat and made their way toward the location of the Tower Hill Tube Station.

When they crested the hill, it wasn't there. Instead, across the cobbled avenue was an ornate glass archway with a mosaic-tile sign: "Mark Lane Underground Railway."

The Tube stations must be different here, Katie thought, sweeping her gaze across the street, searching for the Roman Wall, but couldn't find it either. Maybe the famous fortification hadn't been excavated yet. One sign pointed the way to the Corn Exchange and another to Billingsgate Fish Market.

Toby bought penny-fare tickets at the kiosk and together they descended the granite steps to the polished platform to await the train. The terminal smelled of acrid smoke, making Katie's eyes water. She tried hard to remember what she'd read about the early days of the Underground Railway.

"Um...Toby?" she ventured. "The trains...are...electric...aren't they? I mean they have electric motors, right...?"

He shot her a look. "Not a bit of it. They run on steam. Not to worry, luv. This line has ventilation shafts for all the foul-smelling fumes. You won't die of asphyxiation like some earlier passengers."

She pursed her lips. Was he kidding? People had actually died of asphyxiation down here? She swiveled her gaze, trying to take it all in. The platform was tiled with shiny mosaics and lit from above by an enormous sky-lighted arch, like a giant greenhouse. Running parallel was a similar arched roof but with steel girders that covered the entire length of a ditch below where train tracks stretched as far as the eye could see into a dark tunnel.

An ear-splitting blast, followed by an explosion of gleaming metal, burst from the train tunnel. A steam-engine locomotive roared toward them, chugging and whistling, then ground to a screeching halt. Six linked carriages, like coachman carriages, came to a jittering stop. Doors rattled open, and men smoking cigars poured out. There were no women that Katie could see.

Toby took Katie's elbow and steered her toward the last compartment of the train, which was half empty and didn't resemble any subway car Katie had ever ridden in. The inside was decorated with ornate mirrors, purple tufted seats, and oil lamps. It was as if they were stepping into someone's front parlor. The walls were padded in maroon leather. And the windows were hung with curtains!

Toby guided Katie to a row of seats that looked like sofas nailed to the floor in matching rows of eight. Diagonally across the aisle, a mild, peering little man wearing a silk top hat sank into his seat and tugged a small candle out of his pocket. Placing the candle into a brass holder on the windowsill, he struck a match, lit the wick, and began to read his newspaper.

The candle confused Katie because oil lamps jutting out from the walls blazed sufficiently to read. Several more passengers, all men, took seats across from one another at the rear of the car, pulled out their own candles, and settled them in metal holders on the window ledges.

Katie stared around, awestruck. *"I'm sitting in one of the first underground trains in the world!"* she thought, feeling goosebumps prickle up her arms. Or did New York City have the first subway system? Katie wasn't sure. But this was so cool! Her cousin Collin back home would have loved this. He was a total train junkie. Collin and Aunt Pru collected railway timetables from all over the world. Katie tried not to show her excitement, *but this was amazing!*

"You won't be smiling in a minute, luv," Toby said through gritted teeth. "Especially if you don't relish being shut in." There was a fierceness in his voice.

"I'm *not* claustrophobic. Never have been. This doesn't bother me a bit. I've been on plenty of" — she was about to say subway trains — "underground places. Like caves and. . .tunnels. . .and. . . um. . .stuff," she ended lamely.

"Well, then, this'll be a Noah's ark for you."

"Noah's ark? A walk in the park?"

Toby shook his head. "A lark."

"Yes. It will be a lark," Katie agreed.

Across the aisle, a heavy-jowled, grizzled man with a bristle-brush moustache plunked himself down next to the man in the silk top hat. His shrewd eyes traveled slowly about the compartment, taking in the other passengers, and when his gaze settled on Katie, a flicker of a wry smile formed below his bristly moustache.

The locomotive lurched, then rattled, then thundered away from the platform with a sound like the deafening backfire of a dozen motorcycles. Katie didn't exactly bounce in her seat, but she was definitely joggling to and fro as if she were sitting on a power lawn mower.

"So?" Toby said, watching the heavy-jowled man from the corner of his eyes. "I need you to answer my questions with the utmost honesty."

"Cross my heart and hope to die. I won't lie to you, Toby. Ask away."

The gas lamps winked on and off, sputtered, and went out completely. They were bumping up and down in near darkness, with only the jiggling candles on the window ledges for illumination.

"Are you a spy, Katie?"

"A sp — ? No."

The heavy-jowled man across the aisle tugged out a cigar, lighted it with a sweep of a matchstick against the heel of his boot, and continued staring at Katie.

"Are you the Duke's goddaughter?" Toby asked in a harsh whisper that emanated from deep within in his throat.

"No. I mean, sort of . . . but not exactly."

"Don't feather and hay me, lass. If I find you've deceived the Duke, you'll go down on your knees and beg his forgiveness."

The cigar man cut his gaze from Katie to Toby and back again.

Katie coughed loudly. The tobacco smoke, combined with the acrid smell seeping into the carriage from the belching steam engine, was making her gag.

"Coal dust," Toby whispered. "Like I told you. You won't die from the fumes, but it's not pleasant. I've a mind to travel around and around, back and forth on this underground line, until you tell me the truth. It will get far more disagreeable than this. Some say it's like taking a trip into the cauldron fires of Hell."

Katie gritted her teeth as a fresh wave of nausea hit her full force. She turned toward the rattling window and stared outside, trying desperately to set her gaze on something stationary. But it was black as pitch, and the only thing she could discern was the reflection of the cigar stub, like a gleaming red eye.

"Mrs. Tray says you don't exist. Are you a ghost, then?"

"A ghost? No," Katie sputtered. The air inside the carriage billowed with noxious fumes.

"An angel, then?"

"No, Toby. Not an angel. Nothing surreal or supernatural."

"You're here, but not here. Not of this world. That makes you either a ghost, an angel, a demon, or...*Are you in some sort of secret society, Katie? That's it, isn't it?* There's been talk of subversive social orders trying to do good, but doing ill instead. You're in some sort of society involving the London Stone, aren't you? The stone is probably used for initiation rites."

The man across the aisle leaned forward as if straining to hear what they were saying. He slid his cigar from his mouth and knocked ashes onto the floor, a wrinkle of concentration creasing his beefy forehead.

"No. Absolutely not! I'm not from any secret society," Katie whispered, taking deep breaths to calm her queasy stomach.

"We are twenty feet below ground, lass. Above us is solid, packed earth. There are those who come down into these tunnels who never come up again. I've a flask of tea and brandy in my pocket. It helps calm the stomach. It's all yours if you tell me who you are and why you're here. What's your game? What are you playing at?"

"No game, Toby, I swear." Katie concentrated on watching swirls of smoke curl upwards to the roof of the carriage.

"Mrs. Tray believes you've deceived me, Katie. Deceived the Duke."

"Not deceived...exactly. At least I never *intended* to deceive you. Look, Toby. I'm as confused by this as anyone. More so, probably. I don't know why I'm here other than to stop Jack the Ripper."

"So you *are* from a secret society sent here on a mission? Which is tantamount to being a spy. An American spy. That's punishable by swinging from the gallows."

"I'm not a spy! I'm closer to being an alien from a different... er...time, than a spy." Katie could feel the rapid race of her pulse. She tried to calm herself by taking long, slow breaths, but the air was so smoky and sulfurous all she could do was sputter and gag.

"If we stay underground long enough, asphyxiation from the fumes plays cruel tricks on the mind and the stomach. What's it to be? Tell me the truth, or we stay down here all day. I'll wager you're not clairvoyant either, are you?"

"I'm not clairvoyant. But I *can* predict the future. Sort of. At least where it pertains to those girls who are about to be murdered."

"Was it a parlor trick with the stuffed vulture?"

"Sort of."

"A hoax to deceive me?"

"I guess."

"How did you know what was written on the parchment?"

"If I told you, Toby, you wouldn't believe me."

"Try me."

"I can't."

"Can't or won't?"

"I can't risk it."

He gave a snorting laugh. "The way I see it, Katie, you're a liar and a cheat. Are you a thief as well?"

"Only of time," Katie said under her breath, but he'd heard her.

"A thief of my emotions and of my time. A liar, a deceiver, and a cheat. All in a day's work, eh, lass? Well, I'm washing my hands of you. This is the end. I'll not do your bidding, nor speak to you, nor squire you about. The Oracle of Traitors' Gate was right. You don't exist. Not for me. Not any more."

"Toby. What if I told you I haven't been born yet, would you believe me?"

He turned his back on her.

"What if I told you I don't belong in your world. I belong in *mine*, which just happens to be in another century?"

He continued to ignore her.

"There, you see? You don't want to know the truth! You wouldn't believe the truth if it bit you in the ass! What if I told you I've met your great-grandson, who's also named Toby? Or that I was at Madame Tussauds waxwork museum with him in the twenty-first century?"

Toby exploded. "*Utterly absurd!* And if you believe such nonsense, you belong in an asylum. Perhaps Mrs. Tray couldn't see you because you have a disease in your brain. Bats in your belfry. Loose nails in the coffin of your mind!"

The gas jets sputtered to life as the train chugged and then lurched into the next station. Moments later the doors rattled open. Katie jumped up to leave, giddy with relief to see light outside and feel fresh air. But Toby grabbed her and forced her back into the seat.

Katie took several deep breaths, hating the thought of being closed up in the narrow carriage again. She whirled angrily on Toby.

"What Mrs. Tray *said* was that I'm from the London Stone. And she's right, Toby. I'm a time-traveler. There! Are you satisfied? I don't know how or why, but it's the truth. I'm here because I want to save Lady Beatrix from being slaughtered. If Jack the Ripper isn't stopped, Lady Beatrix will be the Ripper's last victim, the most horrifying and gruesome of all the murders. Can you live with that, Toby? Can you live with knowing you might have saved her?"

"Why should I believe you?"

"I'll tell you everything I know, every last detail, and you can do what you please with the information. I'll return home through the portal in the London Stone. I never wanted to lie to you Toby, or deceive you, or cheat you. I'm not a thief. I'm just an ordinary girl from the twenty-first century!"

Chapter Thirty-six

Green Grass and Flower Names
say the Park Bells of St. James

Toby was silent as a new set of passengers streamed into the train and shook out their newspapers. Then, just as the doors began to rattle shut, he jerked Katie up and shoved her through the half-open door, which snapped closed behind them with a resounding clank.

Katie turned just in time to see the beefy man with the moustache leap up to follow them out, but he was too late. As the train pulled away from the platform, his swarthy face, plastered to the glass, turned white with mottled blotches against his cheeks. He banged angrily against the doors with his fist as his menacing eyes held Katie's through the window.

Smoke billowed from the steam engine. There came a tremendous hiss and clatter as the train hurtled away into the darkness.

"Who *was* that?" Katie asked, blinking and rubbing her eyes.

"I don't know. He followed us from Traitors' Gate. The other man, I *did* recognize."

"What other man?"

"The fawning little toff in the silk top hat with the candle. He works for Major Brown. He was at Mary Ann Nichols's autopsy."

A chill went through Katie. "Do you think they overheard us?"

"No. There was too much noise in the train."

Katie suddenly had a new fear. "What if those men return to Traitors' Gate and question Mrs. Tray? What if she tells them about the London Stone, and about *me*?" Railway steam continued to choke the air and catch in Katie's throat.

"The Oracle of Traitors' Gate would never rattle and pitch. Not Mrs. Tray." Toby took Katie's elbow and guided her up a set of granite stairs into daylight above.

"How can you be so sure? That man with the moustache might rough her up. She's an old lady. No match for —" Katie stopped in midsentence. The jiggling of the train was still with her. The ground below seemed to rock back and forth. She grabbed Toby's arm and waited for the spinning motion to settle down.

"Take deep breaths," Toby said, leading her to a park bench. "You don't have to worry about Mrs. Tray. No one bothers her. Ever. She'd put a right good hex on them if they dared."

"Oh, Toby! There's no such thing as a hex. I know you believe that sort of superstitious stuff, but it's not possible. Trust me, I know more about modern science than you could ever imagine. No one can put a hex on someone."

"But they can travel back in time through a stone?" Toby snorted derisively.

When Katie was almost, but not entirely, over her bout of dizziness, Toby hammered her again. "So, lass. Tell me why I should believe you're a" — he had trouble saying the words, as if they burned his mouth — "*time-traveler*?"

She began to explain, hesitantly at first, about how she and her cousin Collin, and his friend, Toby, had gone to Madame Tussauds in the twenty-first century to see the Jack the Ripper exhibit. Then

Katie started talking so fast, her words came out in a jumble about the waxwork victims and potential Ripper suspects.

"Whoa! Slow down, lass."

Katie took a deep breath, but continued in a rush. "I didn't want to come here, Toby! I didn't *ask* to come here. I went to Madame Tussauds with my cousin and his friend because the London Stone was on display. I only wanted to wish for something simple. I wanted to tell my parents I loved them and...and to say good-bye. Sounds stupid, I know. It's not as if I actually *believed* I could make some sort of cosmic wish and it would come true, but there's this weird legend attached to the London Stone that if you're pure of heart, you'll get whatever you ask for."

Katie took another gulp of air and rushed on before she lost her nerve. "My mom and dad died in a car crash. They were picking up my cousin Collin at the airport. He's a direct descendant of *your* Collin, here in the nineteenth century. Anyway, on their way to the airport in Boston, my parents were in a collision. That's why I put my finger into the Raven's Claw fissure in the London Stone. I just wanted to say good-bye. And I wanted my sister to come home. By mistake, I must have whispered something about Jack the Ripper, because the next thing I knew I was hurtling through time and landed here in your century!"

Toby remained silent.

A spasm of fear shot through Katie. Toby would walk away from her because he thought she was crazy. Deranged. He'd have the Duke commit her to an asylum for the insane.

"Aren't you going to say something?" she wailed, and her voice to her own ears sounded pathetic, like a child begging forgiveness. But there was nothing to forgive. She'd done nothing wrong. Other than conceal her real identity, lie about being psychic, and not tell the truth about where she came from. Minor quibbles in the grand scheme of things.

"I've a question for you, lass."

"Shoot."

"Shoot what?" He stared at her, perplexed.

"No. I mean, okay, hit me."

"Hit you?" Both eyebrows shot up this time.

"I mean, ask your question! Just remember, Toby, as weird as this is to you, it's a gazillion times weirder for me. I'm living it! And unless *you* are Jack the Ripper, I could use a little help here. Go ahead. Ask me anything."

"What's an airport?" he asked levelly, meeting her eyes without a flicker of anger or annoyance or disbelief.

"That's it? I thought you'd be totally pissed off and ready to commit me to an insane asylum. You look as if you actually believe me!"

"I do."

"But why? I mean, *why would you?*"

Toby explained that the last thing Mrs. Tray had whispered to him was that if Katie told him how her parents died, he would know she was telling the truth. And that this truth would be far more difficult to believe than anything he could dream up on his own.

"So," continued Toby, thoughtfully rubbing his chin. "The only idea I could dream up on my own was that you were either a spy, a member of a secret society, a supernatural being such as a ghost, a witch, or a vampire…or you were just plain crazy. But a time-traveler? I didn't think of *that.* So, let me get this straight, your parents were riding in their carriage, which must have overturned —"

"Not a carriage. A car."

"I know what a car is, Katie. It's the cab within a carriage."

"No, it's an automobile. A…um…I think you call it — *or will call it* — a horseless carriage. And an airport is where airplanes land."

"What's an airplane?"

Katie began to laugh, softly at first, then all out. She saw the intelligence in Toby's face, and the humor, too. Gone was the bleak, disbelieving face he had shown her back in the underground railway. She wanted to hug him. No…she wanted to wrap her arms around his neck and kiss him. A cousinly kiss, of course.

She relaxed and, still grinning, said, "An airplane is sort of like a train, only it...er...flies. Through the sky. Through the clouds. Up in the air." Katie held her breath, but when she let it out slowly, Toby just nodded.

"I suppose, lass, if we can travel at lightning speed underneath the ground, it's not much of a leap of faith to believe that we shall someday hurtle overhead in a flying train. Though you won't catch me riding upon one. Not if I have any say in it."

Katie reached over and gave him a hug.

Toby looked startled, then pleased. "Now, lass," he said. "Just because I believe your cock-and-bull story doesn't mean I'm susceptible to your charms. Nor will I allow you to take liberties with my affections. A proper young lady does *not* hug a gentleman in public." Toby tsk-tsked and tugged out his pocket watch. "Best be on our way."

They walked across the street, past the Lyceum Theatre, with its giant billboard advertising *Dr Jekyll and Mr Hyde*, and on through the northern tip of Green Park. As they walked, Katie couldn't take in enough fresh air. She had hated being underground amid the sulfurous fumes, smoke, and roar of the engine.

All around them in the park, autumn leaves rustled. Glossy green grass was turning to golden brown beneath the elm trees. White birches and giant beeches made dancing, leafy patterns against the clear blue sky. Katie felt happier than she had in days.

They strolled down a path flanked by black-eyed Susans swaying in the breeze, their black middles and yellow petals drooping heavily over long, orange stalks. Neat rows of flower beds showed roses still in bloom; spirals of white and purple phlox shimmered in the afternoon light.

Katie smiled as her boots scraped against the paving stones. What was the analogy Mrs. Tray had used to describe Toby's mother? The sound a petal makes when it falls to the ground. Katie glanced at Toby. His sound, if there were such a thing, would be a million oak leaves rustling in the autumn wind, straining to be free.

"What are you thinking about, lass?" Toby asked, his strong nose and handsome face catching the fading rays of the sun.

Katie tried to contain her amusement. "*You.*"

"Well, then," Toby said, his smile steady, his eyes full of laughter. "I'll leave you to your thoughts — as wonderful as they *surely* must be."

Katie laughed happily, and then suddenly stopped as she remembered something else. *Someone else.* Collin. How he would die on the moors in a hunting accident. She thought about her grandmother's family Bible and the historical details recorded there. A year from now, on September 12, 1889, Collin would lose his footing and drown in a peat bog on the moors. And this was *after* he married Prudence Farthington and produced an heir. *I've got to warn Toby. He can save Collin.*

Katie shook her head. *No, I can't tell Toby. At least not right now.* It was enough that Toby believed she could travel through time. And that he believed her about Jack the Ripper. There would be plenty of time later when he trusted her more. Still . . . maybe she could hint at it.

"Toby . . ." Katie took a deep breath. "There's one more thing. Promise me you will never, ever venture out on the moors with Collin. Especially a year from now. Exactly a year from now. Never, ever. Promise?" She didn't mention her grandmother's family Bible, or that Collin would marry Prudence Farthington. Nor did she tell him that Tobias Becket, trusted family friend, would be with Collin Chesterfield Twyford, the third, when he died on September the twelfth, in 1889. *I can't dump one more thing on Toby's plate. He's got enough to swallow right now. And if history can't be changed . . . if we can't stop Jack the Ripper and save Lady Beatrix, there's no hope for Collin.*

Katie stared up at Toby. His strong jaw, glossy black hair, and rugged features made her heart pound. But it was his kind, fathomless dark eyes that just about did her in. *If I tell Toby about Collin's death on the moors, and Toby isn't able to prevent it, how awful is that?* Is it better to know the future or not know? Katie decided that if she could actually change history, even a little bit, by stopping Jack the Ripper, or saving any of those girls, then she'd tell Toby about Collin's accidental drowning in a peat bog—or at least what was recorded in the family chronicle of births and deaths.

With the exit to the park looming in front of them, Toby met Katie's gaze and his tone grew serious. "I think we'd best keep this time-travel business to ourselves. Collin can't be relied upon to keep a secret. And if you go spouting off about the London Stone being a portal into the past, others might think you're a wee bit cracked, up here—" He tapped his forehead. "Have we got a deal, then lass?"

Katie nodded. "It's a jellied eel as long as you agree not to tell Major Gideon Brown. We can't risk it. He's a police officer, which gives him the perfect alibi to be prowling the streets at night. The perfect disguise for Jack the—" Katie stopped when she saw Toby's expression.

Annoyance tugged at the corners of his mouth. "For now," he conceded. "But you're wrong about Major Brown. He's a Cockney who has risen to the top ranks in Scotland Yard. He's totally trustworthy." Toby's eyes fastened on hers. "The very idea that he might be a suspect—"

"Loyalty is a good thing, Toby. But no one, and I mean *no one*, can be above suspicion."

"Or below it."

At the edge of the park, half a dozen gardeners toiled, pushing wheelbarrows full of weeds and carrying watering cans. There were no power mowers in this century, Katie reminded herself. Every bit of work needed to be done by hand.

A bee drifted lazily past. It was fat and striped and brought to mind honey, which was replaced by tea and scones dripping with butter and strawberry jam.

"I'm starving," Katie said, acutely aware of her growling stomach and wanting to think about anything *but* Jack the Ripper and the young women who would soon be slaughtered. *And Collin's impending fate—if the family history was written correctly.*

"Katherine." Toby's voice held a warning note. "My edict still holds."

Big Ben, loud in the quiet park, struck four bongs.

"And what edict is that?" asked Katie, suddenly weary of edicts and deals and promises.

Toby smiled, showing strong, if slightly crooked, white teeth.

"I'm still responsible for your safety, lass. Whatever investigating we do, wherever this leads us, I'm still in charge. You'll do exactly as I say. I've only your safety in mind."

"Of course!" cried Katie with feigned innocence. "I wouldn't have it any other way." She crossed her fingers behind her back. "I'll do whatever you think best, Toby."

If Katie had learned anything in this century, it was this. Girls had to be cunning to outmaneuver the chauvinistic attitudes of Victorian male egos. It was a hazard of being in an old-fashioned century where boys actually believed they were superior.

"So what's our next move, Sherlock?" Katie bit back a smile.

Chapter Thirty-seven

Urchins Will Perch 'neath
the Bells of Christ Church

LATER THAT NIGHT, after a torturously long dinner, Toby found himself consulting his pocket watch as he and Collin climbed onto a horse-drawn double-decker heading for the East End.

They were on their way to warn Miss Annie Chapman of her impending death at the hands of Jack the Ripper on September the tenth, two days hence — at least according to Katie — by the same lunatic who had disemboweled Mary Ann Nichols.

After dinner and the dessert course of strawberry and rhubarb custard, with lemon pudding, the Duke had insisted on singing duets in the library. Katie had pleaded a headache in order to slip away with Collin and Toby, but the Duke, upon learning that Katie could play the piano, was adamant she remain and help entertain his guests.

Katie had pulled Toby aside, pleading with him to rescue her. "*My sister's a rock star!*" she whispered frantically. "I can't play your kind of music. I don't know any songs from this era. I can't very well play heavy metal for the Duke! My own grandmother can't stand listening to Courtney's music. And don't get me started on the Metro Chicks — your great-grandson loves them. The only old songs I know are Beatles songs. Or maybe 'Chopsticks'! What am I going to do?"

"Give the Duke a Viennese waltz or a Chopin mazurka. If all else fails, play something from Gilbert and Sullivan."

"Gilbert and Sullivan . . ." Katie's eye's lit up. "I know a song from *The Pirates of Penzance*. We sang it at camp. But I've never played it on the piano —"

"Camp?"

"Summer camp. Where you learn archery, riflery, horseback riding, sailing, tennis —"

"Riflery! Surely not."

"Riflery and —"

"The future of England — *this England* — teaches girls marksmanship? The British realm becomes militaristic? War mongering?" Toby could only blink at her. What sort of world, future or otherwise, allowed *girls* to shoot rifles? And he had no idea what a rock star was. Perhaps in the future the London Stone was called the London Rock. But what would a rock have to do with stars and music?

When he finally excused himself and said good night to Sir Godfrey, Lady Beatrix and the others, with Collin trotting happily in his wake, Toby caught the flash of frustration in Katie's eyes. She did not want to be left behind. But in truth, it was a relief to Toby. There were so many conflicting thoughts running through his head when he was with the girl that he was glad for the respite.

A spark of perverse satisfaction surged through him as he settled into a seat next to Collin on the omnibus. He would never allow Katie to know how deeply she affected him. Not because she was a time-traveler — though he still couldn't fathom that *not inconsequential* fact — no, it was because, loath as Toby was to admit it, he was falling in love with her. His muscles tensed just thinking about it.

The lass was fearless, and her bluntness, refreshing. Most girls were simpering and superficial and not at all subtle in their desire to catch a titled husband, but Katie was none of these. There was amusement in her voice, and a sparkle in her eyes, but not with the end result of finding a husband — just a murderer, a vicious killer named Jack the Ripper, who might or might not even exist.

Toby sighed. That he should lose his heart to such a one as this ham shank was far more baffling to him than her ability to leapfrog across the centuries. But it was not just Toby who felt drawn to her.

At dinner tonight, Reverend Pinker had seemed overly interested in Katie. Proper etiquette dictated that young ladies did not laugh uproariously at the dinner table, nor offer up opinions on politics, medicine, or science. And yet Katie had done all of these things with an air of appearing interested.

Toby smiled thinking about how Katie had handled herself. During course after course, Major Brown's eyes, like Reverend Pinker's, had been riveted on her. Yet Katie seemed not the least intimidated. Not by Pinker's overzealous attention, nor Major Brown's butterfly-under-a microscope scrutiny, nor even by the Duke's ribald jokes. And much to Lady Beatrix's chagrin, Katie had even been so bold as to dismiss Major Brown's assertion that the feminine brain was not suited to the rigors of mathematics.

Collin was poking Toby in the ribs now, drawing his attention back to the present. Toby consulted his watch again. A quarter past nine. From their vantage point on top of this open-air vehicle, London looked oddly ethereal, wrapped in a smoky white mist that distorted gas lamps and gave the streets from Mayfair down to the brightness of Piccadilly a pale, ghostly appearance.

Collin nudged Toby, harder this time. "I say, old sod. Did you notice what a jackass Pinker made of himself with Katherine at dinner? Ogling her as if she were Venus incarnate! Can't fathom it. Stinker Pinker's always worn his heart on his sleeve for Beatrix. He's a dark horse, that one."

Collin chuckled loudly and continued. "Remember the time old Pinker got me so mad I unhooked the wall mirror from my bureau, climbed out onto my roof, and shone it straight into his eyes as he drove up to the house?" An expression of glee lit up Collin's face. "Old Stink-Pink was driving that glossy two-wheel trap to impress Beatrix. Came prancing up the drive, happy as you please. Ha! The reflection from the mirror darted straight into his eyes! Jolly good fun that, what?"

"I *remember*," Toby said, thinking back on the childish prank, "that the sun bounced off your four-foot mirror directly into the horse's off-side eye, and the poor beast took fright and bolted, sending Reverend Pinker flying arse-over-teakettle into the rosebushes."

Collin beamed. "That crazed horse took off at a speed almost equal to the one at which you chased me halfway round the stable yard!"

"You were lucky I didn't give you the worst walloping of your life, pulling such a reckless stunt. Where's the sport in spooking a defenseless animal?"

"Not to mention old Pinker. But it was a jolly good prank all the same. And you've got to admit, Toby, Stinker Pinker had it coming."

Toby grimaced. "You behaved like a jackanapes. No. Worse. A villainous little brute. Like you always do when someone pays court to your sister."

Collin stuck his thumbs in the armholes of his waistcoat, looking infinitely pleased with himself. "Look here, Toby. Anyone with half an ounce of humor would have seen it for the rollicking good joke it was."

"A rollicking good rum and coke that could have crippled a good horse, or —"

"A pompous old sod."

"A pompous old sod you happen to like."

"Stink-Pink's a good sort, I'll grant you. But *not* good enough for my sister, even if he inherits the earldom from that wretch of a brother, which seems highly unlikely. Quite the nerve, trying to woo Beatrix. But I showed him! And how about that time I put egg froth in the silk top hat of one of her suitors — fellow by the name of Finknottle

— and it foamed all down the sides of his face like a frothy white beard. And remember when —"

Toby sighed. He wasn't in the mood for Collin's tales of tomfoolery. In truth, he wasn't in the mood for Collin. He wished that the Duke had demanded Collin's presence after dinner as well as Katie's.

Toby felt a tinge of disloyalty as he glanced sideways at Collin. With his rust-red hair blowing in the wind; his glacier-blue eyes under their ragged red tufts of eyebrows, and his broad smile showing too many teeth when he laughed, Collin wasn't such a bad egg. *He just has a blind spot when it comes to his sister.* Collin disliked any man who tried to win Beatrix's affections. Toby shook his head. He and Collin had shared the same life, the same roof, the same school for five years. You can't very well do that, Toby reasoned, without some sort of tolerant liking for the other person. Being a dogsbody and general companion to Collin wasn't even difficult. Collin had a temper and got into his fair share of scrapes, but what future lord of the realm didn't? The rules of middling society didn't apply to the nobility. And the Duke, realizing that Collin hadn't the stomach for fisticuffs, had hired instructors to teach Toby the manly art of soft-glove boxing. Which was a right jolly rum and coke. By the time a gent had readied himself into a fighting stance, any Cockney worth his salt — Toby not being the exception — had already knocked the blighter out cold.

Yet Toby never mollycoddled Collin. That would have been demeaning. He just made sure the Duke's grandson stayed out of trouble. That was the agreement Toby had with the Duke.

"Keep the blister out of mischief until he's married and produces an heir. That's an order, young Tobias," the Duke had commanded when Toby was twelve. "After which, the devil take the red-headed imp, for all I care." Yet Toby suspected the Duke was genuinely fond of his grandson, as fond as he was grateful to Toby, especially when Collin got into one of his little "scrapes," as the Duke called them.

Last year Collin tried to trounce a schoolmate for making fun of his purple trousers, claiming Collin must have raided his sister's closet. Then the idiot made a bawdy comment about Lady Beatrix's underdrawers. Collin went at him like a wildcat. Toby intervened, but the boy had it coming. He was a sniggering bully. When the Duke got wind of the story, he bought Collin the pearl-handled pocketknife and told him next time he must use it to defend the Twyford honor.

Next time came soon enough when Collin accused a viscount's son of cheating at cards. The other promptly gave Collin a good thunk on the noggin. Enraged, Collin brandished his pocketknife in the air like a sword-stick, flourishing thrusts and parries with cries of *"En garde!"* and *"Take that, you louse!"* When the card-cheat drew out a small pistol, Toby stepped in, and the future viscount came within an inch of his life. Everyone in the gaming room had cheered.

❖

ANNIE CHAPMAN, CALLED "DARK ANNIE," lived in a dimly lit lane, which curved around to the right toward Christ Church. It was due north of the Mark Street Underground Railway, situated in a narrow row of houses with sagging bay windows and chipped stone steps.

Standing in Annie Chapman's front parlor, with its floral wallpaper and black lacquer table, Toby noticed that the room had been swept and scrubbed. Only a few candles burned in the pewter chandelier, and there were water stains on the ceiling above the sagging windows, but otherwise the room had an air of respectability. There was even a bell-pull next to the fireplace.

Even so, Collin looked ill at ease standing in such modest surroundings. He kept drawing down his sandy-red brows, puffing out his cheeks, and darting sharp glances at Toby, as if to say, *"Go on! Warn her about Katie's phantom killer, and let's get out of here!"*

Toby shot him a cut-it-out look, then settled his gaze on Annie Chapman. She was a tall, high-shouldered woman, whose age was a mystery. She might have been ten years older than she looked — which was about thirty — or ten years younger. Her face was angular and had a slight wasting appearance, as if she had consumption. Toby knew the look. Pale skin with even paler circles ringing the eyes on either side of her high-bridged nose. She had very black hair and very white skin, paper white with a tinge of blue where the veins showed through. Toby thought she might once have been beautiful. Was still beautiful. But it was clear that she wasn't well. And her eyes were so pale a blue, the iris seemed to mingle with the whites — a telltale sign of a consumptive.

Her voice was so soft as to be hard to hear. "So, Tobias, Georgie's grandmother must have told you that Georgie is here. Is that why you've come? Be quick, Tobias, I'm just on my way out."

"At this hour? Mustn't go walking about at this hour, Mrs. Chapman."

"Call me Annie. Or Dark Annie. Everyone does."

"It's not safe, Miss Annie."

She laughed, but the sound was as shallow as eggshells crushed beneath one's fingers. "I've lived here all my life, Tobias. Everyone knows me here. I have but to call out, should the need arise." She moved across the room and took down a paisley shawl from a peg on the wall.

Collin nervously rolled his tongue against the inside of his cheek. "Wouldn't do that!" he yelped.

Dark Annie spun around and again they heard the soft, egg-shell sound of her laughter. "I'll be fine, young man. My late husband was a military man. He taught me how to speak the Queen's English *and* to look after myself."

"We'll go with you," Collin offered.

Dark Annie's brows, like the black wings of a tiny raven, shot up. "I'll just check on Georgie," she said, wrapping her shawl around her shoulders. "He's been ever so agitated today. Poor lad is running a fever. Afterwards, if you care to escort me to Hanbury Street, that will be fine." She turned just as the front doorknocker rang out with fist-pounding ferocity.

"I suspect that will be Major Brown."

"Major Brown? *Major Gideon Brown?*" Toby felt a tightening in the pit of his stomach.

"Yes. He's a friend of mine from the old neighborhood where we grew up. He left a note saying he'd drop by this evening."

"Because of Georgie? You're not going to tell him Georgie is here, are you?"

"Certainly not, though I've a mind to." The doorknocker continued its ceaseless rapping. "Major Brown may have guessed that I'm hiding the lad. He has spies posted everywhere. But I shan't tell him. Are you acquainted with Major Brown, Tobias?" she asked, moving into the hall to answer the front door.

The moment Dark Annie stepped out of the room, everything in Toby's world began to spiral downward. He couldn't have prevented what was to happen, even if he had been forewarned. Which, he realized upon reflection, was the case. Katie had told him precisely what was to transpire. The problem was, she'd gotten her dates wrong.

Chapter Thirty-eight

Swinging Doors and Shame
say the Bells of Clements Lane

KATIE PACED THE FLOOR. *Where were they?* Toby and Collin should have been back hours ago. She scooped up a textbook on ancient Rome from Collin's desk, then another on anatomy, and a third on drawing caricatures of dogs and monkeys and horses. She tossed all three books aside and continued pacing.

It was well past midnight. Collin's elderly manservant, Jeffries, kept popping his head into the room, his eyes sharp and shrewd and suspicious below bushy white brows.

Katie knew she shouldn't be in Collin's bedchamber at this hour, but she yearned to hear what had happened with Dark Annie.

Where are they? Katie hugged her arms around her body and continued to pace. She had spent the evening playing the piano for Sir Godfrey in the library, and the song "The Grand Old Duke of York" was stuck in her head. It was a nursery rhyme in her own century, but a rousing marching song in this one, with extra bawdy lyrics, making

Courtney's *Dangerous Love* music video sound almost tame. But at least Katie had been able to spend some time with Lady Beatrix, who looked so startlingly like Courtney it gave Katie a wistful pang — not of homesickness exactly, but more like a sad ache in her stomach from missing her sister.

Lady Beatrix's singing voice was deeply melodic, with perfect pitch, and she harmonized in a way nearly identical to Courtney's. And when Lady Beatrix turned the sheet music, light from the candelabra had caught the golden highlights in her hair, the brilliant shine in her velvet eyes — so dark a blue they were almost black...

Just like Courtney's.

Katie moistened her lips and unconsciously began to hum.

> *"The Grand old Duke of York,*
> *He had ten thousand men;*
> *He marched them up to the top of the hill,*
> *And he marched them down again —"*

Katie jerked to a halt and gave herself a good shake.

At least the Duke of York song was better than "Drink to Me Only with Thine Eyes," which Katie had had to play half a dozen times. Each time she hit a sour note, the Duke's spectacles had tumbled down his nose, and he rapped his cane on top of the Steinway piano with a thundering *crack!* All in all, it had been a trying evening, especially since Sir Godfrey was tone deaf and his gravelly voice was ear-piercingly off-key.

Now, sighing deeply, Katie threw herself into one of the armchairs next to the fire. As frustrating as the evening with the Duke had been, she had a feeling it was going to get worse. She could feel it in her bones.

❖

FIFTY YARDS AWAY, Toby was running toward the house.

A rustling roar of rain drummed onto his shoulders and trickled down his neck as he hastened past the gatehouse and up the gravel drive, feeling his breath rasp in his lungs. Twyford Manor loomed dim and ghostly white through the sheen of rain ahead. A slant of light flickered in Collin's window, and seeing it, Toby tore across the side lawn to the trellis below, his mind divided between blind panic and seething anger.

Slumped in the armchair next to the fireplace, Katie heard the window creak.

Instantly alert, she jumped from the chair, but her long gown tripped her up as she darted across the room, and she bumped awkwardly against the desk, knocking the textbooks onto the floor. The noise made Katie gasp. The whole house would be up in a minute, and Jeffries would be poking his solemn face into the room again.

She scrambled to pick up *The Artist's Guide to Anatomy*, the drawing manual, and the Roman history textbook. She kicked the desk in frustration. It was anchored dead center in the middle of the room, directly below the gas chandelier. Normal desks skirted walls to take advantage of electrical outlets *for lamps and computers!*

She limped to the window, relief surging through her when she saw Toby's boot push through the open windowpane, followed by a blast of sluicing rain. Katie stared past Toby's wet shoulders, outside into the darkness. There was no thunder or lightning, only a steady deluge of rain.

Toby dropped from the windowsill into the room, and when he turned to face her, Katie knew something was wrong.

Dead wrong.

He snapped the window shut, muffling the roaring sound of rain splashing down the waterspout, and strode to the fireplace with its dying embers, the heavy squelch of his boots reverberating across the polished wooden floor.

Katie stepped in his direction.

She had a momentary impulse to flick on the light switch by the door before she remembered no such thing existed in this century. She blinked across the room and saw the anguished expression on Toby's face as he pitched more logs onto the fire, like a gravedigger chucking earth.

"Dark Annie is dead," he said softly.

Katie's stomach tightened. "That's not possible! She's not supposed to die for two more days!"

"And Georgie Cross?" he said in a low, tormented voice. "When was *he* supposed to die? Two days hence as well? And now Collin —"

"Toby!" cried Katie. "You know I don't know anything about Georgie Cross —" But one thought crowded out all others, surfacing like the gushing rain. "*Omigod!* Where's Collin? Why isn't he with you? He isn't —"

"He's with Dora Fowler at the Cock and Bull."

Katie sighed with relief and pressed on. "Dark Annie is supposed to die on September tenth. If she died today, maybe I got my dates mixed up . . ."

Toby nodded. "That you did, lass. That you did."

Katie ignored his quick agreement. "This can't be right, Toby. How did she die?"

Toby stood facing her in his soaking wet greatcoat. He looked as if he were ready to fight. His legs were braced apart, his hands clenched at his side, and the scowl on his face was as ferocious as the storm outside. "I need to hear every last detail about the man you call Jack the Ripper."

"First off, Toby, I don't actually *know* if he's a man or a woman. Secondly, I told you everything already. Was Georgie attacked as well? Was his throat slit? Was Dark Annie —" Katie couldn't get the word "eviscerated" out of her already dry lips.

Toby lowered his voice. "Dark Annie was slashed like a gutted farm animal. And this" — he struggled out of his soaking wet greatcoat and drew out a small, rectangular pillow — "is how Georgie Cross died."

Chapter Thirty-nine

Open Sores Will Fester
say the Bells of Winchester

TOBY HELD UP THE FEATHER PILLOW and pointed.

Dead center in the middle was the oval impression of upper and lower teeth marks, the size of a half dollar, as if Georgie had tried to holler for help and then bitten into the fabric.

"He was smothered?" Katie asked incredulously.

Toby motioned for Katie to take a chair by the fire and sat down opposite. Rivulets of water trickled down his damp face, but he didn't bother to wipe them away. He stared directly into the flames and thought about Georgie lying on the walnut cot in Dark Annie's back sitting room.

The room had been small, with the shades drawn, and the smell of medicine clinging to the air. When Toby and Collin first entered, Georgie had been very much alive. The wallpaper behind the cot was as clearly etched into Toby's brain as if he were staring at it right here in the flames. Blue, with faded cabbage-rose flowers and dark water stains near the ceiling. On the right-hand wall, as you entered, stood a narrow, red-brick fireplace, its mantel lined with porcelain trinkets. Wedged between the walnut cot and a low chest of drawers sat a rocking chair with a quilted sewing basket stuck full of pins.

Georgie had looked large and bloated in the tiny cot, an old wool scarf wrapped round his neck, which bulged like a goiter above the buttons of his flannel nightshirt. His curly hair fanned outward against the white of the pillow casing, glistening with sweat. Flags of a strawberry rash flushed his cheeks. And his arms, draped over the top of a patchwork quilt, looked soft and plump like dimpled pie dough.

"Damn stuffy in here, what?" Collin had muttered, peering down at Georgie. "Smells like the bloody plague."

It *was* rank, Toby remembered. That's why he had crossed the room, unlocked the window, and cracked it open to let in fresh air. The mottled panes looked out on a small courtyard lined with bricks.

"How did it happen?" Katie asked, interrupting Toby's thoughts. "Talk to me, Toby. What happened? Start at the beginning. You went to Annie Chapman's house with Collin—"

Toby nodded, then slowly filled Katie in, up until the moment of Major Brown's arrival. "Dark Annie rents rooms on the first floor of a boarding house. One in front, two in back, with a shared front door and common kitchen. Collin and I darted into Georgie's room, second from the back. We didn't want Major Brown to catch us there. Georgie had been given an opiate by Dark Annie because he'd been shouting and carrying on, 'all delirious, like,' Dark Annie said. So we slipped across the hall into the back room, out of sight.

"When we entered, Georgie was sleeping. *But he was alive.* His breathing was regular, with grunting snores. After I opened the window a crack, Collin and I stood with our backs to Georgie, and our ears to the door, listening. We could hear Dark Annie and Major Brown arguing. But Georgie must have sensed we were there. He became agitated and began mumbling a French army song and muttering about a girl named Cecilia. I told Collin to stay put, and I stole back into the narrow hallway to hear what Major Brown and Dark Annie were arguing about.

Toby blinked into the fire flames. He took a deep breath and continued: "In the ceiling above my head was one of those trap doors that lead into attics, but Dark Annie's was just a crawlspace used for storage. If you tug on the rope-pull, a set of wooden stairs unfolds. I stood there under the ceiling-door, listening. Three minutes, maybe four. Behind me, with Georgie's door slightly open, I could hear him humming "Aupres de ma Blonde." But in no time at all, Collin joined me in the hallway. He couldn't abide the stuffy room.

"Major Brown was shouting at Dark Annie now, saying she had no business hiding a witness from the crown; and that she'd be thrown into prison if she didn't comply.

"'Will you turn me in, then?' Dark Annie shouted back. She sounded hurt, then clearly bewildered that he was threatening her. They'd grown up together. She begged him not to forget his Cockney roots, but he hollered at her that he had important duties to perform and she was obstructing justice. She became fretful. You could hear the wheeze in her voice as if she were going to cry. In the end, she led him into the alcove where we stood eavesdropping. 'Georgie's in there,' she said, pointing to the half-open door. That's when Major Brown saw us —"

Toby's face had gone pale, with an expression in his eyes Katie couldn't read — a sort of rage, mingled with...indignation? Was he angry at Major Brown? Or just at the senselessness of Georgie's murder? And what of Dark Annie...?

Toby groped at his chair, clenching and unclenching the air above the padded arms. "I think Major Brown killed Georgie," he said softly.

"*What?*" Katie gasped. "Did you see him do it?"

Toby shook his head. His eyes looked haunted. When he spoke, he left off Major Brown's title, as if he thought the man didn't deserve it.

"Brown was furious when he saw us," Toby continued. "Mum and dad. Spitting mad. He cursed me for my 'stupidity' and 'unlawful audacity' and demanded to know why I had insinuated myself — *and Collin* — into a police investigation. When I said nothing, he stormed into Georgie's room as if he meant to wrangle a statement out of him, which, of course, he couldn't, not with the opiate Georgie had been given. Brown stayed in there a long time; when he returned, banging the door shut behind him, he unleashed his wrath first on me, then on Collin, 'What in holy blazes did you think to accomplish coming here and muddying the waters of a police inquest? What you've done is a criminal act of vindictiveness aimed at me...is that it?'

"Then, for some reason impossible to explain, Collin began to laugh. *Yes*, laugh at Gideon Brown, who turned red with rage. I thought he was going to strike Collin. I actually had to position my-self between the two of them in that narrow hallway. It was as if Collin enjoyed taunting his sister's beau. He wouldn't let up. Collin kept laughing in Brown's face. Then he said, 'Hi-ho! What's this?' and reached up and yanked on the rope-pull dangling from the ceiling, and the wooden stairs unfolded like a Chinese fan. 'Maybe I should climb up there and hide like a frightened rabbit? I'm sooo scared of the bullying bobby. Want to tell Lady Beatrix what a cowardly cuss I am? You'd like that, wouldn't you?' "

Toby drew in a long breath. "You'd have thought Collin had challenged Brown's manhood. He exploded, pummeling Collin like a prizefighter in a boxing ring. Collin fell to the ground, gasping for breath. Brown actually kicked him! Kicked him like a dog. And he was down, Katie, *Collin was down*. It was instinct on my part. I lashed out, pinning Brown's arm behind his back, raising it until he cried out in pain. I didn't leave off twisting it until I heard Dark Annie beg me to stop.

"'You've made a grave mistake, Tobias, graver than you can ever imagine,' Brown hissed at me, and when I released him, 'Touch me again, boy, and I shall see you hanged. Both of you.'

"He stormed back to the front parlor, leaving me to revive Collin, still gasping for air, and to soothe Dark Annie, trembling from head to toe. 'Oh, lad?' she cried over and over. 'Why did you want to provoke

Gideon Brown of all people?' She was so distraught she was sobbing. 'Make an enemy of Gideon and yer won't live to tell the tale. I knows 'im all m'life, and I wouldn't put odds on yours, now that you've crossed 'im.'"

Toby was silent now, staring into the fire. Katie could see the reflections of the flames undulating in his dark eyes.

"The evening got worse," he continued, clenching his fists until his knuckles turned white. "I don't understand it, Katie. An honest man doesn't strike a dog when he's down, not like Brown struck out at Collin. He didn't give him a sporting chance, just hammered Collin when he was down and gasping for air. If I hadn't intervened—"

Toby lifted his gaze to Katie's. "Collin can be a boil on a blister, as the Duke likes to say, but he didn't deserve such a thrashing. Brown should have swung at *me*, not Collin. I brought Collin there. It was my doing. Mine alone."

Toby's eyes looked pained. He wrenched his gaze from hers and stared, unseeing, at the flames. "Had you asked me yesterday, Katie, if Brown was capable of losing his temper over Collin's childish antics, I'd have sworn an oath, not. Collin didn't even say anything so very inflammatory—nothing to provoke such violence, and certainly not with Georgie lying sick in the next room."

"So then what happened?" Katie asked, gently.

"Reverend Pinker banged on the front door."

"Pinker? Why was *he* there?" Katie gasped.

Toby explained that Major Brown and Reverend Pinker had shared a hansom cab to the East End. Pinker was on his way to the Mission House for Widows and Orphans, and Major Brown asked him to wait in the cab while he had a word with Dark Annie.

"But here's where it gets tricky," Toby continued, his voice strained. "Dark Annie was crying uncontrollably. When she answered the door and let Reverend Pinker in, she begged him to intervene. 'Don't let 'im hand Georgie over to the authorities until he's recovered. He'll be taken to Bedlam Hospital. I can't bear it!' she sobbed. In the end, after a few words between the two men, Major Brown grudgingly consented, and it was decided that Reverend Pinker would stay with Georgie while the four of us — Major Brown, Dark Annie, Collin, and I — went to Hanover Street, then on to Twyford Manor.

"'Don't disturb the lad,' Major Brown warned Pinker. 'Look in on him only if he cries out. He's got a fever and may be contagious. Give a care, man.' Reverend Pinker nodded, drew up a chair by the fire, and took out his Bible. He said he'd read the good book whilst 'sitting vigil' for poor, young Master Cross.

"The last I saw Georgie, he was alive. After that, the only two people who came within arm's length of him were Major Brown and Reverend Pinker. Both had ample opportunity to smother Georgie. Major Brown, however, was in Georgie's room *a long time*. When he came out, he was pumped up full of energy. His nerves on edge. As if he'd done something terrible. That's why he lashed out at Collin. A sort of scapegoat for his own pent-up emotions."

"But why smother Georgie?"

"Keep him quiet."

"Quiet about what?"

"Lady Beatrix's opera glasses. He'd been searching the entire East End for Georgie. Dark Annie said he had spies everywhere. Maybe Georgie saw him kill Mary Ann Nichols. Georgie's grandmother said one of her tenants heard Georgie arguing with someone who had a Cockney accent, but sounded like a toff. If ever a description fit Gideon Brown —"

"But why kill Mary Ann Nichols?" Katie blinked at him. "What possible motive could Major Brown have for murdering her?"

Toby's dark brows creased over his even darker eyes. "I don't know."

Katie sat bolt upright and gasped. "Of course! I've got it! If Major Brown causes a sensation in London such as Jack the Ripper *did* cause, with the thought of solving it, and thus getting the Queen to award him a knighthood, the Duke will have to consent to his marrying Lady Beatrix! He'd be *Sir Gideon Brown*. That was their deal. I overheard them making it in the Duke's study. It makes perfect sense, Toby. What better way for Major Brown to distinguish himself?"

Toby kept his gaze fully directed on Katie. "But for that plan to work," he said, "he has to —"

"Kill more girls!" she cried excitedly. "The crimes have to get lots of press if he wants to be a national hero when he solves them!"

"If you're right, that means someone will have to swing from the gallows. Major Brown has to make it *look* as if he solved the worst crime in history. The question is, who is he going to frame?"

"It doesn't matter, Toby. The murders never get solved. Major Brown doesn't finish whatever he started. Someone stops him. Maybe that someone is us . . ." Katie took a deep breath. "But if our theory is right, something goes horribly wrong. Beatrix dies at the hands of Jack the Ripper. Why would Major Brown — assuming he's the Ripper — murder his fiancée?"

"Katie. When you described the murders to me, they all fit a pattern. The one that didn't was Lady Beatrix's."

"So either someone else will try to kill her and make it appear to be the work of Jack the Ripper — which in my time is called a copycat murder — or Lady Beatrix discovers what Major Brown is up to, confronts him, and he kills her."

"It's Reverend Pinker," Toby said, his jaw muscles tightening. "Major Brown is going to accuse Pinker. That's why he brought him to Dark Annie's house. To set him up."

Katie nodded. "But we can't rule out Reverend Pinker as a suspect. He was alone with Georgie. Maybe Georgie said something. Or *sang* something that upset him. Maybe Reverend Pinker *is* Jack the Ripper."

"No," Toby said with finality. "It's Major Gideon Brown. I'd stake my life on it. He's setting up the Reverend. It's easy to do. Pinker's weak, he gets befuddled, and he works in the East End. He wears a preacher's collar. He'd be trusted by his victims. That's the way Major Brown's going to present his case."

"If this was an Agatha Christie murder mystery —"

"Agatha who?"

"Christie. She wrote Golden-Age detective stories. Grandma Cleaves says you can always figure out who the murderer is in Agatha Christie novels once you've figured out who stands to gain financially."

"Major Brown gains financially in this case if he marries Lady Beatrix. She has one of the largest dowries in all of England."

"Toby . . ." Katie said gently. "Tell me about Dark Annie. Did you go to Hanbury Street with Major Brown?"

Toby nodded. A film veiled his eyes. "Major Brown made us accompany him to Georgie's grandmother's — he didn't want to let Collin or me out of his sight. But I'd rather not talk about it, Katie. Not now, not ever." He rested his head wearily against the back of the armchair.

"You have to! It could save lives. It could save *Lady Beatrix's* life. Please, Toby. If we work together on this . . . we might save those other girls."

Toby winced, then his mouth settled into a grim frown. He took his time before continuing. "It was like this," he said in a harsh whisper. "The cab splashed up to the curb in front of number twenty-nine Hanbury Street at half-past eleven. It was raining. The first floor windows were alight. I could see a fire-glow through the curtains. Nothing gave me pause. Nothing alerted me to danger . . .

"We left Collin in the back of the cab — brooding. His face was bruised and bloody; his left eye, swollen shut. He refused to come with us. I didn't want to go in, but Major Brown shoved me out of the cab, and I didn't want to upset Dark Annie more than she already was.

"Outside, the pavement was wet and slick. 'Sit there like a toad on a log, for all I care,' Major Brown shouted over his shoulder at Collin. 'The day of reckoning for both you lads will come soon enough.' Then he hollered like a madman, 'You can bloody well run, but you can't hide . . . not from me. Never from me! Idiots, the two of you. More fool me for ever trusting you, Toby. You've ruined any future you might have had at Scotland Yard. I'll go the extra mile to see you're never recruited.'

"I ignored him. He was showing the true colors of a bully. And I'm not afraid of him. Inside, we warmed our hands by the kitchen fire. Major Brown seemed distracted and nervous, and whenever he glanced at me, he was scowling. Georgie's grandmother asked me to fetch some fresh water from the pump out back in the courtyard, but Dark Annie said she preferred to go. I think Major Brown's anger distressed her and she wanted to get away from him. Five minutes later, when she didn't return, Major Brown went looking for her. All seemed quiet enough, but when he returned several minutes later, there was blood on his hands. Mrs. R's back was to him. She was toasting bread over the fire on a long, two-pronged fork. She didn't see him. He motioned me to follow and called out over his shoulder: 'Stay put, Mrs. Richardson. We'll be back in a moment.' His voice was soothing and as if nothing in the world were out of place. . .as if he had no blood on his hands. He led me through a room full of ticking clocks and stacked boxes, out back, down the stairs into a shared courtyard with a recessed garden.

"'There, over there — ,' Major Brown said.

"I heard the clocks ticking inside my head. Through the light drizzle of rain, and in the half-light from the moon, I saw Annie Chapman's body on the ground looking like nothing more than a bundle of wet rags against the dark paving stones.

"'Miss?' I remember saying as if she could hear me. 'Are you all right, Miss Annie?' I thought she'd stumbled. I wanted to help her get up. But of course I couldn't. No one could —"

Toby was silent for a long time.

"Go on," Katie urged, gripping her hands together.

"She was dead. Or nearly so," Toby answered, releasing his breath. Then he sat back with a jerk.

What Toby didn't tell Katie was how he felt when he saw Dark Annie's entrails spilling from her gutted stomach over her hips, onto the wet pavement. It was as if he'd been caught in an exposed place, in front of a firing squad, rifles aimed straight at him. Fear gripped him so intensely, he quite literally couldn't walk. He went down on his knees and crawled to her side. Her cheeks were warm; her eyelids, too. And when he closed them he tried hard not to look at the steam rising from her still warm, pulsing innards, as if her soul was a vaporous mist trying to ascend upward into heaven. But there was no avoiding the moist, coppery smell of her raw, open flesh. Or the fact that her heart was still beating. That's when he vomited.

It was a long while before Toby resumed his narrative. When he finally did, his voice held a tremor of rage.

"Major Brown ordered me to wash my blood-smeared hands at the pump and return to the cab, and then get Collin safely back to Twyford Manor. I was to speak to no one. And like a frightened animal, I blindly did as he instructed. Collin was waiting in the cab. I told him nothing. But I instructed the cabbie to go immediately back to Dark Annie's house, not Twyford Manor.

"When we arrived, Dora Fowler was climbing the stoop, said she was visiting Dark Annie. Collin leaned out of the hansom window, all talkative and animated now that he saw Dora. She invited us to join her after at the Cock and Bull. Collin said yes. I said no and told him he was to stay put.

"When I rang the bell, an upstairs tenant let me in, but the door to Dark Annie's apartment was locked. No amount of pounding could rouse Reverend Pinker, who, I supposed, had fallen asleep, so I stole back outside and climbed into Georgie's window. The one I'd unlocked earlier."

Toby continued staring into the fire. He knew he couldn't tell Katie about this new horror. How Georgie lay dead on the walnut cot. How his mouth, slack in his dead face, still retained traces of the bright, promising young man he might have been. How his arms, draped over the top of the patchwork quilt, were soft and plump, and as lifeless as putty. Yet everything else in the room had looked the same. The faded blue wallpaper. The dark water stains near the ceiling. The porcelain trinkets on the mantelpiece. The sewing basket stuck full of pins . . .

All precisely as before. Except that Georgie's curly hair was fanning outward against the grey mattress. A portion of Toby's brain noticed that the pillow was missing, but couldn't make sense of it at first. Not until he began methodically searching the room and found it wedged in the bottom drawer of the low chest next to the rocking chair.

And so it was that Georgie Cross, the market porter boy from Hanbury Street, who loved to sing and dance, and who fell in love with a different twist 'n' swirl every month. . .had been discovered dead, smothered to death. Toby had hurried into the front parlor, but Reverend Pinker was nowhere to be found. His leather Bible, with its gold clasp, lay upside down on a side table, splayed open, as if hastily thrown down.

Toby blinked up at Katie.

His eyes looked so haunted, she rose from her fireside chair and took his hands. His fingers didn't respond at first, just lay limp in hers. But when she squeezed, and he returned the pressure, she leaned over and brushed her lips across his. He tugged her toward him and returned the kiss, his lips hard and demanding.

All too soon, he pulled away. He kept seeing Dark Annie's consumptive eyes.

"I tell myself she hadn't long to live, Katie. Then I tell myself a dog shouldn't have to die the way that she did. And Georgie. . . Georgie had his whole life ahead of him. Georgie wouldn't hurt a fly. I keep asking myself who could have wanted them both dead?

"The answer is the same person who bashed Georgie's skull in at his grandmother's house. The same person who was looking for something and said, '*Hand it over!*' Georgie had something his attacker wanted. The pawn shop ticket. The opera glasses —"

"*Major Brown*," they said in unison.

Chapter Forty

Go Up and Go Down
say the Bells of London Town

"WE NEED TO TELL THE DUKE."

"*But it's two o'clock in the bloody morning!*"

"No choice, *To-bi-yas*—" Katie enunciated his name, hoping to make him smile. She'd never called him by his given name before. "We've got to tell the Duke about Major Brown."

They argued until Katie finally got her way. The Duke of Twyford was a member of the House of Lords and had been the former Home Secretary as well as Director of Covert Operations for the Crown. He had the Queen's ear and knew every influential person in Parliament. "We need his help," Katie insisted.

Grudgingly acquiescing, Toby threw open the door of Collin's bedchamber and they moved along the hallway in the direction of the west wing. Katie lifted her skirts so as not to trip as they made their way past the marble staircase with its stained glass window and then, moments later, took a dogleg turn down a winding corridor. It was so quiet at this hour that each padded thud of their footsteps seemed to reverberate down the long, drafty passageway. Gas jets in their wall sconces had been turned down so low as to be mere flickers in the gloom, throwing elongated shadows of their tiptoeing silhouettes across the carpeted path.

Leaving the main part of the manor house behind, they moved across bare floorboards, making it impossible to stifle the clumping sound of their footfalls. China bowls brimming with rose petals and orange peel had been set into wall niches to mask the odor in the ancient hallway. And even though the passage was deserted, it felt to Katie as if the ancestral portraits hanging on the walls were eyeballing her. *It's like a movie set*, Katie thought. *Any minute the director will swoop out from behind the wings, shouting at us to take it from the top.*

"Katie?" Toby whispered. "What's wrong? Not getting squeamish, are you? The Duke's bark is worse than his bite...sometimes."

Katie stared at the faded, Rembrandt-brown portraits of her dead ancestors in their starched collars and hilted swords, and had an overwhelming premonition of disaster. Two people had died tonight. And although this was the past, and everyone in it as long dead as the dour-faced Twyfords staring down at her from their gilded frames, the reality of Georgie Cross and Annie Chapman's murders weighed as heavily upon her as if it were all real. *But it is! This is happening in the here and now! It's me who's not real...I haven't been born yet!* Katie's stomach clenched and twisted like a dishcloth being wrung out to dry. She shuddered.

Toby spoke softly but clearly. "Go back to your room, lass. I'll handle this. 'Twas folly on my part to take you with me to speak to the Duke. In all likelihood the guv'nor will take one of his hulking daisy roots, give me a swift boot in the Khyber Pass, and send me packing. Katie?" He peered hard at her. "Have you heard a word I said?"

Katie glanced around the shadowy hallway decorated with frowning ancestors. She still couldn't shake the feeling that a stage door would pop open any minute revealing the film crew of some clever reality TV show. But instead of *So You Want to Be a Millionaire?* this one was *So You Think You Can Go Back in Time?*

"I want to vote myself off this island," Katie whispered.

"Island? What island? Katie, luv. Go back to your room. I'll handle this," he gave her a gentle shove back down the hall.

"My name is Katie Lennox. I was born in Boston, Massachusetts. I'm in the nineteenth century." She closed her eyes and clicked her heels as if, like Dorothy, she could magically wish herself home to Kansas. But when Katie opened her eyes, her own yellow brick road took the form of a gloomy, dark hallway stretching out in front of her.

The low-flame gas jets in the wall sconces flickered on and off like lightning bugs. Katie blinked around. *I can't go home yet. Not yet.*

Toby took her wrist. "I'll take you back to your bedchamber and ring for Lady Beatrix's maid. She'll fix you a tonic to help you sleep."

"No." Katie's voice sounded determined and slightly breathless. She tried to make her racing heart calm down. "I'm fine, Toby. I was just...thinking...maybe *hoping*...this was all an illusion. All these deaths. This house. Even you, Toby. Maybe *you're* not real. Maybe I have a concussion and am dreaming...or maybe I have amnesia."

"Am what?"

Katie blinked at him. Who had coined the term amnesia? Sigmund Freud?

Against the gas-glimmer in the hallway, Katie could see Toby's worried face. "I'm okay, Toby. Come on. We have to talk to the Duke. We have to convince him to help us."

"You risked too much coming here...across time. Leave the rest to me. I'll save those girls...and Lady Beatrix, too. This is a job for a man, not a wee lass."

"I didn't risk anything coming here, Toby. I didn't come voluntarily. But I'm *staying* of my own free will. I can return home any time I want, through the London Stone. But I'm staying. *And as for a job for a man!* Of all the sexist, pig-headed, macho, bull —"

She was about to say "bullshit" but changed it to "bull-ony. Total baloney."

Toby stared at her. Katie's face was pale; her body, rigid with fright or indignation, he wasn't sure. He knew he oughtn't to have let her bamboozle him into coming with him to speak to the Duke, but something about this girl compelled him to do things against his better judgment. When he was eleven, right after his mother died, Toby had been given a gift of a theft-key from his Uncle Kittrick. It was an instrument used to rifle locked rooms at hotels and gentleman's clubs. The tool could unlock a door from the outside, then lock it back again, making it appear as if the room had never been burgled. Toby had never used the pin-wheel contraption, hooked like a darning needle, but the very idea that he owned such an object had given him great satisfaction. And Katie, he believed, was like that theft-key. She held the power to unlock these deaths and lock their secrets back up. She was an unwitting instrument, a tool of some sort, to be used...but by whom and for what purpose, Toby wasn't sure.

Toby took Katie's wrist and began tugging her back to the main part of the house, but she resisted. Straining to wrench free, she began to tug in the opposite direction. A brief contest of wills carried them halfway down the hall until they were standing squarely in front of the servants' staircase. Katie seized the banister rail and held tight.

Toby gripped her wrist more firmly.

"Leave off, Katie. I'll not argue with you. You're to stay away from whatever madness has descended on the Twyford household. I'll not allow you to bedevil my wits again. It was foolish of me —"

"Oh, cut it out, Toby. Give me a break! I'm not some simpering nineteenth-century girl who faints dead away in a crisis. I'm here — I'm not sure why — but I *am* here to see this thing through to the end. I'm going to solve these murders with or without your help. *Put that in your damn pipe and smoke it!*"

Startled, Toby loosened his grip, but not entirely. The girl could blaspheme the very act of smoking!

"Release me, right now," Katie demanded, squirming and tugging.

Toby clamped on harder. The little vixen was not going to have her way this time. Not if he had anything to do with it.

Seeing his mouth set in a firm line, Katie had a jolt of inspiration. "If you don't release me this instant, I'll —"

Toby braced for Katie to yank more forcefully, but instead, she stopped struggling, rose on tiptoe, and planted a warm, moist kiss on his lips. And it was not a chaste kiss, or a sisterly peck, nor even a cousinly hit-or-miss pucker. It was a deep, resolute, single-minded, intense, lip-locking kiss. Toby opened his mouth, and his tongue found hers. A Cockney expression, "When tongues mate, the devil takes your fate," rang through his mind. For a moment he struggled hard with his intense desire to demonstrate a respectful show of propriety, but he rapidly descended past any concern for her honor, her reputation, or even her station in life. The girl had bewitched him, and now she should give a care for her own safety because he had lost all ability to do so.

A door down the hall banged open.

"*God's elbow!*" bellowed a voice from the end of the dimly lit passage. "What in blazes do you two think you're doing? Bloody hell!" roared the Duke, looming large in a dark-green robe and velvet nightcap.

Toby instantly loosened his grip on Katie and just as quickly tightened his grip on the banister. It took every ounce of concentration to turn and face Sir Godfrey without exhibiting any outward signs of physical ardor. He thought about Dark Annie, and the vision of the dead woman cooled his emotional temperature.

"*Tobias!*" the Duke hollered. "You scoundrel! Of all the lowdown, treacherous, deceitful, unreliable —" He took a deep breath and swiveled his angry gaze toward Katie. "*Miss Katherine!*"

"Sir Godfrey?" Katie returned without a tremor. In fact, just the opposite, a bit of humor, or so it seemed to Toby. "Just the person we came to talk to!" Katie said and strode down the hall toward the Duke, chin held high. "We need to discuss something urgent with you, sir."

Toby blinked at Katie's retreating figure. *The lass has guts.* He took a deep breath, squared his shoulders for the harsh reprisal that would inevitably ensue, and followed in the girl's shadowy wake.

"A matter of life and death, you say?" the Duke responded to Katie's assertion when they entered his sitting room. "Your life . . . and this young fathead's *death?* Is that it? Shall I skin him alive? Maybe disembowel the blighter? Just say the word, m'girl. He's a bloody anvil round my neck as it is. I was about to have my manservant fetch the blundering numbskull and demand an accounting of my grandson's whereabouts. But you've saved me the trouble."

Katie blinked at the Duke. Death by disembowelment was an unfortunate choice of words. She glanced over her shoulder at Toby standing in the doorway, and saw it in his face, too. He had paled considerably. They were in the Duke's chambers, in his sitting room.

Sir Godrey tugged off his nightcap and clamped murderous eyes on Toby. "So! Tell me, you insolent little pup, you fatheaded numbskull" — the Duke snorted like an elephant about to charge — "why it is that you arrived home *without my grandson?* Jeffries informed me, over an hour ago, that Collin did not return home, but that you had . . . *alone!* Your one and only job is to stay with my grandson and keep the blistering idiot out of mischief. *Bah!* And now I find you manhandling this little-bitty slip of a girl, *my goddaughter!* What in blazes is going on in that fatheaded brain of yours? You dimwitted Casanova! No! Don't answer that. It's a rhetorical question, you bloody fool. But this one isn't. Where's that nincompoop grandson of mine? What mischief is Collin up to now, eh? I'll skin you both alive, that's what I'll do! Boil you in oil. *God's eyeballs,* I'll rid the world of fatheads if it's the last thing I do!"

The stained-glass lampshade on the only burning lamp in the Duke's chamber was throwing a kaleidoscope of colors onto the wall. Its jeweled glow, mingling with the firelight, made the room appear deceptively inviting. Even the crown of leaves perched atop the marble head of Caesar Augustus above the mantel appeared to blaze in an explosive palette of neon.

"*Miss Katherine,*" Sir Godfrey growled, snatching up his cane. "Will you be kind enough to wait here whilst I have a little chat in the next room with this odious scalawag? What I have to say to him will have nothing to do with a razor strop or the back of my hand—though *God's teeth*, I've a mind to use both. But I assure you, m'girl, you needn't concern your pretty little head with the likes of him again! You have my assurance you'll have no further cause for alarm. I shall banish young Romeo here, from—"

"Oh, he did nothing wrong, sir. I encouraged him to kiss me. In fact, I insisted. I was trying to comfort him. You see, he's had quite a shock tonight. A double shock to be exact. Which is why we're here. Toby witnessed two mur—"

"Your lordship." Toby stepped forward, cutting Katie off. "Let me make this clear, sir. Miss Katherine is blameless. It is I who—"

"Of course the girl is blameless, you fatheaded Lothario!" the Duke roared.

Toby strode forward, his shadow rising over his head as he moved in front of the firelight, passing the Duke, and momentarily blotting out his scowling face. Stepping over the threshold into the connecting bedchamber, Toby turned and shot Katie a warning glance. *I'll handle this. Don't interfere!*

Katie gave a slight nod and watched as the Duke snatched up his cane and clumped across the floor, following Toby into the next room. When he banged the door shut, the bolt hit with such force, it swung back open several inches with a shuddering thud.

"Bah!" the Duke exploded, swiping at the door with his cane, but missing the mark by inches.

With the door slightly ajar, Toby stood in front of the fireplace while the Duke shouted every expletive known to mankind and several known only to the devil himself—or so it seemed to Toby. The ribbon of light shining from the half-closed door had a flicker of a shadow to it. Toby felt sure Katie was eavesdropping. *The lass didn't have it in her to follow instructions.*

"So, m'boy?" the Duke roared, finally ending his tirade. "What in blazes do you have to say for yourself, eh? Where's my grandson, and what's the girl babbling on about a matter of life and death? Speak up, you infernal, ungrateful fathead—"

"Sir," said Toby. "Let me explain." Knowing the value of not saying too much, Toby was brief and to the point, laying out the facts of the evening, including the two murders, from beginning to end. He gave an account of finding Dark Annie's eviscerated body, without being overly graphic; he explained about taking the pillow with the teeth marks that had smothered Georgie Cross; and he calmly put forth his theory about Major Brown.

Toby had expected the Duke to look as startled as if the bust of Caesar Augustus on the mantel had burst out singing. But when the Duke finally looked at Toby, his pallid face showed no surprise. He merely steepled his fingers with a look of deep concentration and began chewing on his moustache whiskers.

Katie, unable to bear the silence another moment, had managed to further nudge open the door and was peeking into the room. The Duke's bedchamber was very dim, awash in the yellow-blue light of gas lamps. The sputtering light fluttered and shrank and sparked off the ornate mirror behind the bust of Caesar above the stone fireplace; it threw long shadows across the four-poster bed in the corner. A smell of old books, old leather, old paint, and stale cigar smoke hung in the yellow-blue gloom.

So engrossed was Katie in looking about the room — her grandmother's bedroom in the twenty-first century — that when the Duke swiveled his head around, she let out a sharp cry of surprise. She could have sworn the Duke was grinning at her. But a second later, Katie thought she could see it for the angry grimace that it was.

"Come in! Come in!" he said testily, waving her into the room. "Why not invite the entire Queen's cavalry while we're at it? Take a seat. Take a seat." His tone was gruff, but Katie detected the slightest softening in his coal-grey eyes as he motioned for them to pull up chairs, then settled himself into a thronelike wing chair by the fire. Adjusting his eyeglasses, he peered first at Katie, then turned his attention to Toby.

"You've got it wrong, son. Stay still and listen!" he barked out. "We've got to work fast. I'd bet my bottom dollar that everything you say about Major Brown is true, but he *won't* try to pin this on Pinker. Burn me if I'm wrong. It will be *Collin!*"

"Collin?" Katie gasped. She looked at the Duke closely and caught the strange expression on his face. Not contemptuous, not bitter, not worried, but a mixture of all three. With his back ramrod straight, arms out, and fingers grasping the ends of the chair arms, Sir Godfrey had the imperious look of a king about to hold court.

"Sir?" Toby leaned forward. "Major Brown wouldn't dare risk implicating Collin, *not* if he has any true feelings for Lady Beatrix. He —"

"Don't say a word, lad. Not one word. Just listen! I've been expecting something like this. But the magnitude, the depth, the cunning. . .*damn his eyes*," the Duke said almost admiringly. "Major Brown is clever. He'll go after Collin like a pitbull after a rat. Has to, don't you see? It's the fastest way for the blighter to achieve his purpose — getting me to consent to his marrying Beatrix. And when he points his finger at Collin with all the might of Scotland Yard behind him. . .what am I to do, eh? It's the perfect blackmailer's ploy. And believe me, Major Brown has used blackmail tactics for me in the past."

The Duke hoisted his feet onto a leather footstool. "Right now, Toby, I want you to find Collin. Oh, I know his penchant for tavern wenches. Just find him. Do not let him out of your sight for a minute. He spits, you spit. He sleeps, you sleep. You'll be my eyes and ears. Any funds you need, lad — the carriage, a stable boy or two to back you up — it's yours. I'll give you further instructions in the morning. I'm forming a bit of a wild plan, don't you see?" He stared thoughtfully into the fire. "This could be a fiasco. . .or we can turn it to our advantage. Major Brown will rue the day he thought to outfox me!"

Katie felt something hot rise in her throat. The hands of the wall clock pointed to half-past four, but instead of ticking, Katie heard only the thumping of her heart.

"Now, then, leave me to my thoughts," grunted the Duke, clasping his fingers around the middle of his cane and raising it as if aiming down the muzzle of a long-barreled musket, one eye winking open, while the other remained shut. "There's more to this rat's tail than meets the eye." He made as if to shoot the bust of Caesar off the mantel. "But apart from all else" — he aimed the cane at the ceiling as if to pick off a pheasant —"I need to keep my grandson safe. My bloodline has lasted six hundred years." *Thwack. . .thwack. . .thwack.* He pretended to hit imaginary targets. "I have a duty to insure future generations make it into the next century. So implicating Collin in a scandal of this magnitude" — he jabbed his cane toward his feet, propped up on the footstool —"is out of the question. And Major Brown knows it."

Katie wanted to shout: *There will be generations of redheaded Twyfords running around.* Her mind flashed on an image of Aunt Pru with her photo albums full of baby Collin, toddler Collin, schoolboy Collin, teenage Collin. Then she thought about the present Collin dying in a peat bog a year from now *after* he and Prudence got married and had a baby. She opened her mouth to say something, but Toby shot her a warning look.

"Off with you, then," the Duke dismissed them, entwining his fingers around the head of the cane. "I have some ruminating to do. This doddering old warhorse still has some fight left in him."

As they were leaving, Katie glanced over her shoulder. A murky, predawn light had seeped into the room, mingling with the sputtering gas light slanting across the Duke's face, which held not a tortured expression, but a menacing, almost gleeful one.

From far away came the muffled crow of a rooster. Closing the door behind them, Toby and Katie heard the Duke's cane tap-tapping loudly against the leather footstool. Then they heard what sounded like laughter.

Chapter Forty-one

Tighten Your Corset
say the Bells of West Dorset

ANNIE CHAPMAN WAS MURDERED by Jack the Ripper on the evening of September 8, 1888.

The next morning, September 9, the weather outside Katie's bedroom window was crisp and clear with a tingling freshness in the air, compared to the rain and gloom of the night before.

Agnes, the ladies' maid, wearing a starched black dress and white apron, marched across the squeaky floorboards of Katie's room, flung open the curtains, and heaved up the window. Leaning over the sill, she drew in a long breath. The air smelled of newly washed laundry.

"Fine morning, miss," Agnes said cheerfully, swiveling round and peering down at Katie lying in the four-poster bed, the covers pulled up to her chin. "Feeling poorly are we, miss?"

Blinking sleep from her eyes, Katie tried to rise up on her elbows. *Was* she feeling poorly? She couldn't tell. Mornings were not Katie's best time of day. Back home she needed a Starbucks Frappuccino to wake up. Then she remembered Annie Chapman and sat bolt upright.

She blinked at Agnes, then glanced around the room trying to forget that she hadn't been able to save Dark Annie. She tried to focus on the small details of the room in order not to think about it. This bedroom was hers for the duration of her visit with the Duke, Beatrix had told her when she first arrived. It was called the "Floral Room." There was a dressing table painted in tulips in the corner, and between the windows stood a wardrobe with a long, beveled, floral mirror. Against the right-hand wall was a massive mahogany chest of drawers, carved with large clusters of flowers, and a marble-topped washstand. The room's festive wallpaper was embossed with giant scarlet poppies, bordered with even larger purple lupines and blood-red delphiniums. Even the bedspread had a floral theme, matching the curtains at the windows, embroidered with crimson roses the size of cabbages. The whole garden-on-steroids effect was garish and a little creepy, Katie thought, like some genetically engineered fluke.

"Miss?" Agnes gave a bobbing curtsy. "Lady Beatrix says you must be feeling poorly on account of you haven't come down for breakfast." Agnes bustled over to the mahogany chest, fiddled around with the contents of a silver tray, and handed Katie a steaming cup of hot chocolate on a delicate china plate.

"Been here thrice to check on you, miss. You've been fast o' sleep like a stone at the bottom of a dark well."

Katie brought the cup of hot cocoa to her lips, grateful for the semi-bitter taste, which had taken her several mornings to get used to. Cocoa was considered a restorative here, and since Katie had trouble waking up most mornings, unsweetened cocoa was Agnes's answer. That, or a cup of beef tea.

Agnes was a cheerful, plump girl in her midtwenties with a face like a scone — or, at least, that's how Collin referred to her. "Old Scone Face." Agnes had been in service at Twyford Manor since she was eleven. At first Katie had felt guilty that so many people in this century were servants, but Agnes seemed overjoyed with her newly exalted status of ladies' maid. She was over the moon with her new uniform and with the fact that Lady Beatrix had taken it upon herself to train her properly. Agnes was illiterate and had been abandoned at the age of seven. She might have ended up far worse off, Katie reasoned.

Katie tugged her mind away from such thoughts. She wasn't here to change the class system. *I'm here to save Lady Beatrix from being murdered. I couldn't save Dark Annie, but maybe I can save Lady Beatrix.*

She took another sip of the bitter cocoa, frothy on top with thick cream, and once again tried to tug her thoughts away from murder. She didn't want to think about Jack the Ripper. There was plenty of time for that later. Right now Katie just wanted to sip the hot chocolate and forget about death and dying.

She leaned back against the silken sheets. The coverlet, fluffy as air, felt like satin against her skin. And though she hated being waited on by servants, the best thing about living here was that she never had to do the dishes or any other chores. Twyford Manor was chock-full of scullery maids, upstairs maids, downstairs maids, tweenie maids, ladies' maids, footmen. The list went on and on. Katie had only to sneeze, and a bevy of servants scurried around her like flies to honey bringing her foot-warming pans, stoking the fire, drawing her bath, helping her get dressed, *bringing her hot chocolate in bed!*

Katie doubted the Ritz-Carlton in London would be this service-oriented, though the Ritz hadn't been built yet. She didn't even have to put toothpaste on her toothbrush. It was all done for her.

Toothpaste.

Katie inwardly groaned. "Paste" was the operative word. Brushing her teeth in this century was an ordeal. The "paste" was actually finely ground powder. Agnes would open a tin of cream of tartar tooth powder, tap a portion into an earthenware bowl, sprinkle in water, salt, and *chalk,* and stir it into a gritty paste. She'd spackle it onto a toothbrush made of swine bristles with a cow-bone handle, and stand there while Katie brushed and spit into a porcelain urn. Next, Agnes would hand Katie a glass of water mixed with baking soda and parsley to rinse with. The bristle-brush toothbrush was stiff enough to take the enamel off her teeth, and the paste gunk tasted like modeling clay before it hardens — *and was more abrasive.* Katie yearned for the creamy smooth texture of Crest Gel with its minty-cinnamon taste. And her favorite soft toothbrush angled to fit comfortably into her mouth.

She brought the hot cocoa to her lips and made a vow that she would never again complain about using dental floss. Yesterday Agnes had caught Katie using sewing thread to floss her teeth after she'd eaten roast duck. Agnes had looked aghast and proceeded to wrench the thread from Katie's clenched fingers, whispering that proper young ladies did *not* put sewing implements into their mouths. "Only heathens would stoop so low, miss!" Agnes had gently scolded.

Having finished the hot chocolate, Katie threw off the covers and squared her shoulders in anticipation of the next ordeal.

Getting dressed.

Half an hour later she was properly corseted, hooked, squeezed, and fastened into an elaborate morning gown with lace appliqués and puffy, leg-of-mutton sleeves. She made her way downstairs to breakfast feeling as if she were carrying lead weights on her hips, thighs, and petticoated legs. If she fell into a river, she would drown from the weight of the excess fabric, most of which covered the skirt's bustle. To Katie, it defied logic to wear a coiled contraption, called a bustle, over her butt — the result of which was a hump projecting from her posterior that continued in a fanlike sweep to the floor.

The dining room at Twyford Manor, though accessed through the same oak door as the one in Grandma Cleaves's condo, was larger and far grander. It was typical of a Victorian dining room, or at least what Katie imagined a Victorian dining room would be. Down the center of a Turkish rug stretched a long, heavy mahogany dining table, with a massive, matching sideboard polished to a purplish shine. Baronial dining chairs skirted the long table. On the walls hung dozens of hunting-with-the-hounds oil paintings. Most of them showed dead rabbits hanging from the mouths of spotted retrievers.

Entering fully into the dining room, Katie was surprised to see Major Brown and Reverend Pinker at the sideboard scooping up heaping portions of poached eggs, roasted tomatoes, kippers, bacon, and sausage onto their plates. Katie wasn't surprised by the amount of food piled pyramid-style on the mahogany sideboard. Breakfasts at Twyford Manor were as elaborate as the all-you-can-eat buffets at fancy restaurants. *More elaborate*, if you counted the intricate flower arrangements spilling down the center of the table, the ornate silver cutlery, the heavy serving pieces and lacy linens.

No, it wasn't the sumptuous food that surprised her. It was seeing Major Brown and Reverend Pinker loading up their plates as if they hadn't a care in the world. *As if last night had never happened!*

Katie stared hard at Major Brown as he moved along the sideboard inspecting the over-laden food platters. If there was anything weighing heavily upon his mind — *such as murder* — Katie couldn't detect it. He was groomed to a spit and polish in his horse guard's uniform. From his shiny boots to his clipped, waxed moustache, he appeared to be the picture of a dashing man paying court to his fiancée. There was even a twinkle in his heavy-lidded eyes, a swagger as he moved to take a seat at the table. Noticing Katie, he called out a cheerful greeting.

"Miss Lennox!" He bowed slightly. "You're looking exceedingly pretty this morning. I trust you slept well?"

"Yes, indeedy," Reverend Pinker chimed in. "You look radiant, my dear Katherine. Fit as a fiddle, as we say at the parish church." Pinker looked longingly at Katie and licked his lips.

Katie wanted to barf.

He's so creepy, she thought. What kind of minister looks at a teenage girl with. . .well, lust in his eyes? Katie didn't know which man was more repulsive to her, Major Brown with his slick, smug demeanor, or Reverend H. P. Pinker, with his smarmy fawning.

Moving to the sideboard, Katie reached for a slice of toast from the silver toast rack and spooned gooseberry jam and a dollop of bright yellow, wobbly butter, resembling an egg yolk, onto her plate.

Then she took a seat next to Lady Beatrix at the dining table. At the other end, Reverend Pinker plucked a rose from the centerpiece and handed it gallantly down the table to her.

"A rose for a rose," he said with a heavy nasal intonation as three pairs of eyes turned to her. Everyone laughed except for Katie.

Ignoring Pinker's ardent ogling, Katie nibbled at her toast triangle smeared with egg-yolk butter and gooseberry jam, but stopped when she heard a loud voice calling out from the doorway:

"*Greetings!* There you are, Lady Bug!" The accent was distinctly American.

"Haven't forgotten our sitting today, have you, Lady B?" demanded a chin-bearded man in an overly hearty voice. And as he strolled forward into the dining room, the French beret angled on his head flapped up and down like a giant pancake. Covering him to the knees was a blousy, paint-speckled artist's smock, and tied round the smock's ruffled collar was what looked like an op-art cravat. But psychedelic scarves wouldn't be in vogue for another century.

"James!" Lady Beatrix laughed, hailing him with her raised hand. "Of course, I haven't forgotten! The easel is all set up in the morning room. Now remember...mum's the word if my grandfather puts in an appearance." She pressed her fingers against her lips and smiled warmly at him.

"Come," she continued, beckoning. "Join us. The blood pudding is divine! Now, let's see...you know Major Brown and the Reverend Pinker, of course. But have you met our American houseguest, Miss Katherine Lennox? Katie, this is Mr. James Whistler."

The man with the goatee and floppy beret strode closer, hand outstretched, beaming at Katie. "A compatriot? By golly, you don't say! Where do you hail from, Miss Lennox? Don't tell me. Let me guess." He squinted his eyes at her, nodded, and declared with confidence: "You're from New York or Philadelphia, am I right? No?" He raised an eyebrow and stroked his pointy chin beard. "Surely not Hartford — *no one of note, save my good friend Samuel Clemens, hails from Hartford* — hmmm...Boston, then! That's the ticket. Has to be.

A beauty such as you can only have been whelped in New England. Charmed. Delighted. *Enchanté!*" He snatched up Katie's hand, which still held the half-eaten toast, raised it to his lips, smooched loudly, and sank into the chair to her right.

"Darned if I don't insist — *insist* — on painting you next," Whistler pronounced flamboyantly. He leaned in close to her ear and whispered conspiratorially, "Don't tell a soul, but I'm from Massachusetts myself. I'll heartily deny it if you breathe a word. Puritanical hypocrites and philistines all — present company excluded, of course."

Katie felt her eyes grow wide. So this was Whistler? *The* James Abbott McNeill Whistler!

"It's a p-pleasure to meet you, sir," Katie stammered, blinking at him. Had he painted his famous mother yet? And why hadn't she known he was an American? From Massachusetts. Somehow Katie had thought that James Whistler was British.

"Confound it!" Whistler roared in an accent that sounded as if he'd stepped off a southern plantation, and not from New England. "Confound it, I say! Have you read the newspapers? Lookie here —" He scratched his pointed little beard, tugged on the mop of brown curls spilling out from under his beret, and unfurled the newspaper curled under his arm.

Major Brown coughed loudly and said to Lady Beatrix in a stage whisper so all could hear, "My dear, I took the liberty of having the morning papers put aside, out of view. Distressing business. Nothing you need concern yourself with." He snapped his fingers at one of the footmen standing at attention on either side of the sideboard and pointed at his empty mug of tea.

"Really, Gideon! You surprise me," Beatrix said with a slightly raised eyebrow. "Pray tell me you are *not* going to be one of those dreadful, antiquated husbands who forbid their wives to read the newspapers?"

"Confound it!" bristled Whistler. "Never took you for a man who believes woman shouldn't bother their pretty little heads with politics and the like."

"Of course not! I merely think that some of the more crude elements of — "

"Of what? Gideon, you frighten me! You sound precisely like the Duke! I assure you my pretty little head is filled with far more weighty issues than fashion and the latest society soirées!" She winked at Whistler. "Though I confess to occasionally reading the *Daily Mirror* for its marvelous gossip!" Her eye held a teasing twinkle. She turned back to Major Brown.

"Now, darling. Don't be a beast," she laughed. "I have a passion for the daily papers, as you well know. How dreary life would be without them! I'm not a bluestocking intellectual, and I *certainly* don't believe women should vote, but I won't abide a husband who believes his wife takes second place. Or that men are the more important members of society! Here now, let me see what all the fuss is about — "

Lady Beatrix reached across to James Whistler on the other side of Katie, but Major Brown said curtly and firmly, "I'll take that." He stood up, rounded the table, and was about to snatch the newspaper from Whistler's grasp, when Katie seized it. She fanned it open and stared at the headline:

MAD SLASHER STRIKES AGAIN!
PHANTOM KILLER VANISHES WITHOUT A TRACE!

In as clear and loud a voice as Katie could muster she began to read:

"London, September 8. **Not since the days of Bloody Mary has our fair city been so terrorized! A mysterious, diabolical killer is prowling the streets of London, slashing the throats of innocent young women, disemboweling them, and then vanishing into the night without a trace. The Metropolitan Police are at a loss to find this fiend whom they have dubbed 'The Slasher Swine.'**

" 'This is the work of an unbalanced mind,' states Major Gideon Brown, assistant chief inspector of the CID, who exhorts the denizens of Whitechapel to remain calm but alert to further outrages. Readers of the *London Herald* are advised to take the utmost precautions until this menacing killer is apprehended."

Katie went on to read the victims' names: Miss Mary Ann Nichols, murdered on the thirty-first of August in Buck's Row, Whitechapel, and Mrs. Annabel Chapman, murdered in Hanbury Street, Spital-fields, on the night of September the eighth.

Katie held up the newspaper so all could see the pen and ink drawing depicting a younger looking Annie Chapman with ear-length ringlets curling around a demure face beneath a straw hat clustered with ribbons and bows.

"Gracious!" cried Reverend Pinker. "Those poor women! Miss Nichols was known to me from my work at the Parish House, and this other lady, Mrs. Chapman, the poor, poor soul, I made her acquaintance only yesterday! I shall pray for her." Pinker had the decency to look grave-faced and solemn even though his face twitched with fear.

Fear of what? Katie wondered. *Did Reverend Pinker know something? Was he involved in the murders?* By the furtive look in his eye, and the gulping of his throat, he looked as if he'd just been caught stealing from the church offering.

Katie paused. There was more to read, but Major Brown had clamped his large hands around hers and was prying the newspaper from her clenched fingers. Further reading was out of the question. A faint flush of triumph — or was that hostility? — sprang into Major Brown's face as he glanced around the table at the others.

"Undoubtedly you can understand why I took the liberty of hiding the newspapers this morning." He shot Katie a reproving look, then slid the paper under his vest.

A stomping noise.

The dining room door banged open, and Collin, dressed in last night's clothes, loomed large in the doorframe.

"By Jove, Collin!" shouted Whistler, heartily. "Confound it! Where have you been of late? Haven't seen you in a donkey's age! Blast it, boy! I've missed our painting lessons. Don't tell me you've changed your mind about becoming a caricature artist?"

"Whistler, old bean!" Collin cried out in return, but his voice was flat and his eyes were clamped on Major Brown.

Lady Beatrix rose from her seat. "Collin! Where *have* you been? Grandfather is sick with worry. Toby's gone out looking for you."

"Yes! Yes!" chimed in Reverend Pinker. "I had an audience with the Duke this morning. He said to send 'those two young cubs' in to see him immediately. He meant you and Toby. Best go see him this instant."

"I've just *been* with the Duke. Heard all he had to say. Actually, quite an earful." Collin glanced from Lady Beatrix to Reverend Pinker to Katie. Standing haughtily in the doorway, a dark cape thrown over his shoulders, Collin looked. . .not bored, exactly, but restive and impatient, with an intense frown scoring the area between his brows. He took a step into the room, his tall boots crusted with mud.

"Good morning, Collin." Major Brown nodded curtly.

"Is it? A good morning?" Collin asked. His right hand slipped inside his cape and pulled out a riding crop with a long, sharp whip end. He strode across the room and, stopping in front of Major Brown, said, "You're as cold as a snake! I'm done with your playing us for fools. You won't get away with this. And what's more, you shan't marry my sister, not while there's an ounce of breath left in my body!" He raised the riding crop and slashed it viciously across the left side of Major Brown's face.

The crop struck with such force that Katie, standing next to Major Brown, heard the singing whoosh of it slicing through the air just before it hit its mark.

The stunned, incredulous silence that followed seemed to stretch out forever.

Not a muscle moved in Major Brown's face, though his left cheekbone showed a fierce welt, rising red and swollen like a burn from a fire poker. He hadn't even flinched when the whip hit him.

Reverend Pinker was the first to move. Leaping out of his chair, he flew to the bell-cord across the room and tugged violently, as if summoning the butler would be of any use.

Chapter Forty-two

Shepherd's Staff and Poles say the Bells of All Souls

In all the confusion of Collin's horse-whipping Major Brown, Toby slipped into the dining room unnoticed and hastened to Collin's side, at the exact moment that Katie strode forward, planting herself protectively on Collin's right.

Toby gave Katie a slight nod and she deftly tugged the crop from Collin's grasp and held it firmly in her own. She glanced at Toby. There was a challenge in his expression as he stood there glaring at Major Brown, almost as if Toby were daring the man to make the next move. But Major Brown did nothing. He stood stock still, the welt on his cheek appearing like a crimson hieroglyph on a stone tablet. *He won't retaliate*, Katie thought. Not in front of Lady Beatrix.

"Gideon!" Lady Beatrix cried, clutching Major Brown's sleeve as if she might swoon. "My darling, are you hurt? Collin didn't mean it! He *couldn't* mean it —"

"Oh, but I did," Collin pronounced in a deep, mocking tone. "Your *policeman* needs to demand satisfaction. What shall it be?" Collin turned frosty eyes on Major Brown. "Pistols at dawn? Fisticuffs at noon? Swords at sunset?" A grudging laugh. "Pick your poison, Major. I've a point of honor to settle with you that has nothing to do with my sister."

Lady Beatrix's hands flew to her mouth. "Collin! Stop this at once. You've gone mad! As crazy as that lunatic who's slashing innocent women!" She began to tremble so uncontrollably, the lace at her throat and cuffs quivered as if from a strong breeze.

Major Brown, Katie could see, was having trouble remaining calm. His face was contorted and so drained of color that the gash across his cheek stood out like an angry red boil against the dead white of his skin.

Katie had an unfathomable urge to laugh. Not because the scene unfolding was funny, but because Major Brown, with his face twisted up and the veins popping out from his temples, reminded her of the Incredible Hulk when he's about to morph into an angry beast.

But Major Brown didn't morph into anything. He just stood there, a furious expression on his face, his fists clenched and white-knuckled at his sides.

It was Reverend Pinker who stepped into the fray.

"Collin! Cease and desist this instant!" Pinker demanded in a low, nervous tone. "Apologize to your future brother-in-law at once, or —"

"Or . . . ?" Collin's tone was bored, but his face held hard contempt.

"Or my name isn't *Horton Philbert Pinker the third!*" Pinker roared, pulling out his Bible and waving it above his head as if to summon God down from heaven. "English common law forbids the practice of dueling! If either one of you is killed, the other will stand trial for murder."

"Juries never convict," Collin said with a gloating sneer. "Juries of *one's peers*, that is. The nobility are *rawther* fond of dueling, don't you know?"

Pinker thumped the Bible to his chest like a shield. "And *you* know perfectly well that Major Brown cannot participate in a duel. As an officer in service to his queen, he would be court-martialed for appearing in a duel. No. No. This is all wrong. Whatever offense has been taken, you shall have to address it in a manner befitting a peer of the realm and the future Duke of Tywford, *not* as some low-life, guttersnipe ruffian." Pinker tugged out a large handkerchief and mopped his profusely sweating brow. "You," he said, turning to Toby, "and I shall escort Master Collin forthwith to his grandfather's study. Sir Godfrey will talk sense into him, by heaven!"

"Very well, escort me," Collin said placidly.

"*Yes. Go!*" Lady Beatrix sobbed, her tear-smudged gaze swiveling from Major Brown's implacable face to her brother's mocking one.

❖

THE DUKE, SMOKING A CIGAR in his study with his feet propped on his desk, was gazing out the window when Toby, Katie, and Collin entered, followed by Reverend Pinker, who proceeded to give the Duke a full account of Collin's transgressions.

"Let that dirty dog be run through with a sword, for all I care!" the Duke thundered. "Let a bullet pierce Major Brown's heart and be done with it!"

"B-but, my lord!" cried Reverend Pinker, thumping his knuckles on his Bible. "Perhaps you don't understand the full extent of Collin's grievous actions —"

"You bloody fool!" the Duke roared. "Leave us! I've no use for nincompoop padres!"

Pinker's neck rose out of his cleric's collar like an indignant turkey. "But, your grace —"

"Out!"

Moments after Reverend Pinker left, red-faced and bristling, the Duke tugged his cigar from his mouth and clamped his eyes on Toby.

"Lad," he growled, squinting down the length of the cigar as if sighting Toby through a telescope. "Burn me! You got it all wrong, son. *We* got it all wrong. Should have seen this coming." The Duke's facial muscles were uncharacteristically twitching.

"Sir?" Toby lifted an eyebrow.

Behind him, Collin scrambled across the floor and plunked himself into the armchair by the fire. With a sound like a snuffling warthog, Collin swung his muddy boots onto the leather footstool. "Bloody fool of a padre!" he chortled. "Have to remember to call him 'Pinker Padre' next time I see him. Touché, guv'nor!"

Without actually rolling his eyes, the Duke glanced at the stuffed vulture on the mantel, then back to Toby.

"Last night, son, you and I put our thinking caps on. I surmised that it was Collin whom Major Brown would go after for those murders. You thought it was Pinker. You were wrong m'boy, by a long shot."

Toby froze and glanced at Collin slouched in the fireside chair. *Was it possible? Brown was going to implicate Collin?* Toby felt the hair on his neck rise up like that of a dog scenting trouble.

"Go ahead," Collin said, cracking his knuckles one by one. "Take a guess who Major Brown is going to try to send to the gallows?" Collin stopped popping his knuckles and plucked up a half-smoked cigar where it lay balanced atop a stack of ledgers, and clamped it between his teeth.

Toby remembered Major Brown's look of triumph last night at Dark Annie's house. And the hatred in his eyes when he spoke to Collin.

"He's going to try to pin this on Collin, sir? I would have bet my bottom dollar against it." There was bitterness in Toby's voice.

"Why's that, son?"

Toby explained about the code of honor amongst Cockneys. "You never rat out a family member — which Collin will be if Major Brown marries Lady Beatrix. He's duty bound to protect the members of his family. Even if Collin were Jack the Ripper —"

"Who?" the Duke demanded.

"Bloke killing those innocent girls," Collin chimed in.

"I read the papers, boy. I thought they were calling that devil 'The Slasher Fiend' or some such?"

"Katherine says that after the third murder he'll be nicknamed Jack the Ripper."

"Does she now?" The Duke puffed on his cigar.

"Conjecture on my part. . .sir." Katie shot Collin a warning glance. "I, er. . .heard. . .someone on the street mention that name."

"Has a catchy ring to it, Jack the Ripper. But *bah!* Enough. What were you hinting at, Toby?"

"Not hinting, sir. Stating a fact. Major Brown is obliged to honor his familial duties — to defend, shield, protect, even break the law if need be, for Collin. It's precisely why Scotland Yard has such trouble recruiting Cockney officers. They'll forsake all else — their sworn allegiance, their oaths of office, *everything,* to protect a family member."

"Rubbish. Major Brown doesn't have a chivalrous bone in his body, if that's what you're implying. He doesn't give a rat's farthing about Cockney moralities or Cockney conventions. He's got his own tinpot rules and wants us all to dance attendance. Don't you see? The only thing standing between my granddaughter, Lady Beatrix, and the fifth largest fortune in England, is *Collin.* With the heir of Twyford out of the picture, and me dead and buried, Beatrix inherits everything! The estate lands in Devon, the castle in Dartmoor, all the grazing land on the moors, the Twyford jewels, an annual income worth a king's ransom. *Everything* except the ducal title. And *burn me* if Major Brown doesn't find some litigious loophole to pilfer that!"

Toby's throat felt dry. "He won't get away with this, sir. I won't let him."

"Oh, he won't get away with it. . .any of it. . .not while there's an ounce of breath left in my body."

That was the exact expression Collin had used right before he slashed Major Brown across the cheekbone with the crop. Toby glanced from the Duke to Collin, and it hit him that the Duke had sent Collin into the dining room to challenge Major Brown. But why? The Duke was from a different era, a generation that chose dueling to settle differences. But even so . . .

"Major Brown is nothing if not tenacious." The Duke glowered. "The insolent, arrogant dog says he can prove Collin murdered those women. *Says* he found a blood-soaked handkerchief with Collin's initials on the last chit's body. Probably swiped it from Collin's room and tricked it out with pig's blood. But *by thunder* when the time comes" — the Duke's voice was choked with a vengeful eagerness — "I shall crush Major Brown like a spider under the heel of my boot. Just watch me."

"Major Brown's lying!" Toby stormed. "I was there. I was at number twenty-nine Hanbury Street. I saw the body, sir. There was no handkerchief, bloody or otherwise, with Collin's initials on it."

Leaning back in his chair, the Duke grabbed his silver-headed cane and began tapping it lengthwise on top of the desk.

"It gets worse, lad. Major Brown claims that Collin was absent during a portion of the play *Dr Jekyll and Mr Hyde*. Says Collin could easily have slipped out, strangled the first girl, and hightailed it back to the theater."

Katie gasped. "No, that's not possible. I was sitting next to Collin. He left his seat for a short while, it's true. But so did Reverend Pinker and Oscar Wilde. Toby, too, for that matter. I didn't see Toby for the longest time. If Major Brown thinks he can implicate Collin on the strength of whether or not he was sitting with me at the theater, Major Brown has another think coming. I'll vouch for Collin. What's more, Major Brown arrived halfway though the second act, giving *him* ample time to have killed that poor girl."

"I'm afraid, lass," explained the Duke, tap-tapping the cane rhythmically on the desk, "it's more complicated than just vouching for Collin. You see, Major Brown believes he can pin this on Collin as easy as pluggin' a tail on a donkey at a birthday party. But he's not going to. I've seen to it. Brown is *now* going after a far easier kettle of fish to fry. Burn me for a fool! I'm getting soft. The old thinkin' apparatus up here" — he pointed a finger to his gnarled temple — "isn't what it used to be. Major Brown is going after the one person I didn't anticipate."

"Who?" Toby and Katie asked in unison.

The Duke opened his mouth, and then hesitated. When he finally spoke, it was in a flat, quarrelsome voice from deep down in his throat.

"*Burn me!* It's you, m'boy!" The Duke jabbed the cane in Toby's direction. "It's you, lad! He's got his sights set on you. He can personally place you at the scene of Mrs. Chapman's murder at twenty-nine Hanbury, and he says he has two witnesses who will swear you entered the back window leading into the room in which Georgie Cross was murdered. There's a pillow in his possession, with teeth marks, which he found in your room above the stables. Says he'll swear in a court of law that that pillow was in Georgie Cross's room when he left the lad *alive*."

The room went silent.

Toby watched the smoky sunlight dance across the Persian carpet.

The Duke sighed. "Major Brown paid me a visit this morning. Laid it all at my feet. You're under house arrest, m'boy. I bought you a little time is all. Won't be long before they march you off to Newgate Prison. Best I could do under the circumstances was negotiate for house arrest."

House arrest.

The mention of those two words sent a chill down Toby's spine. Major Brown was not in the room, but his menacing presence was. The Duke could save only one of them, Toby knew. And he had chosen his grandson. But Major Brown would have his pound of flesh. Toby's flesh. Swinging from the gallows.

Collin sprang to his feet. "It's up to you and me, Katie!" he cried, waving his cigar in the air like a bandleader with a baton. "It's up to the two of us to stop Major Brown, who just happens to be Jack the Ripper . . . and clear Toby's name."

With a thunderous *thwack!* the Duke crashed his cane down on the desk top. The sound of splintering wood reverberated across the room. The Duke's eyes were brilliantly alive. They roved around and around the room from Toby, to Katie, to Collin. "*By thunder*, we're not licked yet!" But his voice cracked just as the wood had a moment before with a sort of groaning, splintering defeat.

Chapter Forty-three

Murder and Mayhem
say the loud bells of Bedlam

"Looks as if it's up to you and me, Katie, old girl," Collin said. "It's up to *us* to stop Jack the Ripper and clear Toby's name. I know you thought I was crazy when I challenged Major Brown to a duel. Don't deny it. I saw it in your eyes. But I won't let Scotland Yard take Toby away. Not Toby. He's my best friend and my cousin, er...illegitimate cousin to be sure, but cousin nonetheless. Major Brown won't get away with this, not while there's an ounce of breath left in my body."

"What nonsense are you spouting off?" the Duke demanded, scowling at Collin. "You're not going anywhere, m'boy. I can save Toby's hide. Just like I saved yours. But you have to make a small, legal adjustment to your lifestyle."

"Legal adjustment? Are you saying I should hand over my legal rights to my bastard cousin...? Because if you are, well...that's a jolly good idea! We'll claim Toby is my legal cousin. We'll fake a birth certificate. Shouldn't be hard to do. Jolly good plan. I'm older than Toby by six months. This way you'll have an heir and a spare, as they say. Fancy that! Give me the documents and I'll sign on the dotted line! Good show, guv'nor. Major-*bloody*-Brown can't go after two ducal heirs!"

"I wasn't thinking of anything so . . . convoluted," chuckled the Duke. "You'll have to sign, all right. But a document of a different sort. A marriage document."

"Bloody hell!" Collin yelped. "I'm only seventeen!"

"You'll be eighteen in December. I was married to your grandmother at nineteen. You shall marry Prudence Farthington, the Earl of Dorchester's daughter. This is not a request or a polite how-d'you-do. It's an order."

"But why on earth — ?"

"Like you said," the Duke roared with laughter. "I need an heir . . . and a spare."

"Bloody hell! And how does this benefit Toby?"

When the Duke didn't answer, Collin turned to Katie and whispered, "Looks like you're on your own with Jack the Ripper, old girl."

Hurrying out of the Duke's study, the three teenagers fled through the conservatory and down the hall into the large lofty library where Toby carefully locked the double doors behind them. When he turned and edged past Katie, their elbows touched, and they both flinched.

Watching Katie stride to the long windows at the far end of the library, Toby was all too aware of her physical presence. And when Katie fingered the velvet curtains and stared out at the garden beyond with its lush, green grass and thick line of willow trees, Toby could think of only one thing — in a very short time he would never see her again.

Now that he was under house arrest and soon to be locked up in Newgate Prison, Toby realized how difficult it would be to lose Katie. Just being in the same room with her made him ache in a way he would never have dreamed possible only a few short weeks ago. What were the odds he would fall in love with a girl from a different century who could travel through time? Or that Major Brown would come after him like a bulldog after a rat for the murder of Georgie Cross? He was doomed, past hope. Major Brown would never back down. And Katie, Toby felt sure, was as far from reciprocating his feelings as the moon was from the sun.

Toby tore his eyes from the girl.

Next to the fireplace, flanked by stone gargoyles, Collin had plunked himself down on an overstuffed sofa and was staring up at the top section of the library with its iron balcony circling above. A tea service had been set on a book table next to the sofa, with a plate of biscuits and a silver bowl brimming with butterscotch toffees. There was a strong scent of wood smoke from the lone log crackling in the fire grate.

Collin reached for a butterscotch toffee, took careful aim, and chucked it into the fire where it sizzled and smoked and sent off a burnt-caramel odor.

Katie continued staring out the window. There was a chill in the vaulted library despite the blaze of sunlight outside in the garden and the fire in the grate. On the trees in the distance, Katie could see fluttering leaves tipped in yellow and gold, hinting at the autumn to come. A sparrow swooped past the upper window. Everything outside looked bright and cheerful and full of promise, unlike inside where gloom had descended as palpable as the chill in the air.

Behind her, Collin tossed another butterscotch candy into the flames, followed instantly by a tiny *pop!* as the sugary glob bubbled and blistered and sent off a pungent toffee smell.

With a sigh, Katie swiveled back to the others, avoiding Toby's eyes. But his face, she saw instantly, was grim and strained as he paced the room. Collin, too, appeared morose as he continued hurling butterscotch torpedoes into the protesting flames.

"*Bloody hell,*" Collin finally muttered, pitching a handful of the hard candy all at once into the fire where it crackled loudly, then burst into a staccato of small cork-popping sounds.

Poor Collin, Katie thought. The Duke had made it clear that Collin had no choice but to become engaged to Prudence Farthington. *And if the family history in Grandma Cleaves's Bible is correct, Collin will marry Prudence, have a child, and accidently drown in a peat bog all within the next year.* There were dark circles below Collin's reddish-blond lashes, making the whites of his eyes, usually so luminous and clear, appear yellow and dull. *I can't tell Collin that he has only a year to live! That's a terrible thing to know . . . like having an anvil hanging over your head that's attached to a ticking bomb. And if we stop Jack the Ripper, that means we can change history. And if we change history, that means Collin's death isn't inevitable . . .*

"It's freezing in here," Collin shouted in a peevish whine. "Ring for Stebbins to add more logs to the fire!" He clamped his eyes on Toby. And although Collin didn't actually snap his fingers, the effect was the same, as if to say, "Do as I say and hop to it!"

Toby shook his head. "No. We need to talk without interruption. We need to formulate a plan. I've been thinking . . ."

"Well, that makes bloody two of us!" Collin grabbed the last butterscotch candy from the bowl and was about to pitch it into the flames when he tossed it high up into the air and caught it in his mouth like a trained seal. "*Katie!*" he slurped, chomping with such fervor, her name sounded like "Kay-we."

"What's that look on your face?" he demanded, sucking harder on the butterscotch. "Like your dog just died."

Katie's stomach lurched. She quickly glanced away.

Toby was standing off to the side, his elbow resting on a middle rung of the library ladder. She met his gaze. He looked calm and unruffled . . . and, well . . . handsome. No matter what Major Brown was about to accuse Toby of, no matter what obstacles he threw in Toby's path, Katie felt sure Toby would win out. *He has to,* she told herself. Otherwise, how would he end up on the moors with Collin a year from now? *I need to warn Toby again. He can't let Collin go anywhere near the moors.*

Toby was looking at her with a strange expression. "All right," he said, "we know — *or at least, Katie has told us* — who the next five victims will be, and when and where the Ripper will strike. We have the *how* and *where* — just not the *why*."

"Or the who. We don't know for sure that Major Brown is Jack the Ripper," Katie said.

"We bloody well do!" Collin shouted, his face flushing purple.

Toby nodded, his dark eyes intense. "If your information is correct, Katie, it shouldn't be too difficult to save those girls."

"And *how* exactly" — Collin frowned — "do you propose to save anyone while under house arrest? Last time I looked, 'house arrest' meant being confined to one's domicile."

"I've some mates in the East End who will help. Let's go over the list again. The next two victims to die at the hands of the Ripper are Molly Potter and Catherine Eddowes on September thirtieth. Is that correct?" Toby turned his full attention on Katie.

She nodded. "A double murder on the same night. Molly Potter on Berner Street in Whitechapel, and then just before midnight, Catherine Eddowes in Mitre Square."

Katie's mind flashed back to the Chamber of Horrors and the hologram woman with the apple cheeks and church-organ voice describing how Molly Potter had been seven months pregnant. The thought of the poor girl's evisceration at the hands of a homicidal maniac sent a chill up her spine.

"*Forget* Jack the Ripper!" Collin sprang to his feet. His red hair, darker at the edges, spiked out around his head like a kid who'd put his finger in a light socket.

"This is all hearsay and speculation. *Clairvoyant* speculation," Collin sputtered indignantly. "And in case you weren't *listening*, my grandfather wants to fry me in oil! Marry me off to Prudence Farthington! This isn't the dark ages. I refuse to be bullied into an arranged marriage. God's eyeballs! I know I'm ahead of my time, but I have this forward-thinking notion that one *ought* to have at least a bit of . . . well . . . *passion* for the girl one is to marry. I suppose you think that's unreasonable. But there you are. It's how I feel. The very idea of an arranged marriage to Horseface Farthington is as hateful to me as, well...drowning in a bedpan full of slops!"

Katie bit back a weak smile. "I remember your telling me you were *fond* of Prudence. And would be very glad if she accepted you. A feather in your cap, you said."

"*Piffle!* I remember no such thing. I'm being forced to marry someone I don't give a fig for! This isn't the olden days! I've got new-fangled, modern ideas. Oh, all right. I'll concede there are some sound reasons for arranged marriages—provided you at least *like* the other person—the nobility must, after all, maintain bloodlines and keep their titles up to snuff. But *God's teeth!* I don't feel the sort of passion for Horseface-Prudence that I feel for...say...er...Dora Fowler. Now there's the girl for me!"

Toby cast a sharp glance at Collin. "*Dora Fowler?* That's a bloody rum joke. Dora can't hold a candle to Prudence. What's more, you've been rattling on lately about how much you adore 'old Prudie.' You said she has smashing Scotch eggs and beautiful pork pies."

"Horseface-Prudence? Nice legs? Beautiful eyes? *Satan's elbow!* I don't give two hoots for old horseface's legs or eyes...or her bones, teeth, or curvaceous...well, never mind. She has a damnable good, er...carriage. But never mind that. I don't give a tinker's toenail about her now that I've met Dora Fowler." Collin marched across the room to a bookshelf and snatched up a bronze ram's head wedged between a two-volume *The Tragedy of King Richard the Third.*

"What chance do I have of happiness"—Collin railed, waving the ram's head in the air—"if I can't be with Dora? And, anyway, I sort of...you know...pledged myself to her. So an engagement to Prudence is out of the question."

"You what?" Katie and Toby said in unison.

Collin replaced the ram's head next to a stuffed snake draped over the collected works of Thackeray on the shelf above, then turned back to the others, but wouldn't look Toby in the eye.

"Dora's not like other girls. She wouldn't have me. . .you know. . .unless I pledged my. . .what did she call it? My applecart. So I pledged my heart like a proper gentleman — or 'gent' as she calls me — and sealed the deal with my signet ring!"

Katie fastened her eyes on Collin's right hand. His signet ring with the Twyford crest was missing; in its place, a telltale band of white skin.

"*You bloody fool!*" shouted Toby. "Dora Fowler, with her ventriloquism and bird whistles, would take you into her bed for far less than —"

"How dare you talk about my beloved that way?" Blue veins bulged in Collin's forehead. "She's pledged herself to me. . .for. . .for all eternity!" He sprang toward Toby, fists clenched, blue eyes fierce.

Toby stepped forward, fists equally raised.

Katie moved to Toby's side and placed a restraining hand on his arm. Her head was level with his shoulder and she sensed the anger inside him — Collin was Toby's responsibility — but fighting would only make things worse.

Feeling the gentle pressure of Katie's touch, Toby dropped his fists to his side. "Collin," he said wearily. "In the name of all that's holy, tell me you didn't offer Dora —"

"My hand in marriage? Err. . .um. . .something quite like it. . .yes," Collin yelped, releasing his own fists and stepping back. "I believe so. I can't remember everything that transpired last night, but I do remember I gave her my ring. . .she wouldn't let me kiss her otherwise. *God's whiskers*, Toby! Don't look at me like that! What would you have me do? I fancy her. She fancies me. True push and shove."

"Well, I hope true love was worth it."

"It was, er. . .yes, *rawther*. Or what I remember of it." Collin gulped and his Adam's apple surged up and down. "We had a few pints at the pub. . .I woke up this morning with a blistering headache. . .and she told me I'd. . .er. . .proposed. And. . .a gentleman. . .doesn't go back on his word, as you well know, Toby."

"What I know is this: Dora pulled the oldest round the stick in the book on you! The oldest trick, ploy, hoax, swindle, deception known to mankind...or, I should say, *womankind*."

"She never!"

"She did, old sod. You were putty in her hands."

"Boys!" Katie stepped between them. She shot Toby a warning look.

"I tell you," sputtered Collin indignantly. "I'm pledged to Dora Fowler, and there's an end to it!" He made a grunting sound, like a sigh, and began tugging on his lower lip with thumb and forefinger. "What's more, I despise old Horseface-Prudie like poison!" He turned and sprang past the book table, bumping against it, rattling the tea set and jiggling the biscuits. One biscuit fell to the floor with a thunk. Collin bent over to retrieve it, then, in frustration, shoved the entire table and it fell over with a crash.

"So you're going to make Dora your bag for life, is that it?" Toby crossed his arms in front of his chest.

"If you mean wife, yes. She'll be the Duchess of —"

"Strife?" Toby was grinning.

Collin rose to his full height and thumped himself on the chest. "Nothing you can possibly say will in any way upset the matrimonial applecart of Collin Chesterfield Twyford, the third, or my name isn't...er, well...Collin Chesterfield Twyford, the third, heir to the Duke of Twyford, and —"

"You're right, old sod," Toby laughed, cutting him off. "Nothing *I* say will make a bit of difference. But the Duke will have more than a few words on that account. He has his own way of dealing with what he perceives as a swinging door."

"A swinging what?"

"What Cockneys call a —"

Katie tossed Toby a sharp glance. *If that's what I think it is, don't say it,* she thought. "Don't even think it," she said aloud, moving forward. But she was too late.

"Whore."

A moment later Collin was raining punches down on Toby, flailing his fists with a fierceness that belied his lanky frame. But Toby came from a long line of fairground fighters. His maternal granddad had been a champion bare-knuckle boxer. Collin was outclassed, outfoxed, outmaneuvered. Toby deflected his blows as easily as if he were dancing around an angry, pecking rooster.

Katie shook her head. Seemingly without effort, Toby sidestepped punch after far-flung punch until Collin grew tired and began to weave off balance. But in a final burst of frustration, Collin raised his right fist and hammered it at Toby's face. Instead of ducking, Toby wrapped his hand around Collin's high-flying knuckles, stopping the momentum as easily as if he were wearing a baseball glove and catching a hard-hit spitball. The move surprised and enraged Collin. He began to howl in anger as Toby twisted his arm and levered him down on all fours. They wrestled to the ground, Collin shrieking, but he could no more fight off Toby than a bear could an elephant, and when Collin was finally pinned and cried uncle, Toby easily released him and strode back across the room to right the tea table, hoisting it up from the floor with one hand.

"Toby! Watch out!" Katie cried.

Toby whipped around.

Behind him, Collin had sprung to his feet and was screaming with such rage, the shrill sound of it set Toby's teeth on edge. It was the piercing shriek of an enraged animal. Collin's face, as he lunged, was twisted with rage and as dark red as if suffused with beet juice.

"You're all in league against me!" Collin screeched, pulling out his penknife and jabbing it in the air like a poker.

Toby's hobnailed boots clattered back across the floor.

Another shrill howl from Collin. "I'll show you who's the boss of me. Not so bold now, eh?" Collin slashed the pocket knife this way and that.

"Put it down!" Toby hissed, circling Collin cautiously. But as he narrowed the distance between them, Collin kicked out wildly at Toby's midsection, forcing him to step back.

Toby continued to circle, slowly, deliberately. "Every Thursday night," he said in a deceptively matter-of-fact voice, "a thousand East Enders pack into Joey's Music Hall. I'll take you someday, Katie." He spoke so softly and conversationally, it was as if he were talking about the weather, but his attention remained riveted on Collin.

"For a shilling I can get us ringside seats. Isn't that right, Collin? You and I like to stand at the back...placing bets. Working-class stiffs number fifty to one against toffs. It's a sight to behold, isn't it, Collin? All the lads wear bright red scarves instead of collars. Not like the tournaments at Albert Hall." His voice was soothing.

But Collin was not mollified. He continued to jab at Toby, his freckled face bathed in sweat, his red hair falling over his furrowed brow. His eyes held a watchfulness that matched Toby's. He was waiting for his moment.

"If anger could win this for you, Collin," Toby said with a wry smile, "you'd be the victor hands down."

When Toby inched closer, Collin saw his opportunity and punched out with his free hand, then kneed Toby in the abdomen. Toby had deliberately gone in close, bracing for the kick — and when it came, it seemed to Katie, he absorbed the blow like a punching bag, inured to the pain.

Emboldened, Collin followed with a jab and a right cross. Toby seized Collin's wrist and pivoted him around into a half-Nelson, then wrapped his right leg around Collin's left. Collin buckled. Twisting his wrist like a corkscrew, Toby ordering Collin to drop the knife. But when Collin stubbornly refused, Toby bent back his fingers one by one, until an expression of agony washed over Collin's face and the pocketknife clattered to the floor.

Chapter forty-four

Kettles of Fish
say the Bells of Shoreditch

IN THE ORCHESTRA PIT at the London Music Hall in Shoreditch High Street, the bandleader raised his baton. The vast auditorium was only half full with Saturday night patrons who had paid a hefty sum to be entertained with bawdy music, juggling acts, knife throwing, sword swallowing, dancing girls, and a rousing ventriloquist act. A half circle of burning lanterns threw spheres of quivering gaslight onto the stage, lending a tremor of anticipation to the charged atmosphere.

Katie, standing next to Collin in the left-hand aisle against a dull brick wall, watched as a dozen black fiddle bows rose from the orchestra pit in unison. Cymbals crashed hard on the opening bar of "Ta-ra-ra-Boom-de-ay," rising with a pendulum cadence and a burst of cheers from the audience as Catherine Eddowes, a striking young woman, sashayed onto the stage and began to sing with deceptive demureness, even as she coyly displayed a flash of her ankles and calves wreathed in lacy pantaloons, and a portion of her prodigious white-powdered bosom, enveloped in see-through silk. Her voice was strong and sweetly feminine as she belted out the lyrics.

> *Ta-ra-ra-Boom-de-ay!* (the cymbals struck again)
> Jack the Ripper's out to play
> He'll take your girl away —
> And slice her up today
> He'll take her organs, too,
> And when he's good and through
> He'll take your sister Lou
> And cut her up for stew
> Ta-ra-ra-Boom-de-ay!
> Ta-ra-ra-Boom-de-ay!

Throughout the dimly lit theater, people whistled, hummed, and clapped to the rousing tune. Collin, too, joined in. An infectious merriment filled the auditorium, which Katie might have felt if it weren't for the fact that Catherine Eddowes, singing with such gusto, was slated to be Jack the Ripper's next victim.

It was the thirtieth of September, the night of the double homicide of Catherine Eddowes, in Mitre Square, Aldgate, and a very pregnant Molly Potter in Berner Street, Whitechapel.

Catherine Eddowes sang the lyrics again, and then launched into a lusty refrain with a sort of kick dance, like the cancan, displaying her long legs and deep cleavage. Bras hadn't been invented yet, Katie knew, but even so, Catherine Eddowes would have been the last person on earth to need a Victoria's Secret push-up.

She went on to sing "The Boy I Love" and "Daisy Bell," and after several prolonged curtsies, Catherine Eddowes exited the stage to a chorus of cheering. Katie cast her eyes about, then nodded to Collin, and together they retraced their steps down the red-carpeted aisle.

The theater was large and amazingly ornate, with plaster molds of cupids and nymphs on the gilded proscenium arch. Poster boards in the foyer announced the return of the Flying Mephisto Brothers with colorful renditions of acrobats in scarlet tights.

Guarding the stage door outside the music hall sat a man in a monk's costume who let them pass into the bowels of the theater when Katie palmed several silver coins into his waiting hand. Inside they moved haltingly down a long, dark passageway, musty with the smell of theater props and scenery. Nobody stopped them as they hurried along past broken rows of orchestra seats shrouded in white dust covers until they came to a set of padded swinging doors. Entering, they could see the side panels of the gas-lighted stage to the right. They were in the wings below a snarl of ropes, levered pulleys, and scaffolding, and could clearly hear laughter from patrons in the front orchestra stalls.

The clang of a xylophone rang out, followed by the thumping clatter of stilt-walkers, dressed like cowboys, stomping across the stage. Peeking through the curtained wings, Katie watched the stilt-walker nearest her at the rear of the stage. He was so tall, she could see only the bottoms of his wooden legs draped in leather chaps, ending in giant spurred cowboy boots.

She drew back. A shadowy figure was approaching from the dark recesses to the rear, moving stealthily under the scaffolding. Emerging from the dimness he looked disturbingly like Major Brown. Katie and Collin ducked behind a curtain wing. There was a stash of props on a side table: a white, ten-gallon cowboy hat, a rodeo-style blacksnake whip, two cross-belt holsters, and a pearl-handled six-shooter. Katie plunked the ten-gallon hat on top of Collin's head, smushing it over his eyes, and ducked behind him into the shadows.

If Katie were to bump into Major Brown in a dark alley, he would have scared her to death. Tall and commanding, he exuded a raw masculine energy that was more than a little menacing. But backstage in this burlesque theater she felt only apprehension and something like anger. What was Major Brown doing here? Had he spoken to Catherine Eddowes? Had he already killed her and sliced her open?

No, Katie told herself. Catherine Eddowes was supposed to die in Mitre Square, just after midnight, not backstage in a dark theater.

"Howdy, buckaroo!" Collin couldn't resist saying in an imitation drawl as Major Brown pushed past.

"Stop that!" Katie whispered, tugging at the back of Collin's greatcoat.

"This here hat is mighty fine!" Collin continued the parody, but luckily Major Brown was out of earshot, having left through the padded swinging doors.

"Quit fooling around," Katie whispered, swiping the ten-gallon hat off his head and replacing it on the prop table. "That was close."

"Sho-nuf, little lady." Collin eyed the pearl-handled six-shooter longingly.

"Forget it," Katie said, shaking her head. "It's only a prop. And stop with the Southern drawl already."

"T'aint Southern!" Collin scoffed. "Can't y'all tell ah'm from Texas?"

"Last time I looked, Texas was in the *South*." Katie tried not to smile.

"*No-sir-ree*, little lady. It's in the Wild West. Don't y'all know anything? Haven't y'all heard of Buffalo Bill?" Collin explained that Buffalo Bill had performed in London last year for the Queen's Jubilee. "*Tarnation*, I saw the show twice! Wish I was a genuine cowboy . . . or maybe a bison hunter! That's the life for me!"

Katie laughed. "Even so, Texas is *not* the Wild West." She didn't know anything about Buffalo Bill except that his name sounded familiar. When she got home, she'd look him up on the Internet. Katie had a vague idea he was related to Annie Oakley. "The only thing worse than imitating a Texan accent," she said, "is a Brit doing it. Come on, let's go."

A dozen firecracker *pops!* sounded across the stage to Katie's right, making her jump. The stilt-walking cowboys were blasting cap-gun six-shooters at one another, all the while stomping long-legged around the stage, as if doing the Cotton-Eyed Joe. The audience rose to their feet, hooting and hollering just as the orchestra started up again.

For a hefty sum, Toby had arranged for Katie and Collin to meet Catherine Eddowes in her dressing room after her stage performance, and then to stay with her throughout the evening—with an even heftier bonus to follow in the morning. But when Katie and Collin arrived at the backstage room where the performers donned their costumes and makeup, Catherine Eddowes was nowhere to be found.

A grim little man in a red clown's costume, wearing black face paint, approached. "If you be looking for Miss Eddowes, she said to tell you she received a better offer, and to say good day to you. Or, should I say, good night." He scurried past several ballet dancers, whose bell-shaped tutus, draped in long pink netting, fluttered outward from their hips.

"*Ballerinas!*" bawled a low voice from the darkness. "*Places! You're on in five!* Hey! You. What you doing backstage? *Places! Places, girls! Half a tick! Wait for it. Wait for it. You're on in three seconds. Two, one—*"

Scampering toward the stage, several ballerinas gave Collin appraising looks. Collin, in turn, stared back at the pink-clad girls, a wolfish grin on his face.

"Wait!" Katie called after the clown man, elbowing past Collin. "Where did Catherine Eddowes go? Did she go home?"

"Not that one," chuckled the clown. "Not by a long shot. Probably taking a stroll past the pubs, see what catches her eye. She likes her gin. Likes it more 'n most. Now me, I'm a pint man, m'self. Don't go in for—"

"Where? What pub?"

"Ten Bells, more'n likely."

Katie thanked the clown-man then narrowed her eyes at Collin who seemed oblivious to anything other than the dancing girls twirling onto the stage in their long, netted tutus, fitted bodices, and pink tights.

Chapter Forty-five

Catch Me if You Dare
say the Bells of St. Clare's

HURRYING DOWN COMMERCIAL STREET on their way to the Ten Bells, Katie and Collin heard the clock of Saint Clare of Assisi strike ten. They had two hours to find Catherine Eddowes and save her from her horrific fate.

Katie whispered a silent prayer that the doorman backstage at the London Music Hall was correct. Catherine Eddowes would be at the Ten Bells Tavern.

A pony cart rattled down the dark street, its lantern light dwindling, then dying away, as the cart turned sharply down Aldgate Lane, out of sight. Katie glanced at Collin, his hand at her elbow tugging her along, and a stab of fear shot through her. *What if we don't find Catherine Eddowes?*

Collin, cloaked head to toe in black, his collar drawn up to his ears, looked precisely as Katie imagined Jack the Ripper would look.

Shrouded in a long cape, the wings of his collar projecting stiffly upward like black raven's wings, he looked —

Katie mentally shook herself. If anything, Collin's clothing made him look more like Dracula. But his flame-red hair jutting out like straw from under his black bowler, shattered the Prince of Darkness image. And yet. . .the expression in Collin's ice-blue eyes below the ginger arch of his brows was murderous.

"What if we don't find her, Katherine? What if. . ." his voice choked.

"I know." Katie nodded. "I was thinking the same thing. But we *will* find her, Collin. We won't let her die."

Collin let go of Katie's elbow and threaded her arm through his. "Not to worry, Katie old girl. If we don't find Miss Eddowes at the Ten Bells, we'll hightail it directly to Mitre Square. . .and wait. We're about to pass through the square now, it's on our way. And you have my word, Katie, I'll do everything in my power — "

"I know, Collin. If only. . ." But Katie didn't say what she was thinking. *If only Toby were here,* because that would irritate Collin, make him think she didn't believe he was capable of thwarting Jack the Ripper. They'd agreed that Katie and Collin would stick like glue to Catherine Eddowes — who had given her promise for a hefty fee to stay with them until past midnight. And that Toby would escape from Twyford Manor — where he was under house arrest — and shadow Molly Potter.

Katie's pulse raced. She started to tremble. They were entering Mitre Square. It would be here, in this dingy courtyard that Catherine Eddowes might die. Katie glanced around. There was no one in sight except a drunken man sprawled on the ground, legs splayed, his back propped against a hitching post. He was snoring loudly, clutching tight to a whiskey bottle, a red kerchief tied atop his head. Streaks of coal dust lay smeared across his eyes and nose like a raccoon mask.

Dimly lit, the cobblestone square was no bigger than half a basketball court, bracketed on three sides by narrow, brick tenement walls, which held the entrances of shops, shuttered and padlocked.

Kearley & Tonge Grocers, O'Fingal's fish shop, and a wardrobe dealer whose name Katie couldn't read because it had been scratched away from the weather-beaten sign hanging over the lintel.

Katie and Collin stopped as they approached the square and scanned the perimeter. The lonely, moonlit square had three entrances: one from Minories Street to the east, the second from a doglegged alley called Church Passage, and the third from a narrow walkway leading from Saint Clare's Place, the last of which they had just walked down.

Collin lit the lantern he'd brought with him. As the flame dipped and rose, it illuminated a stone drinking well in the center of the square.

A cat yowled, and Katie spun around. Collin flicked open the slide-window on the lantern an inch or two, and let the beam of light play up and down the narrow brick walls.

Fear, stronger than Katie had ever felt before, suddenly seized her, making her recoil. She felt an all-consuming sense of revulsion as her gaze fastened on the stone well, similar to the one at Madame Tussauds that had cradled the London Stone. It was here that Catherine Eddowes would die. By some weird illusion of the light from Collin's lantern, the tenement walls rising up behind the stone well looked moist and damp, as if they were sweating tears.

Shaking away her sense of foreboding, as well as the notion that the walls were crying, Katie whispered, "Let's get out of here! It's giving me the —"

"Willies?" Collin whispered back. "Me, too."

Katie was going to say that the place gave her the creeps. She cast a sharp glance around, clutching tight to Collin's arm, and they hastened past the drinking well toward Church Passage.

Collin muttered something under his breath that Katie took for half-oath, half-prayer. She was saying prayers herself.

The drunken man, propped up against the hitching post, cried out in a gravelly, whiskey-soaked voice: "Oy, mate! Got a smoke fer a bloke down on 'is luck?"

"My good man," Collin tut-tutted. "If I had a cigar, I surely wouldn't —"

Katie yanked hard on Collin's arm.

"Er... right," Collin amended. "I left me smokes at 'ome," Collin called out, imitating a Cockney accent. They had agreed, should they meet anyone, that Collin would use a Cockney accent, which he did quite well, having listened to Toby for most of his life. It wouldn't do to sound educated and well-to-do in an area where pickpockets and thieves plied their trade.

"Oy, mate," the man stumbled to his feet. "You two love birds be awful careful, mind." The soot-smeared man belched. "Don't wanna meet up wiff his majesty Jack the Ripper. He's a nasty piece of work, is ol' Jack. Seen him do the dirty deed wiff them girls."

"You've seen him?" Katie asked, turning back. "You know who he is?"

"Course I know him! It's me! Oim Master Jack, his worshipful lordship. Oy! Ain't you a pretty bit of goods?" The man lurched toward Katie.

"Drunken oaf! Leave off!" Collin shouted, shoving the man.

The soot-sodden man tumbled off balance to the ground and let out a throaty roar of rage that grew louder, echoing off the tenement walls. As if licking his wounds, he crawled back to his spot by the hitching post and took a long swig from his whiskey bottle.

As they hurried out of the square, Katie asked Collin if he thought the man might actually be telling the truth.

"Of course not!" Collin shook his head, guiding her forward. "Bloke's nothing but a drunken lout. It would take someone far more clever and virile" — he thumped himself on the chest to indicate his own prowess — "to be Jack the Ripper."

"But, Collin, don't you see?" Katie whispered. "Pretending to be a stumbling drunk would be the perfect disguise!"

They entered the alley leading out of the Square.

"We shouldn't overlook the obvious," Katie insisted. "He might be lying in wait for Catherine Eddowes."

"Look here, old girl," Collin said in what sounded like bravado. "Two hundred years from now when that drunken oaf, and all his grandsons — ours, too — are rotting in their graves, none of this will matter a tinker's curse."

"It *will* matter, Collin," Katie whispered, her throat tightening. "I think violence committed against innocent girls should never be forgotten . . . or forgiven. If we don't stop Jack the Ripper, history will have to find him and track him down . . . if only to honor his poor victims.

"Collin," Katie continued, more vehemently than before, "if it's the last thing I do, I'm going to find out who Jack the Ripper *really* is. Even if we don't save a single girl, at least history will know and condemn him for the sadistic serial killer that he is."

"Sweet, suffering Moses! Let's hope it's not the *last* thing you do." Collin's eyes shone in the gloom as they hurried along. "You sound as if you actually believe the ghosts of those murdered girls will come back and haunt these streets until their killer is brought to justice."

Or maybe a relative of one of the victims — a descendant of Lady Beatrix — will come back and serve up justice!

"I think," Katie answered softly, "that Jack the Ripper and his poor victims will live on for hundreds of years . . . unless we do something about it."

Behind them, from somewhere out of sight, Katie heard a man clear his throat. Katie glanced over her shoulder and caught the vague outline of a shrouded figure hastening down the passageway opposite into the Square. From the dimness rose a strident, arrogant voice they recognized instantly.

In a flash, Collin extinguished his lantern and tugged Katie around the dogleg bend and down a set of steps into a basement stairwell, where they crouched out of sight.

From the far end of the courtyard came the distinct sound of tall boots clicking, long before the man wearing them emerged into the moonlight, black military cloak flapping in the breeze as he strode forth.

Major Gideon Brown.

As he approached the center of the square, Katie caught a clear glimpse of the slightly curved sword protruding down from Major Brown's left hip. It had a woven-wire grip and silver-filigree guard. She saw the holstered pistol, hung like a limp-necked dead bird, next to his billy club.

With a rattle of steel, leather, and hobnails from his boots, Major Brown strode toward the soot-faced man slouched against the post. The bright blade of his rapier flashed maliciously at his side. Its cutting edge appearing needle sharp in the moonlight.

"Angus. I crave a word!" Major Brown spoke bluntly, with an authoritative ring that carried clear across the cobblestones and echoed off the tear-streaked walls.

Crouching in the stairwell, Collin hissed under his breath. "Crave all you like, you filthy swine. The lout's as drunk as a skunk."

"Shhh, Collin. I can't hear," Katie whispered sharply, jutting her neck out to see better.

"Major Brown, sir!" The man shot up, instantly at attention. When he had risen to his full height and was saluting Major Brown, Katie could see it was the same man who had followed Toby and her from Traitors' Gate into the underground railway. The same beefy man they'd escaped from. Major Brown's man.

"Sir! The redheaded lad and the girl. They went that way, down Church Passage." The officer pointed in their direction.

Chapter Forty-six

Clerics Hats and Sheep
say the Bells of Eastcheap

COLLIN WAS ON HIS FEET instantly, the wings of his cloak thrown back as he pushed Katie up the stairwell.

"Run!"

Katie darted along the impossibly narrow alley. If she reached out her fingers, they'd scrape against bare brick walls on both sides. A horse cart blocked the tiny lane.

Panting hard, Katie swiveled back and watched as Collin wheeled the lantern high over his head, swung it around like a light saber gathering momentum, and smashed it to the ground. The glass shattered with a splintering crash. Oil oozed across the narrow passage.

Katie heard the *whick* of a matchstick as it struck against the tinder-box, and watched as Collin flicked the match onto the gooey sheen. Flames rose up, blood-red tongues licking and spitting. Katie blinked, then blinked again. It appeared as if Collin's cloak was engulfed in fire; his face, melting like wax. Terrified, Katie cried out. But an instant later, relief surged through her when she heard Collin's laughter rise up along with the flames.

"Take that, you blighter!" Collin hooted.

It had been an illusion. The only flames engulfing Collin were the spikes of his red hair shooting straight up from his head. His bowler had tumbled to the ground and was rolling by his side. Collin scooped it up and bolted after Katie, shouting: "Run! Run! Run!" A second later, their racing footsteps clattered loudly on the cobblestones, drowning out the hissing fire.

At the far end of the passage loomed an enormous wagon stacked with wooden barrels, stamped with one word: MALT.

Collin took Katie's hand, and they squeezed past the unattended cart, dodging around the back wagon wheel. The owner must have stepped into the Hungry Goblin across the street for a pint. Releasing Katie's hand, Collin hoisted himself onto the back of the open wagon. The large dray horse snorted and pawed the ground.

Pure fury glimmered in Collin's eyes as he shoved barrel after barrel out the back end of the cart where they tumbled down with a loud *thunk*, clattering and rolling into the alley.

With a heavy growl like a mastiff on a leash, Collin jumped down from the flatbed dray and grabbed Katie's wrist. They turned and ran, increasing their pace until Katie felt as if her lungs would burst. Her corset was too tight.

She faltered and stumbled.

Collin slowed down.

They rounded a sharp corner, and only then did they stop. Panting and hidden in shadow, they peeked out from around a boarding house cornerstone and scanned the long, dark street.

With a distance of several blocks between them and Major Brown, they watched the driver of the dray charge out of the Hungry Goblin, howling curses at Major Brown and fisting Brown's assistant in the chest.

Katie glanced over her shoulder. Several women were entering a stark white church across the way on Minories Street. Spiraling up into the misty, dark sky reared the church steeple of Saint Clare of Assisi, its windows lit with candles.

"Collin. Come on!" This time it was Katie who seized Collin's wrist and tugged. As they raced toward the chapel they saw a sign advertising a midnight prayer vigil for the souls of the two murdered Whitechapel girls, *Mary Ann Nichols* and *Annie Chapman*.

Angels adorned the front windows. The church was so small — nestled between crooked houses on either side — that the columns flanking the front doors appeared like giant masts holding up a tiny sailing ship.

This area of the Minories, though not a slum, loomed dreary and smoky with its muddy cobblestones and curbside refuse. Crumbling chimney stacks sat atop tenement houses whose doors were shuttered with iron bars that rattled and groaned in the wind.

"Rot my soul!" Collin shouted. "Look — "

As they approached the church, Reverend H. P. Pinker stood just inside the doorway greeting mostly elderly congregants. When he saw Collin, he gave a hard, sharp look of surprise. Reverend Pinker had been bending forward, murmuring words of solace to two old women and an unshaven man, but he hurried them inside when he spotted Katie.

"My dear Miss Katherine," Reverend Pinker beckoned to Katie, and his long face above the white clerical collar grew heavy and somber. "The East End is no place for a young lady such as yourself. There's a madman on the prowl. Scotland Yard has given us every assurance that this carnage is at an end. But even escorted by young Master Collin — *especially escorted by Master Collin* — there's danger around every bend. I insist on bringing you posthaste to Twyford Manor after I deliver my candlelight sermon. Let me — "

"Stow it, Stink-Pink," Collin roared. "By all that's holy, be a *brick*, Pinker — just this once! We need sanctuary, safe passage, safe haven, not sanctimonious polly-woggle drivel from a — "

"Reverend Pinker, sir," Katie cut in, dropping a curtsy. She was still panting heavily. "Could you . . . would you . . . be so kind as to . . . help us? It's . . . Major Brown. He . . . he —"

"Gideon Brown? *Major Gideon Brown?*" Pinker's tone implied there might be some doubt about whom they meant. "My dear child. What on earth — ?"

Collin scrunched up his face as if trying to come up with a plausible response. "Major — *rot his soul* — Brown was . . . er . . . well . . . treating Katie in an . . . unseemly . . . manner. Yes! That's it! Unseemly. Rough, coarse, and . . . er . . . lustful!"

Reverend Pinker bristled even as his gaze briefly dipped and fastened on the portion of Katie's anatomy where her cleavage — or heart — would have been had she not been bundled up in a wool coat, prim ruffled dress, and whalebone corset.

"Just point us to the rear exit and cover for us, Pinker. If Major Brown comes sniffing about, deny we were here. *Now hurry, Stink-Pink!* We haven't much time!"

"Haven't much time for what? And my dear young lady —" Reverend Pinker bent close to Katie. Too close. "I confess I fail to comprehend why you are here at this hour. What business brings —"

"Ruffian!" Collin intoned. "Major Brown's a ruffian pure and simple. We need to escape!"

Reverend Pinker nodded and gave a grave little bow. "I've always suspected Major Brown was not worthy of the affections of your dear sister, Lady Beatrix. However, young sir," he said to Collin. "I shall not distort the truth, nor shall I tell lies. I will, however, shield you. It is my duty as a devoted family friend and spiritual counselor."

Reverend Pinker's narrow face and elongated neck reminded Katie of a turkey, but above the beaklike nose, his grey eyes held a somber intelligence.

"By God's grace and my own forbears," he said grimly, "I shall give you safe sanctuary. Follow me."

Spotting movement down the street, Katie's eyes clamped onto the shadowy figure of Major Brown in the distance, scanning the dark street that extended south to the river.

Despite her fear as she watched Major Brown step off the distant curb and hasten down the long, dark street, Katie felt an odd sense of relief that Reverend Pinker would shield them, until her mind flashed back to the waxwork figure at Madame Tussauds.

What Manner of Man Could Walk the Streets
OF WHITECHAPEL AND BE ABOVE SUSPICION?

Katie drew in a sharp breath. *This church, so close to Mitre Square, was the perfect place for Jack the Ripper to hide after killing Catherine Eddowes!*

Lifting her gaze, Katie stared into the grey-flecked eyes of the man who could easily be the Right Honourable Reverend Jack!

Seconds later, when Major Brown strode toward the tiny church of Saint Clare of Assisi, Collin snatched Katie's hand and pulled her into the chapel and down the center aisle toward the raised platform with a pulpit in the middle. Two silver candlesticks sat on the dais, a bucket of flowers resting on either side.

As they raced toward the altar, the sacrificial lamb aspect of the scene was not lost on Katie.

Chapter Forty-seven

Half a League, Half a League, Half a League Onward; Death Strikes Again

A COLD BREEZE RUSTLED THE LEAVES. Katie shivered and turned up the velvet collar of her wool coat.

From out of the shadows of the Ten Bells Tavern stumbled two middle-aged women and a stout man in a flattened bowler hat.

"You'll catch your death of cold out here, Mabel!" said the first woman, stepping into the brisk night air. "Put yer cloak on!"

Mabel hiccupped and scoffed. "God's breath! If we run into Jack the Ripper, I'll catch more 'n a cold. Stick close, Rosalynn! Remember what the dailies said. We need to stick together."

"Humph!" scoffed the squat man with the flattened hat. "I'll protect you!"

"You couldn't save us from a bleedin' billy goat if it was about to butt us in the rump!" cried Mabel.

371

"Here now!" cried Rosalynn. "Let's link arms and shove off."

The two women entwined their arms and pushed off into the dark night, followed by the squat man in his crushed bowler.

❖

As Katie and Collin entered the Ten Bells Tavern, the wind seethed behind them. On either side of the front door stood cast-iron dogs, as if guarding the portals.

The pub was filled with cigar smoke and packed with Saturday night revelers: shop girls, factory workers, clerks, butchers, porter lads — all chatting and laughing loudly. An enormous dartboard hung on the left-hand wall. Flanking it were framed prints of eighteenth-century coaching inns — most with darts sticking out of the wooden frames like porcupine quills. Angled near the back wall spanned a lopsided counter doing duty as a bar. Gas jets above the bar flickered with hissing blue flames, throwing elongated light onto a brown staircase.

As Katie and Collin moved forward into the crowd, they spotted Dora Fowler sitting at a table in the corner. Drinking from a pint of ale and wearing a paisley shawl around her shoulders, Dora sat chatting with a man in a blacksmith apron. When her eyes clamped onto Collin's, like a whippet in pursuit of a rabbit, she shot off her stool and forged a path through the jostling crowd.

Dora pushed past Oscar Wilde, who leaned languidly against a side wall where a chalkboard menu hung from a peg. Dressed in a long, plum-colored evening coat, his top hat cocked to the side, Wilde was deep in conversation with a stocky man hidden in shadow and puffing on a cigar.

"*Hoy*, there, luv!" cried out Dora, elbowing her way through the last of the crowd. "Fancy meeting you here!" She patted her dark curls and giggled. "Give us a kiss, ducks."

Dora held out her cheek to Collin and winked at Katie. "He's a proper gent, is my Collin." She nudged Collin in the ribs and asked in a stage whisper, "Who's this then, eh?"

"This is my American cousin, Miss Katherine Lennox. Remember I told you about her?" Collin said, shuffling from foot to foot, looking sheepish and uncomfortable.

"Right! She's the ham shank Toby fancies!" A hint of amusement crossed Dora's expression. "Nice ter meet yer, Katie. Collin calls you Katie, ain't that right? Did he tell you we gots an understanding?" Dora grinned, lifting her gaze trustingly to Collin. "Did you tell 'er, Collie?" she asked, using the pet name that Katie called her cousin Collin back home.

"I . . . er . . . um . . ." Collin stammered, a red flush suffusing his neck and washing upward into his freckled cheeks.

Dora tugged at his sleeve.

"Dora—" Katie cut in, "I saw you give testimony at the inquest for Mary Ann Nichols, and Toby told me all about your talking birds. It's nice to meet you, too. But we're here because we're looking for a woman named Catherine Eddowes. She's a cabaret singer at the London Music Hall—"

"What's it to you, eh?" Dora's eyes narrowed and she clamped her hands on her hips.

"We need to find . . . that is, I need to find"—Katie quickly amended, seeing sparks of jealousy in Dora's dark eyes—"Catherine Eddowes. Do you know her?"

Dora scrunched up her plump face and let out a little laugh. "Whaddya want wiff that old cow? She's close to forty if she's a day. Me mum says, 'Cathy Eddowes is long in the tooth and short on virtue.'"

"You *know* Catherine Eddowes?" Collin stiffened. Katie thought she heard him groan.

"'Course I do! Everyone at the Ten Bells knows Cathy. She's me Uncle Thaddeus's second wife's niece. And the barkeep's cousin." Dora gave a little shrug. "I ain't saying she's a swinging door, mind. Not Cathy. But she likes a bit of the grab-and-tickle wiff the gents, specially the ones who buys 'er gin. She's not for the likes of gentry like you." Dora pointed at Collin and tick-tocked her finger to include Katie.

"Do you know where she is? Can you help us find her?" Katie implored, trying to tamp down the urgency in her voice.

"*Blimey!* She'll be here afore you can say Jack Robinson. . .or should I say, Jack the Ripper?" Again, the impish little laugh.

"How do you know she'll be here?" Katie heard the strain in her own voice.

"Cuz Jago's here."

"Jago?"

"Her new fancy man, what buys her gin." Dora nodded to the short, muscular man in front of the chalkboard menu in deep conversation with Oscar Wilde. Standing in shadow, the only thing visible about Jago was the red gleam of his cigar.

Somewhere outside the tavern a clock began to strike.

The loud gong-notes seemed to float through the Ten Bells Tavern above the noise and laughter. Katie counted the booming bells.

One, two, three, four —

As if sensing Katie's eyes boring holes in him, Jago turned.

Five, six —

The flickering gas globes upon the wall illuminated his striking face.

Seven, eight —

With jowls and a torn ear, Jago looked like a pug-ugly bulldog chewing on a cigar. The tattoos ringing his neck and forming a spiky chain above the canvas collar of his burlap jacket did little to alter the impression.

As the gong of eleven faded into the din of noisy laughter, Jago smiled with a sharp-toothed, underbite of a jaw. Katie had a momentary impression that he might make a "woofing" sound and start barking at her. She quickly glanced away.

"That's him. That's Jago!" cried Dora. "Sells gimcrack south of the Thames."

"Gimcrack? What's that?" Katie asked, sneaking another peek at the man. Gimcrack sounded like some new — *or old* — type of drug.

"A hawker of swag!" A glimmer of laughter sparkled in Dora's eyes.

"Swag?" This time it was Collin's red brows that shot up.

Swag was slang for cocaine in Katie's own century.

"*Blimey!* You two starlings are like baby birds what dunno where to roost! Jago's a costermonger 'oo owns his own pony wagon—the kind you let down the sides and it forms shelves to sell gimcrack—brooches and pendants made o' colored glass." Dora pointed to the large cameo fastened at the front of her paisley shawl. "Jago gave me this *lov-er-ly* pin made o' genuine turtle-bone in exchange for me best talking parrot!" She winked and tapped the side of her nose conspiratorially.

Katie smiled. She remembered Toby telling her how Dora Fowler could throw her voice to make her parrots sound like jabbering chatterboxes.

Dora glanced over her shoulder. "Look. Just like I told you! Her highness just waltzed in."

"Where?" Collin scanned the crowd.

Katie swiveled around just in time to see Catherine Eddowes sashay in from the rear of the tavern, shrug off her fur-trimmed cape, and move with catlike fluidity through a throng of people toward the bar. Her tawny curls, bobbing across pale shoulders and white-powdered cleavage, were threaded with the same glossy red ribbons she'd worn earlier.

Catherine Eddowes gave a slow, curling smile as she glanced around but jerked back when she spotted Katie and Collin. The smile that had been spreading across her face disappeared, and a second later she vanished into a knot of people near the staircase.

❖

ALMOST AN HOUR LATER, Katie was standing guard outside a private little room behind the staircase at the Ten Bells Tavern, watching for Major Brown.

Katie's lace-up boots, where she had been pacing in front of the closed door, had left scuff marks in the sawdust across the floorboards.

An empty wine cask lay upended at the end of the small, confined passageway. Katie dragged it closer to the door and hopped onto it. Only a few minutes left before midnight. She took a deep breath and let it out slowly.

The air in the tiny passage smelled of beer and gin. From her perch on the wine barrel, Katie glanced at the closed door. The room on the other side looked nothing like the main tavern area. Instead of pictures of eighteenth-century coaching inns, a dozen gilt-framed mirrors hung on walls covered in scarlet wallpaper. Long windows, cracked open a half-inch on either side of a smoldering fire grate showed curtains dangling down in dark green velvet.

When Katie first entered the room with the others, it had reminded her of a grim, if plush, parlor in Ebenezer Scrooge's house. Oriental chairs skirted a wooden table that held an hourglass full of sand. Candles glowed in sconces on the walls between the mirrors; in the far corner, opposite the fireplace, stretched a tufted, sagging daybed with several throw-pillows trimmed in red lace.

Katie glanced at the pendant watch hanging from her neck.

Almost midnight.

Catherine Eddowes was slated to die at the hands of Jack the Ripper just before midnight. Katie inwardly smiled. Nothing could possibly go wrong. Mitre Square was a twenty-minute walk from the Ten Bells Tavern, and Catherine Eddowes was secure behind this door with Collin and Dora. Katie could hear her singing a lusty ballad:

> *Soldier, soldier, will you marry me,*
> *With your musket, fife, and drum —*
> *Oh, no, sweet maid I cannot marry you,*
> *For I have no shirt to put on.*
> *So up she went to her grandfather's chest,*
> *And she got him a shirt of the very, very best,*
> *And the soldier put it on.*

Listening to Catherine's husky voice, Katie chuckled remembering how Eddowes had craftily tried to renegotiate a higher fee. But Collin was not without resources and a certain guile of his own. Catherine Eddowes had sauntered into the room and theatrically lowered herself with a flourish onto one of the Oriental chairs at the wooden table. The air in the little room, Katie remembered, smelled — not of gin or beer — but strongly of perfume from the previous occupant.

Lazily crossing her pantalooned legs, Catherine Eddowes slowly raised up a glass of Madeira wine to the candlelight. Batting her eyes at Collin, she began to suck the red liquid through a gap in her front teeth, making air-popping, gurgling noises. It was so blatantly vampish that Katie had had to stop herself from laughing aloud.

She glanced at the pendant watch again.

Was the word "vamp" even used in this century? Katie wondered. She thought about the *True Blood* series on HBO, her sister's favorite show. Ironically, Courtney had recorded a best-selling song called "Femme Fatale," which won an MTV music video award. Dressed as Cleopatra, Queen of the Nile, Courtney had gyrated in front of the cameras to the "Dance of the Seven Veils." In the guise of an enchantress, Courtney had seductively offered an elixir in a golden chalice to all the male dancers. Alternating between Morgan le Fay and the Bride of Dracula, she had danced across the stage, heaving her belly and hips, gyrating her thighs until finally singing out the climactic words of the song that had rocketed her to super stardom: "Bring me the head of John the Baptist!" Whereupon a chorus of nearly naked girls with blood-red fangs had slithered forward carrying silver platters offering up the boy dancers' heads. The music video shot Courtney to the top of the charts and she won the Best Dance Recording Grammy, beating out Lady Gaga.

If only I could have gone to the Grammys!

Katie inwardly bemoaned the fact that she hadn't been allowed to attend. Their grandmother had been so outraged by the scanty costumes and the song — for "its blatant stealing of literary allusions and mixed metaphorical historical characters," that Grandma Cleaves and Courtney had not spoken to each other since.

Thinking of her sister brought a lump to Katie's throat. She fiddled with the velvet collar of her brocade jacket and fingered the cream silk lining. Her old life with TV and VMA awards seemed a distant memory. The nineteenth century felt more real than her own. Ever since her parents had died, Katie had felt more lonely than she'd ever felt in her entire life. But here — even with a mass murderer on the loose — Katie felt alive and more useful than she ever had at home. *And what about Toby?* she mused. *I won't leave until he's cleared of all suspicion, Lady Beatrix and the others are safe, and Jack the Ripper is behind bars. And in a year from now, Toby will have to make sure Collin stays off the moors....*

Katie tugged her mind back to the present. From the other side of the closed door she could hear Catherine Eddowes singing the Jack the Ripper ballad. There was no orchestra as there had been at the music hall, no fiddles playing, no cymbals crashing, but the lack of accompaniment made the lyrics sound more poignant —

Ta-ra-ra-Boom-de-ay! (Catherine's voice was pitched slightly higher)

> *Jack the Ripper's out to play*
> *He'll take your girl away —*
> *And cut her up today*
> *He'll take her organs, too,*
> *And when he's good and through*
> *He'll take your sister Lou*
> *And cut her up for stew*
> *Ta-ra-ra-Boom-de-ay!*
> *Ta-ra-ra-Boom-de-ay!*

Katie thought about how Catherine Eddowes had tried to hold out for more money. Collin had paced the room back and forth trying to decide how to make Catherine Eddowes honor her promise and stay until midnight. There had been a loose-fitting, rusty bolt on the inside of the door and when Collin moved to lock it securely, it wobbled and sagged and pulled free in his hand with a splintering groan.

"I have vowed, madam," Collin said, staring down at the rusty bolt in his clenched fingers as if he couldn't quite understand how it had gotten there, "to keep you safe. And yet, you demand more money! My friend Tobias Becket has already paid you. Your request for a higher fee doesn't appear to be fair *or sporting.*"

"So it's *sport* you want, is it?" Catherine Eddowes lifted her gaze seductively and hiked up her skirt to show a portion of her pantalooned ankle. Then, sniffing at her glass of Madeira in an exaggerated way and swooshing it around in her mouth, she said, "And why should you be wantin' to keep me safe, hmmm? What concern is it of *yours?*"

Katie had glanced at the window behind Eddowes near the fire grate and noticed that the fastening bolts there, too, were as rusty as the one on the door.

"In blunt language, madam!" Collin said, his voice rising. "It's my concern because we hired you. What we choose to do...is...well... er...*our* concern," Collin had sputtered indignantly.

"Tha's right!" cried Dora, jumping into the fray. "We hired you, so you gots no say."

"I gots every say!" Catherine Eddowes boomed in a heavy Cockney accent. She slammed her free hand on the tabletop, and the hourglass jumped and rattled. "It's *me* what's being paid by the hour!" She snatched up the hourglass, inverted it, and banged it back on the table. A *whoosh* of sand began trickling down the narrow tube into the inverted glass bulb below.

Catherine Eddowes didn't exactly bare her teeth, but it was as if she had. "Now you listen to me, Dora Fowler! It bloody well *is* my concern. I needs to know what sort of entertainment I'm being hired for. I'm no swinging door, taking money and not returning honest work in kind."

"Honest work? *Foh!*" Dora scoffed. "Me dog has better scruples than you, Cathy Eddowes, tha's what me mum says!"

"And me toffee-nosed dog chewing on a wasp has a better boat race than you, Dora Fowler. So you can kiss my buttered parsnips of a buttocks! Everyone knows you're nothing but a soppy little bird swindler who was born on the wrong side of the sheets! And you'd have more chance of plaiting fog than getting one of them parrots of yours to say 'cock a snook'!"

Dora looked at Catherine Eddowes, and her face turned prickly crimson as if her cheeks had been stung by bees. She sank down on one of the Oriental chairs, her eyes wide with disbelief.

"How could you say that to me, Cathy Eddowes?" Dora wailed. "You're me Uncle Thaddeus's second wife's niece! How could you?" Clearly Catherine Eddowes had broken some unwritten Cockney law about not airing dirty laundry.

"Look here, Dora Fowler," Catherine hammered. "I was sucking eggs long afore you was even born. So don't go tellin' me my kettle is black, when yours is full of sooty coal. And don't think I don't know why you're wiff this redheaded lad." She poked her finger in Collin's direction. "He gots pots of money, tha's why. So come down off your high horse."

Collin positioned himself between the two. Dora looked as if she would cry. Her face was pinched, and her lips trembled. Katie felt instantly sorry for her.

Outside the long windows came the hollow clop of hooves as horses swept past.

"I quite see your point, madam," Collin said in a placating voice. "But all we want in return for your company tonight is...well...nothing." Collin couldn't very well say he was trying to save her from Jack the Ripper. If Catherine Eddowes thought there was even the slightest chance she might die tonight, she would seek out Jago's protection. And Jago could be Jack the Ripper.

"All we want," Katie said, acting on inspiration, as she stepped forward, "is the pleasure of hearing you sing. It's Collin's birthday," she lied, "and all he wants is to hear you sing. He loves your voice."

Catherine Eddowes, Katie had determined, wasn't used to receiving money and giving nothing in return. But like Courtney and every other musical performer Katie had met in LA, Catherine Eddowes had an ego bigger than the state of California. But the real problem was that Collin had no money left to negotiate. He'd used it all to pay for the private room.

But Collin surprised Katie. With a sort of magician's exaggerated flair, Collin drew a trump card from his hip pocket — in the form of a jeweled watch fob. He held it up leisurely, taking his time to consult the gold watch face, all the while letting the tiny emeralds and rubies encrusted in the fob glisten and sparkle in the candlelight.

And like a cat spotting a juicy mouse, Catherine clamped greedy eyes on the jeweled fob and all but started to salivate.

"If you throws in that worthless little bauble chain," she said, coyly raising her glass. "I'd say you and me got a right fine deal."

"This little bauble chain is worth a king's ransom. But for the pleasure of hearing you sing — until half past the hour of midnight — it is all yours, madam. You strike a hard bargain." Collin turned and winked at Katie. That had been an hour ago.

Now, sitting on the wine casket outside the private little room, Katie listened to the distant clock tower strike twelve midnight. The ringing gong notes were loud in the small confines of the passageway. She shivered a little but then gave a long sigh of relief. Catherine Eddowes was safe.

Hearing footsteps approach, Katie glanced up.

Oscar Wilde, a large crimson flower flapping in his lapel, was motioning frantically.

"Ma cherie!" Oscar cried.

Katie jumped off the wine barrel. "Major Brown? Is he here?" she asked, breathlessly. Oscar had promised to keep an eye out for Brown and tell Katie if he entered the tavern.

"Non, ma petite jeune fille." Oscar shook his head. "Not Major Brown, but one of his minions from Scotland Yard. A repugnant man with a meat-cleaver mouth and ham-hock fists. He barged in, not five minutes ago, demanding to know if anyone had seen you. I directed the dragoon-faced officer to commence his search down the street at the Swan and Whistle."

Oscar pantomimed taking off a wide-brimmed hat and making a low, sweeping bow. "Reverend Pinker is here, too," he said, straightening up. "Looking for you. And that odious Bram Stoker arrived with the glorious James Whistler. But when Bram — the little beast — set eyes on me, he scuttled away like a frightened March hare. Pitiful scribbler that he is. Claims he's here doing 'research,'" Oscar harrumphed.

Katie bit back a smile. Oscar Wilde was here as a reporter as well. Everyone was trying to write about Jack the Ripper — who he might be and where he might be hiding. The Ten Bells Tavern had been frequented by Mary Ann Nichols, the first victim.

Oscar leaned closer and whispered, "Some men, such as Mr. Whistler, cause happiness *wherever* they go. Other men, such as Mr. Stoker, cause happiness *whenever* they go." He flashed Katie a wide smile. "I was ecstatic when that odious stealer of vampire lore turned tail and scurried away."

"Thank you so much, Oscar, for keeping watch." Katie moved down the narrow passageway and peeked out from behind the brown staircase.

In the far corner near the dartboard on the wall, Katie could see James Whistler in his floppy, red beret talking to Reverend H. P. Pinker in his white dog collar.

She turned her head and scanned the tavern to the right.

But it was too late.

Major Brown's man — the beefy one with the bristle-brush moustache from the underground railway — had spotted her.

Chapter Forty-eight

Don't Let Them Fool Ya
say the Bells of Saint Julia

BROWN'S MAN came tearing around the corner. He jerked to a stop when he caught sight of Katie. For a moment his moustache bristled, then his shrewd, dark eyes lit up.

"*You'll not get away from me this time, missy!*" he shouted triumphantly. "Where's your daft boyfriend, eh? Makes no never mind. You're coming wiff me. Major Brown wants a word wiff you." He strode forward, meat-cleaver arms outstretched ready to seize her.

Without hesitating, Katie shoved the wine barrel onto its side. It landed with a resounding *thunk*, and she pushed with all her might. Like a bowling ball, it was supposed to ram into the man, tripping him up — a fast-action maneuver that always worked in the movies. But the wine barrel didn't roll. It quivered and bounced to the side like a bowling ball into a gutter.

Oscar raised his arm over his head in a Statue-of-Liberty gesture, and stepped between Katie and the man.

The man snorted like a disgruntled bull. "Move aside! In the name of her Majesty the Queen, *move aside*."

"Move aside yourself, little man!" Oscar retorted, his right arm held high as if clutching a torch.

"Who're you calling little?" The man grasped Oscar's velvet lapels and gave a hard shake and an even harder shove. Oscar fell arse-over-teakettle over the wine barrel, legs splayed in the air, the ostrich plume in his glossy top hat sticking straight up like the tail of a spooked cat.

Oscar groaned loudly.

The man hoisted him back up by the scruff of his velvet collar and waved a menacing fist in his face.

"*Hoy there!*" James Whistler came striding around the corner with Jago in tow. "Unhand my friend!"

"Shove off!" the man snarled at Whistler, twisting Oscar's collar like a tourniquet until the poet's face became suffused in an ugly, purplish wash of color. "I've got orders to —"

"Shut your mug, or I'll shut it for you!" Jago stepped closer, fists raised. "Let go of me friend or you'll be sorry for a long grease and grime."

"I'm an officer of the law!"

"I don't care if you're an officer of the devil! You ain't welcome here. Bluebottles ain't never welcome at the Ten Bells. It's *you* what needs to shove off, mate — or get down on your chips and peas and start praying!"

"I don't take orders from the likes of you!" The man released Oscar, and began throwing punches at Jago. Oscar stepped away from the fray, clamped both hands dramatically to his throat, and began coughing loudly.

Hearing commotion, Collin cocked his head out from behind the door of the small, private room. "God's elbow, Katie! What's going on?" He was breathing hard and his carrot-red hair hung limp over one eye.

Katie wasted few words explaining the situation. "We've got to get out of here!"

Collin nodded. "It's past midnight. Dora and Catherine — er, I mean *Madam* Eddowes — are safe. But I'll have Dora stay with her here all the same." He ducked back into the room.

When Collin returned, closing the door behind him, James Whistler was shouting and beckoning. "Follow me! I've got a horse trap waiting out back."

Collin grabbed Katie's hand, and they moved swiftly down the back hall to the rear entrance.

Katie glanced over her shoulder. Jago had wrestled Major Brown's officer to the floor, and Oscar Wilde was charging down the passageway to join them, the ostrich plume in his hat quivering.

Tethered outside the back door of the Ten Bells Tavern stood a speckled horse harnessed to an open-air carriage.

"Jump in!" Whistler called to Collin and then helped Katie climb aboard onto the front-facing seat. It was a two-wheeler with front- and rear-facing seats. Oscar Wilde flipped up his velvet cut-away coat and clambered onto the back-facing seat. James Whistler flicked a long-handled whip, and the horse trotted into the mist.

"Where to, young pup?" Whistler asked Collin. "Twyford Manor?"

Collin's mouth pinched together at the word "pup." He slanted his eyes to Katie sitting next to him. She nodded and answered, "Berner Street, Whitechapel. Can you take us there, Mr. Whistler?"

Berner Street was where a pregnant Molly Potter would be lying dead if Toby hadn't been able to protect her. As the carriage swept southward along Osborn Street, Collin pointed ahead. "Turn left onto Whitechapel Road."

James reined the horse sharply around the next corner.

Katie grabbed the padded side rail. The open carriage was like a teacup carnival ride, swiveling them this way and that. The cold night air whipped her bonnet sideways and her hair across her face. She buttoned her wool coat up to her neck and thought about Toby. The plan was to meet him at Traitors' Gate if anything went wrong. So far so good. But the logical next step was to go to Berner Street to make sure Molly Potter was not lying eviscerated with her womb slashed open and the fetus missing.

Katie shuddered. *Toby's too resourceful to let Molly die*, she assured herself. But Toby was being pursued by the police. What if he was in jail right now? *No, I won't think about that.* If Toby wasn't able to save Molly Potter, the scene they were about to come upon would be gruesome beyond words.

The night was eerily quiet except for the thump of the trap's iron-rimmed wheels clattering over cobblestones.

"Not to worry, my young friends!" James Whistler said with a chuckle as they turned down a narrow, gritty lane of crooked cottages with laundry hanging in side-yards. "I know a shortcut to Berner Street. Indeed, I was there earlier this evening."

"You were?" Katie and Collin exchanged glances.

Whistler nodded. "At the Working Men's Institute — it's an educational club. I exhibited a landscape painting there last year when the Royal Academy banned my work in their hallowed halls. Claimed my art was indecent! High-brow cretins. They'll regret their caustic barbs, their condemnation! Mark my words!"

Katie inwardly smiled. James Whistler would indeed have the last laugh with the artistic elite. His paintings would be priceless in the twenty-first century.

"Giddyup, Gulliver!" Whistler shouted to the horse, then turned to Collin. "Speaking of artwork, how are your drawings coming along, young cub?"

Collin winced. "I've been studying the books you gave me, James. But perhaps you could oblige me on one small, insignificant matter... I'd prefer it if you didn't call me 'cub' or 'pup.'"

"What shall I call you then?" Whistler laughed, and the beret on his head — like a colorful, large pizza — flopped up and down.

"You can call me the Archbishop of Canterbury, for all I care, just don't call me —"

"Splendid! Splendid!" cried Oscar from the rear seat. "We shall call you *Archie*, after the Archbishop!"

Snapping the reins, Whistler turned to Katie and began telling her about the club he had visited earlier on Berner Street. He explained that every Saturday night the Working Men's Institute held lively debates — religious, political, educational — that often went far into the night. Saturday night was the only time members were allowed to bring their wives or lady friends.

"Look! There's the club, up ahead."

Katie glanced into the gloom to where James Whistler was pointing. It was a brick and timber building with a large, wooden, gatelike door. On the opposite side of the narrow enclosure leading up to the club's front facade were several shops — a tallow shop, a mirror-maker, a tailor — with brass plates on the front doors and iron bell handles hanging down. A high stone wall loomed at the end of the lane, intersecting with the triangular wedge of a clock tower, giving the illusion that the narrowing street came to a dead end.

The only illumination, aside from slivers of moonlight, was the faint gleam trickling out from the club's first floor windows.

"I came here earlier," Whistler continued. "Because the members espouse ideals I'm rather fond of. They believe in worker ownership and equal access to resources for everyone."

Oscar laughed from the backseat. "Are you spouting more of your proletariat claptrap?" he asked in a teasing tone. "Friedrich Engels would do better to stop preaching his working class drivel — that wealth through exploitation creates an unequal society. Of course it does! A toddler in knee-breeches knows as much. Who needs an equal society in which every plebeian fancies himself the equal to an aristocrat; every aristocrat to a god! Imagine a world where all musicians believe they'd be better suited as politicians, and politicians yearned to be poets!"

"You mustn't mock those of us who wish to make the world a better place," James Whistler shot back.

"Why mustn't I? The height of selfishness is not living as one wishes to live, but asking others to live as one wishes to live."

"The members of this club are sincere in their sentiments, as am I, Oscar."

"Of course you are, James! But a little sincerity is a dangerous thing, and a great deal is absolutely fatal!"

Just then the horse shied.

Whistler muttered a curse. "There's an obstacle in our path. Jump down and poke around with this." Whistler handed Oscar his long-handled whip.

"Wait!" Collin cried. "I'll go with you."

They jumped down and Collin lit a match.

Oscar peered into the gloom, then back at Katie and Whistler in the carriage. He looked troubled as he drew in a long breath, and his eyes appeared almost black in the moonlight.

"You don't suppose . . ."

"Of course not." Whistler wound the reins around the whip-stock. "Looks like a bundle of clothes left in a heap. Something's dropped off a costermonger's cart, I'll wager. A bundle of firewood or some rags perhaps." Notching the wooden drag-break, he climbed hastily down from the carriage. Before he could mutter for Katie to stay put, she had scrambled down herself.

In the distance, the clock in the tower struck a long, single, plaintive note.

One o'clock.

"Looks to be a tailor's dummy or a mannequin used for dress-making," Whistler said, taking off his floppy beret and running a hand through his dark hair.

The horse pranced and whinnied, ears flicking.

Oscar Wilde took a deep breath and strode forward, Collin at his side. Katie and James Whistler followed behind. Oscar poked at the heap with the long-handled whip.

It wasn't a bundle of clothes, or twigs, or a tailor's mannequin.

Peering down at the figure lying in the street, Collin's hand shook so uncontrollably, the match flame wavered and guttered out.

With unsteady fingers, he lit another.

The dead girl lay on her side, knees drawn up, feet pressed against the curb, a straw hat partially covering her face. Her clothes were wet, and her head rested in line with the carriage's right wheel. Blood had seeped into the paving stones around her head, saturating the ground like a dark glistening halo. A blue jacket with a white fur collar was buttoned tightly across her slender waist, but gaped open at the neckline. And her dress, of a dark green material, had forget-me-nots embroidered into the fabric. A long, white petticoat peeked out from under the edge of the hem. She was not visibly pregnant.

Katie felt an irrational flood of relief.

"She doesn't look —"

"Eviscerated?" Collin gulped hard. "She isn't."

James Whistler knelt down next to the body.

"It appears as if a knife or other sharp instrument has been drawn across her throat, severing her windpipe and carotid artery. The blade may have cut open her esophagus."

"From whence cometh this extraordinary wealth of medical knowledge?" Oscar Wilde raised an eyebrow.

Whistler shot his friend an annoyed look. "I'm an artist. In order to paint live people one must first study dead ones — which I did extensively in St. Petersburg. I learned to draw the human body from plaster casts, live models, and an occasional cadaver. I got a first class mark in anatomy."

Collin nodded. The match flame jiggled in his unsteady hand. "James gave me an anatomy book to help me draw caricatures."

"That's right, young pup — er, Collin." James Whistler nodded. "You can't be a painter without studying the anatomical insides of humans and animals. Look here," he said, pointing to the halo of dark blood on the ground circling the girl's head. "What does this tell you?"

"That there was a lot of hemorrhaging at the root of her neck?" Collin asked hopefully, like a student seeking approbation.

"Correct. *Severe* hemorrhaging. Also, that the blade was very sharp, possibly cutting through her windpipe. See here," Whistler said, pointing to the body, "from the collarbone to the lower edge of the Adam's apple? The knife's laceration caused serious injuries to the large vessels in her throat. Beneath the skin, in the middle of the neck, lies the trachea and just behind it, the gullet."

Katie held her breath and inched closer. She reminded herself that this couldn't be Molly Potter because she wasn't seven months pregnant, and that whoever it was had been dead for over a century. She knelt down next to Whistler whose cuffs appeared paint-splattered like his beret — deep crimson splotches — and peered at the body.

A dark trickle of blood showed across the girl's throat in such a jagged manner that it appeared as if a spiky piece of barbed wire had been branded into her flesh. Courtney had a similar looking barbed tattoo circling her biceps. But this jagged line wasn't a tattoo.

Katie reached out and felt the girl's wrist. The skin wasn't warm, but it wasn't stone-cold either. She hadn't been dead very long.

Katie gently tugged the straw bonnet away from the girl's face. Collin gasped. Katie blinked and blinked again.

The violet eyes staring blankly out from a bone-white face were those of Elizabeth Stride! The girl from the pawn shop. Busy Lizzy! What was going on? Lizzy Stride wasn't supposed to die tonight. *It's September thirtieth!* Had Toby managed to save Molly Potter only to have Lizzy die in her place? Did this mean they couldn't change history, just rearrange it? Would the outcomes be the same, but the dates of the deaths changed?

If we can't change history, how can we can save Lady Beatrix? Or prevent Collin from drowning?

Katie closed her eyes. Her mind flashed to the future. She was standing in Madame Tussauds, the musty smell of the museum in her nostrils. *"You can't alter history, Katie!"* the future Toby had warned her. *"You can only change small things, inconsequential things."*

Katie's eyes flew open.

She glanced from Collin to Oscar to James and then at the dead girl whose bloodless lips were puckered as if in a twisted kiss or the throes of agony.

I can change history! I know I can, Katie told herself. *I have to!*

She just didn't know at what cost.

But all too soon, in the predawn hours when one's mind plays tricks and time seems to bend and mold to accommodate nightmares, Katie would find out. And she'd wish with all her might that she hadn't tempted fate.

Chapter Forty-nine

Sailors and Oars
say the Bells of Saint Flores

"I'll fetch the police," Oscar said, the feather in his top hat quivering. "There's a constable box around the corner."

"Why didn't the girl cry out?" James Whistler asked. "With a constable so close. And look. There are lights on in the club. Someone would have heard her scream for help, surely."

"Perhaps she knew her assailant," Katie ventured.

"Or perhaps the killer looks harmless," Oscar said. "The very *essence* of a successful murderer is that his victim sees a smiling face."

"Or *her* victim." Katie nodded. "The killer might be a woman."

Whistler turned, grim-faced and apologetic, to Katie. "You shouldn't have witnessed this, Miss Katherine. I'm sorry. I forget my-self sometimes. I should not have let you —"

"It's all right, Mr. Whistler. I'm fine. I've seen —" Katie was going to say worse. But of course she hadn't, not in real life, only on TV. In advanced biology, she'd seen an autopsy performed in real time on a video cam.

Collin tugged Katie by the elbow, telling Whistler he agreed that this was no place for Katie, and that they would wait in the carriage. But they didn't climb back into the varnished two-wheeler. They both knew that as soon as Oscar summoned the constable, the entire street would be swarming with police.

And they were right. For the next twenty-four hours both Berner Street and Mitre Square would be teeming, not only with the Metropolitan Police, but with angry vigilantes demanding justice, amateur detectives looking to solve the murders, social do-gooders, voyeurs, newspaper reporters, ministers preaching the evils of sin, thrill-seekers, and dozens of law-abiding citizens demanding that Scotland Yard catch the murdering, evil fiend who was Jack the Ripper.

Instead of climbing into the carriage, Katie and Collin hastened to Mitre Square, where Catherine Eddowes was supposed to have died tonight. Catherine Eddowes, Katie knew, was safe.

But will we find another girl dead in Catherine Eddowes's place?

They headed west on Commercial Road and south toward Minories Street. It was a fifteen-minute fast walk to Mitre Square, but Collin led the way down side streets and through several backyards, and they arrived in under ten minutes.

Katie wondered who would be lying dead in the Mitre Square instead of Catherine Eddowes? Had they saved Eddowes only to postpone her death in exchange for another innocent victim?

When they reached Minories Street, Collin led the way to Fenchurch, overshooting Mitre Square and thus coming upon the dingy courtyard from the corner of Leadenhall Street, due north of the Tower of London.

Katie's pulse raced. A cat yowled in the distance.

The moon, low in the sky, gave pale light through the fog-filled air. Church Lane Alley, where they'd escaped from Major Brown earlier, doglegged into darkness; the rear entrances of Kearley & Tonge Grocers and O'Fingal's fish shop were shuttered and padlocked.

To the right of the pitch-black alley, Katie could see the back walls of tenements rising up, the bottom bricks — glossy with white-wash — showing more clearly in the moonlight. She could just make out the stone drinking well anchored in the center of the cobbled square. The pump handle, jutting out from the slime-crusted side of the well, looked like the crooked spout of a teakettle.

Katie held her breath.

A shadowy figure leaned menacingly over another shadowy fig-ure that lay prone on the ground in the exact spot where Catherine Eddowes was to have died. Was the person bending over, silhouetted in shadow, Jack the Ripper?

Collin snatched up Katie's hand in his own damp, shaking one.

The rattle of something familiar, like the tap of hobnail boots, sounded in the distance. Katie's heart raced; her spine tingled. They both stood still, listening. But the sound was so faint, Katie thought she must have imagined it. Clutching Collin's hand tightly, she tugged him forward.

The moon overhead showed, then hid, then showed itself through dark clouds scudding across an even darker sky. Katie peered into the gloom. When they were several yards from the stone drinking well, she let out a strangled gasp.

It can't be!

But it was.

Toby was bending over Catherine Eddowes, whose body lay in a pool of blood near the stone drinking well. Lying on her back, her head cocked at an unnatural angle, Catherine Eddowes stared straight at Katie with blank eyes. No. No, that wasn't right. *One* eye. Cather-ine Eddowes had only one eye. The other had been gouged out.

Katie felt a thrumming in her ears, a roaring as the blood rushed to her head. She told herself to look away, but it was no use. She couldn't help herself.

The dead woman's pantalooned left leg was extended, while her right was bent at the knee. Both arms, stripped of their sleeves, ex-tended outward as in a crucifixion, palms up. Catherine Eddowes's throat had been badly mutilated, and there was a long gash across her face from the nose to the curved angle of her cheekbone. Her left eye had been gouged out, and her right ear was missing. The flaps of her abdomen lay exposed, the entrails spilling out like coils of dark rope. A handkerchief lay on the ground by her open left palm.

"It's Catherine Eddowes," Toby said heavily.

From his crouched position next to the body, Toby peered up at Collin with a faint inflection in his voice that might have been suspicion. "You weren't able to save —"

"But we did! I swear it!" Collin sputtered. "She was alive at midnight!" Trembling shook his words.

"She's stone cold," Toby answered, his voice composed but with a terrible fierceness in it.

Collin hunched up his shoulders defensively. "I swear to you, I don't know what happened! Katie was keeping watch. Catherine Eddowes was singing most of the night. I tell you, Toby, she was with us at midnight. She can't be stone cold. We were together less than an hour ago." But he said this as if it were a rehearsed speech. As if he felt guilty about the poor woman's death. As if it were somehow his fault. He went on in a rush. "I don't understand it, Toby. I don't. There are elements of the supernatural at work here. That's the only explanation." Collin's face was pale, Katie noted, almost inhuman in the moonlight.

Collin pointed a shaking finger at Toby. "You've got blood all over you!"

"Elizabeth Stride's blood. I went to Berner Street. Lizzy Stride from the pawn shop...she's dead. She was bleeding badly when I arrived. I tried to stem the tide of blood, but it was no use. She'd been slit from ear to ear. So I came here and found—"

"And what's that?" Collin yelped. "In your hand?"

"My dagger," Toby answered, his lips twisting in a strange way.

"Your...dagger?" The steel blade glistened with blood stains. "What's it doing — ?"

"Precisely."

Then Toby did something very odd. He threw back his head and laughed.

"I hardly find this amusing," Collin bristled. "A dead woman lying at our feet, who, not an hour ago was singing robustly at the Ten Bells. Have you lost your mind, Toby? There's nothing laughable about this!"

"Isn't there?" Toby seemed to smile and frown at the same time. "Can't you just see the spectacle at the coroner's court? This is *my* dagger stained with blood. My clothes are awash in even more blood. I was seen entering Berner Street, and now I'm here. Coincidence . . . or planned? It appears as if I've played right into the hands of a puppet master whose tricks are far superior to my own." Toby narrowed accusing eyes at Katie.

Katie reached out her hand to him, but Toby jerked back. Katie wished with all her might that she'd never traveled back in time, never gotten Toby and Collin involved in the hunt for Jack the Ripper.

Toby's eyes, as he stared at her in the waning moonlight, showed a boiling rage even as he continued with that strange, twisted smile on his face. "Jack the Ripper is not a slap-dash, spur-of-the-moment killer, nor supernatural, but a cold-blooded person tugging on strings behind the curtain of this deadly farce, someone I underestimated but who carefully planned every piece of this. The Ripper is brutal and cunning, but flesh and blood, I assure you."

"Major Brown!" Collin cried. "He's trying to frame you!"

The muscles down Toby's jaw tightened. "Hasn't the Duke told you? If anything happens to you, I'm to be his legal heir. Jack the Ripper has no choice but to pin this on — "

"Both of us." Collin bent down and scooped up the handkerchief near the dead woman's open palm. He turned it over, exposing the monogrammed initials "CCT."

"It's mine. *Collin Chesterfield Twyford*. We'd best get out of here — "

Too late.

The shrill of a police whistle was followed by the familiar rattle of steel, leather, and hobnail boots. A moment later, the yellow glare of a bull's-eye lantern caught them all squarely in the face.

The lantern's light dazzled in a stinging sort of way, making Katie squint and hold up her hand to shield her eyes, as if from the burning rays of the sun. Like a pantomime, the three teenagers stood there frozen in a tableau of guilt, caught in the glare, with Toby hunched over the dead woman, dagger in hand, blood stains splattered across his clothes.

The bull's-eye beam was lowered. But it rendered the shadows in the courtyard so heavy that Katie could scarcely make out Major Brown standing across the way, clutching the lantern to his side.

Major Brown began to swing the lantern back and forth. To their left, the whitewashed walls glimmered in the light's swinging arc. To and fro, the wink of the swaying lamp created puddles of light around the dead woman's stomach — making her bulging intestines appear as wet and slick as the skin of an eel. Katie felt bile rise up her throat.

Hoofbeats pounded in the distance. Footfalls sounded closer, fast approaching.

Two police officers raced into the square from Minories Street. Major Brown stepped forward and raised the lamp again, letting the beam's light shine directly into their faces.

"Stand fast! Tobias Becket, put down your weapon! In the name of her Majesty the Queen, you are under —"

That's when everything became a blur.

For the second time that evening Collin began shouting, "*Run! Run! Run!*" But he was screaming these words at Toby.

In the glare of the lantern, Katie watched Collin charge headlong into Major Brown, toppling him over.

Toby took off like a shot. And it was this image of a cannonball that made Katie scream at the top of her lungs: "I've been shot! I've been shot! You have to help me!" It was all she could think of as a diversion. "I'm dying! I'm dying! Help me!"

One of the constables stopped in his tracks and came rushing to Katie's side. There remained only the second officer to pursue Toby. Katie fell into a pretend swoon onto the cobblestones not two feet from the lifeless body of Catherine Eddowes.

Chapter Fifty

Mustn't Climb the Wall
say the Bells of Saint Paul

THERE WERE THREE EXITS out of the moonlit square. One led into Minories Street to the east; the second, through the doglegged alley where Toby had disappeared; and the third, down a narrow footpath bracketed on either side by towering brick walls.

Pressed against the blood-soaked cobblestones, her face inches from Catherine Eddowes's body, Katie eyed the dark footpath and made her decision. Even though it meant she'd have to scramble around the corpse and race through the courtyard, Katie knew she'd have to take the risk. And it would divert attention away from Toby.

Luck was on her side.

The heavyset constable lumbering toward her jerked to a halt when he caught sight of the corpse sprawled in a pool of blood, abdomen sliced open, bowels glistening in the moonlight. Katie heard the whooshing intake of his breath, the sputtering wheeze of disbelief as he took in the carnage.

The momentary pause allowed Katie to spring up from the shadows, vault over the dead woman, and race to the footpath. Running blindly forward she stumbled slightly in the mud, then regained her footing when the path became firmer, until finally she burst into the open byway of Fenchurch.

Gasping, Katie darted south to Tower Hill.

She ran past Barty's Stable Yard, smelling of wood smoke, then through a tiny graveyard with a burnt-out church, whose steeple, balanced on half-demolished timbers, poked defiantly upward into the blue-black sky.

Lodging houses sprang up and disappeared as Katie raced around corners, zigzagging left and right, half blinded by the wind slicing into her face. Despite the grit whirling into her eyes, she pressed forward, running as fast as she could, her skirts flapping like sheets on a clothesline. She found that if she kept her head lowered, her bonnet helped shield her face from the biting wind, but it also rendered her blind to what was in front of her. Finally, when she felt her breath would burst in her chest, and when she couldn't hear footsteps behind her, Katie stopped.

Bending over, hands pressed to her shaking thighs, Katie panted until her heart stopped thundering. Judging by the clock-beats in her head, she guessed that she'd been running for five to six minutes.

Still taking in gasps of air, she glanced around, trying to get her bearings. If Toby escaped from the pursuing police officers, they were to rendezvous at Traitors' Gate. *At least that was the plan.*

Traitors' Gate was located at the southern end of the Tower of London — a ten-minute walk from Mitre Square. But Katie had made so many turns, and had cut through so many back alleys in an effort to elude anyone following her that she wasn't sure where she was or in which direction she was heading. She knew to proceed in the direction of the Thames, but where exactly was the river? In front of her? Behind? Katie was totally disoriented.

Up ahead was a cast iron arch. Katie pressed on at a fast clip. There were more cast iron arches in the distance and a stable yard to her right. Barty's Stable Yard. *Oh, no! I've run in circles!*

Approaching the burnt-out church, she slowed down. There was ankle-deep mud everywhere, with thick steam rising from the ground around the gravestones. All was deserted and dark as she turned around and hurried back the way she'd come. Veering past tethered horses, she picked up her pace to a steady jog, passing houses whose dark windows threw back reflected gleams of light from the gas lamps across the street.

Turning the corner, Katie felt as if she were being swallowed up into darkness, but she could smell low tide on the river. As she hurried along a long line of broken fences, pinpoints of light from the river showed through the cracks. She was almost there!

Guiding herself cautiously toward a break in the fence, she found a gate and pushed. A spring-lock handle clicked open. *I'm safe now*, she told herself, moving down a narrow road with ivy-covered stone walls rising on either side. *I just have to make it to the river!* She headed straight down the center of the lane, but at the corner came a swaying carriage, fast approaching. The coachman waved his whip and shouted, "Stand clear!"

But the lane was so narrow, with no sidewalks, that she had literally no place to stand clear. She had only seconds to react. She flattened herself into a recess in the stone wall. Coach lamps cast swaying cones of light onto the paving slates at her feet as the carriage rumbled past. The coachman at the front, and footman at the rear, paid her no heed. Muddy and disheveled, she didn't exist, or it was beneath their dignity to take any notice of her.

With the thundering noise of hooves fast receding, Katie glanced down. She truly *was* a sorry sight. Her grey gloves, once soft as silk, were greasy and muddy; her dress and cloak, caked in grime.

A shadow swooped overhead.

A seagull?

She hastened down yet another narrow pathway, following the cry of the gull overhead, but came to a grinding halt when she heard the faint noise of words lost on the wind.

Angry words.

She raced on until she came to a lonely corner with a statue of Eros on a pedestal.

The sound of her approaching boots clattering on the cobblestones made a woman standing under a streetlamp glance up.

The woman, whose face was in shadow, had hiked her skirts up at the prospect of soliciting business, but when she saw it was only Katie crashing down the street, she let her petticoats drop to the ground with a whoosh. Katie wanted to scream for her to go home. *Jack the Ripper killed two women tonight! He could easily—*

Katie suddenly realized that she, too, was alone. *She, too, could be the Ripper's next victim.*

Katie was about to scoot past the woman when she heard the voices again, and recognized them. She ducked behind the statue of Eros, where she crouched, her head drumming, her lungs aching. Katie read the inscription at the base of the statue: "ANTEROS: ANGEL OF CHARITY." *So it wasn't Eros,* she thought. *It was his twin.* Katie thought about the twin Collins in her life and shuddered. Where was *her* Collin now?

"You're all a pack of blithering idiots!" came the voice, all too familiar. *Major Brown's voice.* "You lost all three of them!"

So Collin and Toby had escaped!

Katie felt an urge to shout for joy, but made her breathing go shallow. She didn't want to make a sound. The smell wafting up from the gutter behind her made her want to gag. She put her fist in her mouth and forced herself to stay perfectly still.

"Return to the Ten Bells," Major Brown shouted to the two officers at his side. "See if they doubled back. I'll head down to the river and have a talk with Mrs. Tray. If anyone knows where Tobias is, she will."

"Won't tell you nofink. Not Mrs. Tray from Traitors' Gate."

"Oh, she'll tell me," said Major Brown with authority.

"She'll put a hex on you, she will," said the second officer.

"Superstitious hogwash. Who's that?" came Major Brown's voice.

Katie held her breath as Major Brown passed within feet of her. She could see his profile in outline. The long, hollow face, the eagle nose.

One of his officers lit a match and it curled up into flame. "'Tis only a street walker, sir."

"Get her out of here. Take her home, sergeant. It's dangerous."

The other man sputtered. "Who give's a rat's curse about a gin-soaked harlot? Let her —"

"I care, Sergeant Drummond. Do as I say — *now!*"

"But, sir. 'Tis naught but Mary Jane Kelly!" The sergeant made a sneering gesture.

Mary Jane Kelly?

Katie squinted in the gloom, peering around the statue, trying to make out Mary Jane's features. Mary Jane Kelly was going to be the Ripper's next-to-last victim, a brutal and gruesome murder. Katie shuddered. Mary Jane, age twenty-five, would be flayed alive, and then her limbs amputated and her organs sent through the post to the police.

Sergeant Drummond strode up to the girl and gave her a powerful shove. "Move along, Mary Jane!"

"Stop that, sergeant," barked Major Brown. "You shall escort Miss Kelly to her lodgings. It's not safe for her to be out tonight. And you will comport yourself like an officer of her Majesty the Queen."

"She's rip-roaring drunk, sir!"

"More's the reason to escort her home, sergeant," Major Brown said with grim resolve.

The officer moved to grab Mary Jane's arm.

"You cursed son of a swine! Take your 'ands off me," screamed the alcohol-soaked voice of Mary Jane Kelly as she reached into the bosom of her blouse with fingerless gloves and tugged out a gin bottle.

Consoling herself with a long pull from the chipped bottle, she hiccupped twice and belched.

The shutters on the bottom window of a padlocked storefront behind Mary Jane began to bang in the wind. Katie blinked in that direction. A reflector lamp, with a candle, showed itself in the second floor window. A minute later the window was thrown open, and a man wearing a stocking cap thrust his head out.

"Pipe down!" shouted the man. "I'll set the police on you, I will!" An instant later the window slammed shut, but the reflector lamp, with its candle, continued to burn on the sill like a cheery beacon at Christmas. Only this wasn't Christmas, and nothing about the scene was cheery.

Mary Jane stumbled sideways, closer to Katie, and Katie almost gasped. In the moonlight the girl was so strikingly beautiful she could have been a movie star. Golden-haired and strong-boned, she looked like a Norse goddess. So unexpected was her exquisite face that Katie would have been rendered speechless even if she weren't trying to be silent.

The girl's clothes were of good quality: a claret-colored velvet bonnet and matching short cape. Again Katie had to blink several times. In an age of disease-ravaged skin, Mary Jane Kelly's features were as perfect as a china doll's — with pink dimpled cheeks and shining dark eyes under arched eyebrows, and a full painted mouth above a round chin. She was a dead ringer for Anna Nicole Smith or Marilyn Monroe.

When she spoke, all resemblance to a china doll or a celebrity disappeared. Standing with her feet planted apart, Mary Jane Kelly let out a string of curses in a gravelly, demonic voice. Katie could see that several of her teeth were missing, and her remaining eyetooth was black with decay.

Sergeant Drummond bristled beneath his three-collared policeman's coat and grabbed Mary Jane Kelly.

Mary Jane screamed and screamed just as a flicker of lightning flashed in the distance, lighting up the Thames.

The river was so close; Traitors' Gate, even closer.
If only I could slip away....

Chapter Fifty-one

This Could Be Sinister
say the Bells of Westminster

TEN MINUTES AFTER Sergeant Drummond led Mary Jane Kelly away from the corner lamppost and the Angel of Charity statue, Katie found herself stealthily following Major Brown to the river.

At first she hung back, darting into doorways and ducking behind trees, shadowing him like they do in the movies. But when Major Brown strode down the muddy slope of the Thames embankment, Katie moved rapidly to close the gap between them.

Instead of veering toward Traitors' Gate as Katie had expected, Major Brown made a sharp detour toward a row of oddly shaped houses close to the river. Bigger than lean-tos, but smaller than cottages, the structures resembled gypsy caravans anchored on stone foundations, with chimney stacks that pointed straight into the dark sky like witches' hats — the thatching along the rooflines like the straw of a broom. In front of the fenced-in yards was a long line of crooked trees, hunched and bowed over as if the wind had pummeled them for years in a downward direction. Moonlight slanted through fast-moving clouds making everything appear blue-black and murky.

Katie peered out from behind one of the gnarled trees and watched as Major Brown strode toward a house in the center of the row and knocked loudly. A dwarf-sized door flew open and a moment later, stooping low to get under the lintel, Major Brown disappeared inside, and a candle appeared at the window.

Darting from one tree to the next, Katie crept forward until she was forced to hopscotch across the gnarled roots bulging up from the ground. She had an irresistible urge to race across the yard and peek into the window, but held back. The house was so small that a face peering in from outside would be like a goblin jumping out of a jack-in-the-box — conspicuous and startling.

Still . . .

She edged closer, her eyes fixed on the spot of light from the candle flickering on the sill, even as the wind blew against her eyelids.

Maybe if she put her ear to the door . . .

Then, as if someone were listening to her thoughts, the candle window opened outward like a small door, beckoning. As she neared the front stoop, every crunch of gravel set Katie's teeth on edge. She tiptoed to the window and crouched beneath a flowerbox that was bursting with blood-red geraniums.

"*Tell me where he is, Mrs. Traitor!*" boomed Major Brown's steely voice through the window, followed by the twinkling, church-organ sound of Mrs. Tray's.

"Why, Gideon! You haven't called me Mrs. Traitor since you were a boy in knee-breeches!"

"I'm on official business, Mrs. Traitor — as you well know. Where are they?"

"They?"

"The three young people. Tobias Becket, Collin Twyford, and an American girl named Katherine Lennox. They are together, no doubt. And I'll wager you know precisely where that is. I should have come to you earlier. Toby's been hiding here, hasn't he?" Major Brown's voice sounded odd, almost hoarse.

Katie straightened up slightly, the better to hear the stomping, scraping noises coming from inside — as if Major Brown were hauling furniture around.

"Ha-ha! Caught you!" she heard Major Brown snarl. And then, "What the blazes! *You?* What are you doing here, Molly Potter? Where's Toby?"

"Molly arrived this evening, Gideon," Mrs. Tray stated. "Tobias brought her. Molly and her unborn child are under my protection. No one shall harm them."

Molly Potter? Katie almost bumped her head beneath the flower-box. *She's here? She survived the Ripper!*

Katie felt a rush of relief surge through her. She wanted to high-five the air, but a moment later, the doorlike window banged shut, followed by the rusty sound of a handle-latch snapping into place.

I need to hear what they're saying!

Katie crept around the side of the house, mud-bubbles gurgling up through the gravel at her feet as she moved through an opening no bigger than the width of her body, down a narrow path hemmed in by a neighbor's sidewall, and into Mrs. Tray's backyard.

But the back door — down a narrow stairwell — was shuttered and locked, so Katie retraced her steps. She was just about to round the corner to the front of the house when she heard the front door burst open.

"Tower Bridge? Are you *sure*, Mrs. Traitor?"

Katie shied back.

"So be it," came Major Brown's voice, followed by the stomp of his boots echoing away into the night.

Katie counted slowly under her breath. When she reached fifty-Mississippi, she peeked out from around the side of the house and squinted into the distance. Major Brown was just a blur in the predawn light.

"Katherine? Katie-of-the-Stone? Is that you?" came the old woman's voice. "Come here. Come here. There's no time to waste."

Katie rounded the corner fully. She blinked at the old woman standing in the doorway dressed all in black. "Mrs. Tray —

"Toby's not at Tower Bridge, Mrs. Tray," Katie said, forgetting for a moment that the old woman was blind.

"Of course he is, my dear." The woman stared in Katie's direction, a watchful tension in her wrinkled face.

"No. We agreed to meet at —" Katie stopped. She wasn't sure she could trust the Oracle of Traitors' Gate.

"Tobias is *not* at Traitors' Gate, Katie-of-the-Stone, if that's what you think. He is hiding under the pilings on the construction pier below the scaffolding on Tower Bridge."

"But Major Brown wants to arrest Toby! Wants him to hang for the murders of —"

"Stuff and nonsense," came the church organ voice. The old woman's eyes were as grey and foggy as the mist rising off the Thames in the distance.

"There's no time, Katie-of-the-Stone, so I shall speak quickly. There will be a death at the bridge tonight. Either Gideon Brown shall perish, or —"

Mrs. Tray's plump little hands, in their fingerless black gloves, motioned to Katie. "Quickly. Let me explain."

"But if Toby's at the bridge, I've got to get there!" Katie cried. "I've got to warn him."

A small, feminine voice called out from inside the house. "Mrs. Traitor?"

"Just a minute, Molly, dear. We have a visitor." Mrs. Tray compressed her wrinkled lips, then peered at Katie through the cloudy formations in her sightless eyes. "That's Molly Potter. Tobias brought her earlier. Don't be alarmed. Molly is perfectly safe here. Her baby shall arrive in a fortnight."

"But Mrs. Tray!" Katie gasped. "If Major Brown knows that Molly Potter is here —"

"Yes, my dear?"

"He's Jack the Ripper! He'll kill her! He'll slice—"

"Goodness! Is that what you think?" The fog swirls in the old woman's eyes seemed to twirl round and around in a hypnotic kaleidoscope. "I'm afraid, my dear, that you—"

"I've got to go, Mrs. Tray. I've got to warn Toby!"

The old woman put her hand out and touched Katie's shoulder, level with her own as she stood a foot above Katie on the stoop.

"Katie, my dear. I had trouble seeing your aura when first we met at Traitors' Gate, but not now. Which means you must return home— *to your home*—immediately. You have so little time left. When the sun breaks fully in the sky, it will be too late. You must return to the London Stone at once. You haven't a moment to lose."

"But I can't! Toby's in danger. If he's at Tower Bridge and Major Brown is on his way there...Oh, Mrs. Tray. I know you didn't mean to, but you've put Toby at risk! Major Brown's going to arrest him. He'll be...hanged."

The old woman's voice rose and fell and rose again like a church organ at a funeral. "When you are safely back in your own time, my dear, I shall explain everything to Tobias. Go now."

Katie turned to leave. But the thought of a pregnant Molly Potter meeting the same fate as Catherine Eddowes—slashed and eviscerated—made Katie stop in her tracks. "Mrs. Tray, about Molly Potter...She's *not* safe. You may have saved her tonight, but she's still in danger. If Jack the Ripper isn't stopped, Molly Potter will die."

"She *is* safe, my dear. I promise. She and her baby, a boy she will name Harold, will live long, full, productive...and perhaps," said Mrs. Tray, chuckling, "even *charmed* lives."

"How can you be sure?"

"It's already been written. It's in the cards." Again the soft, tinkling laughter. "Of course, Molly can't play cards as she can't read or do sums. But she *will* be safe. I promise. And her son will grow up to be a fine young man—as will his great-grandson. You shall have to trust me on this, my dear." Again the chuckle.

Katie took a deep breath remembering Mary Jane Kelly's being led away cursing and hollering by Sergeant Drummond.

"If you can save Molly Potter, can you save a girl named Mary Jane Kelly?" Katie asked. "She's supposed to die on November ninth. Her death will be horrible. She'll be...tortured."

The misty whirls in Mrs. Tray's sightless eyes swirled faster. "I know Mary Jane Kelly well. But I'm sorry, my dear. There is no hope for poor Mary Jane."

"But—"

"Leave now, Katie-of-the-Stone. Before it is too late."

"But what about Toby? Is he going to be all right? Will he be charged for these murders? Have I caused history to be changed?"

"Only *you* can determine that, my dear...by your actions on the third pier near the scaffolding at Tower Bridge. But afterward, you must go as quickly as you can to the London Stone. Don't tarry. I fear it is already too late." Her words fell with a heavy, chilling weight. But what Mrs. Tray did and said next was even more unnerving. She hobbled off the stoop and rooted about the ground until she found a jagged rock embedded in the muddy gravel and held it out to Katie.

"You, my dear...you who are *of* the Stone and *from* the Stone. You have my blessing to use this—" She handed Katie the heavy rock. "Nothing and no one is who they appear to be. But remember this, Katie-of-the-Stone. When you return to your own world, you must choose *the hard right over the easy wrong.*"

And with that, Mrs. Tray hobbled back onto the stoop and disappeared into her tiny cottage.

Chapter Fifty-two

You Gave Your Promise
say the Bells of Saint Thomas

AMID THE GLOOMY DARK WAVES and shadows rippling across the River Thames, Katie could see pale gleams of light from bobbing boat lanterns. By day this vast waterway would be overflowing with sewage and teeming with tug boats, barges, cargo vessels, and clipper ships, whose tall masts would sway and soar and puncture the sky like giant church spires.

At sunrise, the clatter of horses' hooves would mingle with the shouts of boatmen and the lap of the tides — but for now, in the predawn dimness, the only thing Katie could hear was the dying-goose wail of a foghorn competing with the clinkity-clank of buoy bells.

The hard right over the easy wrong. What had Mrs. Tray meant by that? Katie wondered as she hurried along the embankment toward the river. *And why did Mrs. Tray give her this heavy rock?* She reached into her pocket and felt the jagged edge of the stone.

With only the sharp scent of wet earth to guide her along the footpath, Katie veered away from the embankment down a sloping expanse of grass toward a gravel causeway running parallel to the river. She was brought up short minutes later by a fenced-off area with "Danger!" signs posted on wooden crosses in the mud flats beyond. The split-rail fencing, enmeshed with wire, showed spiky points across the top. Katie squinted, trying to discern objects and shapes in the gloom on the other side of the fence. In the waning moonlight, she could make out piles of bricks and metal crossbars, beams, pulleys, swags, and chains scattered across the green-glimmering slime of the riverbank — the skeletal bones of what would soon be the most talked-about bridge in the world. This was the construction site for Tower Bridge. The turrets and battlements of the famous structure had not even been built yet — in their place, nothing but dark sky.

Closer to the water's edge, Katie could hear boats moored along the riverbank creak and crack, their ropes groaning. But with the fence barring her way, Katie had to scramble back up the grassy slope to the embankment, where just ahead stood a hansom cab.

Katie hastened toward the black cab for no other reason than that the horse tethered to it was the only living, breathing creature in this lonely stretch of deserted river bank. When she was almost abreast of the carriage, she noted that the coachman was not sitting on his perch, and that the horse, a tired old nag, was tied to a post next to a stone hut.

Katie moved cautiously forward.

The hut — shaped like a rectangular shoebox and resting on concrete slabs — had a flat tin roof with wavy ridges dipping low. Bales of wire and planks of wood lay strewn around the ground in front. Katie was reminded of a construction trailer she had visited with her father when she was twelve. Her dad had insisted that she wear a hard hat. When they entered, there had been a drafting table in the center of the room, charts on the walls, and a coffeepot percolating in the corner. Was this structure the equivalent of a construction trailer?

Would there be a drafting table inside, but no coffee maker? Katie wondered. Then she heard something that made her heart race.

A feeling of dread surged through her.

It was Catherine Eddowes singing "Ta-ra-ra-Boom-de-ay!"

But it couldn't be. Catherine Eddowes was dead.

Katie listened with shaking nerves. Someone was singing. Someone who sounded exactly like Catherine Eddowes! If Katie closed her eyes, she could almost imagine it *was* Eddowes with her lusty, throaty bravado.

But a moment later, from out of the carriage window, popped Dora Fowler's laughing face and bouncing brown curls. "'S'at you, Katie? Whatcha doing 'ere? Cor! The whole bloomin' city of London is 'ere!"

The whole city of London? The street was totally deserted.

Katie hurried to the carriage. "Dora? What are *you* doing here?"

"I came wiff Collin! Not ten minutes ago. Then, sure as you please, Major Brown comes waltzing on past, followed by that hollow-faced, eagle-nosed reverend!"

"Pinker?" Katie gasped. "Reverend Pinker?"

"The very same!" Dora hooked her elbows out of the cab's window and giggled.

She doesn't know that Catherine Eddowes is dead, Katie thought and moistened her lips in order to break the news. But Dora leaned further out the window.

"Whatcha doing here all alone?" she demanded. "You best come in here wiff me. 'Tis nice 'n' warm inside this cab. Collin gave the Westminster Abbey a few quid to get a pint o' beer at the pub round the corner, so I'm all by me lonesome."

"Collin went to Westminster Abbey? But —"

Dora giggled. "Not a bit of it. Collin gave the Westminster Abbey a few quid to make hisself scarce."

"Dora, I don't understand —"

"Westminster Abbey — the cabbie! Collin gave the cabbie bread 'n' honey to —"

"Okay. Okay. I get it." Katie was in no mood to wrap her mind around Cockney rhyming slang. "Collin gave the coachman money to get a drink at the pub."

"Tha's right! So it's joost you 'n' me. Gives me the fair shivers to be out here alone at night, so I'd be ever so grateful for your company. Leastways till Collin returns."

"I can't stay, Dora. *I've got to find Toby.*"

"He's hiding up there on the upper pier. That's where Collin went. Said he had somfink important to tell Toby." Dora pointed to the double set of pilings covered in scaffolding jutting out into the water, the top structure rising high above the lower like unfinished highway roads leading to nowhere.

"Did you tell Major Brown?" Katie gasped.

" 'Course not! Blimey. I ain't no itchy snitch. Didn't tell the vicar neither."

With a sigh of relief Katie continued. "Dora. I've got to get up there. How do I do it? Do I climb the scaffolding? And how do I get over the fence?"

"You can't do neither. That fence will cut you to shreds sure as I'm a bird seller. T'aint safe, Katie. It's what we calls French fencing. It's got barbed wire woven into it. Sharp steel points to keep people and animals out."

Katie bit down on her lip. "I don't have a choice. Toby's in trouble."

"Toby can fend for hisself, better 'n most. Don't you go worrying 'bout him. He's as slippery as the devil and just as strong."

"How did Collin get through the fence?"

"There's a hidey-hole. But I ain't showing you where. T'aint safe, I tells you."

Katie blinked at Dora and realized that Dora was in danger as well. If Madame Tussauds' waxwork plaques were correct, Dora would die near the construction pilings of Tower Bridge at the hands of Jack the Ripper in exactly two weeks. But everything was so upside down in terms of history's rewriting itself, maybe the Ripper would strike again tonight. Maybe Dora was next . . .

"Dora!" Katie reached up and tugged on the carriage handle. "You've got to come with me."

"I ain't getting out of this 'ere warm cab."

"Dora. *Please*. Let's stay together."

"Thank you, no," Dora said primly, shrinking back inside the carriage when Katie swung open the black lacquer door.

"Dora. We need to stick together. Did Collin tell you anything about me?" Katie improvised. "Like that I have second sight?"

"Every Cockney and his Great Aunt Fanny claims to have the seeing eye. If I had a farthing for every time a fortune-teller claimed to know me future, I'd be rich as Croesus."

"But I'm different," Katie bluffed. "I *am* clairvoyant."

"T'aint no one clairvoyant save old Mrs. Tray at Traitors' Gate."

"Precisely, Dora. And I've just come from Mrs. Tray's house. She agrees with me. Someone . . . I don't know who . . . is going to be murdered by Jack the Ripper at this exact spot any minute now . . . in a . . . Westminster Abbe —" Katie said, still improvising. "In a cab. I see it as clearly as I see you now."

"Are you saying the cabbie is Jack the Ripper? I don't believes you!"

"Ask Mrs. Tray. Some poor innocent girl — who shall remain nameless — is going to die in a . . . in a . . . er, right here. Any minute now. I don't know about you, Dora, but I'm not chancing it. You can . . . well, suit yourself. It's been nice knowing you."

"Eeeeek! I ain't staying here by me lonesome!" Dora shrieked. In a flash she had scrambled out of the cab. "Like you said, Katie, we oughts to stick together." Dora glanced around nervously. "You don't really suppose that fellow . . . the cabbie . . . is Jack the Ripper?"

Katie gave an I-don't-know shrug. "Let's not wait to find out."

Dora clutched the ring hanging down from her neck on a gold chain that glinted in the moonlight. "Collin wouldn't take kindly to nobody trying to murder me afore we dot and carry."

"Dot and . . . ?"

"Marry," Dora explained as they hurried down the slope of lawn toward the water's edge.

"We needs to stay close. It's slippery," Dora said. "When we're on the other side" — she pointed to the spiky fence — "and we gets to the pier, if you fall into the river, the current will carry you away and you'll die quick as a wink swallowing the filthy muck floating in it."

Katie nodded. Dora was telling the truth. The River Thames was a sewage funnel for most of the city. Marine life couldn't live in it. The polluted water carried typhoid and cholera. And although there was a new underground sewer system in London, most factories and open drains still emptied human waste directly into the river.

Dora pointed to a gaping hole in the fence. She told Katie it was where Collin and, later, Major Brown and the vicar, had ducked through.

"Careful, now," Dora warned. "We don't wants to get tangled up in that barbershop wire — sharp as a blade on a straight-edge razor. Falling into the river would be a far pleasanter way to die than getting cut and slashed to ribbons." Dora pointed to what looked like twisted jagged points of metal protruding from the fence.

Katie blinked at Dora. If Jack the Ripper wasn't stopped, it would be *exactly* how Dora would die: *cut and slashed to ribbons*.

It took several long minutes to wriggle through the opening in the fence because of their long, billowing skirts. After hiking them up around their waists and each helping the other step gingerly through the hole, they shook out the folds in their skirts and headed for the double set of pilings at the water's edge.

Dora began to chatter nervously, "You wouldn't thinks to look at us, but Collin and me gots true . . . heavens above."

"Heavens above . . . love?"

Dora nodded. "Collin's a right decent bloke, even if he does wear them funny swallows and sighs."

Katie stopped in her tracks. "Swallows and sighs . . ."

"Collars and ties!" Dora chuckled. "Blimey, Katie, you're as *la-di-da* as Collin. Let me gives you a lump of ice —"

"No, Dora." Katie sighed. "Let me give *you* a lump of advice. You and Collin will need a bag full of fruits and nuts — guts — to get past Collin's grandfather. The Duke of Twyford has his mind set on Collin's marrying the daughter of an earl."

Dora made a face. "Collin told me all about horse-face Prudence. Makes no never-mind if she's the daughter of *Gawd* Almighty. Collin says she's a petticoat lane in his bottle of rum."

Katie raised an eyebrow. "A petticoat lane — *pain* — in his...bottle of rum? What's that?"

"You know! His kingdom come. His fife and drum. His queen mum."

Katie shook her head. "You lost me."

"His bum!"

"Ah...of course." Katie bit back a smile.

Dora giggled. "I tells you, Collin hasn't even had a decent muddle wiff horse-face Prudence."

"Muddle?"

"Kiss and a cuddle!" Dora tittered gaily. "And he's had plenty wiff me, I can assures you!" She nudged Katie playfully in the ribs. "So? Is that what you Americans say — fruits and nuts?"

Katie shook her head. "I just made it up."

Dora raised a quizzical eyebrow. "Why would you do that? Make something up? Why not just say Collin and me will need enormous orchestra stalls to marry wiffout the Duke's blessing?"

"Orchestra stalls?" Katie blinked at Dora.

Dora sing-songed, "Balls."

Minutes later neither girl was smiling or laughing. They were both breathing heavily. They climbed over piles of rubble, moving slowly toward the scaffolded piers, one rising high above the other. Red mud held fast to their boots and clung in waxy clumps to the bottoms of their long skirts. A stinking odor of rotten eggs and excrement rose off the water.

Chapter Fifty-three

No Words Profane
say the Bells near Mark Lane

A SWATH OF FOAMY MUCK ran parallel for some thirty feet along the muddy shoreline to the truncated wharf.

Katie and Dora staggered forward, skirts hiked high, as they threaded their way around construction rubble to the bottom of the pier. The wooden pilings, Katie could see, were studded with clumps of barnacles.

All around them, seaweed clung to the wet pier. Above their heads, wind pummeled the planks of the pier like fists of rage.

A feeling of dread swept through Katie as an image of Catherine Eddowes's eviscerated body flashed into her mind. The prickle of fear tingled along Katie's scalp, down her arms, and right into the tips of her gloved fingers. She took a deep, shuddering breath and tried to stay calm, even as the sense of something terribly wrong — or something about to go terribly wrong — invaded her thoughts.

Dora began to shiver as if she felt a sudden foreboding as well. She shot Katie an anxious glance. As if with one thought, they craned their necks to stare up at the double set of piers, with risers holding up a timbered construction platform high above the water and looking as insurmountable as Mount Everest.

Taking another deep breath, Katie strode under the pier toward a slimy set of stone stairs.

"Not that way, Katie. 'Tisn't safe. Too slippery by far. Me dad's an oarsman for the river ferry. I've been down here afore. Likely as not, them rails over *there* are a better way to climb up." Dora pointed to a pebble-strewn area beneath the pier that gave way to an iron ladder, bolted between a set of pontoons, which cut right up through the middle of the jetty. The ladder reminded Katie of the kind that ran up the sides of giant water tanks.

"Onward and upward," Katie muttered, leading the way. She remembered her grandmother repeating a similar sentiment when faced with an obstacle in her path. But this wasn't just any ordinary obstacle, this was a perpendicular iron ladder rearing straight up the inside of a slimy, barnacle-crusted jetty!

Katie bunched up her skirts again and stuffed them into the waistband of her bodice, and moved in the direction of the iron ladder.

Hoisting herself up the first few rungs, Katie took a deep breath and continued to climb until the ladder stopped at the top ridge of a metal platform that opened onto a sort of wooden catwalk. Katie turned and helped Dora up onto the platform, and they both scurried down the catwalk toward a second platform that led to another set of risers. When they reached the top structure, they were a full three stories over the water. They could hear the sound of waves slapping against the pilings far below — a rhythmic, repetitive, whooshing sound like a dishwasher.

Dora cupped her mouth with both hands in order to be heard above the roar of the wind and said, "Now, remember. When we gets to the end of this platform, mind your step. If you fall into the river and the current doesn't drag you down and kill you, the foul sewage will, as sure as if you had the pox. No one falls in what lives to tell the tale. So mind your step."

"Gotcha," Katie said under her breath as she squinted downward, listening to the waves below. The odor of creosote wafted off the tar-smeared pilings, and the stench of dead fish was overwhelming. Ahead of them loomed rough-hewn planks extending farther out over the water.

Katie's insides went queasy. She took several deep breaths, but the rancid odor assailing her nostrils made her feel as if she were seasick.

"Let's keep going," she shouted as they moved toward the second open platform farther along the catwalk. Another bolted ladder reared straight up the side of the jetty. To access this next ladder, they had to maneuver along a slippery set of cross-planks. Metal rings had been woven into the rope-handled banister on either side of the catwalk. Katie held tight to these stirrup-shaped handles, which gave off a sharp rattle and clash when she let go of one set to grab onto the next.

"Gawd's truth, Katie!" Dora wailed behind Katie's shoulder. "I can't take another step!"

With water crashing against the pilings far below, and the wind whistling in a harmonica chorus above their heads, Katie's bravado — as well as her heart — began to sink. Toby and Collin could be anywhere on this crazy structure. What if she and Dora were headed in the wrong direction?

"Can you swim?" Katie asked, more to distract Dora than anything else. Katie knew that swimming was not an option. They were much too high up.

"I ain't no bleedin' porpoise!" Dora cried incredulously. She was panting from exertion and trying hard, like Katie, not to slip on the wet, cross-hatch slabs beneath their feet. "What sort o' girl do you take me for? And where would I swim, if'n I could? Not in the bloody Thames! Swallow one drop of that bilge water, and me own birds would be peckin' the skin from me gangrenous bones!"

Approaching the next ladder, Dora folded her arms over her chest. "I ain't movin' another step. I can't swim, nor climb like a monkey neither. I ain't movin' another step, not for nothink." She plunked herself down on an upside-down wheelbarrow, anchored with chains to the catwalk. Having sunk down on top of the inverted barrow, Dora refused to budge.

"I'm staying right here till you gets back."

Katie tried to reason with Dora, but it was no use. Dora pointed to a lantern light glimmering on the upper platform. Katie promised to return as quickly as she could and began to climb the ladder, determined to head in the direction of the flickering light. She hated to leave Dora alone, but forged ahead, hoping to find Collin and Toby.

Minutes later, Katie had climbed twenty-five feet straight up the ladder when she heard movement coming from below. She clung tightly to the wet rungs of the ladder and listened.

Nothing.

Had Dora had a change of heart? But the sound was too far away. And what was that clunking, dragging noise?

With a fresh surge of adrenaline, Katie hoisted herself up the last rungs until she came to a crosspiece with a steel hook shaped like a U, which, when she skirted around it, gave way to a ramp that opened onto another catwalk. But this one was made of iron mesh, not wood.

Movement ahead!

A gas torch flickered in the distance, faint yet distinct. *That's got to be Toby and Collin!* Katie thought, relief surging through her. She inched cautiously forward toward the lantern. As she approached the flickering, firefly light, she saw a flash of red. The wooden handrail to her right, braided with nautical rope, was wrapped in red flannel. The damp flannel was easier to grasp, less slippery. As she clung to it and pulled herself along, Katie could hear voices. Collin's voice? Her spirits soared. She was close! But when she stopped in her tracks, the figure behind and below her stopped as well.

She took several quick steps forward and stopped, several more steps and stopped again. The repeated echo of footfalls stopping and starting beneath her on the lower catwalk sent a shiver up Katie's spine.

Someone, with a much heavier footfall than Dora's, was following her. Katie could just make out the outline of a cape as it flapped like a dark sail around the silhouette of the person below who was...stalking her?

With the wind buffeting her body, Katie felt shaky and unsteady, but she pushed steadily forward.

The footsteps behind her started again.

If the person in the cape was a strong climber he'd be on her level in just a few minutes. Katie squinted over the railing into the gloom below. The figure beneath showed the upsurge of a tall man clothed all in black, like an undertaker. The gleam of his brass-headed cane rose up as if lifted to strike. Then the cane swung up and down like a baton leader's in a marching band.

"*You there!* You up there. Halt. Halt, I say!"

It was Reverend Pinker's voice. Katie could almost see his gulping Adam's apple. And for a brief moment, relief flooded her. But she quickly regained her senses. Some warning mechanism made her hasten forward toward the firefly lantern light.

Then the sound of a thud...someone falling beneath her in the gloom. A startled cry floating upward.

A vision of Dora sprawled on the catwalk below flashed into Katie's mind. Had she left Dora alone and utterly exposed to danger? Was Reverend Pinker Jack the Ripper? The image of Pinker sliding a knife across Dora's exposed throat made Katie stumble. She gripped the flannel handrail just in time. Righting herself, she bolted toward the lantern light that danced and flickered like a beacon of hope at the end of the construction platform that jutted out above the water. With her boots crackling and crunching on the grooved surface of the catwalk, Katie raced headlong toward the light of the lantern.

Chapter Fifty-four

Tin Soldiers and Tea
say the Bells of Chelsea

As she got closer, the light pooled downward, guiding her steps along the catwalk toward a platform with a sheer drop-off.

This far out over the water, Katie could feel the change in the wind. No longer buffered by steel risers or a shoreline below, it blew straight up, whipping Katie's skirts and making a tangled mess of her hair. Strands of curls that had been piled atop her head whipped against her face, stinging her cheeks and eyes.

With each step she took, the wind gained momentum, whirling around the precipice at the end of the construction pier as if around a giant cliff-edge. Blinking and squinting, Katie slowly pressed forward. The lantern ahead was just dim enough to turn dark shapes into flickering illusions. The closer she got, the more the firefly glimmer danced, distorting the distance to the edge of the platform.

And what was all that movement up ahead?

The blustery wind seemed to loom with newfound ferocity, only to lash down on her, impeding her progress. Katie braced each time she sensed it whirling upward for the inevitable crashing down, like the ocean waves that used to frighten her as a child.

Pausing to catch her breath, Katie glanced over her shoulder, squinting into the gloom, fearful that she would see Reverent Pinker closing in.

She saw nothing, nor did she hear the clatter of his footsteps.

She gave a shudder of relief and continued headlong into the wind toward the light. . .but if the sound of Pinker's heavy footfalls had sent a shiver up her spine, the noises up ahead made her breath catch painfully in her throat.

Katie could hear fists hammering, blow for blow. The landing of punches coming one after the other. Silhouetted by the dancing firefly flames, Katie saw two figures exchanging vicious blows.

Hunching her shoulders into the wind, she inched closer toward the end of the platform.

More dancing light.

On either side of the drop-off, set down upon upended barrels, were fish-oil bowls with floating wicks. The light dancing off the wicks combined with the lantern's to make the end of the walkway look like a dimly lit, narrow stage — dull, flickering footlights for the death scene in *Macbeth*.

Katie shook herself. Lightheaded, she had a sense of déjà vu. She'd been on this very pier before, looking out toward the cliff-edge drop to the crashing waves below.

"This isn't real," Katie told herself, scrunching her eyes so tightly she felt the wince of pain from the heartbeat pulse thrumming behind her lids. *I'm dreaming. This is all a dream. I'm in my own bed in the twenty-first century. I'm dreaming bad things are happening. This is all a spoof in my mind's eye because I watched a* Pirates of the Caribbean *movie last week. My brain's playing tricks on me.*

Katie began to laugh. She threw back her head in the whipping wind, and in an overloud, raucous voice, she howled with laughter like a crazy person. Perhaps she was a lunatic locked up in some insane asylum — where each jab of the needle, each stab of electric shock treatment, sent currents of laughter rippling from her mouth. *That's it!* Katie thought. *I'm on some kind of hallucinogenic drug.*

The effect of her outburst brought the two fighters ahead of her to a halt.

"God's eyeballs! What are you doing here, Katie?" Collin sputtered, fists clenched and held high on either side of his nose. "Go back! Go back!" he cried, and for a moment, with only the fish-oil lamps lighting his face, he looked as crumpled and withered as an old man. With nostrils flaring, he called out again, *"Turn back, Katie!"*

Major Brown, recovering from the split-second shock of seeing Katie, let fly a fierce left hook that landed against Collin's chin.

Behind them, Katie could see Toby lying unconscious on the ground near one of the barrels, blood oozing from a deep gash at his temple. Katie's first instinct was to run to him — he could be dead or dying and not just unconscious — but instead she stood frozen, watching in horror as Major Brown let loose a vicious punch that connected with Collin's cheek, splitting it open.

Collin roared with rage, but instead of conceding or stepping back, he flew at Major Brown. In a burst of fury, Collin began pummeling angry blow after angry blow, landing a cracking right-handed fist to Major Brown's nose, drawing a gush of blood, like red rain.

With a chill that shuddered up her spine, Katie realized that this was no gentleman's fisticuffs with rules of conduct. Collin was swinging punches in a mad rage, left and right. The vehement wrath emanating from both men was as palpable as the crashing waves below. And it was clear from the look on their faces that they meant to kill each other.

Murder was in the air.

With the frenzied howl of a wolf braying at the moon, Collin lunged and swung out at Major Brown with such force that when his fist missed the mark, his entire body collided with Brown's, knocking him to the ground.

In one fluid movement, Major Brown reached into the calf of his boot and drew out a dagger. Collin kicked at it, and it clattered to the ground. With a heaving grunt, Major Brown attempted to haul himself up, but not before Collin snatched the blade and held it aloft. As Brown staggered and rose to his full height, Collin took aim.

The only thing that saved Major Brown from being stabbed in the throat was his instinctive sidestepping to the left, so that the knife ripped through the collar of his military jacket. The lantern's gleam flashed on the blade as Collin lifted the dagger once again. But Major Brown had reared up like a bear. In sheer height and bulk, he had the advantage. Just as Collin lunged, Brown kicked him ferociously in the groin.

And it was over.

In a fit of heaving agony, Collin dropped to his knees, clutching his midsection. Then he fell sideways to the ground in a fetal position.

Except for the wind, all was quiet. Deathly quiet. The only thing competing with the whoosh of the blustery air was the sputtering, choking sound of Collin mewling in pain, like a baby animal caught in a steel trap.

Katie blinked at Toby lying unconscious on the ground next to one of the barrels and then at Collin softly weeping and doubled over, near the end of the platform. Katie's feet felt like lead. *She couldn't move.* If she stayed still long enough maybe Major Brown wouldn't notice, giving her enough time to formulate a plan. But what plan? All three of them — Toby, Collin, and Katie — were up here alone and at the mercy of Jack the Ripper.

It was then that Major Brown, slowly and with great deliberation, reached for the dagger and moved haltingly toward Katie. For a brief, terrifying moment, Katie could see her own slashed and eviscerated body being hoisted over the edge of the pier and dropped into the rushing, dark waves below.

But when Major Brown took another step in her direction, Collin surprised her. He made a diverting, howling noise, drawing Brown's attention. With great gasping effort and a strange semblance of dignity, Collin staggered to his feet and stared calmly, almost happily, at Major Brown. But the voice that choked off Katie's cries of protest was anything but calm. "Stay out of this, Katie!" he screamed. "Major Fathead's quarrel is with me, not you."

Major Brown clamped his eyes on Collin, and before he could even clench his fists, Collin charged at him with his own fists at the ready.

Watching what transpired next made Katie feel as if her head would explode. She gasped, struggled for breath, and felt a searing, aching, physical pain in the pit of her stomach as if Major Brown had landed a blow to her own stomach, instead of Collin's.

Paralyzed with fear, Katie was certain that Collin would keep fighting until Major Brown finished him off.

I have to do something! But what?

Frantically, Katie looked around. She was powerless against Major Brown's brute strength, his anger, his flying fists. . .and the knife that would surely slice her open.

She reached into her pocket and felt the jagged edge of Mrs. Tray's rock. She yanked it out of her pocket, then watched in horror as Major Brown cocked his fist back like a pistol hammer and put all his strength into a right cross to Collin's chin. Had it landed, it would have broken Collin's jaw, so powerful was the arc of the swing. But Collin's head, like Jell-O on a stick, wobbled and bobbed as his legs swayed and staggered beneath him, and the punch didn't land on his chin. It landed with a sickening crunch in the soft flesh just under his left ear. Collin, his brain dazed, his limbs loose and floppy, reeled backward like a rag doll and fell into a heap at the very edge of the wooden pier.

Major Brown moved menacingly toward him.

By rights Collin should have been paralyzed. . .or dead. But instead, he began thrashing about, trying once again to rise up. Any minute now he'd pitch himself over the edge by accident — or design, in order to thwart Major Brown's *coup de grace*.

There were no ropes or guard rails cordoning off the sheer drop at the end of the pier. The only thing standing between Collin and the precipice was an upturned wheelbarrow — beyond which Katie could see the vast, dark abyss of the Thames and could just make out the masts of schooners bobbing in the distance.

Stay still, Collin! Stay still! Katie silently prayed as, hunched over and clutching his stomach, Collin wobbled unsteadily to his feet and began to lurch this way and that.

With Major Brown's back toward her, Katie inched closer. She could see the sheer drop at the end of the pier, and it gave her vertigo just thinking about plunging over the side — which Collin would surely do if he didn't hold still. One wrong step . . .

Tall and menacing, Major Brown loomed in front of Katie like a gladiator as he slowly moved in for the kill.

Collin, swaying on his feet, his face and neck smeared with blood so bright and glistening it made the red of his hair look mud-brown, stared at Major Brown with fatalistic determination.

No! Katie silently screamed. She could see it in Collin's eyes. He meant to go after Major Brown again. It would be his last act on earth.

The slippery boards beneath her feet began to shake, the hand-rail to tremble. Katie realized with a jolt that it wasn't the pier that was shaking, but her whole body shuddering convulsively.

Do something! Do something! Do something! her mind screamed.

Clutching the jagged rock tightly in one hand, Katie scooped up the lantern from its pole with the other and swung it wide. The firefly flame jumped and jiggled, making both Collin and Major Brown pause for a split second. It was all the time she needed. She swung the lantern so the beam of light settled full into Major Brown's bloodshot eyes. She gave one last quick glance at Collin, sluggish blood oozing from his cheekbone.

Then Katie did the unthinkable. She closed her eyes.

Unthinkable by her father's standards, who had taught Katie to throw a baseball — and throw it hard.

"Never close your eyes, Katie! It's fatal!" Her father's words ricocheted in her head.

It had taken an entire summer to rid Katie of the habit of screwing up her eyes after taking aim. But that was exactly what she did now. She wound her arm back, took aim...and squeezed her eyes shut, letting the rock sail through the air.

The stone made thudding contact at the same instant that Katie willed her eyes to flick open—in time to see the rock smash dead center into Major Brown's forehead. Stunned and reeling, Major Brown blinked like a dazed Goliath and began batting his hand in front of his eyes. Collin saw his opportunity and flung himself straight at Brown. The force of it sent them both tumbling over the upturned wheelbarrow.

Collin rolled to the side and kicked out.

Major Brown tried to scramble up just as a foghorn blared in the distance. Collin kicked out again, smashing his boot into the man's kneecap. Major Brown buckled and fell to the ground.

The dagger was in Collin's hand.

Grabbing a fistful of Major Brown's hair, Collin yanked the man's head back. He was about to draw the blade across Brown's exposed throat when a thin, clear voice called out from the darkness behind.

"Don't do it, Collin."

It was Toby's voice.

"But he deserves it!" Collin screamed at the heavens.

"Don't," Toby repeated, limping toward them.

Collin hesitated. He let go of the knife. As the blade clattered to the ground, Collin's mouth split into a defiant, triumphant grimace, and he shoved Major Brown with all his might.

The taller, bulky man flailed, grabbing at air, but was off balance. Behind him loomed the yawning chasm of the pier's drop-off into the Thames—a sharp plunge, straight down, like the nosedive of a roller coaster. There was no tension wire or safety rail, nothing to grasp. Just wet, slimy wooden boards, sheared off at the end.

Collin gave another heaving thrust as if pushing a giant boulder over a cliff, and Major Brown toppled off the edge, a pinwheel of arms and legs. A scream of rage, not fear, echoed eerily back up at them until Major Brown's body hit the surface of the water far below with a thudding splash.

Katie's lantern caught Collin's white face, turned sideways. "*May he rot in hell*," Collin said hoarsely. He sank down to his knees and began to cry, slowly at first and then with deep, shuddering gasps. Across the horizon, grey-white clouds hung against the moon, which was dipping slowly into the water's edge on the opposite bank of the river.

Dawn breaking.

Katie hastened to Collin's side. Hard sobs wracked his body. Whether from happiness, pent-up fear, or gratitude that the man who would have killed him was sinking into the watery depths below, Katie didn't know.

All she knew was that Collin was alive. Toby was alive. And so was she. *We're safe now.*

Katie knelt down shakily and threw her arms around Collin. "I thought you were going to die. I thought Major Brown was going to kill you."

"*Have a care, old girl!*" Collin sputtered through his tears. "I wasn't...about to...let that blighter kill me. I showed him a thing or two!"

Katie bit back a smile. She wasn't going to tell Collin that it was Mrs. Tray's rock that had turned the tide. Instead, she hugged Collin harder. Close to his torn and bloodied ear, Katie whispered softly, "It's going to be all right, Collin. Everything's going to be all right now, I promise."

A moment later, she held his shoulders at arm's length and looked directly into his eyes. "We did it, Collin! Molly Potter, Dora Fowler, and Lady Beatrix are all safe now. Just think about it. We stopped the most infamous serial killer in history! We stopped Jack the Ripper."

But of course, they hadn't.

Chapter Fifty-five

Puppeteers Make Fun
say the Bells of Newington

KNEELING NEXT TO COLLIN, just inches from where the pitted boards gave onto the crashing waves below, Katie stared at the floating wick in the fish-oil bowl. Smoke rising from its tiny flame flickered like a question mark reminding Katie of the incense sticks Courtney used to light back home in Boston. *I miss my sister! It's time to go home!*

"It's not over," came Toby's expressionless voice from behind her.

Katie dragged her eyes from the hypnotic dancing flame with its pungent, rancid-oil smell, and swiveling her head around, peered into the shadows. "What do you mean, it's not over?"

"Jack the Ripper isn't dead," Toby shot back.

Katie felt cold rising inside her that had nothing to do with the moaning wind. She could see Toby across the way, supporting his weight against the handrail that ran the length of the pier up and down on either side. His left arm was dangling by his side at a crooked, awkward angle. *It's broken*, Katie thought with a shudder.

Toby's good arm was resting on a tangle of nautical rope coiled around a metal strut jutting out from the railing. With his dark hair plastered across the deep gash in his forehead, and his eyes shooting daggers at her, Toby looked more menacing than Major Brown had just moments before.

"But, Toby! Major Brown went over the side. No one could have survived that!" Katie blinked at him. *He must have a concussion.* "I guarantee you," she said more gently. "Major Brown can't hurt anyone ever again—"

"He's...right...Katie," came Collin's rasping voice so close to her ear she felt the prickle of his breath like a tickling feather against her neck.

"Major...Brown...not...the...Ripper," Collin choked out, his chest heaving from the exertion.

"*Omigod!*" Katie sputtered. "Reverend Pinker! It's Reverend Pinker, isn't it? *I knew it. I just knew it!* Dora's all alone. We have to go back and find her!"

With an adrenaline rush that precedes gargantuan feats of strength, Katie hoisted Collin to his feet, then half dragged, half pulled him away from the edge of the pier, his boots raking over the wooden floorboards with a stumbling clatter. But she managed to put a distance of only six feet between them and the drop-off brink.

Still too close, Katie thought. She could easily see beyond the wet-slimed swath of the timbered edge to the black expanse of water below. She moistened her lips, and the taste of salty air was all-pervasive like beads of sweat. She raked the back of her hand across her mouth to rid herself of the moisture, but her fingers only managed to smear her face with more watery brine.

"I knew it was Pinker! *I just knew it.*" Katie's heart pounded. She swallowed the salty wetness on her lips, acrid and sticky.

"No," came Toby and Collin's voice simultaneously.

Toby pushed himself away from the handrail and limped to the spot where Mrs. Tray's rock lay. With his good hand he scooped up the stone, and it disappeared into his clenched fist.

"Jack the Ripper is very much alive. But he's *not* Reverend Pinker."
There was a strangled, dark look in Toby's eyes as he hobbled closer,
which deepened into something more fierce: *Sorrow? Anger? Pity?*

"Who, then?" Katie demanded, struggling to prop Collin up as
the wind whipped her hair around her face.

"In a manner of speaking—" Collin said, swaying unsteadily. "I
suppose you could say it's *two* people." He glanced at Toby and smiled
weakly. There was a strange sort of relief in his voice, even as his body
quivered. "Two of us. Isn't that right, Toby?"

"What are you talking about?" Katie let go of Collin's elbow and
instinctively stepped back—from disbelief or fear, she wasn't sure.
Collin, unable to stand without her help, lunged to the waist-high railing to their left. Clutching the wooden handrail, rigid in his intensity,
he locked stares with Toby, ten feet away. The only thing separating
the two boys was the expanse of pitted grey boards at their feet.

Katie glanced from one to the other.

To the east, a pale, buttery orb of a sun began to rise up out of
the Thames. With it, the groan of the wind died down. Katie could
hear buoy bells clanking in the distance and anchors being hoisted up,
chain against chain, like the clatter of pots and pans.

There was a pause as if they were all standing still in awe of the
sunrise. In the momentary lull, Katie peered down the long boards to
where the pier dropped off into the sea. The Thames looked more like
the yawning span of a misty golf course than a crashing river—bright
green in patches where beams of sunlight sparkled. The image of the
Thames as a golf course made Kate laugh. But it was a bitter, mirthless
laugh. Before her father died on his way to pick up Collin, he had
given Katie a present: a titanium driver with a graphite shaft, a Python
Light Speed.

"So what do you say to that, Katie?" Collin's voice pierced her
thoughts. She hadn't heard a word he'd said.

"You never guessed it was us, did you, Katie?" Collin continued.

Us . . . ? Katie yanked her thoughts back to the present. She felt
oddly disconnected. As if she were here, but not here. Like one of

those near-death experiences where you float above a hospital room watching doctors try to revive you. *It's like that,* Katie thought. *I just want to be left in peace and float away. I don't want to be revived. I just want to go home!*

But the two faces peering back at her, both grim and splattered with blood, no longer resembled the boys she knew so well — full of pranks and mischief, bravado and heroics. It was as if, in the space of several hours, Collin and Toby had grown into full manhood. Standing across from each other, on either side of the long pier, their expressions looked like mirror images — bleak but resolute, full of anguish and grief...triumph and determination.

"Who are you talking about?!" Katie shouted, scared to her very core of the answer she might receive.

Toby smiled, but it was more a grimace than a smile.

Waves sloshed against the lower pilings.

Who? Katie silently screamed.

Collin was the first to break the silence.

"I guess you could say...the one who set it all in motion...was the Duke," Collin said, his face ashen as he leaned against the left-hand rail of the pier, the sun rising up behind his shoulders.

"The Duke?" Katie cried incredulously. "That's not possible." *The Duke can hardly walk. He uses a cane. He's not nimble enough to be all over the East End, slashing women and then disappearing from sight.*

With a grunt of pain, Collin straightened to his full height, bracing his feet and legs against the wooden slats of the railing. He was breathing hard. "The Duke hatched a plan...that went wrong. Dead wrong. Isn't that right, Toby?"

The breeze carrying up from the water below smelled chokingly of burnt toast, garlic, and dead fish. Katie clenched her stomach, trying hard not to dry heave.

Toby stared at Collin. "The Duke is not Jack the Ripper. He may have unwittingly set plans into motion. He's not blameless in the death of Mary Ann Nichols. But he never physically touched any of those girls."

"True enough, Toby, old sod. True enough," Collin said in a tired voice with a sort of bitter inflection. Then, from his torn vest pocket, he tugged out the knife that had clattered to the ground when Major Brown went over the edge, and held it aloft — a parallel image of Toby's holding up the rock in his clenched fist.

"Because Jack the Ripper is none other than" — Collin dropped the one monosyllable Katie least wanted to hear into the frozen stillness — "*You.*" Collin's eyes grew wide with a sneaky look. "You did the Duke's dirty work for him, Toby. You're Jack the Ripper. But your luck's run out, old sod."

Uncomprehending, Katie blinked from one to the other. "Collin! Are you insane? Toby is no more Jack the Ripper than I am!"

"'Fraid not, old girl. Toby's going to hang."

"How in all blue hell do you figure that will happen, Collin?" Toby asked in a flat, emotionless tone, but a vein in his temple began to twitch.

Collin's red brows shot up. He pantomimed shock that Toby could even ask such a question. "Because of Dora's testimony. *And mine.* I can *prove* you're the Ripper. Dora's a witness. She's going to give Queen's evidence against you."

"And when she does, you'll plant an emerald the size of a pigeon's egg on her wedding finger, is that it, Collin?"

"I, for one," Collin persisted, swinging the dagger from his left hand to his right like a surgeon weighing a scalpel, "shall take great delight in your undoing."

"And I'll see you on a morgue slab with that knife in your heart first."

"Not before I watch you swing from the gallows."

"You're a damn fool if you think so." There was naked contempt in Toby's voice. "Dora would no more give evidence against me than fly to the moon. There's a code amongst Cockneys — *not to rat each other out* — or have you forgotten?"

"As the future Duke of Twyford, I'm prepared to sign a statement that I saw you standing over the body of two of those murdered girls, knife in hand. There's already a great deal of evidence against you, Toby." There was a vicious eagerness in Collin's eyes, matched only by the look of pure hatred in Toby's.

"And as for Dora," Collin continued, "I think her loyalties will lie with those poor, dead Cockney girls. *And* with me. It won't matter a fig if you're her Great-Aunt Fanny's nephew, thrice removed."

"Are you so sure about that?" Toby grunted.

"Of *course* I am! Dora would play the part of a Cherokee maiden if I asked her to. But she saw what she saw. *You* bending over two of those murdered girls. I suppose you'd like to tell Katie that it's me. That I'm Jack the Ripper. But it won't wash, old sod. Katie was with me at the Ten Bells Tavern. She knows I couldn't possibly have killed Catherine Eddowes. That took someone as evil and cunning as Satan."

"On that, we're in total agreement. But you'll be shaking hands with the devil long before I will. Go on, Collin. Tell Katie. Tell her what you told Major Brown. That you never meant to kill the first girl . . . how it was an accident."

"So? You want me to babble? Spill the beans? What's to be gained by it?" In the soft glow of the rising sun, Collin's face appeared veiled.

His voice was icy as he said, "Why don't *you* tell Katie, Toby? Tell her how it's possible that I could be in two places at one time? How could I have killed the first girl tonight, Lizzie Stride, and then slit Catherine Eddowes's throat? Katie was with me at the Ten Bells. Unless you think I'm a ghoulish phantom who can float through walls and be in two places at once. We kept Catherine Eddowes singing until half after midnight, in the back room at the Ten Bells. I came out and got Katie five minutes *after* Catherine Eddowes finished her last song. The whole evening, up to that moment, I was at the Ten Bells Tavern."

"That's true!" Katie interjected. "I was outside the door the whole time. I heard Catherine singing. Just minutes after her last song, when he heard Oscar Wilde fighting with Major Brown's officer, Collin came flying out the door. Collin couldn't have killed Catherine Eddowes. I was there. Dora was there. There wasn't time for Collin to do anything, let alone murder two woman, cut them up, and leave their bodies blocks away from the Ten Bells. Unless...unless Collin had help. An accomplice."

Fear shot through Katie like a sharp pain in her side. She blinked at Toby. *Toby is either Jack the Ripper...or he's Collin's accomplice!* Her throat tightened. Tears stung her eyes. The revelation struck her like a jab from the knife in Collin's hand. *They're both Jack the Ripper!* The thought rattled around in her brain like pebbles in a tin can.

She stared at Toby with revulsion and something more: a deep, desperate, wrenching feeling of betrayal. She had cared deeply for him. More deeply than she had ever imagined possible. *I always lose the people I love!*

Toby saw it in her eyes. The hurt, the anger.

Katie clenched and unclenched her fists. The horror that Toby was Jack the Ripper overwhelmed her. But a burst of outrage, blind and furious, overrode her repulsion. She made a step to fly at him, both fists raised.

Collin lunged toward her and grabbed her wrist. "Have a care, Katie. We can't have him slicing you up as well." Collin's voice was emotional and passionate, but not altogether convincing.

Katie turned and stared at Collin. An angry flush suffused his blood-smeared face like a crimson mask. Red on red.

She knew. She knew by the sneer broadening his mouth, by the slow shake of his head, by the look in his eyes as cunning and frightening as anything Katie had ever seen there before.

"It was *rawther* ingenious of me, don't you think, Katie, old girl?" Collin's voice rose half an octave as he yanked her to his chest and jabbed the tip of the dagger into her throat. She could feel the twitching pulse of her heartbeat where the blade pressed into her flesh.

"But it can't be you, Collin. It can't be!" Katie wailed, droplets of blood trickling like tears down her neck, wet and warm. *"I was with you at the Ten Bells!* There wasn't time for you to murder two girls."

"Wrong again. The door was closed. You were outside, listening. *Listening*, mind you. Foolish, foolish girl. You didn't hear Catherine

Eddowes singing. You heard Dora Fowler. She's a natural mimic and ventriloquist, remember? When I first met Dora, she made it appear as if one of her parrots was a veritable chatterbox — I told you all about that, Katie. She can manipulate her voice so it sounds as if its coming from her birds. Dora can imitate anything or anyone."

Katie's mind raced back to the Ten Bells Tavern, and Catherine Eddowes singing a lusty version of the Jack the Ripper song. Then she remembered approaching the hansom cab earlier. Dora was in the carriage singing "Ta-ra-ra-Boom-de-ay!" For a brief, agonizing moment Katie had thought it *was* Catherine Eddowes singing. Dora was more than adept at mimicry, she was a talented ventriloquist. That's how she sold her parrots!

"But the others? How did you do it, Collin? And why?" Katie stopped struggling and began breathing slowly in and out. *Stay calm, stay calm.*

"As to the others," Collin sputtered, loosening his grip across Katie's collarbone, "Toby can tell you how I pulled it off. You and he will have an eternity to discuss it at hell's gate or heaven's door — doesn't much matter which."

Toby stepped forward. "I bet she'd rather hear it from you, Collin. Tell Katie how you never meant to kill the first girl, Mary Ann Nichols. Tell Katie what happened. It *was* ingenious of you."

He wants to keep Collin talking, Katie thought, catching the cajoling inflection in Toby's voice.

"So . . . ? Toby's not the Ripper?" Katie squeaked out. "He didn't help you?"

"*Pheff,*" Collin sniffed. "Toby could crush a man twice his size and not even break a sweat — everyone knows that. But he'd never lash out at anyone who hadn't lashed out at him first. No. It took someone far less principled and far more cunning than Toby."

Toby's not the Ripper! Katie's heart soared, then plummeted as the flat of the blade pressed against her throat.

Toby nodded almost imperceptibly, and Katie continued in a coaxing tone, "And . . . Mary Ann Nichols . . . ?"

"Ah...yes. The first girl I ever killed. I almost bungled that one."

"But why kill her?" Katie persisted, trying not to flinch or squirm under the pressure of the knife. "What did Mary Ann ever do to you?"

Collin shifted the knife closer under Katie's chin, and Toby quickly took up the narrative.

"She double-crossed you, didn't she, Collin?" Toby's voice was low, almost a whisper, but with underlying urgency. "Mary Ann Nichols went back on her word, didn't she? The Duke hatched a plan to discredit Major Brown. He paid Mary Ann a hefty sum to *claim* that she and Major Brown were recently betrothed, thereby invalidating Brown's courtship of your sister. Reverend Pinker introduced Mary Ann to you. She was a regular at his East End Charity Mission. Pinker knew Mary Ann was desperate to get away from Mad Willy. At the inquest we learned that Mad Willy had fisted her in the mouth, loosening several teeth."

"Precisely," Collin said, with a flash of excitement. "It was concluded at the inquest that Mary Ann knew her assailant or she would have cried out. Mrs. Green, the owner of a boarding house, stated she was sitting in her front parlor and would easily have heard Mary Ann scream for help."

Toby nodded. "Witnesses claimed that on several occasions preceding her death they saw Mary Ann stepping out with someone who appeared to be a toff — that was you, Collin. Am I right?"

"Of course it was!" A superior smile twisted on Collin's lips. "Even her own father testified that his girl had foolish pride, thinking she was above her class. Mad Willy had popped her a good one more than once, so she wanted a hundred quid to get out of London and start a new life.

"The plan was for Mary Ann to arrive at the theater the night we all saw *Dr Jekyll and Mr Hyde*. As we were leaving the Lyceum, Mary Ann was *supposed* to make a scene on the steps outside the theater, insisting that Lady Beatrix stay away from Major Brown. Mary Ann was to present Beatrix with the opera glasses and tell her that Major Brown had given them to her that very day as a token of his affection. Beatrix would recognize the man she loved as a liar, cheat, and thief, and break off all ties with him."

"But Mary Ann Nichols never arrived at the theater. What happened?" Katie sputtered, squirming ever so slightly from the pressure of the cold steel at her throat.

"The stupid strumpet had a change of heart. She sent a note to her friend, Molly Potter, the orange seller at the theater, to tell Reverend Pinker to meet her at Buck's Row. Pinker showed me the note. I thought the silly chit was holding out for more money. So when Pinker exited the theater and hailed a cab, I took the underground railway. It's quicker than a cab through traffic, as you discovered Katie when you rode on the underground train with Toby. You said yourself how much *faster* it was below ground than above. So I beat Pinker to the punch, *so to speak*." Collin began to laugh maniacally. "I didn't punch her — a gentleman doesn't hit a lady. I slit her throat." More echoing, crazy-sounding laughter.

Collin's insane, Katie thought.

Collin stopped laughing, his voice a low snarl. "When I arrived in Buck's Row, Mary Ann told me she didn't want more money. She tried to give back the opera glasses. Claimed she couldn't undermine Major Brown because he was a fellow Cockney and a hero in the East End, having risen so high in the ranks of Scotland Yard. I would never have killed her had she not praised Major Brown to the heavens. Ballyhooed his name as if he were a veritable god! It was too much. *Too much*, I tell you! I lost my temper. Who wouldn't have?" Again the low, hissing snarl. "Ah, yes. . .my famous temper that you keep hearing about, Katie. *And that you've seen first hand*. I used my pocketknife to slit her throat — but like a fool I made a mistake. In my haste, I forgot Beatrix's opera glasses. I knew Reverend Pinker would arrive any minute, so I raced down the street to the underground railway on Tower Hill, and arrived back in the West End at the Lyceum Theatre, where I slipped quietly into my seat and resumed watching the play. But you noticed my absence, Katie. It was *almost* my undoing."

Katie shuddered. Waves sloshed and sucked against the pilings below the pier. "And Reverend Pinker?" Katie prompted, feeling the pulse in her neck quicken from the downward force of the blade.

"Hah!" Collin snorted like a horse at a starting gate. "Good old Stink-Pink arrived in Buck's Row, but never saw me. He inspected the girl, got scared, and returned to the theater believing it was some random act of violence. Blood must have transferred to his sleeves — *blood you saw*, Katie, and commented on, drawing attention to the good Reverend. Stinker hasn't an ounce of intelligence. He never thought for a moment I'd done the deed. Why would he? And later, when we left the theater, that stupid, pregnant orange seller, Molly Potter, almost brought me down low. She asked Reverend Pinker if he'd received the note from her friend, Mary Ann Nichols. I shoved her hard to shut her up. You saw that, Katie, but didn't put two and two together. It all might have ended there. Gone no further, but for Georgie Cross who pilfered the opera glasses. My *sister's* opera glasses. The only tangible thing that could link Mary Ann's death to me and my family, and that sorry excuse of a porter lad stole them off a dead girl! The vile, despicable, thieving fool."

"So Major Brown had nothing to do with any of the deaths?" Katie asked. *Keep him talking. Keep him talking.*

"Major Brown?" Collin sneered. "With all his militarism and sanctimonious sense of superiority he couldn't gut a fish, let alone a flesh-and-blood girl. But Brown eventually figured it out. He was on to me at Dark Annie's house when I suffocated Georgie Cross. Oh, how he was on to me! But being a Cockney, he couldn't hand me over to the authorities because he believed I would soon be his brother-in-law! The blighter wasn't good enough to lick my boots, let alone my sister's, yet he *dared* to presume he could ask for her hand in marriage! My sister is the great-great-grandniece of a king! And Major Brown — a mere commoner from the lowest of tenement slums."

"But why," asked Toby, inching closer, "kill Georgie Cross?"

In the distance a five-mast schooner swayed on the waves like a ship on the open sea.

"Ah, there's the rub, Toby!" Collin chuckled, shifting his weight. "You might have saved Georgie Cross. Yes, *you*. If you hadn't left me alone with the addle-brained nincompoop when we first entered his sickroom at Dark Annie's house. So you can chalk up Georgie's death to your own incompetence."

"How...so...Collin?" Toby asked between clenched teeth.

Toby was having trouble keeping his voice steady, Katie could tell. She swiveled her eyes and tried to focus her gaze along the shoreline below, silvery white and speckled with seaweed and rocks.

Collin, one arm wrapped around Katie's waist, the other gripping the dagger at her throat, shouted at Toby not to come any closer, and resumed his narration as if talking to Katie alone.

"Here's what happened, Katie," Collin hissed, his breath prickly against her ear as he tugged her tight against his chest. "When Toby and I entered Georgie's sick room — which smelled like the bloody plague — Georgie was asleep. His breathing was regular. He might have lived to a ripe old age, if not for Toby. I turned my back in case the young fool woke up and recognized me. But the idiot porter boy must have sensed we were there in the room because he became agitated, half-mumbling a French song and muttering about a girl named Cecilia. Toby told me to stay put, then he stole back into the hallway to eavesdrop on Major Brown who was shouting at Dark Annie, telling her she had no business hiding a witness from the crown."

"But why smother Georgie?" Katie cried.

"It was the opera glasses! After the inquest I went to Georgie's grandmother's house — I knew the address because they read it off at the inquest. Mrs. Richardson told Toby that one of her tenants had overheard Georgie arguing with someone who had a Cockney accent, but who sounded like a *toff*. That was *me*. You've heard me imitate Toby's rhyming slang a hundred times. And as you so aptly pointed out, Katie, I sound like an aristocrat pretending to be a Cockney. That's exactly how Mrs. Richardson's neighbor described the person who attacked her grandson. You and Toby thought the description fit Major

Brown. But he's a Cockney pretending to be an aristocrat. There's a big difference.

"Georgie Cross refused to give me the opera glasses. Disavowed all knowledge of them. But since Mary Ann had them on her when I'd killed her — and it was a fair bet Reverend Pinker didn't nick them — it had to be Georgie. We argued. I smashed his head against the kitchen wall so hard it addled his wits, concussed his brain."

Katie swallowed hard, squirming ever so slightly. "Go on," she said in an urging tone.

"I'm growing weary of talking."

Katie glanced at Toby standing several feet away. She saw in his face that he was as repelled as she by Collin's confession, but was trying with great effort not to let on.

"So," Toby continued. "When Mrs. Richardson learned that the police were looking for her grandson because he hadn't shown up at the inquest, she spirited him away to Dark Annie's house. In his stricken condition, Mrs. Richardson was afraid that the peelers would put Georgie in Bedlam Hospital and he might never come out." Toby took a deep breath and went on.

"At Annie Chapman's house Collin stayed with Georgie while I went into the hall to eavesdrop on Major Brown. But Georgie sensed Collin was there in the room and became increasingly agitated. Collin didn't want Georgie to regain consciousness and spill the beans. Isn't that right, Collin?"

"Precisely," Collin sneered, "Georgie started to wake up and was mumbling some silly French song. Any minute he'd have recognized me as his attacker — the one who'd given him that thumping crack on the head."

Toby nodded. "Georgie had been given laudanum, so it was nothing short of child's play for you to take a pillow, place it over his face, and smother him. Later, when Major Brown stormed into Georgie's sickroom, leaving us all out in the hall, Brown saw the pillow and hid it in the corner cupboard, where I found it much later. He concealed it because it had Georgie's teeth marks embedded in it. Even with all the laudanum, Georgie struggled for his life, didn't he, Collin? Which is why Major Brown realized it had to be you. He knew I wouldn't hurt Georgie. As you just said, Collin, I wouldn't lash out at anyone who hadn't lashed out at me first. Major Brown knew I'd never hurt a defenseless boy, and never in a million years would I hurt Georgie Cross, a lad I'd known since my youth. So Major Brown rightly assumed that it was you."

Collin threw back his head and laughed. "And when Major Fathead came barreling out of Georgie's room, he saw me and was furious. Mum and Dad as you put it, Toby. Spitting mad. He cursed me for my unlawful audacity. He said, 'What you've done is a criminal act of vindictiveness aimed at me, is that it?' I just laughed in his face. I knew he couldn't hand me over to the authorities. Beatrix would never forgive him, nor *marry* him if he exposed her brother as a cold-blooded murderer. Cockneys live by different sets of rules. They hush things up where family members are concerned. Once I became part of Major Brown's extended family, in his mind, he was duty-bound to shield me from the law. Knowing this, I goaded him: 'Want to tell Lady Beatrix what a cowardly cuss I am?' I knew he wouldn't turn me in. I knew I could taunt him as much as I pleased. But my jeering drove him over the edge. He pummeled and lashed out, giving me the thrashing of my life. Might have killed me, too, if Toby hadn't intervened."

Katie remembered how miserable Toby was when he had described all this to her later. "*Had you asked me yesterday, Katie, if Brown was capable of losing his temper over Collin's childish antics, I'd have sworn an oath, not. Collin didn't say anything so very inflammatory — nothing to provoke such violence.*" But Collin *had* done something to provoke Major Brown. He had killed Georgie Cross.

"Then! The evening got even better!" Collin crowed. "Reverend Pinker arrived. Dark Annie didn't know Georgie was dead, and she begged Pinker to intervene on his behalf. 'Don't let 'im hand Georgie over to the authorities until he's recovered. He'll be taken to Bedlam Hospital!' Major Brown couldn't let the cat out of the bag, at least not then — not while suspicion might land on his future brother-in-law.

'Don't disturb Georgie,' Brown warned Pinker. 'He's got a fever and may be contagious.' Humph!" Collin snorted. "Georgie was no more contagious than you or I — *because he was dead* — but it was enough to insure that Stink-Pink wouldn't set foot inside that sickroom. Major Brown needed time to come up with a strategy while he wrestled with his conscience, trying to decide whether his allegiance to Beatrix was greater than his allegiance to the law. His Cockney ethics must have been warring within him — God rot his soul."

"And Dark Annie?" Katie choked out. "Did you kill her, too?"

Collin nodded.

The muscles in Toby's face tightened as he forced a smile. "Tell us about Annie Chapman."

"Ha! That was an easy one. But I'm weary of telling this tale. The two of you will have all eternity to dissect the minute details of my scurrilous — though dare I say, brilliant — crimes!"

"Wait! The others. . .? Lizzie Stride and Catherine Eddowes. You killed them as well?" Katie asked.

"Yes and yes! But I won't hurt Dora, even though *you* predicted her death, Katie."

"You'll marry her, then?" Katie asked, stalling. She could see Toby from the corner of her eye, slowly raising his fist, clenching Mrs. Tray's rock.

"Hah!" Collin spat out. "The Duke can't dictate to me, by thunder. But in this instance, he's right. I shall marry Prudence. She's an earl's daughter after all, with a private fortune, country homes, and farmland to boot. But as to Dora. . .Have no fear from that quarter, Katie. I'm too fond of Dora to kill her. She'll be my Scotch warming pan, as the Cockneys say."

Collin laughed and poked the knife into Katie's throat, pricking the skin until she cried out. Then he turned to Toby and shouted, "Drop the rock in your hand, Toby! Unless you care to see Katie bleed to death." Collin made an exaggerated twisting motion of the knife at her throat.

Toby let the rock clunk onto the pitted boards at his feet.

"Go to the end of the pier, Toby," Collin continued barking orders. "Get down on your knees. Raise your hands above your head. *Do it now!* Do it, or I slit her throat from ear to ear." Collin yanked his grip tighter around Katie's waist.

Toby moved haltingly to the edge of the wharf, knelt down, and put his hands up. Katie could see the crooked arc of his broken left arm. To raise it must have been excruciating. But Toby's face was as implacable as the stone he'd just dropped.

Collin spun Katie around so that she faced him, her back to Toby. "I want to gaze into your eyes when I kill you." Again the maniacal laughter.

"So! Toby?" Collin continued, his breath warm and sickeningly moist against Katie's cheek. "I'm going to ask you nicely to jump off the cliff edge," he shouted. "If you do, I give you my word of honor — as a gentleman — that I shall kill Katie quickly. She'll feel no pain."

"Then you'll eviscerate her?" Toby shouted back. "Gut her like a slaughterhouse calf?"

"Of course. I need this to appear as if Jack the Ripper — you, Toby — killed her, and I wrestled you over the side. So, what's it going to be? A fast, easy death for Katie, or an agonizingly slow and painful one?"

Katie remembered a ruse from a TV show. She gaped past Collin's shoulder and shouted, "No! Major Brown, *don't!* Collin's got a knife!"

Collin gave a snorting laugh. "Nice try, Katie, old girl." He made a heavy gesture with the knife, drawing a new gush of blood at her collar bone.

"She's right!" Toby shouted. "Major Brown is behind you."

Uncertainty sprang into Collin's eyes, then quickly faded. "You want me to turn around so you can jump me? Well, I'm not so easily tricked. Major Brown is dead. Anyone who plummets into the Thames at this height hasn't a snowball's chance in hell. You'll have to try something more original, old sod. Now, let me explain the plan once again —"

"Drop the knife!" boomed Major Brown's voice from behind Collin.

Collin shoved Katie aside and whipped around.

There was no one there.

But in that split second, Toby sprang forward. Katie lunged and shoved Collin with all her might. Collin let out a billowing whoosh of air as Toby grabbed his wrist and twisted it back until the bone snapped. The dagger fishtailed through the air and landed tip-down in the pitted boards where it thrummed like the shaft of an arrow. They were perilously close to the side, waves thundering below.

"*Get down, Katie!*" Toby cried.

Katie dropped to all fours, her fingers gripping the ribbed boards, damp and slippery beneath her open palms. She heard the crunch of fist against flesh. Then came a whomping thud as Collin toppled over her arched back.

She turned her head in time to see Collin's arms flapping in the air, followed by a screech of pure terror as he wheeled over the edge of the wharf.

Then the sound of his body hitting the current below with a gurgling, loud splash.

And it was over.

On her hands and knees, Katie scrabbled across the uneven boards and stuck her head over the side. Swirling dark water dipped and slapped, black tinged with gleams of silver where the waves crashed against the lower pier. She squinted hard, scanning the depths, but it was impossible to see anything more than the shades and shadows of the water rising and falling, and crashing back, whitecaps foaming.

Bending low, Toby reached out a strong hand, and Katie clasped it tightly in her own and rose up slowly, clamping her free hand to her bloodied neck. Some dim recollection, a déjà vu feeling caught her up short. *Major Brown! He's alive!*

Katie whirled around. "Major Brown . . . ?" she called out.

Farther along the pier, sheltered from the breeze, Dora popped out from behind an upturned barrel. "I heard what that murdering devil said. He killed me best friend, Mary Ann!"

Katie's heart thumped wildly. The small nicks at her throat throbbed.

It was Dora! Dora had thrown her voice to mimic Major Brown's, and Collin had taken the bait. He had fallen for it, literally.

Katie raced down the pier, wrapped her arms around Dora, and hugged her. "You saved our lives! Thank you, thank you, thank you, Dora."

"You would'a done the same for me," Dora said. "Collin deserved far worse. He ought to 'ave been skinned alive and salted! And as for a Scotch warming pan . . . I gots me pride, I does."

Dora disentangled herself from Katie's embrace. "I wouldn't hurt nobody, not for nuffink. Not even for this here ring!" She held up the ring with an emerald the size of a pigeon's egg. "Course it's mine now, good and proper. May Collin rot —"

" — in hell," they spoke in unison.

Katie thought about Major Brown. He was innocent, but he too had died at the hands of Jack the Ripper. She swallowed hard. *I threw that rock at him. If I hadn't thrown it, he might still be alive . . .*

Sunlight streamed through the overhead clouds as Toby limped forward. "It's time to go home, lass."

"But Major Brown —" Katie's stomach lurched.

"He died as he lived. It's time for you to return home. Where you belong."

Home.

Katie nodded, but felt helpless and oddly alone — helpless because she had unwittingly assisted Collin, and alone because when she returned to her own century, everyone here would be dead. She would never see Toby again. Her time with him was drawing to a close, trickling away like the blood oozing down her neck.

Toby, Lady Beatrix, Collin, the Duke. . .everyone and every-thing here would be a distant memory, consigned to history. But at least Jack the Ripper's reign of terror was over.

Or so they thought.

Chapter Fifty-six

Tell Me My Fate
say the Bells of Traitors' Gate

AN HOUR LATER Katie would be back in the twenty-first century. But if she thought she was finished with Jack the Ripper, she was wrong.

Dead wrong.

After devising a makeshift sling torn from Katie's petticoat for his broken arm, Toby guided Katie and Dora down the slime-coated ladders traversing the truncated construction pier.

Descending the slippery metal rungs was easier than climbing up. At least for Katie. Every few steps Toby would wince from the pain shooting up his arm.

"Hurry, lass, we haven't much time!" Toby whispered to Katie when they reached the lower level. "Mrs. Tray told me you needed to return to the London Stone *before* the sun was full in the sky. And by the look of things...she wasn't wrong."

Katie glanced down.

With a gasp of surprise, she realized that Toby was right. Her skin — especially on her arms, showing through the torn patches of her sleeves — seemed to be fading in and out. The molecules were... flickering like a fuzzy TV picture that blinks and crackles and eventually goes blank.

What's happening?

Dora, too, noticed. She kept giving Katie sideways glances and muttering about having had too many drinks at the Ten Bells. "Me vision's a wee bit bleary," she kept repeating, blinking and rubbing her eyes.

When they finally reached the muddy bottom below the pier, Katie looked out past the shoreline across the dark water where a five-mast schooner bobbed on the waves. Ferry boats passed in both directions, their whistles blowing like mournful bagpipes.

Toby told Dora to go to the Tower and ring the bell for the river police. "Tell them to look for two bodies. Major Brown's and Collin's. Can you do that, lass?"

Dora nodded. "Me dad's an oarsman on this river. I knows me way around the Thames like the back of me hand. The closest bell is at Traitors' Gate. I'll ring it till me hands fall off. But whatchya want me to *really* tell 'em, eh, Toby?"

"The truth."

"I'll give 'em an earful, I will. Collin was a nasty piece of goods. May he sizzle in hell for what he did to my poor Mary Ann and them others. And to think it could have been *me* what got her throat chived from ear to ear."

Katie took a deep, shuddering breath just thinking about the fact that Dora *would* have been Collin's next victim.

Toby gave Dora a gentle nudge. "Best hurry, Dora."

"Don't you worry, Toby. I'll summon the River Police quick as a wink. Lord! Think of all the attention this will get once the newspapers hear of it. I'll make a pretty penny selling my side of things. And the inquest...I'll wear me best bonnet, I will! I shall be known far and wide as the lucky girl who outwitted Jack the Ripper."

"On the other hand, Dora. . ." Katie said casually, too casually. "As long as Toby's name is cleared and he's not under any suspicion, I'll bet the Duke of Twyford would pay far more than any newspaper to keep his grandson's name *out* of the press." Katie was thinking about her own cousin back home, and how he'd hate it if he knew Jack the Ripper was his ancestor. "I'd wager the Duke might even set you up in your own little shop."

Dora giggled. "Now why didn't I thinks of that? Blimey, wiff all the terrible goings on, I seem to have lost me wits. You'd make a right fine Cockney, Katie. A Robin Hood East Ender."

"Robin Hood. . . ?"

"Good," Toby whispered in her ear. "You'd make a good Cockney." There was pride in his voice as together they watched Dora trot off in the direction of the Tower of London, sand crunching beneath her feet as she disappeared into the swirling mist.

Toby clamped a firm hand on Katie's elbow and guided her in the opposite direction, through piles of construction rubble along the shoreline, mud oozing at their feet, clam bubbles gurgling up through the muck.

Halfway up the rocky slope of the embankment, Katie glanced over her shoulder. She could see Dora's hazy form hastening toward the Tower of London, which seemed to rise out of the early morning mist like a giant sandcastle; the archway of Traitors' Gate, with its dock and ferry landing, was blanketed in ribbons of swirling fog.

Katie caught movement from the corner of her eye. Something was barrel-rolling in the waves close to shore.

"Look!"

They both stared out across the water.

Tangled in a web of seaweed as if caught in a fishing net, Collin's lifeless body bobbed in the waves.

Katie gasped and began to choke and sputter from the sulfur fumes and the smell of dead fish as they watched Collin's body rise and dip with the foam rolling in with the tide. Then, with a swooshing, sucking sound, the current tugged his bulk beneath the surface.

They waited, but Collin's body never popped back up. The seaweed and the weight of his clothes had dragged him under.

Collin can't hurt anyone ever again! Katie thought with relief as they scrambled up the rest of the embankment. *Dora Fowler, Lady Beatrix, the pregnant Molly Potter, and Mary Jane Kelly are all safe now!*

At the top of the slope, Katie glanced down at her hands. The skin on her wrists was flickering. *Everything will be okay*, she told herself. *I just have to get to the London Stone!* She took several deep nervous breaths, filling her lungs with the salty air until, like a pumped up balloon, she felt ready to burst. "We did it, Toby!" she cried. "We stopped the most vicious serial killer in British history. I only wish we had saved Major Brown. . .and the others."

"Major Brown died as he would have wanted to, Katie. In the line of duty. He was one of the bravest and shrewdest men at Scotland Yard. There is no more honorable way to die. He knew the risks. He took an oath. It will be the same for me when I join Scotland Yard. I'll take risks to serve and protect. Major Brown died a hero's death."

Katie nodded. "At least now, Collin can't hurt anyone ever again. We made that happen, Toby. We changed history."

But by nightfall — in her own century — Katie would rue the day she'd ever attempted to change history.

❖

MINUTES AFTER WATCHING COLLIN'S body disappear beneath the waves of the Thames, Katie and Toby climbed into the horse-drawn carriage that Collin had paid to wait by the construction pier, and as the horses clip-clopped through the narrow streets of London, and the choking smell of the incoming tide receded, Katie thrust her head out the window trying to take in every last sight and sound before returning home. Her work here was finished. They hadn't saved Major Brown or Elizabeth Stride or Catherine Eddowes, but they had stopped Jack the Ripper and ascertained his identity. Lady Beatrix and the others were safe. *That's why I came here. That's what I wished for at the London Stone. To go back in time and save Lady Beatrix!*

Katie's eyes misted as she stared at the scene unfolding outside the carriage. Fish stores, pastry shops, boarding houses, and a butcher shop, whose peaked roof was outlined like a sharp dagger against the early morning sky, sped by until the carriage pulled up to the curb in front of St. Swithin's.

And there it was.

Protruding out of the side of the church's outermost wall, nestled in a niche behind black wrought-iron bars, sat the whitish-grey boulder. *The London Stone.*

Whether it was the rock that King Arthur had drawn his sword from, or a Druid altar used for human sacrifice, or the Stone of Brutus — Katie would never know. But one thing was certain. The craggy edifice, known for centuries as the London Stone, had paranormal powers.

Clutching Toby's hand tightly in her own, Katie followed him down the gravel path, through the moss-covered headstones in the churchyard strewn with honeysuckle and roses.

"This is where I first met you, Toby," she said, stopping to breathe in the heady scent of the flowers. "I thought the other Toby and my cousin — my real cousin — were playing a joke on me. I thought this was all part of a multimedia exhibit at Madame Tussauds."

"A multi...what?"

Katie smiled and squeezed his hand. She thought about the first time she'd ever laid eyes on Collin Twyford — the future Duke of Twyford — Jack the Ripper! She remembered how his red hair, parted with razor precision down the center of his head, had been slicked back on the sides. She had a clear image of Collin's stiff winged collar, his frock coat, his floppy necktie — and how she thought at the time that it was some sort of wardrobe costume change. She hadn't for a moment believed — at least at first — that she had traveled back in time. *If only I knew then what I know now!*

She stared over Toby's shoulder at the side door of the church. It was on those steps that she'd first seen Reverend Pinker trotting down the granite risers with Lady Beatrix. Beatrix had been wearing the exact same dress as the one in the portrait hanging over the mantelpiece in Katie's bedroom back home. The half-finished portrait that Katie now knew had been painted by James Whistler.

"It's time to go, pet," Toby said, pulling her gently forward until they were standing in front of the London Stone.

A breeze swept past, and Katie felt something prickle up her neck. Early morning sunshine dappled the graveyard with sparkling glints of light, warming the air, but Katie felt something ominous and cold and dark...as if something were lurking just around the corner.

Toby glanced at her inquisitively. Behind him, Katie could see the church steeple piercing the pale sky above his head, clouds swirling around the spire.

She tugged at Toby's hand, drawing instinctively back.

What is it? What am I feeling? Katie wondered. Sadness about leaving...or something else? Something was floating on the fringe of her consciousness like the diaphanous clouds overhead. *But what?* The sensation was like searching for a word on the tip of your tongue that won't materialize. Something...something...something she'd known or had sensed all along...

"What is it, ham shank?" Toby looked concerned.

Katie swallowed hard, focusing her attention back to the present. She smiled at the Cockney word for Yank. She was a Yankee about to return home...but not to Boston, to London. Her London. Her time period. "I'm going to miss you, Toby. I'm going to miss everyone and everything in this century. But most of all, I'm going to miss you."

"I know that, lass. But it's time. You may have —"

"Worn out my welcome?"

"Not that. Never that. But you're fading in and out. Disappearing, like. If I were a superstitious bloke, I'd say you were a witch...or a ghost."

"*I am a ghost.* Or will be."

"I think it's *me* who will be the ghost," Toby said, his voice unbearably sad. "I'll be long dead and buried in a pauper's grave by the time you return to your own century."

"Hardly a pauper's grave, Toby. You're going to be a great success in whatever you do. You'll probably be a famous detective at Scotland Yard, known far and wide for your ingenious methods of detection. Like Sherlock Holmes. When I get home I'll Google you on the Internet."

"You'll what?"

"I'll look you up in the...er...history books...at the library. Also, your great-great-grandson — the other Toby — might know what became of you."

"Good luck with that, Miss Katie. Rattling skeletons, like teacups, in the old family cupboard is never a good idea. Now give us a kiss, lass — and let's get you on your way."

"Write to me! Leave a message in the Duke's stuffed vulture. I'll read it as soon as I get home. Promise me you'll do that?"

He nodded and nudged her closer to the stone.

But Katie didn't want to leave. She clung to his good arm and motioned to his other in the sling. "You've got to see a doctor and get your arm put in a cast."

"A what?"

"Don't you have casts in the nineteenth century?"

"We have splints. They'll straighten the bone and secure my arm using plaster of Paris."

"Ouch."

"Don't worry. It will mend. It's my heart I'm bleedin' fearful of. It won't mend any time soon."

"Because of Collin and Major Brown?"

"Because of you."

That's when he kissed her. A slow, deep, lingering kiss. A kiss that set off sparks and made her legs wobble.

"I'll never forget you," Katie whispered, feeling dizzy and off balance as tears spilled down her cheeks.

"Nor I, you."

"Promise you'll write? Something. Anything I can remember you by." Katie was sobbing.

Toby nodded and bent closer. "Here's another promise for you, lass. In my heart, I shall love you forever. Throughout time, throughout history, throughout eternity." And with that, he gently guided her index finger through the metal bars toward the pitted hole in the London Stone.

Katie's pulse raced.

Love you forever? *Is that what Toby had said?*

And a moment later, Katie was hurtling through time and space.

Chapter Fifty-seven

Mountebanks and Liars
say the Bells of Blackfriars

A DEAFENING EXPLOSION. Shock waves pounded through Katie's body. She was falling, falling, falling, her limbs and torso tumbling this way and that as a cacophony of roaring sounds reverberated in her head, along with familiar words: *Beware of what you wish for...!*

When the gut-wrenching sensation of free-falling finally subsided, Katie took a deep, shuddering breath, but kept her eyes shut against the intense bright light flashing against her lids.

A voice was shouting at her.

And what was that smell? Peanut butter and smoky cheese?

The shouting grew louder as if a tin can were rattling inside her skull, clanking and banging.

"You all right, luv?"

"Stop yelling!" Katie moaned, clamping her hands over her ears and squinting her eyes open a crack.

"Not shouting." It was Toby — the twenty-first–century Toby — peering at her in an odd way.

Katie gave a weak smile. "Just whisper, Toby. Please. It sounds as if my eardrums will burst."

Toby was standing in front of her, his black duster skimming his ankles, his dark hair falling to his shoulders. With his strong jaw and piercing brown eyes, he looked like her own Toby, only taller, less broad across the chest. His nose wasn't crooked like *her* Toby's; his front teeth weren't chipped; and his complexion was clear — no knife scars or pitted indentations from childhood diseases. Katie felt a pang of regret that swirled in her gut until Toby turned his full dark gaze on her and said, "How do you know my name?"

Katie froze, then slowly lowered her hands from her ears.

"What do you mean?" she choked out in a hoarse whisper. "Of course I know your name."

"Well, I don't know yours. And unless I was totally stoned out of my gourd when I met you, I'm sure I'd remember a twist 'n' swirl with such a beautiful boat race."

"Toby, it's me! Katie."

"Pleasure to meet you."

"Shit! Don't you know who I am?"

He looked blank.

"I'm Collin's cousin!" Katie cried. "Katie Lennox."

"Sorry, luv. Dunno anyone named Collin. Care for a Milk Dud?" He held out his hand, but she noticed it was shaking slightly. He was nervous. Or worried. Or lying.

What's going on? Katie wondered. "Is this one of your stupid rum and cokes, Toby? Because if it is, it's not funny."

Again the blank look, but the hand holding out the chocolate candy was definitely not steady.

"I'm Collin's cousin," Katie said slowly, patiently. "His American cousin. His ham shank cousin? Please tell me you're pulling my leg, Toby."

"I'm sorry, but I really don't know anyone named Collin."

"Collin Twyford. He goes to school with you."

Toby shook his head. "Sorry, luv." He took a step closer. "Look. You're looking a bit green around the gills. Pale as a ghost, actually. There's a god-awful little tea shop downstairs, soupy little biscuits, but if you'd care to —"

Katie's stomach tightened. "There's no time for . . . *tea!* I need to find Collin." Her eyes swiveled to her backpack on the ground. She lunged for it, and tugged out her cell phone from the inner pocket.

"No mobiles allowed in the museum," Toby warned.

"I don't give a crap," Katie said, feeling oddly emboldened. "I just helped push the most notorious serial killer in British history over the side of a pier. I don't have time for cell phone rules. I need to know —"

She held up her iPhone and scrolled down the list of her contacts. No Collin.

There's a glitch in my phone, she told herself, and hastily tapped in his number, which she knew by heart, but got someone else's voice message. She swiveled her gaze back to Toby.

"*Omigod!* Collin hasn't been born! I mean, he *couldn't* have been born. I killed his ancestor. His direct ancestor! Collin never married Prudence Farthington. So my Aunt Pru —"

"Slow down."

"No, you slow down! What am I going to do? I can't go back and change everything to the way it was, like you did, Toby. I can't!"

"What do you mean . . . like I did?"

"You told me the London Stone transported you back in time as well — but in the end, you had to go back and undo everything. You asked me if I'd ever read 'The Raven's Claw.' It's a short story about —"

"I know. I know. It's about a guy who changes history then uses his last wish to return everything back the way it was. But about time travel . . . I never told anyone —"

"Well, you told me."

"I swore on my grandfather's grave, I wouldn't reveal it to anyone. What did I tell you . . . exactly?"

"Oh, Toby. I can't remember *exactly.* Something about Madeleine Smith who killed her lover with arsenic in the eighteen hundreds."

"Yes. Okay. Now I believe you. We've obviously met before. Tell me about this cousin of yours...?"

"His name's Collin, and I just helped push his ancestor over a very high construction pier — where the future Tower Bridge will be built. *Has been built.* It was built, right?"

Toby nodded. "Why did you push —"

"He was Jack the Ripper!"

"Who?"

"You never heard of Jack the Ripper?"

"Nope."

"Does that mean there's no Jack the Ripper exhibit here in the Chamber of Horrors?"

"There's a gruesome one about an ax-murderess, the Demon Duchess of Devon. But no Jack —"

Katie grabbed Toby's sleeve. "What am I going to do? I can't go back and change everything to the way it was! I can't —"

"You can. And you have to. At least that's what I did. If generations of your cousin's family have been wiped out, it doesn't look as if you have a choice, Katie. I went back and undid all the harm I'd caused. Just like my grandfather did when he was my age."

"Your grandfather *knew* about the London Stone? Did he...by any chance...learn about it from his...father?"

"*His grandfather.* My namesake. Tobias Becket."

"Jeez! I just kissed your...er...um...I was just talking to your great-great-grandfather. He promised...oh, never mind. Look. I can't go back and undo everything. If I do...innocent people will die. Lady Beatrix, Dora Fowler, Molly Potter, and Mary Jane Kelly will all have their throats slit and their bodies eviscerated. And Molly Potter is pregnant!"

"Katie, luv. If your cousin was alive when you left, but isn't now, you've likely wiped out far more than four people —"

"But he's related to Jack the Ripper! Maybe it's for the best! Maybe my cousin Collin has these, like, weird genes that shouldn't be passed on!"

"Do you really believe that?"

"Wait! Maybe Collin *was* born after all. But has a different name. You told me that I could change small things, but not big ones. Maybe—" But Katie couldn't dismiss the uneasy feeling in her gut that she'd wiped out generations of her cousin's family.

"Katie. Tell me what happened. Tell me everything. Start at the beginning."

Katie took a deep breath and began talking fast. Very fast. She told Toby the saga of what happened in the year 1888 when Jack the Ripper began his rampage. And though she rambled a bit, when she finally came to the part about Collin's tumbling over the edge of the pier into the Thames, Toby nodded his head.

"Katie," he said, his voice grim and low. "You've got to go back and change things to the way they were."

"No. Not until I've checked. Maybe Collin's here. Or maybe there's a reason he's not here. Maybe he's not *meant* to have been born."

"Can you really play God? Can you actually say this person should live, and that person not? The only sensible thing to do is return things to their natural order."

"You're right. I know you're right. I just have to double-check. I need to go home to my grandmother's house and make sure. If it's true...if Collin was never born, can I actually just go back and undo everything?"

"Yes. That's what I did. And if it's any consolation, you can go back and explain everything to this other Toby, my great-great-grandfather. If he's all that you claim he is, he'll see to it that this Ripper lad—the future Duke of Twyford—doesn't harm any more girls *and* produces an heir. That's how I did it when I went back. I asked Madeleine Smith—"

"That's it! You're a genius! I remember reading in the family Bible that Tobias Becket—your ancestor—was with Collin on the moors when Collin died. He fell into a bog and drowned. He was only twenty-one. Collin had married Prudence Farthington the year before, and they were in Dartmoor, at Bovey Castle, because their baby had just been born — a boy they named Collin! That's what actually happened. I mean, that's what the family Bible recorded."

Katie took a breath and continued. "When I went back in time again, I warned Toby never to let Collin go anywhere near the moors. I didn't want Collin to die so young and without ever getting to know his son. I didn't have a clue that Collin was Jack the Ripper. So, if I travel back to Victorian London one last time — to a day or so *before* we pushed Collin over the pier — and lay it all out at Toby's feet, maybe he can save Lady Beatrix and the others. Keep them safe. He can do it. I know he can! Then, after Collin produces an heir, Toby will make Collin's death on the moors appear to be an accident!"

"That's asking a lot of this other Toby bloke — my ancestor."

Katie smiled thinking about Toby. *Her* Toby. "He'll make it happen. He's the most amazing person on the planet. I know it sounds silly, but he's my *hero*."

Toby grinned. "Must be in the genes, this hero stuff. One never thinks of one's ancestors as being really cool dudes. . .but of course, he would be, if he's anything like his twenty-first – century namesake!"

"Except for the modesty gene, you're actually very much like him," Katie laughed, then grew serious. "OK. Here's the plan. I need to go home before I make any decisions. Maybe we've got this all wrong. . .or backwards. Maybe Collin was born after all. . .maybe we're missing something."

Toby sucked in his breath and let it out slowly. "I think you should go back now, *this instant*, and undo —"

"No. I'm going home first."

"Don't go home."

"Why not?"

"Because it won't change anything. You're still going to have to travel back in time and undo what you've done. There's a Latin inscription at the bottom of the Stone, hardly legible: 'Beware of what you wish for.'" Toby's jaw clenched, then he continued, "My grandfather told me — as his grandfather had told him — that the London Stone always gives you what you wish for, but not in the way you wanted it."

"Obviously. I get it."

"I don't think you get it at all." He stared hard at her. "Look, Katie. When you touched the London Stone that first time, what *exactly* did you wish for?"

"I wanted to catch Jack the Ripper.'"

"Are you sure?"

"Of course, I'm sure. I was thinking: 'How hard could it be to catch Jack the Ripper?' Knowing what I know in the twenty-first century and having watched lots of crime shows on TV, I thought it would be easy to figure out who the Ripper was and save Lady Beatrix. I put my finger into the fissured hole in the London Stone, wriggled it around, and *poof!* I landed in the nineteenth-century to chase a serial killer."

"That's all? Think, Katie. *Think.* What else did you wish for?"

Katie's cell phone rang out, startling them both. The peeling ringtone was totally unfamiliar. A loud, roaring car engine. A pedal-to-the-metal *vroooom-vroooooming* sound. Katie glanced at the number but didn't recognize it.

She slid her finger across the bottom of the iPhone.

"Hello?" she said tentatively.

"Katie? Sweetheart." The voice was deep and masculine. "Where have you been? You forgot to leave me a note. Did you go to the museum after all?"

Katie's mouth dropped at the same instant that the phone slipped from her hand and smashed with a resounding *thwack* onto the tile floor. It bounced and crackled and spun toward the corner. The battery light blinked. . .and just before the phone went totally dead, Katie heard the familiar voice once again:

"*Katie. . .?* Are you there?. . .Can you hear me?" A pause. "Can you hear me now, sweetheart?"

Chapter Fifty-eight

Grimace and Glower
say the Bells of Clock Tower

KATIE STARED AT HER iPHONE on the floor in the corner behind the London Stone. Her entire world began to spin out of control. *The voice on the other end had been her father's!* Was it possible her dad hadn't died in a car crash on the way to the airport to pick up Collin . . . *because Collin had never been born?*

Katie felt a surge of joy, followed by a plummet of sheer panic. She scooped up her backpack and cell phone and raced out of the glass-enclosed room, nearly knocking over an old woman with a cane who looked vaguely familiar.

Toby helped the elderly woman right herself, apologized, and hurried after Katie. He caught up with her near a wrought iron bench in the hallway just outside the Chamber of Horrors.

Katie stopped dead in her tracks and motioned to the neon sign over the arched entrance, electric candles flickering in brass candelabras on either side:

The Demon Duchess of Devon
the most notorious murderer in British History!
Enter If You Dare!

"Toby!" Katie cried, pointing to the sign. "This is where the Jack the Ripper exhibit was."

At the thought of having changed history so drastically, Katie felt a chill shoot through her. She turned to Toby. "The voice on my cell phone was my dad's. If Collin was never born, my parents couldn't have died on the way to the airport to pick him up. They're alive!"

"Katie," Toby said, taking hold of her hand. She pulled away.

"Something similar happened to me when I traveled back in time," Toby continued. "It doesn't matter if your parents are alive. You need to go back and change things to the way they were because —"

"Not in a million years," Katie choked out. "If my mom and dad are alive...I'm never, *ever* going back." She turned away from Toby and ran down the hall, past a row of steel elevator doors. On the Plexiglas staircase, taking the steps two at a time, Katie shouted over her shoulder at Toby who was close on her heels.

"That old woman back there...near the London Stone. She looked...familiar."

"She was blind, Katie! You barreled over a blind woman!"

"A blind wom —?" That's when it hit her. *The old woman looked like Mrs. Tray from Traitor's Gate!* But Katie couldn't think about that now. *I have to get home!*

Racing past the ticket counter and the waxwork policeman near the entrance, Katie jumped over the exit turnstile and burst through the front doors. Outside, she found herself blinking in near-blinding sunlight. She tried to get her bearings, but the wail of traffic from all directions drew her up short. She rubbed her eyes. There were no horse-drawn carriages, no cobbled streets, no small shops and narrow-fronted houses with lynch gates and iron-rail fences.

In front of her, Marylebone Road yawned as wide as a canyon with fast-moving cars, trucks, taxis, and buses all careening past — horns honking, tires thwacking, exhaust fumes billowing. And all around her came the eerie shuffling, laughter, breathing, hollow tumult of footsteps — the thunk of flip-flops, the squeak of sneakers.

"Give yourself time to adjust," Toby warned.

Katie's knees began to shake, then her legs buckled. She would have fallen had Toby not held her tight, one arm wrapped around her waist. "Easy now," he kept repeating.

A parade of tour buses rattled around the corner and seemed to be bearing down on them. But it was the *whhhhooooing* roar of a police siren in the distance, picking up speed in rising waves, that made Katie clasp her stomach. The deafening din of the twenty-first century was making her physically sick.

Toby tugged her away from the curb.

"Take a queen's death — a deep breath. Take your time, Katie. It's overwhelming at first, I know. Take it bright and breezy."

She bent over and took several deep breaths. Bright and breezy? Did that mean take it easy. . .or don't get queasy? Katie wanted to laugh — in order not to cry.

When she finally straightened up, she was able to gasp out her grandmother's address.

Toby nodded. "Want to take the tube, luv? Or walk?"

"Walk," Katie said without hesitation. The thought of being underground with steam engine fumes made her want to retch all over again. *No! Steam fumes are in the nineteenth century, not this one!* Still, the idea of descending down into a dark, cavernous place — like a crypt — sent a shudder through her body.

Heading down Baker Street, Katie's eyes darted back and forth. Her heart pounded, her temples throbbed. Toby made a joke about

Sherlock Holmes living at number 221b, but Katie wasn't listening. *I've got to get home. My dad's alive.*

Right?

Moving at a fast clip, Katie tried not to think about the reality of what she might find at her grandmother's. She blinked around in order to distract herself. It was all so different here. The concrete buildings were enormous, and there weren't any churches on the street corners. In Victorian London, hundreds of steeples dotted the skyline in every direction.

"It's so big and loud and noisy here, and the architecture is so ugly, not like the nineteenth century—"

Katie stopped herself. She'd spoken aloud. When she was nervous she tended to say whatever popped into her head. It used to annoy her cousin Collin. At the thought of Collin, Katie felt an ominous dread in addition to wrenching anticipation. When she and Collin first visited Madame Tussauds, Katie hadn't cared about Jack the Ripper. She had wanted to see the London Stone. She knew the legend attached to the ancient stone was nonsense—a ridiculous myth—but she told herself she only wanted to ask for something simple. What harm could come of it?

I wanted Courtney and Grandma Cleaves to get along so we could be a family again! I wanted my sister in my life.

But what Katie had really wanted, in her heart of hearts, was to change history. She wanted her parents back. *I never got to say good-bye. Never had the chance to tell them I loved them.*

Katie ran trembling fingers through her loose hair. There were no pins or hair adornments pricking her fingertips, no ribbons or heavy strands of pearls looped around her head.

Had the London Stone granted her the very thing she'd wished for? The reason she'd gone to Madame Tussauds in the first place?

Through a haze of tears, Katie could just make out a taxi stand across the street, but instead of a long line of horses dangling feedbags, she saw a row of shiny black cars, roofs domed like old-fashioned bowler hats.

Stop it, she chided herself. *Stop comparing the two centuries! This is now, that was then. And if my parents are alive. . .I'm never, ever going back!*

When they arrived at Twyford Manor House, Katie sucked in her breath. She knew exactly what the condo building would look like, but still it gave her pause. The sweeping front lawn had been replaced by a parking garage. The high stone wall, pierced by iron gates, was nowhere to be seen. Gone was the stable yard, the carriage house, and the top-hatted footmen standing at the ready. No gargoyles jutted out from the roof; no battlements stood on each corner; no stone lions flanked the entrance.

Katie swiped her key-card, and they entered the lobby, which had the same black-and-white tile floor spanning out in all directions like a giant chessboard, but it was so chipped and worn as to be hardly recognizable. To their left, no grand staircase rose like butterfly wings to a balconied second floor. Instead, there was a cinderblock wall with a row of metal letterboxes. Katie moved cautiously through the lobby to a door at the far end that opened onto a doglegged hallway.

She dug out a metal key from a chain attached to her backpack, and pushed open the second door on the right. They were in the west wing of the apartment complex.

Inside her grandmother's condo, the tiny front hall was tiled in green marble, but unlike Twyford Manor, there were no suits of armor flush to the walls, no double doorway leading down a center hallway to the conservatory.

"If," Katie whispered to Toby, "my dad's here, I'm never going back."

"Never is a long time."

"Don't look at me like that, Toby! I'm never, *ever,* going to change things back...if...my parents..." She couldn't finish the sentence. It seemed crazy to think that her parents might be alive. It just wasn't possible.

And yet...

Every fiber in Katie's body wished it were so as she hurried down the hall, her sneakers slapping against the tiled floor. She turned and beckoned impatiently to Toby who had stopped in his tracks behind her, scanning the hallway.

"Have I been here before? I have this déjà vu feeling..."

Katie nodded. "You were here with me last time I traveled back in time — I mean forward in time." She took his sleeve and tugged him down the hall in the direction of the library, and was about to call out to see if anyone was home, when a grandfather clock against the wall struck a chime like a ship's bell, startling them both.

Passing the tall clock, still clanging like a bell, they approached the drawing room — a small, graceful space that was her grandmother's favorite. Katie peered in. She recognized two pieces of furniture from the Duke's house: the writing desk in the corner and the oyster shell bureau by the window. She took a deep, gulping breath of air and held it in her lungs. There was no smell of coal gas stirring in her nostrils. No hissing gas jets from the wall sconces, no hollow pings from popping valves. Katie tore her gaze away and continued down the hall to the library, Toby at her side.

The door was closed.

Katie blinked down at the old-fashioned keyhole.

How many times had she and Courtney peered through that keyhole when her father and mother and grandmother were having family discussions? Or at Christmas when the tree and presents were off limits until Christmas Eve?

Katie gripped the crystal knob and shoved open the heavy oak door.

The air was thick with the smell of old leather books. There was no coal gas closing in. No wood smoke. In the corner stood an old-fashioned armchair, padded in red leather. Katie remembered it as the one her father loved to sit and read in. And the iron fender around the fireplace...was that in her bedroom at Twyford Manor? No. She was mixing up her centuries.

A slight, rumbling cough came from the shadows in the far right-hand corner.

Katie's heart skipped a beat.

Standing with his back to her, in shadow, holding a book, was a man. And when he wheeled around, Katie's pulse began pounding in her ears, like the rush of the waves in the Thames. She had a strong impulse to scream, but flew across the room instead and leapt into her father's arms, sobbing uncontrollably. She cried and cried and cried. She clung harder and tighter than she ever remembered doing when he was alive.

He's alive! I did it! The London Stone did it. I'm not going back. My parents are alive and that's all that matters. She put Collin out of her mind. Losing him was a small price to pay for having her parents back.

She stopped clinging when she felt her father stiffen. But she didn't stop crying even when he held her at arm's distance and peered into her face, anxiety and alarm stamped across his features.

"What is it, Kit-Kat? What's wrong? Katie! Sweetheart! What's happened?"

Worry and fear pressed into his forehead in little horizontal wrinkles. *Oh, how she'd prayed to see this face again!* She had forgotten about the furrows that creased his forehead when he was worried. How could she have forgotten? She'd thought about him a million times since the funeral, but never once remembered those deep grooves in his forehead.

"Daddy!" she wailed, though she hadn't called him that since she was little. Now she just kept saying it over and over again, as if he might disappear...or fade away into the oak paneled book cases...or dissolve into mist. "I missed you. I missed you. I missed you!"

When she finally calmed down enough for her father to ascertain that she wasn't hurt and nothing bad had happened to her, he said, "I missed you too, sweetheart. Though it's only been...What? Two hours? Three? Now what's all this about?"

"Oh, Dad! I love you, I love you, I love you. Where's Mom?"

Her father checked his watch. "Should be here any minute. She's with Grandma. They're doing that fund-raiser for the Widows' and Orphans' Charity in the East End. Remember? The one you had a hissy fit about? You refused to go? That one?"

"Oh...er...um...yeah. That one." It was Katie's turn to hold him at arm's length and study the face she had yearned to see, along with her mother's, for so long. So long it hurt. As if someone had been twisting her insides, tugging the entrails out of her body...eviscerating her with a sharp knife...*for three long years.*

Katie swiped her hands across her eyes, trying to drink in every last detail of this man she loved so much. He was wearing a navy cardigan with holes in the elbows, his favorite for sitting by the fire and reading. He was middle-aged and handsome in a classic sort of way: solid, regular features, keen hazel eyes. And when he smiled at her — as he was doing now — his square face molded into an expression that Katie *did* remember. One of absolute love for her.

"*John Carter Lennox was a man devoted to his daughters,*" the minister had said at his funeral. "*Courtney and Katie were the pride and joy of his life.*"

"Katie?" Her father's baritone voice broke into her thoughts. "Truly, honey. Why all the tears? Is everything all right?" He looked so unbearably worried, it pierced daggers into Katie's heart.

"Everything's fine, Dad. I was just...missing...you. And I had...er...this horrible premonition that something happened to you...and mom."

He lowered his head thoughtfully and Katie noticed the hint of a double chin. She remembered him saying that all the men in his family — when they grew older — had a tendency to have jowls. *When they grew older.*

"You're going to grow old, Dad. I promise," Katie said aloud, though she hadn't meant to. It just popped out.

"Well, I plan on it!" His hazel eyes twinkled with amusement. "Now, sweetheart. Why don't you introduce me to this young man hovering in the doorway. And if he's in any way responsible for my precious girl's tears, I'll string him up."

"No. He's not responsible for anything. That's just Toby. The other Toby. I mean...er...Tobias Becket."

"The other Toby?" Her father's eyebrow shot up. "How many Tobys do you know? How many *boys* in London do you know? We just arrived yesterday."

"Toby is...um...related to a friend of mine from school. He's British. I mean, she's British...my friend at school. She asked me to look him up."

"Really?" Her father smiled.

"We've been communicating on Facebook-of-the-Future, sir," Toby said quickly, striding into the room and extending his hand. "It's a sort of time-travel, social-networking portal."

"Then you're a better man than I, Gunga Din. To quote —"

"Kipling, sir. And why is that, sir?"

"Yes. Kipling. Nice to see young men still read these days. You're a better man than I because my own daughter defriended me on Facebook. Imagine! If I were a fighting man, we might have to duke it out with fisticuffs." Again, the twinkle in her father's eyes.

He was trying to be funny.

Katie laughed. Her father's humor used to drive Courtney crazy. She and Katie would roll their eyes at him. Now Katie was laughing so hard that happy tears streamed down her cheeks. She threw her arms around her father's neck and hugged him all over again. "I *love* your jokes, Dad. I always have. All of them. Even if they are —"

"Fantabulous?"

"Fantabulous." Katie squeezed harder. She used to squirm when he used that word, especially in front of her friends.

"I love you, I love you, I love you," she whispered in his ear.

Looking over his shoulder, Katie caught sight of Lady Beatrix's portrait hanging above the mantel — instead of in her bedroom as it was when this longest day of her life had begun. Clutching her father's arm tightly in her own, she tugged him across the room to the fireplace.

Katie wasn't about to let go of him, not even for a nanosecond. She stared up at the oil painting, with its brass plate that read "1865–1933." It was completely finished, but the signature was still missing.

"Dad? Did you know Whistler painted this?"

Her father chuckled. "If that were so, lambkins, we'd be millionaires. No. It was probably done by one of those second-rate portrait painters back in the nineteenth century. It's a shame it was never signed, though. Maybe you and Grandma Cleaves can take it on that *Antiques Roadshow* program. Might be worth something after all. But Whistler? I highly doubt it."

Katie met his amused gaze then swiveled her eyes back to the painting. Faded, with tiny cracks in the surface, Beatrix's face appeared more animated and happier than the earlier rendition. There was no arrogance or defiance in the tilt of her chin, no hint of accusation in those dark blue eyes — so dark a blue they were almost black — just like Courtney's. And in this painting, unlike the other, Lady Beatrix's expression seemed suffused with wonder and a sparkling sort of contentment. Katie smiled. Beatrix must have found happiness. The world had been good to her.

"It's amazing how much she looks like Courtney," Katie said, taking in the beauty mark above Beatrix's top lip.

"Who?" her father asked.

"Lady Beatrix. In the portrait. She looks just like Court —" but Katie stopped herself. "Courtney? As in the lead singer in the Metro Chicks? . . . as in your daugh —"

"Is that one of those girl bands?" her father asked, peering up at the painting. "You know I'm a die-hard Tom Petty fan. Stuck in the past, as your mother says. What sort of music do they play?"

"Dad! Dad, look at me! Do you know *anyone* named Courtney? *Anyone at all?*"

"Don't think so," he said. "Funny you should ask, though. That's the name your mom almost gave you. She loves that name. Always said she was going to name her firstborn daughter Courtney. But when you came along, we went the traditional route and named you after your grandmother."

Katie's pulse raced. Dread spiked through her body as she frantically scanned the photographs lining the bookshelves. Framed in silver, not one family photo included Courtney.

Courtney's not here!

Katie gritted her teeth against a violent wave of nausea. Bile rose up her throat and she tried hard not to gag. The dark, ugly truth of what she had done loomed in front of her like an oncoming train. With sudden clarity, she remembered that her parents had been visiting Aunt Pru in Paris when Courtney was conceived. But if Prudence Farthington never married Collin in 1889, generations of little boys named Collin and girls named Prudence had never been born! Aunt Pru never studied at the Sorbonne in Paris. Therefore, her parents never visited her there!

My sister doesn't exist!

"Dad?" Katie cried, holding both his hands so tightly in her own she could feel the gold band of his wedding ring digging into her fingers. "W-what if you had a moral dilemma — a terrible, terrible decision to make — and you didn't know what to do?"

"That's an interesting question, Katie. I suppose. . .after weighing all my options. . .I'd try to do what I thought was right."

"What if you didn't *know* what was right?" Her voice held a pleading whimper.

Her father raised a quizzical eyebrow.

Katie bit her bottom lip so hard it drew blood. "What if. . .you had *two* daughters. . .not just one. . .and you could save the oldest daughter — *but you'd have to give up your own life* — what would you do?"

"But I don't have two daughters."

"Hypothetically, Dad. What if it was *me*? What if someone with a magic wand came along and told you I could live. . .but you'd have to forfeit —"

"My life?" Her father looked thoughtful. "I'd do what any man who loves his child would do. I'd gladly sacrifice anything for my children. If I had just you or if I had ten. It's hypothetical, I know. But I'm your father. I'd trade my life for yours any day of the week. But as that's not going to happen, Kit-Kat, let's not hear any more of it."

"But what if *I* had to make the decision?" Katie wailed, the urgency in her voice growing louder.

"I don't follow you."

"What if I could keep you and mom alive . . . but I had to sacrifice others . . ."

Horizontal lines creased his forehead. "Katie. My sweet, sweet Katie. When faced with life-altering decisions, you need to look into your heart. Always choose the hard right over the easy wrong . . ."

The hard right over the easy wrong. Those were Mrs. Tray's words.

Chapter Fifty-nine

Illness and Loss
say the Bells of Charing Cross

TWO HOURS LATER Katie was standing in front of the London Stone at Madame Tussauds, tears streaming down her face as Toby, towering next to her, clamped his hand over hers and guided her trembling index finger toward the pitted hole in the Stone.

"It will be all right, luv. You're doing the right thing."

Katie smiled weakly. "You sound like your great-great-grandfather."

"Give him my regards, eh?" Toby winked and kissed her softly on the cheek.

"I don't think I can do this."

"Yes, you can."

"What if you're wrong?"

"I'm not."

"But what if —"

"Do you want to take that chance, Katie?" Toby inclined his head. "You're already starting to fizzle in and out. Like a doomsday sparkler. You don't have much time."

Katie looked down at her hand, then her wrist. It was as if the molecules in her skin were dancing.

"If you *don't* go back and change things to the way they were, there's no guarantee your parents won't die in a car accident tomorrow or the next day. And then where will you be? You'll have lost your parents *and* your sister. Not to mention your aunt and cousin."

"You don't understand. If I do this, I'll lose my mom and dad all over again." Katie yanked her finger from his grasp, scooped up her backpack from the floor, and raced out of the glass-enclosed room.

Half blinded with tears, she shot down the hall toward the bank of stainless-steel elevators, past the Old Curiosity Gift Shop, and didn't stop running until she came to the Chamber of Horrors where fake candles flickered on either side of the arched entrance, throwing shadows on the neon sign above:

The Demon Duchess of Devon
The most notorious murderer in British History!
Enter If You Dare!

Katie blinked at the sign. It should have announced the Jack the Ripper exhibit. *But I can't go back,* she told herself. *I won't.* Her heart pounded furiously against her ribcage. Behind her, flush against the wall facing the entrance, was the Victorian-style bench she had sat on with Toby so long ago. . .another lifetime it seemed. She took a deep breath and made her way to the bench, but stopped midway and tugged out her iPhone. Pressing the Safari app, she Googled Jack the Ripper.

Her hands shook, making the iPhone jiggle in her fingers, but she kept scrolling and searching, all the while trying to ignore the fact that the molecules in her hands seemed to be jumping, absorbing and reflecting light. Like an optical illusion.

Katie scrolled faster. The only hit she could find about Jack the Ripper was a short passage from an obscure religious periodical stating that in the year 1888, a murderer dubbed Jack the Ripper by the London press was believed to be a Cockney officer at Scotland Yard named Major Gideon Brown. "Brown's short killing spree ended when he drowned himself in the Thames out of remorse for his evil doings."

Major Gideon Brown, Katie thought. *He was innocent, and I helped kill him!*

Feeling sick to her stomach at the thought of Major Brown, Katie sank down onto the bench. She felt the *thump-thump-thump* of her heartbeat pounding furiously against her ribcage, the queasy clenching of her stomach. Drawing her knees to her chest, she closed her eyes and pressed her eyelids into her kneecaps until she saw black spots.

She thought about her parents, who *hadn't* died in a car crash on their way to pick up Collin...because Collin had never been born.

Aunt Pru had never been born.

Courtney had never been born!

At the sound of heavy footfalls, Katie glanced up and saw Toby striding toward her, his duster coat rippling in his wake like a Victorian cape. And as he lowered himself onto the bench next to her, dull light from the fake candles at the entrance to the Chamber of Horrors made long striations in the hollows below his cheekbones.

A minute later, a group of school children scampered down the dark hallway, their voices high-pitched and excited as they pushed and jostled and lined up to see the Demon Duchess of Devon.

"Way cool!" came a little girl's voice at the front of the line. "A real live ax murderess!"

"Double-cool!" came another young voice.

"Is she real?" asked a boy.

"No, William." This from a school-marmish woman dressed in a navy skirt and blazer. "These are just wax figures."

"But she was real in the old days?" the boy persisted.

"Yes, William. Now remember, children. The Duchess of Devon was a wicked young woman, but she deserves our pity, not our condemnation."

A snicker rose from the group, followed by a giggling whisper: "Teacher said condom! Teacher said condom!"

"Are we going to see her dead body? Are we?" came William's eager voice, shrill and excited.

Katie watched the children plow through the archway, their high-pitched squeals fading as one by one they disappeared into the exhibition chamber. Murder and mayhem seemed to thrill all ages, all genders, all centuries. Whether it was Jack the Ripper or an ax-murderess, murder knew no boundaries.

Toby, slouched on the bench next to her, turned penetrating eyes on her. "For what it's bloody well worth, Katie, I know exactly what you're going through."

"You don't know," Katie whispered, fresh tears pricking her eyes. She pounded the bench with her fists. "How could you possibly know what it's like to lose your parents a second time? I can't do it, Toby. I can't go back in time and have them die all over again."

Toby leaned in closer. A lock of dark hair fell across his forehead. "A year ago I lost m'dad, Katie. He fell off a frickin' scaffold, painting a house. That was his job. He was a house painter. I never told this to anyone, but after he died I came here — well, not here, but the Victoria and Albert, where the London Stone was on display. And I traveled back in time just like you."

"I know that, Toby. You told me the last time we sat here, on this exact bench."

Toby swiveled his eyes up and down the dark hallway, then clamped them back on Katie's face. "We've been down this frog and toad before, have we, luv? Sitting on this bench? In this exact Loch Ness? Just you and me? Bloody hell. Thought I was going rental."

"Rental?"

"Mental."

"Loch Ness?"

"Mess."

"Don't tell me...frog and toad?"

"Road," they both said in unison.

Katie smiled through her tears. "We were here. Sitting just as we are now—only the Chamber of Horrors was a multimedia exhibit about Jack the Ripper. You were blowing smoke rings from an imaginary cigarette.

Toby grinned. "Sounds Isle of Wight."

"Isle..."

"Right. Sounds right."

"Isle of Wight. Got it." Katie swallowed hard, remembering the other Toby. The long-dead Toby. "You look so much like him." Her gaze took in his strong nose, wide mouth, dark eyes. "Except for the nose...you look just like your great-great-grandfather."

"Had a god-awful fireman's hose, did he?"

"Not such a bad nose. Just a broken one."

"Bit of a Molly Coxer, was he?"

Katie nodded. "He was a bit of a boxer, yes."

"Shall we do this, luv?" Toby entwined his fingers in hers. The skin on her hands was settling back now. It looked less jumpy. *Soon I won't be able to go back.*

"In life, as in death," Toby said, leaping to his feet, tugging Katie up with him, "there's always a soupçon of pleasure and rain."

"A what?"

"Soupçon means—"

"I know what it means." Soupçon, along with pedantic, was one of Katie's vocab words this week. "I meant pleasure and—" Katie stopped herself. She knew instinctively what pleasure and rain meant.

Pain.

"Toby. I'm not going back to the nineteenth century. I can't. I won't. I've made up my mind." But she tightened the grip of her fingers, interlaced with his.

"Okay, lass. Close those beautiful mince pies of yours and think back to what your father said to you. His exact words. Remember?"

Katie closed her eyes and envisioned herself back in the library at her grandmother's, standing in front of the fireplace with her father. After he told her to always choose the hard right over the easy wrong, he had hugged her and whispered the old English nursery rhyme he used to recite to her.

> *If wishes were unicorns*
> *Maidens would ride*
> *If you call forth dead ancestors*
> *They shall abide*
> *But long ago ghosts*
> *From their graves shall collide*
> *So if wishes be unicorns*
> *Please do not ride.*

Then her dad had held her at arm's length and said with a touch of wistfulness, but in the kindest voice imaginable: "Beware of what you wish for, Kit-Kat."

"Because it might come true," Katie had whispered back.

Chapter Sixty

Once a Wish, Twice a Kiss, Thrice a Letter, Four Times Something Better

Dizziness. Searing hot pain.

Katie tugged her finger out of the fissure in the London Stone and made a dive for her backpack on the floor.

Had she done it?

Had she changed things back to the way they were?

She tore open the nylon flap at the top of her backpack and rummaged frantically through the contents, then unzipped the front pocket and finally found it. Her cell phone. She tried to scroll through her contacts, but her palms were so sweaty, the phone kept sliding through her fingers like a bar of soap.

Get a grip!

She spied the empty water bottle in the mesh side pocket of her backpack. Her mouth was cotton-wool dry, her throat parched, her hands sweaty. *I'd kill for a mocha Frappuccino!*

Kneeling on the cold tile floor, Katie tried again to scroll down her list of favorite contacts.

And there it was! Courtney's cell number.

Katie let out a giant sigh of relief and raised her hand to high-five the air. *My sister's alive!* But an image of her parents' car crash popped into her head, and her throat closed up. She gasped hard, trying to fill her lungs with air, sputtering and coughing. When she was finally able to take a normal breath, she glanced around. There was no smell of gas fumes in the air, only the musty, mothball odor of the museum.

The hard right over the easy wrong reverberated in her head.

Katie hoisted herself to her feet.

Her feet.

She looked down.

No longer laced into stiff, bone-crunching, ankle boots, but soft, red, high-topped sneakers, Katie wiggled her toes. *I'm home . . .*

She slung her backpack over her shoulder and hurried from the glass-enclosed room, not even bothering to glance back at the London Stone.

I never want to see that stupid rock again!

When she'd left Victorian England, the Duke of Twyford had been busy planning Collin's wedding to Prudence Farthington. Major Brown was alive and pledging his troth to Lady Beatrix. And Toby had vowed to make sure Collin didn't murder any more girls.

After laying all the facts at Toby's feet and convincing him that Collin was Jack the Ripper, Katie had helped Toby hatch a plan to ensure that after producing an heir, Collin would meet with a fatal accident on the windswept moors near Bovey Castle.

At the thought of Toby's sending Collin to his death a *second* time, Katie shivered. Toby was on his own.

But *now* was the future, and that was the past.

Had he succeeded? Katie wondered. *Had he managed to make Collin's death appear an unfortunate accident and save Lady Beatrix and the others?*

There was one way to find out.

Katie shot down the hall toward the bank of elevators that gleamed like stainless-steel refrigerators. Sweeping past The Old Curiosity Gift Shop, where a girl stood in the doorway wearing combat boots and earrings the size of Hula-Hoops, Katie turned the corner and raced toward the Chamber of Horrors.

As she approached, she could see electric candles flickering on either side of the archway, but couldn't make out the neon sign above. A slow-moving line of elderly people shuffled toward the entrance with an air of courtesy alongside a faster-moving gaggle of children pushing and shoving with clumsy anticipation.

Katie lifted her gaze. And there it was. The sign above the exhibit:

Jack the Ripper.
The most notorious murderer in British history.
Enter If You Dare!

Ignoring the disdainful glances as she cut the queue, Katie elbowed her way into the exhibit hall, shrill and noisy as a toy store. A row of waxwork people dressed in Victorian costumes stood in arched niches up and down the walls on either side of the room. She hurried into the gallery and stopped midway. She stood very still. *What if he didn't do it? What if Toby couldn't save those girls?*

Katie remembered the expression on Toby's face when he'd kissed her just minutes ago. They had been standing in the churchyard of St. Swithin's saying good-bye. Knowing the identity of Jack the Ripper and the task set before him, Toby's face had looked cold and hard and determined.

Until he kissed her.

I'll never forget you, lass. And in my heart, I'll always love you . . .

That's when his tongue probed hers, and she tasted the tart sweetness of apples on his breath, smelled the rich essence of him — like salt sea air and saddle leather.

There had been a soft lurch as his body pressed against hers and he guided her finger into the fissure of the London Stone. The last thing Katie saw before hurtling through time and space was Toby's face in profile: the crooked line of his broken nose, the strong jaw, the muscular, ropy neck. He looked so composed. But she could feel the beat of his heart, see color burning on the crest of his cheekbones. And at that exact instant, Katie felt a strange sort of grief, persistent and overwhelming, as if she were drowning. Their eyes met, and a moment later Katie was hurtling through time and space . . . until she landed with a thunk in the musty, mothball smelling world of Madame Tussauds.

Katie opened her eyes and peered around at the crowd. Adults and children, pushing and pointing, shoving and laughing. The long gallery was illuminated by low-hanging chandeliers giving off a fluorescent, neon-yellow glare. Extending down the middle of the room was a flat, glass-topped display case with Jack the Ripper memorabilia.

Katie inched closer.

Nestled in velvet in the case nearest to her, lay a Bible with a gold clasp. *Reverend Pinker's?* And there were the opera glasses! *Lady Beatrix's opera glasses.*

Katie peered into the case and read the inscription:

Replica of the opera glasses believed to have been found upon the first victim, Mary Ann Nichols, Later Pawned by a Market Porter Boy Named Georgie Cross. Initials in the Handle, BFT, Unknown.

No mention of Lady Beatrix, Katie thought. She studied the replica of the rose-gold opera glasses. The tiny faux rubies and diamonds, the mother of pearl handle with the initials.

The case also held an artist's anatomy sketch book.

Collin's?

Katie hurried toward a group of people waiting in line to view the first victim. Each waxwork figure was positioned well back in an arched niche along the far wall. But in order to fully see the display you had to stand directly in front of the alcove, sunk deep into the wall.

When it was her turn, Katie hastened to the first wax statue. Larger than life and with a realistic expression painted on her face, Mary Ann Nichols had green marble eyes that glistened with reflected light from the chandeliers above.

Mary Ann Nichols. Died at the hands of Jack the Ripper,
August 31, 1888, in Buck's Row, Whitechapel

Wearing a feathered hat and clutching a parasol, with a red petticoat peeking out from below her brown skirt, Mary Ann Nichols seemed to be smiling down at Katie.

Katie swallowed hard and continued along the line to the next waxwork victim.

Annie Chapman. *Dark Annie.* Tall, thin, and high-shouldered, Dark Annie's eyes held a measure of realistic fear. Katie forced herself to study the wax face. The artist had captured her angular, frail features and pale skin with blue veins showing through. With an embroidered cap, lacy shawl, and long, white gown, she looked like a frightened bride.

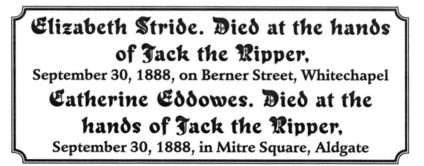

> ## 𝔄nnie 𝔈hapman. 𝔇ied at the hands of 𝔍ack the 𝔎ipper,
> September 8, 1888, on Hanbury Street, Spitalfields

Katie shuddered, remembering how Dark Annie had tried to protect poor Georgie Cross. *This was a mistake,* Katie thought. *It's too painful. I knew this woman!*

She forced herself to move on.

The next two victims were standing side by side on a double pedestal. *Elizabeth Stride and Catherine Eddowes.*

> ## 𝔈lizabeth 𝔖tride. 𝔇ied at the hands of 𝔍ack the 𝔎ipper,
> September 30, 1888, on Berner Street, Whitechapel
> ## 𝔈atherine 𝔈ddowes. 𝔇ied at the hands of 𝔍ack the 𝔎ipper,
> September 30, 1888, in Mitre Square, Aldgate

The caption below hailed their deaths as a despicable double murder. They had died on the same night. Katie blinked up at the wax figures, trying to be impartial and detached. But one look at Catherine Eddowes and Katie couldn't help but feel overwhelming anger at the brutality of her death.

The artist had captured Catherine's face and buxom figure so realistically, Katie's breath caught in her throat. The wide-spaced eyes, sensual mouth, enormous white-powdered cleavage. *It's as if she's alive!* Katie thought. Any minute now, Catherine Eddowes would step off the raised platform, coyly flash her pantalooned calves, and start belting out the lusty lyrics of "Ta-ra-ra-Boom-de-ay!"

Katie forced herself to continue.

The next Ripper victim was Mary Jane Kelly. The waxwork face showed how strikingly beautiful she was. With delicate hands pressed to her cheeks, and lips forming a perfect, round "O," Mary Jane Kelly looked like a heraldic angel.

𝕸𝖆𝖗𝖞 𝕵𝖆𝖓𝖊 𝕶𝖊𝖑𝖑𝖞. 𝕯𝖎𝖊𝖉 𝖆𝖙 𝖙𝖍𝖊 𝖍𝖆𝖓𝖉𝖘 𝖔𝖋 𝕵𝖆𝖈𝖐 𝖙𝖍𝖊 𝕽𝖎𝖕𝖕𝖊𝖗,

November 9, 1888, in Miller's Court, Dorset Street, Spitalfields

---

Toby obviously hadn't been able to save her. Katie quickly moved on.

And froze.

She blinked. And blinked again.

At first Katie showed no outward reaction, but when the prickles of unease at the back of her neck slowly died away, she fisted the air over her head, jumped up and down, and hooted, "He did it!" Her knees felt like jelly. She had to stop jumping. She grinned so hard her cheeks hurt. Emotions swirled inside her, a whiplash of joy and triumph. *He did it!*

The Ripper had taken only five victims: Mary Ann Nichols, Annie Chapman, Elizabeth Stride, Catherine Eddowes, and Mary Jane Kelly.

Toby saved Lady Beatrix, Dora Fowler, and the pregnant Molly Potter.

"You are the man!" Katie whispered under her breath. "You are *my* man," she cried aloud.

"Who's your man?" came a low, masculine voice from behind her.

Katie spun around and saw Toby striding toward her — *the twenty-first century Toby* — his duster coat rippling in his wake.

"We did it, Toby!" Katie shouted. "We did it! Your great-great-grandfather —"

"Do I know you, luv?"

His words drove into her like nails.

Oh, no! What have I done now? Katie cast her mind back trying to think what she'd done wrong. Had she forgotten to tell Toby — *the other Toby* — something important? Katie's nerves were blazing. Her eyes swept over the crowd, frantically searching for a thatch of red hair.

Toby grinned. "S'right, Katie. I know who you are. Just having a bit of a rum 'n' coke."

Katie whirled on him. "You jerk! You idiot! I could rip your head off! Don't ever scare me like that again."

"Can't a bloke have a bit of a leg-pull with a beautiful twist 'n' swirl?" He was laughing, grinning from ear to ear. "You should see your face, Katie. Like a wet hen about to peck my eyes out. Sorry, ham shank. I couldn't resist."

"Where's Collin?" Katie demanded, glaring at him.

"Round here somewhere. Look, Katie. Let me make it up to you. There's a teashop downstairs with soupy little biscuits. Care to join —"

A vibrating ping rang out.

"Hold up, luv —" Toby tugged his cell phone out of his pocket and glanced down. "Text message." He quickly thumbed a reply and shoved the phone back into his pocket. "He's a bit of a wonk, but he's the only tartan plaid I've got."

"Tartan plaid? Dad?"

"Tha's right. Now about those soupy little biscuits and —"

"Your father's alive?"

Toby looked startled. "Wasn't brown bread last I looked."

"He didn't fall off a scaffolding painting a house?"

"Huh?"

"He's a house painter, right?"

"No. He works for Scotland Yard. I come from a long line of —"

"Toby! Do you know anything about your great-great-grand-father? I know it was a long time ago, but —"

"Course I do. He was my namesake."

"W-what happened to him? I mean . . . do you know anything about him?" Katie crossed her fingers.

Toby glanced down at her fingers and shook his head gravely. "Came to a bad end, that one. Lost his arm to gangrene and was mixed up in some sort of skullduggery. Prosecuted for murdering his best friend. Poor sod died a penniless drunk and was buried in a pauper's grave."

Katie gasped. She felt a stab of pain deep in her gut. *This is all my fault! I've got to go back!* Then she saw the smile spreading across Toby's face.

"Sorry, luv," he laughed. "Couldn't resist. No worries. My great-great-grandfather, Tobias Becket, rose from humble beginnings to become the Commissioner of Scotland Yard. He was best known for apprehending the Demon Duchess of Devon, a Victorian ax-murderess, but he solved a slew of other famous cases. He was eventually knighted by the king."

"You mean the queen. Queen Victoria —"

"Nope. The king. King Edward. For his service to the crown. He lived into his eighties."

"Does that mean you're actually Sir Toby Becket?" Katie felt so relieved that Toby — her Toby — hadn't died in a pauper's grave, she wanted to hug his great-great-grandson.

"My namesake, Tobias, was awarded a life-time peerage. Meaning you can't pass the title to your sons. It dies with you in the grave."

In the grave.

Toby was in his grave now. But he'd lived a long, prosperous life. Katie reached up and threw her arms around his great-great-grandson's neck. "I'm so happy for him."

"You sound as if you knew him." Toby raised an eyebrow. "The old geezer died a few decades before you and I were born. But if you're interested in ancient stuff like that, there's a rather good — if stern — portrait of him at Scotland Yard. Not much to look at, but sharp as a tack, from what I've been told."

Katie linked her arm through his and tugged him across the room. "I *am* interested. OK, smart aleck. Any idea who Jack the Ripper really was? If you guess correctly, I'll let you take me to Starbucks for a mocha Frappuccino." It was Katie's turn to grin ear to ear.

"Bloody good gambit," Toby said as they moved toward the row of waxwork suspects on the other side of the room. "Seeing as nobody knows who the Ripper really was."

"Ah . . . come on," Katie teased. "Take a guess."

They traversed through the crowd, toward a sign that read

Who was Jack the Ripper?
Was he a supernatural phantom who could materialize at will? Or a flesh and blood man bent on harrowing destruction?

Katie hurried over to the first niche in the wall. Standing upon a pedestal was an exact likeness of Reverend Pinker. Tall and gaunt with a white clerical collar; the light from above caught the bulge of his Adam's apple.

Was Jack the Ripper a Minister?
Authorities at the time suspected several clergymen, among them, The Right Honourable Reverend H. P. Pinker.

The next sign read

Or Was Jack the Ripper a Butcher Lad?
Butcher boys proudly walked the streets of London, their trademark leather aprons smeared with blood.

This waxwork figure showed a boy wearing knee-breeches, cap, and vest, with a blood-crusted apron looped around his waist.

Or Was Jack the Ripper a Writer?
Novelist Jack? . . . Journalist Jack?

This platform depicted two waxwork suspects, Oscar Wilde, flamboyantly dressed in maroon velvet with a red gardenia sprouting from his lapel, and Bram Stoker in a vampire cape and top hat.

Katie laughed.

Toby shook his head and frowned. "Bleedin' far-fetched, if you ask me. These two were mortal enemies, for one thing. Just because they were famous and living in London at the time shouldn't make them suspects. Says here they were questioned by the police because their books were full of scenes of grotesque and supernatural death. That's a right good Turkish bath."

"A total laugh, I agree." Katie nodded, thinking how Oscar Wilde and Bram Stoker would have hated being showcased on the same platform.

The next plaque read

Or Was Jack the Ripper a Police Officer?
Several members of the Queen's own Privy Council postulated that a Cockney officer at Scotland Yard, Major Gideon Brown, was Jack the Ripper. Rumors ceased after Major Brown married a member of the nobility, Lady Beatrix Twyford.

Here Katie paused. The waxwork display looked exactly like Major Gideon Brown. *So he married Beatrix after all. . . .* She smiled, wondering if Toby had had a hand in that as well.

"But at least he lived," she murmured to herself.

"As opposed to died?" Toby chuckled. "They're all brown bread now."

The last waxwork figure was the most interesting.

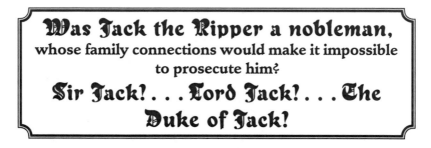

Was Jack the Ripper a nobleman,
whose family connections would make it impossible to prosecute him?
Sir Jack! . . . Lord Jack! . . . The Duke of Jack!

This statue showed a perfect likeness of the *Duke of Twyford!* Though younger-looking and less formidable, the duke had the same sour expression on his bulldog face, the same bald head and protruding stomach.

Could the Duke of Twyford have been the most vicious murderer in British history?
Mid-century historians hypothesized that the Duke or one of his henchmen in Queen Victoria's government was responsible—or at least aware of who the culprit was.

Katie smiled. She knew exactly who Jack the Ripper was.

He wasn't a butcher boy.

Or a minister.

Or a writer.

Or a police officer.

Or a duke.

From over Katie's shoulder came a voice she knew only too well.

"My money's on that old guy, the Duke of Twyford. Madness ran in his family, that's what the sign says. Whoever killed those girls *must* have been crazy. Someday scientists will discover a mutation or a gene that runs in families for things like serial killers and psychopaths."

Let's hope not, Katie thought, spinning around.

Standing behind her was her cousin Collin, his flame-red hair spiking out in all directions, his face peppered with a gazillion freckles. He wasn't wearing a stiff winged collar; his hair wasn't parted with razor precision and slicked flat back; and his eyes weren't a steely, heartless blue . . . but a coppery color above his long, freckled nose.

Katie threw her arms wide to embrace him, but he ducked out of her reach, looking alarmed. Collin hated displays of emotion.

If he's not careful, Collin will grow up to be a decayed little prig, Courtney used to say of their cousin. Katie inwardly chuckled. "I'm leaving now," she said to both boys. "I've got a date —"

She was about to say "with destiny," but decided against melodrama. *I've had enough drama for a lifetime!* Katie just wanted to get home as fast as possible and read Toby's letter — the one he promised to leave for her in the stuffed vulture.

"A date?" Toby frowned.

"Not a date," Katie said. "More like an assignation with an old . . . manuscript. Something I've got to read, waiting for me at home."

"At least let me walk with you." Toby gave her a crooked grin. "We can stop for mocha fraps."

Katie nodded.

"Well, count me out," Collin said, looking miffed. "I haven't seen the London Stone yet. Toby, want to join me?"

"No!" Katie and Toby said in unison, then eyed each other with an equal measure of suspicion and curiosity.

"Suit yourselves." Collin tugged on his lower lip. He dug his hands into the pockets of his purple striped shirt — a gift from Aunt Pru — and started to saunter away.

Katie called after him, "Collin! How's your mum?"

Collin swiveled back around, one red eyebrow feathering upward like the arch in a robin's wing. "She's working on a new photo album of . . . me." He had the good sense to look sheepish about this.

Outside the museum, the air was crisp and clean. Marylebone Road was a whirlwind of honking cars, hooting taxis, clanking trucks, and rumbling buses. On the sidewalk all around them came the shuffling, laughing, breathing, happy sounds of pedestrians enjoying the sunny afternoon.

Katie smiled.

Toby smiled back. "Shall we take the tube, luv? Or walk?"

"Walk," Katie answered. But as they were about to step off the curb, her cell phone rang out with the lyrics to "Dangerous Love," Courtney's first hit single.

"I *love* that song," Tody said, hearing the ringtone. I'm in *lust* with the lead singer Courtney from the Metro Chicks. Cut off m'left arm just to meet her."

Katie whipped her backpack off her shoulder and tugged out her phone.

"Courtney!" She all but shouted into her iPhone.

"Hey, baby girl," came Courtney's throaty, sing-songy voice. "How goes it, baby sis?"

"Courtney!" Katie squealed.

"Listen, Kit-Kat. I've got some smokin' hot news for you. I'm coming home."

"Home? To London? When?"

"Next flight. And hold on to your friggin' blue-painted toenails, I just bought a condo —"

"Where? In LA?" Katie took a deep breath. Courtney already owned a house in Beverly Hills and a condo in Malibu.

"London, baby sister! How cool is that? But here's the totally rockin' news: I bought a flat in Twyford Manor House —"

"Grandma Cleaves's building? You're joking...?"

"Nope. It's weird. I've been having these, like, goofy vibes lately. Like Dad's voice is in my head or something. Hey, look. I'll explain it all when I get there. I've missed you...and...well...when Mom and Dad died, I guess I was so caught up in my own grief I just sort of threw myself into my career...and, well, I'm sorry, Katie. I haven't exactly been there for you. You'll be going off to college in a year or two. So I thought we might hang together until then. Like a real family. I know Grandma Cleaves hates my guts —"

"That's not true, Courtney! She loves you."

"*Puh-leeze.* The old bat doesn't approve of my music *or* my lifestyle. She can take a flying leap, for all I care. I just want you and me to be together."

"Courtney...I love you...I mean it. There isn't a day goes by...I don't miss you."

"Are you crying, Kit-Kat? Come on, baby girl, don't go all boo-hoo-hoo on me. Jeez. Talk about guilt-tripping me. Between your bawling and Dad's friggin' voice in my head...cripes! And before you go all mush-gush on me, I've gotta be in London for another reason. I got this new gig —"

"I don't care why you're coming, Courtney. Just get here!"

"Aren't you going to ask me about this new gig?"

Katie laughed through her tears. "OK. What's the new gig?"

"I got a commission to write the score of a new movie being filmed in London. It's one of those gothic, steampunk flicks."

"Well, that should be easy for you, Court. Gothic and steampunk are right up your alley."

"Yeah. That's why they're paying me the big bucks. And since you're the family bookworm, Katie, I was hoping you'd help me do some research. Know anything about the Victorian era?"

"Yes!" Katie shouted. "It's kind of. . .my. . .er. . .specialty. I mean, I've read a lot about the nineteenth century. I've actually lived there. . .in my head, I mean."

"That's cool, then. I need you to research what was being sung in the music halls and bawdy houses, that kinda thing."

Katie thought about Catherine Eddowes and her lusty lyrics. "I can *definitely* help you with that."

"The melodies need to be historically accurate."

"I can sing tunes with lyrics that are *totally* from that era." Katie felt a tingle of joy. The whole world seemed full of sunshine and roses. *A happy, safe place*, Katie thought.

"So you'll do it, then? You'll help me? The movie's about some dude named Jack the Ripper."

The End

Notes to the Curious

THIS NOVEL ATTEMPTS TO PORTRAY, through the medium of a time-travel mystery, an accurate picture of life at varying levels of society in the year 1888, during Jack the Ripper's reign of terror. The story may vary from accounts of Jack the Ripper with which the reader is familiar because of the nature of a back-in-time/forward-in-time narrative, where a character's actions in the past can and do alter the future. Rest assured, however, that the women who fall prey to Jack the Ripper by novel's end are the actual true-to-life victims. The order in which they were murdered, the precise locations of the murders, and the actual dates are all historically accurate. Their ages and circumstances have been changed slightly in deference to the plot. As my writing teacher and best-selling author Bill Martin taught me: "Never let the facts get in the way of a good story." For this bit of factual tinkering, I beg the reader's indulgence.

With the obvious exception of Twyford Manor and one other place, every street, every location, every scene is an actual one the reader might have encountered had she or he lived in London at the time of the murders. And though the manners, customs, clothing, modes of transportation, speech patterns, and Cockney rhyming slang have changed almost as much as the London skyline, I have tried to convey a true sense of the time period, filtered through the eyes of Katie Lennox, with her twenty-first–century sensibilities and perceptions.

The historic figures of the day who tread lightly (or, perhaps, with heavier footfalls) through the pages of this novel — Bram Stoker, Oscar Wilde, and James Whistler among others — all resided in or around London in the year 1888. Bram Stoker (before he wrote *Dracula*) was the theater manager of the Lyceum Theatre, and would in all probability have been there at the opening of Robert Louis Stevenson's highly anticipated new play — the same night Mary Ann Nichols's body was discovered in Buck's Row. Oscar Wilde may have been at the Lyceum as well, given that he was an aspiring playwright and theater critic.

And as Katie witnesses firsthand, on the very night that *Dr Jekyll and Mr Hyde* opened at the Lyceum Theatre, newspaper boys were running up and down the gaslit Strand waving newsprint and shouting: "Murder! Murder! Read all about it!" The fiendish Jack the Ripper, like the shape-shifting Mr. Hyde, was about to enter the annals of famous Victorian murderers. In his case, life truly mimicked fiction.

The London Stone

THE LONDON STONE — the portal through which Katie travels back in time — does exist and is purported to have supernatural properties. For 900 years the stone has resided in the heart of London. Often called the Stone of Brutus, it looks like an ordinary boulder. You can see it today wedged in a wall alcove outside 111 Cannon Street. But it is no ordinary lump of rock. Ancient legend has it that if the stone leaves London, the city will cease to exist. "So long as the Stone of Brutus is safe, long will London flourish."

Historians differ as to the stone's original purpose, believing it was either an ancient Druid altar or part of a religious stone circle, like Stonehenge. For centuries it was believed to be the stone from which King Arthur withdrew his mythic sword, Excalibur.

What we do know is this: The earliest written mention of the London Stone hails from the tenth century. Maps dating back to the eleventh century depict it as a landmark in the heart of London; ancient manuscripts tell us that it was used as a place where deals were forged, proclamations made, and oaths sworn to King and Queen. The pitted indentations referred to as raven claw fissures, on the surface of the stone (that Katie plunges her finger into) were forged by repeated sword blows during medieval pageants.

Shakespeare, Dickens, and many others have written about the famous stone. In Tudor times, Queen Elizabeth I (arguably the greatest English monarch) believed the stone had mystical powers.

What appeals to me most about the London Stone is the fact that for 900 years, through bouts of war, turbulence, fires, cannon blasts, and air-raid bombings, the London Stone has remained intact and unscathed.

In 1888, when our story takes place, the London Stone was encased behind an iron grille set into the south wall of St. Swithin's church, where it remained until the Second World War. In 1941 (on the very day my own mother, a very young girl, was evacuated from London) a bomb was dropped during the Blitz, hitting its target: St. Swithin's. The church was totally demolished and reduced to rubble. Yet, miraculously, the London Stone sat amid the burning ruins unscathed. Three centuries earlier, in 1666, the iconic lump of rock survived the Great Fire of London. Then, as in 1944, the stone lay unharmed amongst smoldering devastation.

Uniformed guards kept vigil over the stone in earlier times, lest it be chipped away at by people who believe it had mysterious powers and might bring them luck. Sadly, the boulder has been neglected in modern times, relegated to the status of "quaint relic from the past." And though visitors from far reaches of the globe still make pilgrimages to see and touch the stone, few Londoners today give it so much as a passing glance as they hurry along the busy thoroughfare of Cannon Street where the stone resides in the shadow of a towering office building, half hidden behind a decrepit iron grate.

The gas-lit, swirling fog that once engulfed the London Stone in 1888, when Jack the Ripper struck fear in the hearts of millions, has been replaced by modern exhaust fumes billowing from the heavy traffic roaring past; its only illumination now, the yellowish sweeping glare of motorized headlights.

The True Identity of Jack the Ripper

IN THE YEAR 1888, Queen Victoria had been England's reigning monarch for fifty-one years, and would continue to sit on the throne for another thirteen. Hence the name given to an era that spanned a good portion of the nineteenth century: The Victorian Age.

In the autumn of 1888, fear gripped every corner of Great Britain because of a series of gruesome murders perpetuated in London by an unknown assailant, dubbed Jack the Ripper. Newspapers on both sides of the Atlantic chronicled the horrific mutilations with a fervor boarding on obsessive. The shocking nature of the murders was unparalleled in the history of crime and criminals. Jack the Ripper attacked his female victims without warning, slitting their throats and eviscerating their bodies, and then was able to slip away undetected, even though police officers were close at hand.

Hailed as "a reprobate, half beast, half man, with an insatiable thirst for blood," Jack the Ripper invoked terror, as did the mere mention of his name. People throughout England, Europe, and America talked of little else save the fiendish monster who sliced up women in such a gruesome manner.

Women in London at this time dared not venture out after dark unless they had no other choice. Those who plied their trades or earned their living at night — such as factory girls, actresses, music hall performers, midwives, or ladies of the night — lived in fear of being attacked.

Queen Victoria beseeched her female subjects to stay indoors after sundown, but should they have to venture out in the evening, to always walk in pairs. Scotland Yard instructed women to hail a police officer to escort them safely to their destination. The Metropolitan Police were doing double and triple shifts, manning every corner on every street in the Whitechapel District of the East End. But to no avail. Jack the Ripper eluded the authorities at every turn.

Outraged at the ineptitude of the police, members of the community — including ministers, priests, clergymen, students, news reporters, and members of "vigilance societies" — began roaming the streets at night in order to apprehend the fiendish killer, but with equally poor results.

How many murders did Jack the Ripper commit? There is no agreement on this subject. Some believe eight; others, eleven; and still others, fourteen. Scotland Yard pronounced the official toll to be five, listing the first victim as Mary Ann Nichols, followed by Annie Chapman, the double murder of Elizabeth Stride and Catherine Eddowes, and then the last and most gruesome murder of all, of Mary Jane Kelly.

These five victims died within earshot of a police officer or someone passing by. All but one of the murders was committed on the street. Many women at this time carried whistles for sounding an alert. Scotland Yard implored girls and women to scream or blow a whistle at the merest hint of provocation. And yet none of the victims called out. Why didn't they cry out for help when help was so readily available?

What we know is this: Because of the vicious nature of the wounds, the perpetrator would have been covered with blood. Therefore, Jack the Ripper either had a reason for walking the streets at night wearing blood-soaked clothing — such as a doctor, midwife, or butcher lad whose leather apron would be smeared with blood — or he was wearing a large cape or cloak to disguise his bloody clothing.

After the third murder, Scotland Yard, the newspapers, and the queen stepped up efforts to warn women to walk in pairs at night and not to trust any man whatsoever, not even their own kinsmen.

The last three victims were terrified of Jack the Ripper. They knew the risks they were taking walking after dark. Mary Jane Kelly told friends that she couldn't sleep at night, believing she might be murdered in her sleep by the Ripper. A neighbor heard Mary Jane singing in her room late at night, the very room where she was found dead, brutally chopped up, several hours later — all while a police officer walked up and down the street outside her window.

Surely the Ripper's victims, if they believed themselves in danger, would have screamed bloody murder. Did these women know and trust their assailant? Could Jack the Ripper have been a minister, a priest, a clergyman? Another woman? A man dressed as a woman? Perhaps a trusted member of the community? A police officer? Someone above reproach, whom they least suspected?

We shall never know for sure because Jack the Ripper was never caught. After the murder of Mary Jane Kelly, the Ripper seemed to vanish into thin air. His or her identity will remain forever a mystery. Unless, of course, we are lucky enough to come upon a time portal, such as the London Stone, that might transport us back to London in the year 1888....

Acknowledgments

First and foremost, to my parents, Julia and Richard McNiven, who read, commented, and encouraged me throughout early drafts of *RIPPED*. To my British grandmother, Clarice Cleaves Carr, whose wit and charm and stories about England made me fall in love with all things British, particularly four o'clock tea and Golden Age detective fiction. To my grandfather, Daddy John, for introducing me at an early age to the mystery surrounding Jack the Ripper and to the possible Ripper suspects who might have "dunit."

To Julia Dickson for her unwavering support, for reading the manuscript countless times, and for her belief in her ink-slinging old Mum. To Coco Karol for editing the penultimate draft and making extensive notes, all the while producing and dancing in the Red Soles promo video for *RIPPED*. To Chelsea Lennox who, with her teenage insights and joie de vivre, insisted I change the ending to a happily-ever-after version, and hounded me until I tweaked it.

To Kerry and Wooda McNiven, Lynn Centa, and Russell Grossman, my eagle-eyed readers and supportive sibs, many thanks.

To Ned Berman, freshman at Dartmouth and first official young adult reader, who skipped classes because he couldn't put the manuscript down (music to a writer's ears).

To my writers' group—you know who you are—thank you, one and all.

To my salon sisters at the Vermont College MFA writing program—hats off.

To my near-and-dear buddies at the Huntington Theatre Company—you rock.

To my WGBH and Masterpiece Trust colleagues, especially those involved with *Sherlock* and *Downton Abbey*—your love of romance, intrigue, and historical drama inspires me.

A shout out to Bill Martin, who taught me "everything I know about writing" in his master class at Harvard Extension. To Gregory Maguire, who, over lunch at Papa Razzi, encouraged me to "defy gravity" on a broomstick of my very own; and to Dotty Frank for her wicked writing wit and wisdom.

To the brilliant, hardworking, professional team at NBP: Nan Fornal, Annie Card, and Jon Albertson, thank you for being incredibly patient with me and meticulous with the care and handling of my book. To Chris Gall, the gifted illustrator of *RIPPED*, much gratitude.

To Phyllis Westberg, the reigning queen of agents and mystery writers, for her efforts to place this book. I hope we can work together again.

To my Sisters in Crime: Ellen Flynn for her artistry and editing acumen; Fancy Zilberfarb for her "fancytastic" organizational skills (everyone should have Fancy on their team); Carol Deane for her friendship and support and love for London theater—hugs and more hugs.

To the "Risley Gang of Nine": Judi, John, Annie, David, Dotty, Peter, Stephen, and Steven. The much-needed breaks from writing were a godsend. The laughter, fun, frivolity, and general debauchery . . . all appreciated.

To my long-suffering husband, Steven, who put up with my locking myself in our garret to finish this book. Thank you for believing in me, supporting my writing, and bringing me hot tea and encouragement in the morning. You are my everything.

About the Author

SHELLY DICKSON CARR was just ten years old when she read *He Wouldn't Kill Patience*, the classic mystery by her grandfather, John Dickson Carr. Since then she's been hooked on the genre and thinking about the mystery she'd one day write. *Ripped* is her first novel.

The idea for *Ripped* came while on a scouting trip. As a board member for the Huntington Theatre in Boston Shelly has traveled frequently to London with theatre members in search of interesting new plays. While in London, the author began researching the mystery surrounding Jack the Ripper, one of the greatest unsolved murder cases in history.

Shelly's fascination with the nineteenth century started when she was a young girl, in a rambling Victorian house in Mamaroneck, New York. Her British mother, an author and bibliophile, filled every room in the house with floor-to-ceiling bookshelves. Leather-bound classics abounded. Her friends called it the library house. In third grade Shelly read all the *Just So Stories* by Kipling—because she could reach them on the lower shelves.

A founding member of The Masterpiece Trust that enabled *Downton Abbey* to be aired on PBS, and a supporter of Masterpiece Mystery's *Sherlock*, the author has a deep love of all things British.

She has three daughters and lives with her husband, their youngest daughter, and their bulldog, Becket, on Beacon Hill in Boston. Shelly has an MFA in writing for children and young adults from Vermont College, and an undergraduate degree in education.

When not reading or writing or busy with community arts projects, Shelly, aka Michelle Karol, likes to spend time with her horse, Tucker. She also loves to ski and travel with her husband.

CPSIA information can be obtained at www.ICGtesting.com
Printed in the USA
BVOW082116060213

312602BV00002B/53/P